*Perfect*

# PROPOSALS

## BE MY BRIDE

# *Perfect*
# PROPOSALS
## COLLECTION

March 2016

April 2016

May 2016

June 2016

# Perfect
# PROPOSALS
## BE MY BRIDE

Natalie
ANDERSON

Jessica
STEELE

Kathie
DeNOSKY

MILLS
BOON

First Published in Great Britain 2016
By Mills & Boon, an imprint of HarperCollins*Publishers*
1 London Bridge Street, London, SE1 9GF

BE MY BRIDE © 2016 Harlequin Books S.A.

*The Right Mr Wrong* © 2013 Natalie Anderson
*A Most Suitable Wife* © 2005 Jessica Steele
*Betrothed for the Baby* © 2006 Kathie DeNosky

ISBN: 978-0-263-92153-3

09-0416

Harlequin (UK) Limited's policy is to use papers that are natural, renewable and recyclable products and made from wood grown in sustainable forests. The logging and manufacturing processes conform to the legal environmental regulations of the country of origin.

Printed and bound in Spain
by CPI, Barcelona

# THE RIGHT MR WRONG

## NATALIE ANDERSON

**Natalie Anderson** adores a happy ending—which is why she always reads the back of a book first. Just to be sure. So you can be sure you've got a happy ending in your hands right now—because she promises nothing less. Along with happy endings she loves peppermint-filled dark chocolate, pineapple juice and extremely long showers. Not to mention spending hours teasing her imaginary friends with dating dilemmas. She tends to torment them before eventually relenting and offering—you guessed it—a happy ending. She lives in Christchurch, New Zealand, with her gorgeous husband and four fabulous children.

If, like her, you love a happy ending, be sure to come and say hi on facebook/authornataliea, on Twitter @authornataliea, or at her website/blog:www.natalie-anderson.com

# PROLOGUE

*Christmas Day, five years earlier.*

THEY WERE ALMOST all there. Her parents. Oliver's family. Oliver's friends. The only one missing was Stella, her rebel sister, whose name hadn't been mentioned once in the four years since she'd left.

Victoria Rutherford looked at the pile of presents under the tree. There wouldn't be one for Stella, of course, but she hoped there was at least one for Oliver's friend. She stepped closer, scanning the tags for his name.

Liam.

She really shouldn't worry about it. He was Oliver's friend, Oliver's guest. Of course his parents would be polite enough to have something for the guy who'd only arrived in England this week.

'You're not going to start shaking the boxes, are you?' a low voice murmured behind her.

She started, a smile irresistibly springing to her lips. It shouldn't. It really shouldn't. But he made her laugh with his comments—even just the wry expression he could shoot from his way-too-warm eyes. She'd had to stifle shivers when he'd looked at her in a way he shouldn't. Not that he did now.

Unfortunately he'd looked at her that way the first moment they'd met—when he'd not known who she was. She was still trying to get over the embarrassment of him coming across her in the guest bathroom wrapped in nothing but a towel. He'd had clothes on but that hadn't stopped her from noticing things she really had no business noticing.

'Your streamers look awesome, by the way,' Liam added.

'Thanks.' She'd stayed up way too late the other night to finish them. With a not-so-little helper.

She swallowed, suppressing the memory of the moment just before she'd taken herself to her small guest bedroom super quick. *Nothing* had happened. She had nothing to feel guilty about. And yet.

He was her boyfriend's best friend. A guest in her boyfriend's home for Christmas. The *last* person she should look at.

As everyone gathered around for the present sharing there were the usual joke gifts, a tradition in Oliver's family, as well as the 'proper' gifts. And the gifts for guests—including Liam.

And then there was only one little box left. She figured it was one for Oliver's mum. In the lull and under the cover of various conversations, she couldn't help a quick glance at Liam. Massive mistake because he gave her a quick flick of his eyebrows from over his new ugly knitted Christmas jersey.

She turned away, biting back her giggle.

'I think this might be for you.'

Victoria jumped as Oliver suddenly appeared in front of her.

'You've already given me a present.' Victoria blinked, taking a minute to pull back from the dangerous place her mind had wandered to.

Then she saw Oliver was on his knee in front of her. Why was he on his knee? His blue eyes were dancing and everyone around them had fallen silent.

'Victoria, you know how much I love you.'

She smiled, but inside she was stunned. Was this—? No way was Oliver about to—

'Will you marry me?'

Victoria stared at him. Somehow she kept the smile on her lips.

Oliver, her first boyfriend, who she knew and trusted. And here, in front of her parents, his parents and—

'Victoria?' Liam interrupted.

*OMG.* Don't look at him. Don't.

She couldn't resist.

His eyes were fixed on her. His too-warm, gold-flecked intense eyes staring right through her as if he could read her every thought. Every doubt.

Every desire.

'Do you mind?' Oliver sounded more stunned at the interruption than annoyed. 'I'm asking her a question.'

But Victoria's eyes were locked on Liam. She should look away, but she couldn't. She sensed restlessness ripple through the people surrounding them. *Her parents.* Any second now someone else would speak. Would question.

Oliver cleared his throat. Oliver, the one perfect for her, who had their future mapped out. She couldn't hurt him, embarrass him. Him or any of them.

'Victoria?' Oliver said. Now he sounded slightly annoyed.

Victoria immediately, mutely, looked back to Oliver, the guy right before her. She smiled—automatically soothing because that was what she did. And she wanted to because she loved Oliver, right? She wanted everything that he wanted— what they all wanted and expected—didn't she?

Oliver smiled back. And as she sat flushed, yet frozen, he repeated the question.

'Will you marry me?'

# CHAPTER ONE

'YES, OF COURSE,' Victoria answered brightly, ignoring the burning muscles in her hand. 'Absolutely.'

She'd do whatever it took. That was what entrepreneurs did, right? Made sacrifices. Worked all night. She'd read *You Too Can Be a Billionaire* months ago, so she knew. Not that she wanted to be a billionaire or even a millionaire. She'd settle for solvent—no more of that screaming red ink on her bank statement, thanks.

Anyway, writing another five place cards in flourished copperplate was nothing on the number she'd already done. So long as those passed their impending inspection. They'd better. So much depended on this.

Victoria watched her client, Aurelie Broussard, cross the ornately furnished room to the large writing desk where she nervously waited. Like everyone else who'd ever been in Aurelie's presence, Victoria couldn't help staring. The 'in-another-realm' woman glowed in a long white summer dress and navy shrug. Her hair fell to the middle of her back in long, loose curls. Its colour matched her eyes, as glossy and dark and sensual as hot fudge sauce. Athlete, model, businesswoman. And about seven months pregnant judging by the graceful swell of her belly. Victoria hadn't known about the baby, but then she didn't know much about the former world-champion surf star other than that she was getting hitched in five days' time. Victoria deliberately didn't take an interest in water sports—they flowed too close to deep-buried, sharp-edged memories.

She'd never met a more beautiful woman. Or anyone with the power to improve her business so drastically—or destroy it. If Aurelie liked her work, she'd be set. If she didn't, Victoria was screwed. And brides were notoriously picky—especially brides with squadrons of celebrity friends and a 'super wow factor' wedding to pull off in less than a week.

Victoria slowed her movements to hide her nerves, carefully laying out some of the completed cards on the antique wood. Aurelie silently studied them. They'd taken Victoria more hours than she could count, working under bright lights all through the night to get them finished. She'd been contracted at the last minute—not ideal for a calligrapher whose craft required light, space, time and serenity to get it right.

'They are beautiful.' Aurelie finally gave her verdict. 'Exactly what I wanted.'

Victoria rapidly blinked back burning tears of relief. Two hundred and thirty-four painstakingly calligraphed cards—so many in such a short time she *was* in pain. But she wanted to be sure all were perfect.

'I've done them exactly as they were written on your list but someone will double check them?' she asked. She didn't want some A-lister offended by having her name incorrectly spelt.

Aurelie nodded. 'My assistant. Perhaps you can do the extra five while you're here?' She slid open the top drawer of the desk and drew out a sheet of paper with a list of names typed on it.

'Of course I can…' She'd brought her pen and ink and spare card with her, but the implication of five more guests suddenly hit and caused tunnel vision. 'Umm…with the extra guests…' Victoria's innards shrivelled. 'Does that mean you've changed the seating plan?'

That plan had taken so very, very long already. One large board with all those two hundred and thirty-four names written

yet again in flourished copperplate, plus titles for the table—
surf beaches. The thought of redoing the entire thing sent
Victoria's brain spinning. The nerves in her hand shrieked.

'Yes.' Aurelie turned her beautiful face towards her, and
drew up to her full height—almost a head taller than Victoria. 'Will that be a problem?'

'Not at all.' Victoria somehow stretched her mouth into a
smile and lied. She'd stitch back her eyelids and work round
the clock for the next five days and nights to get this done—
and she was going to need every one of those hours to do it.

She remembered being a bride, wanting everything to be
perfect. She'd work as hard as she could to help Aurelie have
everything the way she wanted. But while Victoria's own ceremony had been fairy-tale pretty, her marriage to Oliver hadn't
been perfect. It had been a slow-imploding mess.

Working on Aurelie's wedding would help her recovery,
financially at any rate. There were so many privileged people coming, with her best work on show, she might get more
commissions.

The irony of having a career where she helped people create their perfect weddings wasn't lost on her, given her own
spectacular matrimonial failure. But she wasn't cynical. For
the right couple, a wedding was a wonderful beginning.

Hopefully Aurelie's fiancé was a decent guy. Victoria knew
even less about him than she did about Aurelie. She hadn't
looked up any Internet info—the turnaround time was so tight
she'd had to get straight on with writing. But she'd recognised
the names of some of their guests—elite sports people, ce-
lebrities, models.

'I'm sure I can count on you.' Aurelie smiled.

It was one of those smiles with an 'I'll kill you if you screw
up' edge. Well, while Aurelie was counting on her, Victoria
would be counting on coffee—dump trucks of it.

'I can do the cards here and now if you'd like, but I'll need
to redo the table plan at home. I don't have the supplies here.'

Aurelie nodded. 'I'll get my assistant to email you the changes for that.'

'And I'll bring it here as soon as it's done.'

'And when will that be?' The ice cool question, the smile. No pressure at all.

Victoria hesitated, desperate to please but not wanting to over-promise. 'Well in time for the wedding.' Victoria clung to her smile as Aurelie looked at her for what felt like hours.

Finally Aurelie smiled back. 'Thank you.'

*Great.* Victoria put her bag on the chair and took out her pen case and ink bottle. Five cards shouldn't take that long and she'd please her client. Then she'd rest up on the train and study the seating changes at home. And call by the shop on the way to load up on stay-awake supplies.

'Do you like the candles?' Aurelie suddenly asked.

Victoria turned. Aurelie had opened the lid of a big box stacked beside the desk. It was filled with tissue-wrapped cylinders neatly packed end to end. Aurelie lifted one out and unwound the delicate covering and revealed a candle in a gorgeous soft white.

'They're surfboard wax scented.' Aurelie giggled. 'My favourite.'

Victoria grinned at the quirkiness. To be married in a French chateau by candlelight with handwritten calligraphy and lace and silk everywhere? Not to mention fireworks and orchestra and fountains? Aurelie might be doing some things slightly out of order, but there was a lot that was traditional in her plans—and fun. She was having it all. Good for her.

'They're beautiful. This whole place is beautiful. It is going to be enchanting.' Victoria meant it, she really did.

Aurelie put the candle back. 'It is going to be *parfait*!'

'It is.' Victoria drew in a breath for courage. 'Now, the menu hasn't changed, has it?' she asked, mentally crossing every crossable part of her body as she waited for the answer.

'No.' Aurelie laughed—a peal of infectious amusement

that had Victoria smiling again. 'I see why you were recommended,' Aurelie said. 'You don't get flustered. You just say yes.'

Victoria maintained her smile despite the tweak on her nerves. In two minutes Aurelie had nailed her. Victoria had been so good at saying yes. To her parents, to Oliver. To the people she'd been desperate to please more than anything—more than herself. And then what Aurelie had said registered.

'I was recommended?' Who'd have done that? She'd only been in Paris seven months—most of her income was derived from the secretarial work she got from an agency. She'd only recently relaunched her online calligraphy and personal stationery design business. Perhaps it was a contact from when her company had been flying high in London? Either way she was grateful—despite the last minute panic that Aurelie had just dumped on her.

But Aurelie didn't answer, she'd swiftly crossed to the window. Now Victoria too heard the crunch of the gravel outside. A car.

'Oh, no,' Aurelie gasped. 'He's here. He can't see any of this. If he comes in here, hide it. *Everything.*' With superior athletic grace, even with that burgeoning belly, Aurelie ran from the room.

Victoria blinked at the suddenly empty atmosphere. Presumably *he* was the groom. Curious to see what kind of guy had landed the incomparable Aurelie, she walked over to the window and peered down the two levels to the grand entrance.

The discreet-but-gleaming black car parked right in front was empty. As she watched, one of the conservatively clad assistants strode across the courtyard towards it. No doubt he was going to park it somewhere where it wouldn't ruin the picture-postcard perfection. While it might be a 'miniature' chateau, it was still one of the grandest buildings Victoria had ever been in. Surrounded by formal gardens with long avenues and hidden nooks and a selection of trick fountains, it was gorgeous.

She went back to the desk, picked up the completed cards and dropped them back in their protective box. She didn't want any damaged; she had too much to redo already. She took out several blank cards from the other box she'd brought in case, frowning as she arranged them. The desk was beautiful, but it wasn't angled like her one at home. It'd be better if she could do these there, but she wasn't about to say 'no' to Aurelie.

She prepared her pen, drawing up ink, and worked on a practice card—warming up her fingers and getting the ink to flow smoothly.

'Aurelie, you in here?'

Victoria froze, her pen digging into the card. Shock curdled her blood. Ink spilled but she hardly noticed. Because she knew that voice. That warm, laid-back, confident call.

She turned her head as he walked into the room. Her heart paused for a painfully long time between beats. She held her breath even longer.

*Liam?*

Utterly gorgeous, absolutely unattainable Liam?

Her eyes were so wide they wanted to water. But that wasn't happening. Not in the presence of this particular guy. Never ever.

He paused, barely noticeably, before walking towards her. But, as always, Victoria noticed *every* tiny thing about him, so she saw that slight hesitation. She also saw his height—his tall, lean, muscled physique. He'd always been an athlete and more competitive than most. *Dangerously* competitive. Liam Wilson wanted to win, no matter the cost.

And he'd won the best, hadn't he?

*Aurelie.*

His sunflower-flecked brown eyes locked on her. Staring right back, Victoria saw the trademark easy-going stubble covering that sharp-edged jaw. She saw the dark brown hair,

cropped closer than it had been the last time she saw him.
Only vaguely did she take in the jeans and white tee because
she was fully mesmerised by his expression—that intense,
purposeful focus.

*OM freaking G.*

Liam Wilson. She couldn't believe it. Completely thrown,
she looked down for a sec to collect her scrambled thoughts.
How could he have grown even more attractive? How could
she take one look and *want* all over again?

Pulling the plug on the visual didn't work. Because now
she *remembered* so much of a time that had been so short.
Now she wanted to hide. No one had ever exposed her the
way Liam once had—with just one look.

'Victoria.'

She fixedly stared at the ink-splodged mess she'd made on
the card, aware he'd stopped a few feet from her chair.

He cleared his throat. 'Long time, no see.'

She heard the smile. He'd always spoken with that easy-
as smile. That innate confidence had been part of what had
drawn her to him. The kind of confidence she'd never had.
She'd been jealous of his 'I-don't-give-a-damn-what-you-all-
think' attitude too, because she'd *never* had that.

Focused, hungry, *fascinating.* Liam had an edge Victoria
hadn't encountered before or since. Tall, strong, determined
to do what he wanted, he'd sliced through any opposition.

Until Oliver. And her.

Unable to resist, she chanced a glance back at him. That
element of danger? It was still there—now lethal. Because,
despite that smile, his eyes weren't just focused and relentless, they were hard.

There was no point clearing her throat. It wasn't going to
work. *Nothing* in her body—especially not her brain—was
working this second. Or the next.

'How've you been?' he asked.

Oh, he had to be kidding. Five years since she'd last seen

him, five years since he'd interrupted her own wedding proposal and here he was five days from *his* wedding and he was
greeting her like some old schoolmate?

Then again, how else to handle it?

She looked at the blank cards on the desk, glad she'd packed
the others away. Aurelie hadn't wanted him to see them.

Aurelie. Liam.

Aurelie Broussard was marrying Liam Wilson.

Liam was the father of Aurelie's baby.

Liam was getting married.

*Why* was it so hard to compute?

She'd once had the chance to say yes to Liam. Not to marriage but to *something*. She hadn't. She'd said yes to someone
else and life had moved on for all of them. And she was okay
with that, wasn't she?

*Yes.*

She straightened, ignoring the churning riot of recollections
and emotions inside. She was *happy*. And she'd act like it.

'Fine, thanks.' *Score.* Her voice sounded almost normal.
'How are you?'

'Stunned to see you.'

Hardly stunned. He was still standing, tall and fit in those
blue jeans and soft leather boatshoes and an eye-wateringly
bright white tee with seams that had to cling hard to contain
his broad shoulders. It ought to be impossible, but the guy
was *more* gorgeous than he'd been back then. But what really
stunned her was the glint in his eyes. He blatantly stared—at
her hair, over her face, seeming to take in each feature—lingering on her mouth and then dropping below, taking in her
figure. Was he sizing her up as he had that very first time
they'd met? Back then it had been excusable—he'd not known
who she was. But now?

Victoria tensed beneath his inspection, willing her body
not to let the remnants of that old attraction show. Because

that was all it was, like muscle memory—an imprint of an old infatuation. Not real. Certainly not *worse*. It couldn't be.

'It's been a long time,' he said. 'And, as impossible as I'd have thought it, you're even more beautiful now.'

Her breath quickened as her body absorbed his words—words that mirrored her thoughts of him. Her system responded *so* inappropriately. Heat shot everywhere—most of all deep and low in her belly.

Her brain clicked more slowly, taking too long to realise that it was meaningless, just his usual flirt talk. That was all it had ever been. *Talk*. But he had no right to tease her. Not that she could put him in his place the way she wanted to. Not when it was his fiancée she was working for. No, she was going to remain calm and professional and brush him off politely.

'You're looking good too,' she said crisply. She even smiled. She could handle this unfortunate coincidence and she could handle him. Of course she could.

He leaned against the table right next to where she sat. Her feet tingled, her legs itched. But she wasn't running, not showing how badly he got to her. She knew he was playing. He'd played with her before. She remembered that exact roguish expression from the first night she'd met him in the guest bathroom at Oliver's parents' place. Then, as now, Liam looked like a wicked cat who'd just spied a juicy mouse and he was going to have fun devouring it ever so slowly.

Victoria Rutherford was never going to be a mouse again.

'Thank you,' he drawled.

Her eyes narrowed as anger seeped through her polite armour. He really was the same game player? After all this time? Even now he was about to get married?

'Victoria,' he murmured softly, as he'd once murmured her name before. Now, as she had then, she steeled her heart.

How could she be this affected again by his mere presence?

Victoria froze as he moved, leaning across her—far, far too close. She held her breath but it was futile. He still smelt of ocean spray, sunshine and freedom. A heady, intoxicating mix that had once made her almost crazy high. The ultimate, *forbidden* temptation. Her boyfriend's best friend.

As her client's fiancé, he was even more forbidden now. So her suddenly over-excited hormones could just go back into dormant mode. Liam Wilson—even if he was single— would *never* be hers.

'What are you doing?' she squeaked—totally mouse—as he came closer still.

His gaze didn't leave hers; his mouth curved as he moved into her space. She was transfixed by that intense, challenging look. And he was so close now, she could see the individual, unfairly long lashes that framed his dangerously warm eyes.

'Mind if I take this?' He pulled the pen out of her clenched fingers with a sharp tug. 'It's looking a little like a weapon there. You stabbed me in the heart once. I'm not chancing it again.'

She gaped. As if she'd hurt him? Quite the reverse. He'd hurt her. And Oliver. He'd thrown a spanner between them— damaging the bond that was never fixed quite right after. But he didn't need to know how much he'd mattered.

'I hurt *you*?' She pulled herself together and faked a light laugh. 'No woman has ever hurt you.'

A single eyebrow lifted. 'You think?' He shook his head. 'Aren't I as vulnerable as anyone else?'

'No,' Victoria said bluntly.

'Come on,' he drawled. 'You know exactly how human I am,' he purred.

'Are you hitting on me?' she whispered—utterly amazed— and aghast. 'Seriously?'

When his seven-months-pregnant fiancée was in the building and he was getting married in less than a week?

Screw the prospects this job might bring. As far as Victoria was concerned, Aurelie didn't need flourishes. She needed a new fiancé.

'Liam!' There was a squeal and a vision in white darted across the room. Aurelie really was too swift for a heavily pregnant woman, not to mention perfectly chic and elegant even in her third trimester.

'Hey.' Liam wrapped his arms around Aurelie for a tight hug before pushing her back to arm's length and gazing at her adoringly. 'You. Look. Amazing.'

'I look huge but I don't care.' Aurelie laughed and leaned closer, smiling openly up at him. 'And I'm so glad you're here.'

Victoria's stomach twisted. Because he was a flirt cheat—not that she was jealous. There was nothing to be jealous of. She was happily divorced. Happily single. The last thing she wanted to do was revisit past mistakes and Liam Wilson had been an almighty mistake.

A mistake that *Aurelie* was about to make. Aurelie, whose features appeared brighter—her lips shinier. She'd disappeared for those few moments to touch up her make-up? Someone had to warn her about him. Only Victoria couldn't—she could never go there. Instead she loudly scraped together the blank cards on the table.

'Don't worry, Aurelie,' Victoria interrupted the scene, not wanting to watch them indulge in more PDA. 'He's not seen anything.'

Aurelie and Liam turned, the spell between them broken.

'All the surprises are safely hidden,' Victoria continued with determined firmness. Why were they looking at her as if she were speaking Martian?

'I've put everything away...' she faltered.

Something had flashed in Liam's face—a frown? A flicker of anger? It had passed so quickly Victoria couldn't decide. And now came the smile—the one that charmed everyone.

'Yes, don't worry, I left the groom downstairs.' Liam jerked his head to the door. 'But he'll be up here in a second if you don't hurry to see him.'

But Aurelie didn't hurry. She gazed up at Liam, her palm

flat on his chest. 'It is so good to see you. I wasn't sure you'd come.'

'I didn't want to miss it.'

'Yes, you did.' She laughed again and patted his chest a couple of times. 'But I am glad you're not. Thank you.'

'Anything for you.' He winked and gently brushed the back of his hand along the edge of her fine-boned jaw. 'Now you'd better go stop him from coming up and spoiling any of your surprises.'

As Aurelie left the room Victoria sat in a swelter of confusion and defiance and embarrassment.

'You thought I was Aurelie's fiancé?' Liam walked back towards her, his smile had widened yet he managed to look less friendly.

Could he blame her when Aurelie had said 'he'd' arrived and then Liam had walked in as if he owned the place?

'You thought I was marrying her?' He stepped closer, suddenly very tall and a lot like a roadblock. 'And playing you?'

Victoria tried to glance behind him but it was impossible. He was fully in her face and expecting an answer with his eagle eyes. The only thing to do was play it cool. *Frigidly* cool. 'Do you blame me for thinking that?' She arched her brows as if that could make her taller. 'You have form.'

His eyes narrowed. 'I could spend some time arguing that, but why bother?' He stayed in place, right in her space. 'Just as I was five years ago, Victoria, I'm here as a guest.'

A *guest*. He truly wasn't Aurelie's fiancé.

For a second relief flooded her. But then mortification screamed back. Her cheeks burned under his mocking scrutiny.

Of course she'd thought he was the groom. In the rare moments she'd ever let herself think of him in the last five years, he'd *always* been the groom. The guy she'd never said yes to and refused to ever regret.

'Your name wasn't on the guest cards,' she said defensively.

'I didn't think I was going to be able to make the wedding,' he explained. 'That's why I'm one of the late additions.' He pointed to the sheet of paper Aurelie had put on the desk.

He hadn't made it to Victoria's wedding. She wasn't sure he'd even been invited. Not after what had happened. It was the only time she'd seen Oliver uncontrollably angry. She'd gone upstairs and the rest of the family had retired to change for lunch. Oliver and Liam had gone outside. Victoria had pressed close to her bedroom wall, secretly peering out of the window.

Liam had taken the blow without putting up any physical defence. The spot on his jaw had reddened, but all the while he'd quietly insisted to Oliver that nothing had happened. That she'd done nothing. That his interruption wasn't her fault. It had been his mistake alone.

He'd been facing the house. He'd glanced up, seen her. Their eyes connected for one split second.

Withdrawing. Apologising. Leaving.

He'd never looked at her again. Until today.

But had she done nothing? Really? Who had made the bigger mistake? Whose fault was it really? She'd been scared. She'd never had the strength to stand up to any of them—her parents, Oliver. Even Liam. She'd always done as they bid because she'd needed their approval. And all of them had steam-rollered over her. But she'd let them—she'd *helped* them. That wasn't happening again. Only now she did look at the list Aurelie had handed to her. The third name down?

Liam Wilson.

'Oh.' She faked a bright smile. 'I thought—'

'I know what you thought,' he said, easing back into position against the desk. 'You never thought much of me, did you?'

That wasn't true but she couldn't reveal what she'd thought of him all those years ago. She couldn't admit it then, she couldn't now.

There were five names on that list: three men, two

women—one of whom had the same surname as another of the guests. The other woman's name was written last, beneath another man's name. Liam's name stood alone in the middle there. Was he coming to the wedding without a partner?

She didn't need to know. She really didn't. Because it didn't matter.

That didn't stop her glancing at his hands—his fisted fingers. Bare knuckles didn't mean anything for men. Many guys didn't wear wedding rings or, if they did, only when convenient. And even if they did wear them?

Victoria knew all too well how a wedding ring wasn't necessarily an obstacle as far as another woman was concerned. Or for a husband who was no longer satisfied in his marriage. Liam's lack of ring meant nothing. Nor did his lack of date.

But still that unwanted excitement heated her blood and anticipation zinged through her veins. What was she, some teen girl going to meet her fave ever boyband?

But he might be free. And now? So was she. There was nothing to stop them from finally exploring this *thing*...

Only the ten tonnes of baggage she was constantly pushing in front of her. And the baggage he'd worked into some kind of bullet-proof vest that he wore beneath that easy-come, easy-go attitude.

'I'm sorry.' She looked up at him. For today, for all those years ago. For what could never have been and never could be. She'd moved on; she didn't want to go back to the doormat she'd been. She had *plans* and they didn't involve anyone else. Not him. Not any man.

Liam looked right back at her, his mouth curved in that slight, sexy smile. Time shifted—five years disappeared in that unspoken communication. She was drawn right back into those feelings that should have been forgotten—warmth, want, desire.

And she had to get out of there before she did something really dumb.

He wrapped his fingers right round her wrist—halting her just as she moved. 'I'm not anyone's fiancé.' His grip was sure and warm. 'That means I'm free to flirt with whoever I want,' he added.

'Not with me,' she said huskily, swallowing to ease the dryness in her throat. She didn't want to flirt with anyone.

'Yes, you.' His smile was oddly gentle. 'You're not anyone's fiancée either, or wife.'

So he knew her marriage had ended.

'I can't believe you still blush like this—'

'I'm not here to flirt,' she interrupted him quickly. 'I'm here to *work*.' The emphasis was for herself as much as for him. She couldn't afford to be distracted by this quirk of fate.

His gaze rested on her for a long moment, as if he were weighing the truth of her words. His grip remained firm—could he feel her pulse accelerating?

He let her go. 'Then let's see you in action.' He handed back her pen.

As if.

'I can't do this with you watching.' Her palms were damp; she'd already smudged ink everywhere just from hearing his voice. She'd be less competent than a two-year-old with a pack of finger-paints right now.

'You always had a problem with me watching.'

She tensed, hoping to stop him from seeing her all-over tremble. She *had* always been aware of the way he watched her. 'It's not you,' she lied sassily. 'I don't like anyone watching me work.'

'In case you make a mistake?'

'Not at all.' She lied yet again. 'I'm not afraid to make mistakes. I've made many.' Too, too many.

'Then you're fine to write in front of me. Write my name.'

She shook her head. She wasn't going to make *more* mistakes. She had to focus now.

'You're still a chicken,' he jeered.

'You're confusing cowardice with being sensible.' She had always tried to do the sensible thing. No shame in that, right? 'And with these smudges?' She held up her fingers. 'Why would I waste my time and resources?'

He glanced at the table. 'You're really into all this?'

'I want Aurelie to have what she wants.'

'So you've not been put off weddings and all that's wonderful about them?'

'Of course not,' she mocked. He was the cynical one, not she. 'You think because my marriage didn't work out, I'd go all bitter and anti?'

His lips twitched. 'No. I just…wouldn't have expected you to be so into weddings, I guess.'

'I'm into *other* people's weddings,' she said smoothly, putting her pen back into its case. 'And you're still not into weddings at all.'

His shoulders lifted. 'And yet here I am. Happy to enjoy someone else's wedding.'

'That's an improvement on the last time I saw you. You didn't seem to want anyone to marry then.'

'And I was right, wasn't I?' He casually picked up a candle and breathed in the scent.

She took that hit. 'You couldn't have foreseen what was going to happen.'

'Couldn't I?'

No. She rejected the idea totally.

'You and I both knew it wasn't right,' he said softly, lowering the candle and coolly looking at her. 'Even Oliver knew it wasn't right.'

'I think it's best if I go home and work on these in my studio,' Victoria said through gritted teeth.

'Where are you staying? Paris?' Liam asked, his lips curving in that suspiciously sinful way. 'I can give you a lift.'

'You're not staying here?'

He shook his head and straightened, looking all man-of-action. 'I have some things in town I need to do.'

She couldn't possibly get a lift with him. Never. The train was the only option.

Victoria looked up to meet his gaze and saw the mockery written all over him. But as she was about to answer he laid a finger over her lips.

'What are you so worried about?' he taunted slyly. 'You'll be stuck with me for less than an hour. What harm can come?'

To be stuck in a car with the guy who'd once tempted her so completely? She'd be mad to contemplate it. She had to think of some excuse.

'With you driving?' she tried to tease archly. 'You always travelled too fast, Liam. So I'd say all kinds of harm could come.'

'Oh, well.' His answer came lazy and insolent. 'If it's speed you're afraid of, why don't you drive?'

# CHAPTER TWO

LIAM TRIED NOT to hold his breath as he waited for her answer. Victoria Rutherford—the only woman he'd wanted, but had never had. The one who'd got away. It was such a cliché, but face to face with her for the first time in five years?

He still wanted.

She was even more beautiful now. Until today he wouldn't have thought that was possible.

'Sure.' Her very pretty chin tilted upwards as she finally gave him an answer.

Liam had to suppress more than a sigh of satisfaction—there was a burn in his blood and in his gut as well. Last time he'd asked her something it had been a denial she'd issued. Not today. And, as crazy as it was, Liam had more to ask of her. Much more. He wanted to hear 'yes' from her mouth many times over.

Maybe then his mind would be freed from all those memories.

Victoria willed confidence. Of course she could drive that big black car. It might have power but it'd also have every safety feature ever invented. And no doubt it had a fancy satnav system and automatic clutch. It'd be a cinch. 'I'd love to drive.'

Yeah, she just oozed faux confidence—refusing to show how flustered she was.

She carefully packed her gear into her bag. Shame she

didn't have some light leather driving gloves to don with chic aplomb. Gloves would hide the almost permanent ink stains. 'Let's get going. I've got a lot of work to do.'

But the car that an assistant brought to the front entrance of the chateau wasn't the big black machine she'd seen from the window. It was a tiny two-seater.

Victoria eyed the sleek gleaming silver with its explicit promise of speed and seduction and turned to Liam. 'Who do you think you are—James Bond?'

Even she, no car fiend, recognised a vintage Aston Martin when she saw it. No automatic clutch, no sat-nav, no airbags. No roof even. And no chance she was driving it.

He held open the driver's door for her. 'You don't think it's gorgeous?'

That wasn't the point. 'Is it yours?'

Of course he had some zippy racing thing. The guy only knew one speed—supersonic.

He shook his head. 'It's a rental. But I figure that's no reason to be boring.'

As if he could ever be boring. Still, the ownership gave her an out from the nightmare. 'Then insurance won't cover me. I'm not taking the chance of damaging a rental car.'

'But you wouldn't mind damaging mine?'

Her gaze clashed with his. He didn't look away. Nor did she. Like swords crossed to the hilt, their eyes were locked. Neither would disengage.

'You're driving,' she spoke through lips that barely moved.

'See, you are a coward,' he answered equally softly.

'I choose not to take unnecessary risks.' She broke the fierce challenge by walking round to the passenger side, yanking open the door and sliding into the seat. She really couldn't afford a bill if she pranged. And given how shaky her hands were right now, a prang seemed inevitable.

After a minute that felt like an hour, she glanced over to

where he still stood by the open driver's door. He was smiling as he stared at her.

'If you're not willing to drive either, please let me know so I can catch a train,' she said impatiently. 'I need to get home to get on with my work.'

'Of course,' he answered ever so politely.

Frankly, she didn't see how a guy with legs as long as his could actually fit into a tiny roadster like this. But he did with a way-too-sensual ease, pulling sunglasses from a small compartment and putting them on. That was when she registered the next problem. The two-seater was a close fit. It wasn't big enough for her to be able to slink into the far corner. Instead his shoulder was merely inches from hers.

Too intimate.

Swallowing, she glared out of the window. She'd focus on the external view, not the Greek-god-gorgeous guy sitting so close.

He revved the engine and cruised down the gravel driveway. Victoria breathed again, inhaling the fresh summer air. They'd be on the motorway and he'd put his foot down and they'd be back in Paris in no time and this would all be over. As they reached the end of the drive she braced herself for the acceleration. But when they hit the road, Liam didn't quit the leisurely pace.

'What's with the speed, Grandpa?' she finally asked. She wanted away from him as soon as possible. 'Are we anywhere *near* the speed limit?'

'If I drive too fast, I won't be able to hear you.'

Hear her what? Breathe? She wasn't about to have any kind of deep and meaningful conversation with the man. As far as she was concerned, the less they talked, the better. Her overly sensitive nerves didn't need to hear more of the laughter that was always audible in his voice. So she sat silent, keeping her eyeballs glued to the window. After five minutes they were still going at that ridiculous pace.

'You'll get pulled over for holding up the traffic,' she finally muttered.

'There aren't any cars behind me and, if there were, there's a lane for them to overtake me.'

See, there it was. That latent lazy humour. As if everything was warm and easy with him. Well, if he was going to insist on the snail's pace—and he clearly was—then she might as well quench some of the curiosity burning out her brain. 'Why are you at the chateau so far ahead of the wedding? Isn't your life so busy you could only fly in the day before?'

'I'm on holiday. Thought I'd help her out with some arrangements.'

As he'd helped prepare for that Christmas years ago? He'd worked alongside her—helping out in all kinds of ways. As if he, like she, couldn't cope with sitting around idly all day. She'd always wanted to feel needed. But she didn't think he craved other people's approval in the same way she did. 'You don't want to laze on the beach?'

He shook his head. 'I'd want to be on the water.'

'You're not good at having a holiday.' He'd always sought out something to do.

'I prefer to keep busy.'

'Why's that? You can't relax?'

She glanced at him. His eyes were hidden by the sunglasses, but his mouth curved into that wicked grin.

'I can relax,' he said softly.

'By "getting busy", right?' she asked sarcastically, knowing that was exactly what he was thinking of. 'But you can't cope with quiet? You scared of being alone with your thoughts?

'I'm a professional sportsman, right? Therefore I don't *have* thoughts.'

Oh, he was no brainless jock type. He was smart, successful—you didn't need to note the expensive watch and discreet-but-mega-expensive clothing labels to know that.

'So what have you been keeping busy with these last five years?' Once more she gave into her urges and asked.

'You don't know?'

She sent him a cool look. 'No. You left on Christmas Day and that was that.'

His brows waggled above his sunglasses. 'You mean you didn't Google me?'

'No.' Laughter bubbled out at his irrepressible arrogance. 'I'm sorry to deflate your ego, but I haven't spent the last few years cyber-stalking you.' Which wasn't to say she hadn't ever thought about him. But she'd resisted curiosity then and pushed him from her mind. Now his answer made her wonder. 'Did you ever Google me?'

He smiled at the road ahead, his fingers rhythmically tapping the steering wheel.

Oh, my. 'You *did*.' She twisted in her seat and stared at him. '*When* did you Google me?' It would have been easy to find her. She hadn't changed her name—something that had really bothered Oliver. She had a website—it even had her picture on it. And she was on Facebook like anyone. She frowned, drew her lip between her teeth. What had Liam found out about her online? What info was out there that she didn't know about?

'When I heard you and Oliver had broken up,' he said.

All that time later? A lone butterfly fluttered in her stomach. 'How did you hear about that?'

'I'm still in touch with some people in London.'

But not Oliver? 'You know he's gone to Canada.'

He nodded.

So he probably also knew Oliver hadn't gone to Canada alone. What else did he know?

Suddenly cold, Victoria didn't want to find out. She didn't want to think what some of her old acquaintances might have said about how it all fell apart.

'How do you know Aurelie?' She turned back to stare out of the windscreen, folding her arms across her tummy.

There was a pause. 'I'm one of her ex-boyfriends.'

Victoria clenched her fingers into fists, glad they were hidden under her arms. She kept her eyes firmly on the window. So he had wanted Aurelie. He'd *had* Aurelie. Then she remembered the expression that had briefly flared in his eyes when she'd interrupted him hugging Aurelie. Was he hurt because his former love was marrying someone else?

Victoria released the breath she'd held too long. 'You're still friends?'

'We're close.' He inclined his head and briefly glanced at her. 'Is that hard to believe?'

Frankly yes. What woman could be 'just friends' with Liam Wilson? He was too intensely attractive.

And what surprised her more was that he chose to remain in touch with Aurelie. He'd been the burning bridges type a few years ago.

'Is she the one who got away?' She tried to joke but it sounded flat to her. 'Do you still hold a torch?'

'I care very much about Aurelie, but—'

'You care about yourself more?' She couldn't help interrupting rudely—she regretted asking anything now. She didn't want to know.

He chuckled. 'What is it about me that threatens you so much?'

'Nothing. You don't. I'm not bothered by you.' Lord, could she sound any more flustered?

She tilted her head back and hoped the breeze would cool her cheeks.

'No? I bothered you once. I made you want something you thought you shouldn't.' His smile was still there but all sense of joking was dead.

'As arrogant as ever, I see.' And a game player. He'd considered her sport. He'd done it because he couldn't help himself—consumed by that driving need to win. Even over his best friend. Oliver had told her about the new sailor who'd come into the team—that he was driven like no one else.

He was driven to win in everything.

But even though she knew that to be the truth, her heart puckered. Surely it hadn't entirely been a game? That attraction had been intensely fierce. Surely there was no way it had only been her feeling it for real?

And the night they'd first met, Liam hadn't known she was Oliver's girlfriend. Not until that heated look and those soft, searing words had already been exchanged.

'You'd be disappointed if I wasn't.'

She rolled her eyes but she couldn't help those urges again. 'So you and Aurelie?'

The wry smile on his lips told her he was amused by her curiosity. She lifted her chin and ploughed on anyway. Because, damn it, they'd shared something. They weren't mere acquaintances. A moment of connection had forged a thread between them. Incredibly, she almost felt a *right* to know. He'd once interfered in her personal life—didn't that give her certain leeway in return? 'How long were you together?'

'On and off, almost three years.'

She snapped her mouth shut, almost as shocked as when she'd first seen him walk into that room at the chateau. He'd been with Aurelie longer than she'd been married to Oliver? He must have loved her.

Liam chuckled. 'I've surprised you.'

'Yes.' She drew a breath and nodded. 'You have. But in a good way.'

'Why good?'

'You committed that long.'

'You didn't think I could commit?' His brows shot high, an odd note sounding in his voice.

'It doesn't fit with your image.'

There was a pause. 'What's my image?'

Victoria swivelled in her seat again to look directly at him, determined to play it up and ease them back into that slightly wary, almost joking mood. 'Untamable. Challenging. Arrogant.'

There were so many more adjectives she could add to his definition. But she wasn't going to feed his ego any more.

'And that makes me seem like I wouldn't commit?'

'Well, you're such a flirt,' she said bluntly.

He laughed and his hands tightened on the wheel. 'Only with you.'

'Yeah, right.' That was a prime example of his flirt talk just there. And it totally wasn't true. He'd had them all eating out of his hand all those years ago. She'd seen how the other girls there had watched him. They'd looked at him the same way Victoria had covertly looked at him. With dazzled hunger.

She couldn't believe he'd been with Aurelie three years. What had happened to break them up? Why was she marrying someone else? Victoria thought she already knew. Liam wasn't the marrying kind. Not even to a total dream-girl like Aurelie. He'd never be pinned down by any woman—not for life. No doubt there were too many other challenges—races, trophies, women.

'Are you in a new relationship now?' That curiosity got her once more.

'No,' he answered with a soft drawl. 'I have commitment issues.'

She couldn't help it. She laughed. Even though she knew it was the truest thing he'd said all day.

'What about you?' he asked. 'Are you with someone new?'

She shook her head. 'I have commitment issues too.'

Now his laughter rolled.

'Well, you can't blame me for being wary now.' She smiled wryly.

He stopped laughing immediately. 'No.' He turned his attention to the road ahead. 'I'm sorry it didn't work out.'

'I thought you were all "I told you so"?'

He shook his head. 'He was an idiot.' There was a silence. 'We were all idiots.'

Victoria shrank in her seat. She'd been the biggest idiot. She'd been unable to stand up for herself and say what she'd really wanted. And in some ways, what she'd really wanted had been neither of them. She'd needed freedom and independence and she'd been too afraid to reach for it. But she had it now and she wasn't giving it up.

'The calligraphy's going well for you?' He changed the subject.

'Yes,' she said proudly. It mightn't be world famous but it was doing okay.

'It's an interesting way to make a living. Doing the purely decorative.'

'It's nice to make things beautiful for people. Life shouldn't just be functional,' she declared, knowing he was deliberately provoking her and responding regardless. 'Anyway, it's no less meaningless than sailing from point A to point B as fast as possible. You're hardly securing world peace with that career.' She tucked a stray strand of hair behind her ear with an affected gesture. 'At least what I do makes a difference to a few people—it makes them smile.

'I make people smile too, you know,' he said slyly. 'I make people cheer. And scream.'

She bet he made many women scream. 'Is that why you do it?' She couldn't resist a little provoking either—asking him in terribly polite tones, 'You need the adulation?'

His resulting chuckle made her smile inside. 'I just like to win.'

He hadn't won with her. He still wouldn't.

She looked at him. 'Not everyone can win all of the time. Not even you.'

'That's not going to stop me trying.'

No. Hadn't he made a play for her even when he knew she

was with someone else—someone who was supposed to be
his best friend?

But once more her conscience niggled because he could
argue he hadn't made a play. He'd not said or done anything
out of line once he knew who she was. Then again the man
was so devastating he hadn't *needed* to do or say. He'd only
needed to *look*. And when he had finally spoken? In front of
everyone? She sighed. He was the one who'd got away.

'This the street you meant?'

Despite his determined effort to fly well under the speed
limit for the entire journey, they were indeed finally in her
neighbourhood.

'Yes.' She directed him to her apartment and he pulled up
outside.

Her heart thundered. Her silly hands were actually sweating as she unclipped her seat belt. She was going to say goodbye to him again. For ever. Good, right?

He turned in his seat and faced her. She should get out of
the car. She should open the door and walk away. But she
couldn't; somehow she needed to see him—see his eyes. See
if that look was there.

And he knew it. He took off his sunglasses, meeting her
eyes. His were serious, but there was that glint of laughter
and of something else.

Determination. Desire. *Challenge*.

She recognised them all. But she couldn't let this happen.
Even if she was *dying* of curiosity inside. She'd resisted him
once, she could again, right? She had a new man-free plan
and she was sticking to it.

'Victoria—'

'No.' She pre-empted him. She was not inviting him in. She
was not touching him. She was not letting him—

He smiled. Reaching out, he touched her burning cheek
with just the tips of his fingers.

She clamped her jaw together.

'Even now you want to resist it?' he murmured.

'You can't just pick up with five years in between when we last saw each other.' Did she have to sound so breathy?

'Why not?'

'Because…' So much had gone down between then and now.

'I'm single.' He glanced at her hands in her lap. 'You're no longer attached.'

'And you're pleased about that,' she said tartly.

He clamped his hand over hers, a quick frown pulling his brows. 'Of course I'm not. Believe it or not I wanted you to be happy. I wanted you both to be happy.'

She swallowed, conscious of the strength of his hand pushing on hers. The heat of it. 'We were,' she said hoarsely, but honestly. 'For a while.'

'I'm sorry it didn't work out. But it not working out was nothing to do with me.'

'I never said it was.' And she wouldn't. But the edges of her heart shrivelled because, while Oliver had been the one who'd cheated, she'd been the one who'd withheld part of herself. She'd not been honest with him. Or herself. Or anyone.

Liam leaned closer. 'Don't make me pay the price of him hurting you.'

'I'm sorry?' She narrowed her eyes. 'What is it you want to do?'

'What I've always wanted to do.' His shoulders lifted. 'From the second I first saw you in nothing but a towel and steam. At least I'm honest enough to admit it.'

She felt the steam now as heat surged through her body.

'This thing between us?' He shook his head. 'Still the same, even after all this time. You can't deny it.'

Of course she'd deny it. Self-preservation was a basic instinct. 'I can.' Because she knew all that was important to know about Liam, yet he knew nothing of what was important about her. Like the fact she wasn't about to let herself get distracted. 'You don't know me now, Liam. You don't know what I want.'

'So you're going to take the easy option and avoid it? You're good at that.'

She shook her head. 'You thought you were so clever. That you saw it all. But you saw nothing of what was really going on with me. You didn't know me.'

'I knew enough,' he argued. 'I still do.'

'And what do you think you know? That I was sexually attracted to you?' She kept her head high despite another flare of heat in her cheeks. 'You intrigued me then, yes, I admit it. But I'm not interested now.'

'Then prove it.' His gaze locked on hers. 'Come closer without blushing.'

'Oh, please.' She covered up with a laugh. 'I don't need to prove anything to you.'

'What about to yourself?' he challenged right back, his expression wicked and tempting. 'Isn't that part of what you're doing now? Isn't your move to Paris all about proving things to yourself?'

'You still think you're so smart.'

'No, but I know when I'm right.' He brushed that strand of hair behind her ear for her. 'You're out here on your own. Proving you can do it. You can handle it.'

'And I can,' she whispered.

He smiled. 'Yet you won't even try to handle me.'

# CHAPTER THREE

'You do not have to see me to my door.'

'Yes, I do.' Liam wasn't letting Victoria walk out of his life again. At least, not yet. Not when there was this much unfinished between them. He was going to get *something* from her today. Even just an admission. He wanted to hear her say it only the once, a whisper even. She reckoned she didn't want him? She reckoned wrong. He knew that as well as she.

'I have to work.'

He knew that too. 'I'm not asking to stay the night.' Though he would if she offered. One night was all he'd need. Why she could do this to him, he didn't know, but from the first second he'd seen her it had been there. That hot response in every cell of his body.

*Want.*

But he wasn't the kid he'd once been. He wasn't going to lose it as he had back then—he was in control of everything now, right?

He'd experienced lust plenty of times. Course he had. Had acted on it too. But it had never been as extreme as it had that night he'd first met Victoria. When she'd opened her mouth and answered him back? When she'd been as enthralled as he had?

She still was. He'd seen it flash in her eyes when he'd walked into that room, before she'd had a second to school her face. He saw it now in the way she went out of her way to avoid touching, or even looking at, him.

But he looked at her. And he wanted to touch. In fact he wanted to provoke—that would only be fair. Because that rampant lust was back as bad as it had ever been.

He followed her up the stairs, trying hard not to stare at her sweet curves. Instead he glanced around, checking out her digs. The distraction was not good.

The stairwell was poorly lit but he could still see the grimy, peeling paintwork and he could smell something horrendous—like several stale dinners mixed with the stench of wet wool. How many tiny apartments were squished into this ugly building? They passed a million doors as they marched on. No wonder she was looking fit given all these stairs she had to climb.

'So you're doing the garret-in-Paris thing?' He ground the feeble joke out. This place was hardly the Left Bank and giving her a nice view of the river.

'I'm not starving. I'm doing very well,' she said as they finally got to the top floor. She unlocked her door and paused. 'And calligraphy is a craft as much as it is an art. I'm happy.'

'Good for you.' He ignored the 'goodbye' in her tone and walked right past her, into the shoebox of an apartment—a child's shoebox at that. 'But there are better garrets. With better views.' He frowned, learning all there was to know in a swift glance. One room with a cupboard for a kitchen and another for a bathroom. The place sucked.

'I don't need a better view. I only need good light.'

She'd set up a small workspace in the room. The biggest bit of furniture was her desk. Angled and pushed against the window to maximise use of the natural light. On a flat desk beside it was her computer. Against the far wall—as if it were an afterthought—was the smallest single bed he'd ever seen.

The place wasn't miniature doll's-house cute, it was cramped.

'How can you work in here?' He looked away from the itty,

bitty bed. 'It's hardly a "studio" is it?' It wasn't big enough for anyone to be comfortable in. Not even petite blondes with leaf-green eyes.

'That's exactly what it is.' Her chin lifted high, as if she was just waiting for the criticism.

Confronted with that expression, much as he wanted to criticise, he found he wasn't going to. She was trying—independent and alone. Far more than she'd been five years ago. Good for her, right? Except for some reason it annoyed him more. Why should it matter? Couldn't he, of all people, understand the need to succeed?

'Why don't you come to my hotel and work there? I have a suite—it's three times the size of this place.' He knew before he'd finished saying it that it was a mistake. He knew how she'd react—call him worse than a flirt. Thing was, he meant it. Grudgingly. It wasn't a line.

'Oh, please, that was so unsubtle.'

Yep, she boxed him right back into flirt mode.

'But we wouldn't have to share a bathroom this time.' He walked up to her, giving into her expectations—and his own need to provoke. And stand closer. 'Unless you wanted to.' He smiled and lifted a hand to her jaw, unable to resist touching her again. 'Now, that was unsubtle.'

He'd never forget the time he'd walked in on her in the bathroom. It had been his first night there that Christmas break. To his relief she hadn't screamed the place down. She'd been mortified. In truth so had he. He'd covered up by joking, of course. But he'd soon got derailed. The towel had covered her most private parts—parts he'd ached to see. But there'd been so much damp skin on show and with the steam and the sweet scent of her soap? Of course he'd made a play. A huge one.

It wasn't until the next morning that he'd learned she was Oliver's girlfriend—the one he'd been with for a couple of years. Who Oliver's family loved and expected him to marry.

The good girl who slept in her own room when she stayed—not Oliver's. It was all so *perfect*.

But it was already too late. Liam had been young and dumb and so callow. He'd mistaken insta-lust for love at first sight. He'd been unsubtle in his attention. Unable to stay away.

'That wasn't just unsubtle.' Victoria lifted her chin sharply, so his fingers slipped from her skin. 'That was sledgehammer.'

'This is a dodgy neighbourhood,' he said, wishing he could see her out of here.

'Don't try to get me there under the pretext of caring for my welfare.' She looked amused.

There was no shifting her. And—albeit reluctantly—he respected that. 'So where do you see it—' he waved his hand at her desk '—in a few years?'

'You want to know my business goals?'

Yep, oddly he did. 'How are you going to expand when it's so dependent on you? What happens if you sprain your wrist or something?'

'I have business insurance. In terms of expansion—is it necessary? I only need to make enough for me to live comfortably.'

A single bed was never comfortable, no matter how slight she was. She clearly needed to make more than she currently was. 'How are you going to factor in holidays? When you own your own business, it's very easy to forget about holidays.'

'How do *you* factor in holidays?' She laughed at him.

'I love my work. Work *is* a holiday for me.' Sailing was and always would be his first, his ultimate, passion. He loved the challenge on the water. It was his home—the place he felt safest. And the most free.

She turned and looked at him. Her green eyes were very bright—he felt their power right into his bones.

'And you don't think it's possible for me to feel the same about my work?' she asked.

Frankly? No. 'Not in this environment.' This place was

stifling at best. 'But maybe it doesn't matter to you. Maybe you only see what you're working on.' He walked over to the scrupulously tidy desk. 'You're very good at what you do.'

Victoria couldn't get over his nerve. He couldn't try to make it better now with flattery. Not when he hadn't even seen her work. He'd only seen that mess on the card at the chateau. She'd boxed the others away and right now her desk was completely clear. So he had no idea how good she was. Unless—

A horrible suspicion occurred to her. 'Did you recommend me to Aurelie?'

He stilled.

'You did. You Googled me. You found my website. You—' She broke off.

For once the self-assured expression was wiped from Liam's face. He looked guilty. He *was* guilty.

Victoria gritted her teeth. She couldn't back out of Aurelie's job now, but a huge part of her wanted to.

'I didn't think I was going to make it to her wedding.' Liam offered an explanation. 'And I never expected to see you even if I did. But, yes, I wanted to help.'

Help who—her or Aurelie?

It shouldn't bother her. It really shouldn't. But she didn't want to feel beholden to him. And she'd felt so stupidly proud to have gotten this commission. That she was succeeding independently and on her own merit. Oliver had implied that her early success in London had only been because of his contacts. Not the quality of her work. She'd thought this job an antidote to that bite.

'I mentioned your name when she was boring me with wedding details one day.' Liam fiddled with one of the tins she had on her desk, pulling out the pencils one by one and dropping them back in. 'She looked you up herself and decided whether or not to hire you. She likes your work.'

Victoria swallowed. She couldn't let pride ruin this. She

could still get business off the back of Aurelie's wedding. Her work *would* speak for itself.

He glanced at her, his sharp eyes assessing. 'You're unhappy with me.'

'Not at all,' she lied. 'It was very nice of you to suggest me to her. I'm amazed you could even remember my name.'

'Come off it, Victoria.' He stepped closer.

She instinctively retreated. Because sometimes he saw too much—past her polite veneer to what she was really thinking. And wanting.

'You're so determinedly independent now?' he asked, his brows lifting at her attempt to put distance between them. 'Can't accept anyone's help?' A muscle worked in his jaw. 'Least of all mine?' He let his gaze slowly lower—trailing over her body.

She stood her ground, hoping to school her response and this time truly hide her thoughts from him. But once again he seemed to know.

'What are you so afraid of?' he baited. 'You have nothing to fear from me. It would only be the once.'

Victoria smiled, keeping the rest of her expression smooth. 'Why? Isn't it going to be very good?'

His attention snapped back to her face. 'I've done the convenient relationship. It doesn't work. One-night stands do.'

The 'convenient relationship'? So he hadn't been in love with Aurelie? Or was this his way of hiding his own deep hurt?

'I'm not a one-night stand person,' she answered honestly.

'Maybe you should try it. Once.'

She held his gaze—still feeling that pull towards him, but she was older and wiser and stronger now. 'You don't like to give up, do you?'

There was a slight hesitation. 'No. I told you I like to win.'

'And that's what this is?' She gestured—fluttering her fingers towards him and then herself. 'Like an event to be won?'

'If we don't explore it, there'll always be that curiosity. Be honest,' he drawled, taking another step closer. 'You're dying of curiosity. That burning wonder of what might have been.'

'So poetic?'

'It's the Irish ancestry in me. And I'm right. We both know that.' His voice dropped. 'We also both know how good it's going to be.'

'Liam.'

His lashes lowered. 'It's always going to be like this,' he muttered. 'It's inevitable. It always has been.'

No. She'd ceded control of her life for too long—always doing what others wanted. She was in control now.

He'd stepped near enough to touch her and now he did. Reaching out to brush the tips of his fingers on her shoulder.

'Only once, you say?' she asked, letting some tease out. Determined to make him pay for this casual attitude. As if all this was was sexual curiosity that could be assuaged in one hit.

'Feel free to make me change my mind.' His mouth quirked. 'Love to see you try.'

She stepped back.

'No,' she said. 'Not happening.' She folded her arms across her chest. 'Feel free to make *me* change *my* mind,' she threw at him. 'Go on. Do your worst.'

Startled, he stepped after her. 'Victoria—'

'Was this only ever lust? You're so driven by base urges you ruined your friendship with Oliver? You almost broke up a relationship? For a quick fling?'

Or was it even less than that? She took another step from him, using the last bit of space behind her and bumping the backs of her knees against the small cot she called her bed.

'Was it just your overblown need to win?' she continued. 'You're so insanely competitive, did you need to get one over him? Was I nothing more than the trophy of the day?' She kept her smile on but it was slipping. Quickly.

'No.' He frowned.

That didn't satisfy her. 'Then don't cheapen this. Don't cheapen *me*.'

Now he looked angry. 'I didn't betray Oliver.'

No?

'I didn't seduce you,' he argued, standing so close she could feel his warmth and almost taste the salty ocean breeze that he always seemed to evoke. 'And I could have.'

'You think?'

'I can't give you everything you want. I can only—'

'You don't know what I want.'

He shrugged one shoulder. 'Marriage, babies, Labradors.'

'I tried that. It's not for me.' Maybe she just wanted acknowledgement of what could have been between them. That this had been *more* than just a sexual attraction. That somehow, unbelievable as it might have been, there had been a real connection between them that week.

'So what do you want?'

'A career. My business.' She lifted her chin. 'I was making headway before the divorce. Oliver hated that I was more successful than he was.' The banking crisis had hardly been her fault. Hundreds in the city had been laid off—Oliver had been one of them. But for whatever reason, her little enterprise had gained traction. But after his affair and the divorce she'd lost it. Now she was back at the beginning. But she believed in it. In herself. 'I want to build this up into something great. And to do that I need to finish this for Aurelie. That's what I want. To have work coming out of my ears. For people to love my work.'

He was silent, his eyes boring into her, for a long moment. Then he glanced around her small room again. The plain, utility style room with her neatly lined tins and stacks of paper and materials.

'That's all you want?' he asked.

'That's all I have time for.'

'No time for anything else?' He suddenly smiled, wicked-incarnate again. 'Not even one night?'

'Typical.' She rolled her eyes, her good humour lifting at the swift return of his. 'You just want to bang the one who got away.'

'What, and you think you're unaffected?' he teased. 'I see how you look at me.'

She averted her eyes immediately. 'Unbelievable.'

'But true nonetheless.' He nodded. 'Look, I respect your aims. And you're right, you have no time. But let's clear the air a little.'

In what way exactly? That wicked look in his eye was only growing.

'I don't think the air needs clearing,' she said firmly.

'One kiss,' he tempted. 'We never even kissed.'

That was true. She'd turned away. She still didn't know how she'd managed it. But she was repeating it now—there'd be no kissing.

He laughed at her expression. 'Don't look so worried. It might be a huge let-down.'

'I thought you were too much of a Casanova to let any woman down that way.'

'You might let me down,' he taunted.

'You're questioning my abilities?' She winced at the high pitch of her attempted comeback. Not exactly sizzling.

His smile came so quick, so lethal it shot heat into her abdomen. 'Well, how good are you?'

'Better than you.' She snapped the obvious answer straight back—smart all the way and unwilling to concede a thing.

His smiled broadened.

But hers faltered. She thought about what she'd said. Fact was she was more fizzle than sizzle. The fantasy was shattered. She wasn't good at all. She'd had one lover in her life—Oliver. And he'd gone and found greater warmth with another woman.

'Victoria?'

Liam's smile had died. Was it concern that he was looking at her with? She looked away again. She didn't want that. She didn't want a pity kiss, she didn't want to be a disappointment.

'It's not going to be good.' She cleared her throat and then glued on a smile so he'd think she was feeling it as an easy joke. 'So let's just keep it as an unfulfilled fantasy.'

He muttered something, she didn't know what. She just wanted him to leave now. She had a headache coming on, she had so much work to do. And the emotional spin he'd put her in? It was like going through the washing machine on heavy duty. Only he wasn't washing away all those old emotions. He was hauling them out again—the stains of the past. Want and desire and silly things that she'd forgotten about.

Except she'd not forgotten. And it still wasn't the right time. It never would be.

He touched her. His hand cupping, then lifting her chin. She couldn't look at him. All that sass-talk of a few minutes ago fled, leaving her empty inside. Doubt flurried into the vacant spaces within. He might have stuck with only one girlfriend for a while, but he was still vastly more experienced than she. He'd laugh at how hopeless she was.

He stepped closer, into her space. 'Look at me.'

She swallowed, trying to suck back the stupid pity moment. She lifted her chin herself, working her stiff mouth into some kind of smile, summoning the words to brush him off and escape this embarrassment. She didn't need to be mortified. She didn't need to kiss him and be exposed. He knew too much as it was.

'Liam, I—'

He put his hands on her waist. Firmly. Her gaze collided with his and was captured. Whatever she'd meant to say slipped away.

Silence. Heat. Sensation.

Light from the late summer sun streamed through the window, encasing him in a golden glow. There was no hiding from his scrutiny, or his expression. And his expression revealed desire. Naked want.

Victoria blinked but couldn't tear her focus away from the fire in his eyes. His hands slid over her firmly, shaping her hips. Her hands were useless—her fingers curled into fists. She held them pressed tight in the space just beneath her breasts. She stood as still as a small bird aware of a predator too close by.

He swept a hand to the small of her spine and then downwards. He pressed her forward, until her hips collided with his. She trembled at the searing impact—the shocking, undeniable proof of his attraction. That big bulge pressed against her— instantly scattering some of her doubt. Her dry lips parted so she could draw in a shaky breath. He stared, his focus fixed on her eyes.

They must have shown him something good, because his mouth eased, one corner lifting slightly.

He pressed her closer, then eased the pressure before pressing her against him again. He didn't break contact with her, but the rippling rhythm intensified the sensations cascading through her. Her skin felt scalded—as if she'd been plunged into a pool of boiling water. She couldn't look away from him, from the way he was watching her so intently. Lulling her. Inviting her. Making her feel as if it was all going to be okay.

It was going to be more than okay.

Breathing became difficult, as if the heat between them had burned all the oxygen. She tried to draw more air in. But breathing deeper took her chest closer to his. She lifted her hands—pushing them against his rock-hard heat. But slowly, unable to resist the urge, she stretched out her fingers to splay them over his broad chest. Through the navy cotton she could feel his skin burning, and she could feel the strong, regular drive of his heart. She pressed her lips together again—firmly, trying to ease the swollen feeling of them as her blood pulsed faster to all her most sensitive extremities.

He shifted, planting his feet wider. Both his hands were at her back now. Bending her into his heat. Saying nothing in words but everything in actions. She felt the impact right to her toes.

*I've wanted to kiss you for so long.*

She heard the words in her head though his mouth hadn't moved. Nor had hers. Did he say it? Did she? Or had she just dreamed it?

Her throat was tight; she couldn't have spoken if she'd tried. But she felt the most intense yearning deep within herself. And within him.

She was so hot. And that heat slid in greater waves over her skin as he teased, pulling her closer, closer, closer. Stringing out that searing tension. Tormenting her with his steel-strong body.

Until she could no longer bear it.

Until she lifted her chin.

Until her lips broke apart as she gasped in defeat.

Until in hunger she pressed her mouth to his.

He instantly moved, wrapping his arms right around her, locking her fast into his embrace. One hand held her core against him, his other swept firmly up her spine, to her neck and into her hair. Tangling there. His lips rubbed over hers, firm and warm and possessive. His tongue teased—a slide across her mouth, then a stroke inside—tasting, taking.

She quivered at the intimacy. Her nerve endings sent excitement hurtling along her veins and deep into her belly. She slid her hands over his shoulders, exploring their breadth before smoothing her palms on the back of his neck, his head. Holding him. She'd dreamt of holding him so many times—but never had she imagined she'd feel as hot as this.

Her breasts were pressed to his chest. She shivered in delight as her taut nipples rubbed against him. Her pulse sprinted.

It was too quick, her heart thumping too fast, too hard. She couldn't breathe at all. She didn't want to. She didn't want to break the seal of her lips to his. The moan came from some place buried a mile within her.

Such a long time.

The kiss grew hotter, wetter. So did she.

Her body weakened, strengthened, slid. She wanted to fall to the floor and lock her legs around him. Wanted the weight of him, all of him on her, inside her. Most of all she never wanted it to stop.

He held her close, taking her weight with his large, strong hands. Kissing her the only way a woman should be kissed in France—stroking her tongue with his, nipping her lips. She felt the spasms inside, the precursors to physical ecstasy. It wasn't going to take much—but she wanted it all.

She felt flayed, so hot it felt as if her skin could be peeled from her. It was so much more than a kiss.

Nothing sounded in the room but roughened breathing and the occasional moan pulled from that locked place inside her. It threatened to burst out of her completely. He pulled her closer, crushing her against him. Her fingers tightened on him as uncontrollable desire smashed into her. She wanted him. Everything. Now.

'Liam.'

He broke away, his head snapping back with a violent jerk. His eyes went straight to her mouth. 'I've bruised you.'

He hadn't. She liked the kissed-to-full feeling. She wanted more of it. She wanted him to fill her in every way imaginable.

His eyes were wild and wide, but his face was surprisingly pale. He coughed. 'I'm leaving now.' His breath came fast and uneven.

'Okay.' Her wits were completely scattered. And it wasn't okay. She didn't want him to go.

He cleared his throat. 'You have to work.'

Work? Oh, yeah. She did. 'Okay.'

'So I need to go. Because if I don't go now…' He looked at her.

'Okay.'

'Victoria?'

'Okay.' She just sat where she was, landing on her miserable, single bed. Her legs felt wobbly, her brain fried.

He hunched down in front of her and looked into her face. 'Okay if I stay or okay if I go?'

She stared at him. Then her glance slid past, to her table—and she remembered all the ink and pens and pretty card she had to spend hours over.

'I'm going to go,' he repeated roughly, standing.

She looked back at him—encountering his long, strong, legs. 'Okay.'

Cold descended on her. If he hadn't made that decision, if he hadn't pulled back, she'd be beneath him right now and not caring at all about the deadline hurtling towards her. Well, not 'til she'd come floating back to earth.

Then she'd feel bad.

'Your timing is so lousy,' she said softly. 'It always was.'

He whirled away, scooping up her small bag from where she'd slung it on a chair when they'd first got in.

'What are you doing?' she asked.

He'd unzipped the bag and pulled out her phone. Now he tapped the screen. 'If you don't want people playing with this, you should put a password lock on it.'

'That slows me down.'

'And you don't like to go slow?' A whisper of a chuckle. 'We're not so different, you and me.' He tapped the screen a few more times, then walked closer, stretching out his arm to hand her the phone but staying well out of touch zone.

She took it, watching his face but unable to determine a thing.

He looked back at her. With a small sigh he took one step closer and ran a finger along her lower lip. 'I'll be in touch.'

'Okay.' Victoria tossed the phone onto the bed before she dropped it from her trembling fingers. How was she supposed to work now? How could she possibly hold her pen with a steady hand? She clenched her fists.

He'd gone already. The door banged, she could vaguely hear the thuds as he headed down the kazillion steps. And what was she doing sitting here like a lemming?

All she'd been able to say was okay. Okay, okay, okay.

She punched the jelly feeling from her legs and stood. She was as pathetic as she'd been all those years before. So meekly acquiescent. All her progress had been obliterated in less than a minute. From what—some kissing? To just swoon in his arms and say *okay*? It was beyond pathetic.

Why hadn't she shoved him away and said enough? Or, given she'd really wanted it, why not haul him close and have him completely? What was with the passivity? Why had she let him make the decision for her?

She *wasn't* the malleable, eager-to-please girl she'd once been. She couldn't revert to that type. She had more focus and strength than that now. But that weak part of her whimpered—*so good*. It had been *so good*.

Fantasy, she told herself. Just fantasy. Even though she'd blocked him from the forefront of her brain, she'd built him up. Finally being in his arms, it was sensory overload. Anyway, it had been so long since she kissed a man. Over a year. Maybe it wasn't *him*; maybe it was hormones? Her body saying she needed to get out more, score herself something of a social life?

Or just score.

She closed her eyes and pulled on some strength. She'd work. She'd fake it. That was what she did these days. She'd get this work done. Then she'd find a love life.

And she'd never see Liam Wilson again.

# CHAPTER FOUR

COLD SHOWERS. MANY, many, cold showers. Showers to wake her up, showers to keep her awake and—most importantly— cool her down and keep her thoughts from straying into the forbidden hot zone. But that part of her feeling socially deprived needed some happy thoughts, so she mentally planned, listing the nightclubs she'd go to once the job was done. She'd head out on Saturday night when Liam was at that wedding. There'd be hotter looking guys than him at those clubs.

*Liam.*

Damn, she was thinking about him again. She bent closer to the huge sheet of card in front of her, narrowing her eyes as she prepared to write the next, the forty-fifth, name on the seating plan. She almost had the nib down when her phone rang.

Surprised, she lifted her pen quickly and checked. No blot or mark. Good. She scooped up her phone and put on her 'professional' voice.

'Victoria Rutherford Design.'

'How many have you done?'

She squeezed the phone hard so it wouldn't slip from her fingers. Her heart squeezed harder. He'd always been an early riser and even over the scratchy connection she could hear his smile. 'Pardon?'

'Names on the table plan. How many?'

'A few.' Not enough.

'How many?'

'Who do you think you are?' she said, trying to recapture some smarts. 'I don't have to report to you.'

He chuckled. 'You never used to argue back. I remember you used to do everything anyone asked of you. Obedient and unquestioning. Eager to please.'

Victoria braced herself against the subtle suggestion in his last sentence. She hadn't done what he'd asked her to. But she was hardly going to remind him of that. 'Yeah, well, I've grown up a bit since then.'

She only did what others asked of her now if she wanted to. Like this work for Aurelie. Ultimately it was Victoria's choice. But she knew part of her was still eager to please. She'd been so weak in Liam's arms last night. If he'd asked she'd have done everything, and let him do anything. She'd wanted to please—and be pleased.

Not going to happen. Not with him. Not at this time.

She straightened up from bending over her desk and twisted from side to side to ease the kinks and literally strengthen her spine.

'Do some stretches,' he instructed.

She froze. 'Pardon?'

'You'll get stiff if you don't take regular breaks. Walk around the room while you're talking to me.'

She immediately bent back over her desk. 'I just told you I don't do everything anyone asks of me now.'

'But this is for your own good.' His amusement sounded louder. 'Don't take the independence thing too far. Just because it's not you but someone else who suggests something doesn't automatically make it a bad idea.'

Victoria tried to stiffen, to resist the sound of his smile. Him calling her like this was *not* good for her. 'You don't need to do this, you know.'

'Do what?'

'Act like you're interested.'

'Victoria,' he chuckled. 'It's no act.'

Yeah, but it was only the one thing he was interested in. One thing, one night. He couldn't have made it clearer. 'Well—' she gritted her teeth '—*I'm* only *interested* in finishing my job. And I need to get back to it now.'

She ended the call, afraid that if she didn't she'd say something she shouldn't. She drew in a deep breath and pushed it out in a sharp, frustrated sigh. She didn't want him to phone and distract her. Yet part of her was glad he had. That part of her wanted him to think of her. To want her.

Because she still wanted him.

*Fool.*

She mocked herself. She wasn't going to act on it. Instead she looked at the board.

*One letter at a time.*

Three hours later her phone rang again.

'Time for another break,' he said before she'd finished giving her name.

She pressed a fist to her chest, as if the pressure could settle her skipping heart. 'What makes you think I haven't been taking regular breaks already?'

'I know the lengths you'll go to, to keep someone happy. I remember you staying up almost the whole night to make enough streamers for Oliver's mother to hang in the hallway.'

Oh, Lord. Victoria chuckled. She remembered that. The endless rolls of crêpe paper had nearly killed her. In the end Liam had come and helped her. He and Oliver and the others had gone down to the local pub for a few. Victoria had opted to stay and help. She'd needed some space from the stranger who made her feel so self-conscious with the way he watched her, teased her, tempted her.

The boys had got home late. Oliver had staggered straight up the stairs to his bed, drunk. Liam hadn't. He hadn't been drunk. He hadn't left.

Victoria had determinedly kept on going with the darn decorations, trying to pretend he wasn't there. But Liam hadn't let her. He'd chatted—easily maintaining a one-sided conversation for the first fifteen minutes, until she'd got over herself and actually giggled. Then it had been a fun tease.

Until she'd tried to move out of the chair. She'd not realised how stiff she'd got sitting still so long, folding ribbons of the thin paper over and over.

That was when Liam had come to help. That was when he'd rubbed her shoulders to ease the ache. That was when he'd stood too close and touched too much and that ache had become a burn.

That was when he'd turned her in his arms and looked at her—

*Don't.*

Victoria closed her eyes and banished the memories. 'I've learned to take care of myself better now,' she said briskly. 'I even use a timer.'

'So efficient.' The old amusement was audible.

She didn't want to hear that tease. It had always melted her, always made her smile. She should hang up—but she couldn't yet. 'How is your holiday going?'

'It's pretty frustrating.'

'Oh?' Her heart slammed against her ribcage.

'There's no water.'

'Are you drowning on dry land?'

'Pretty much.'

She laughed. 'You get itchy when you're away from the water too long.'

'Yep.'

'Why is that?'

He was silent for a moment and she knew he was actually seriously considering the question. 'It's my home.'

'You're a merman? Mr Atlantis?' she joked lamely.

'It's where I'm free. It's where I can be in control of my own destiny.'

'You can't be in control of your destiny on land like nor-mal people?'

'On land there *are* other people. In my boat, I'm alone.'

Solo sailor. He'd gone for months at a time without seeing anyone as he'd circumnavigated the globe solo. In his team events, he was the captain. Reliant on his crew, yes, but ulti-mately the one in charge.

'You don't want to have to factor anyone else into your life?'

'I am that selfish, Victoria.' There was none of the tease now, none of the amusement. It was a warning—as loud and clear as a foghorn.

But she didn't know whether to truly believe him. The Liam she'd met five years ago had been fiercely competitive, fiercely determined. But he'd also been helpful. Yes, he'd been on the fringes, watching how Oliver's family—and her fam-ily—played out. But he'd helped, he'd wanted to be involved. Was it merely to have something to do?

'Why don't you ask Aurelie if there's something you can do to help her get organised?'

'Not necessary. There's a wedding planner here. She's scary.'

'Scary?' Victoria chuckled. As if Liam would ever be in-timidated.

'Seriously scary. Check this out.'

A second later her phone pinged. She swiped the screen and smiled. He'd sent her a picture of the chateau. Uni-form-clad minions were busy constructing a big marquee. There were white chairs everywhere. There was one ultra-efficient-looking woman in the middle of it all with clipboard in hand, wireless phone piece in her ear and her hair ruth-lessly scraped back. She was very attractive in a headmis-tress sort of way.

'She's not scary.' Victoria cleared her throat. 'She's gor-geous. And she looks like she's fabulous at her job.'

'She's a robot,' Liam answered shortly. 'And she has everything under control. There's nothing that needs doing.'

'It looks like it's going to be amazing,' Victoria said.

'It will be.' He suddenly sighed. 'So you'd better get back to your writing.'

Victoria held onto the phone for a couple of minutes after he'd rung off. Was his abrupt switch from joke to sigh because of that in-his-face wedding scene? Because of Aurelie?

Her skipping heart ached.

A few hours later Liam couldn't help placing another call just to hear her voice. Over the phone she sounded blood-pumpingly breathy yet brisk at the same time. Just hearing her got him hard and he couldn't resist it any longer.

'I think you should take twenty minutes and come and see me,' he said the second she answered. And what he really wanted was to see her *come*.

He'd been deliberately bold the other day. He'd wanted to bait her. Get a reaction from the woman who provoked him to insanity with just a glance. Get her to admit the vibe between them for once.

But he'd done more than provoke. He'd unleashed them both. He'd had to stop when he'd realised she wasn't going to say no. It had nearly killed him to pull back, but it hadn't been the right time. He didn't want either of them to have regrets. But the right time was going to have to be *very* soon.

'Twenty minutes?' Victoria answered in an unimpressed tone. 'That's all you want?'

He grinned. It'd be more like two given the state he was in. And frankly? He'd settle for anything now.

'For the first round,' he amended for form's sake. 'Then we could settle in for the rest of the night.'

'Have you been drinking?'

'You know I don't.' The way his father had drunk? Obliterating reality from his mind? He hadn't been an abusive father in a physical sense, he'd simply been negligent. Never there. Either at the wharf or at the pub, he couldn't have been less interested in his only child. Liam shook off the memory and focused on his much more appealing immediate future. 'Why try to ignore the fact that the genie is out of the bottle?'

She'd said yes the other night. Not in words, but in actions—she was all the way to yes.

'Throw another cliché my way,' she answered snappily. 'That one doesn't work for me.'

He laughed. 'When did you get so tough?'

'I told you, I finally grew up.'

Had she? She'd been so sweet back then, soft and pretty and pleasing. She'd been all things to all people. She'd had to be—her parents had demanded perfection. Liam looked out over the gardens, his eyes narrowing as he wondered about how that whole thing had played out for Victoria. 'How are your parents? Do you see them?'

There was a moment before she answered. 'I see them occasionally.'

Her answer was too diplomatic, too reserved. 'Are they unhappy about you and Oliver?' He pressed the phone closer to his ear, trying to catch the nuances.

'Very.'

Did they blame her? He bet they did.

Oliver had told him that Victoria had a sister who'd left home as a teen. A total rebel who'd fallen in with the kind of people Victoria's family would have nothing to do with. So they'd then had nothing to do with her. The sister had become persona non grata—her name never mentioned, memories of her life expunged from the family home. And then Liam had watched Victoria—seen the way she'd deferred and smiled and obeyed. Too afraid to ever rock the boat. But she'd spoken up with him that first night when she hadn't known who he was. Without fear she'd been a spitfire. In company, she'd been meek. It still annoyed the hell out of him. His annoyance grew at the thought of her parents blaming her for her marriage break-up. But he couldn't resist asking her one last question. 'Do you ever see your sister? Did you ever track her down?'

She'd wanted to. Working late on the crêpe decorations that night, she'd mentioned the sister—and that desire—so briefly after she'd asked about his background. Then they'd both changed the subject.

Now there was silence.

'Victoria?' he prompted.

'Yes, we met up a while ago.'

She spoke too cheerfully.

'Was it okay?'

'It was fine.'

'Are you still in touch?'

'We're very different people. I send her a Christmas card.' Her words came faster and lighter. 'Look, I'd better go now, I'm still behind on where I need to be.'

Two seconds later Liam pocketed his phone and looked at the almost luminous green lawn. Knots turned in his stomach as if he were land-sick. He hurt for her—she was alone and she shouldn't be. He wished it didn't bother him. But it did.

Victoria's phone rang the next morning at five-thirty. So he knew she'd be awake and working already? She answered on the first ring, an unstoppable smile leaping to her lips. 'You must be really bored.'

'I'll come and pick you up. You have to stop for a food break some time.'

'Food? You're going to take me to lunch?'

'I was thinking sooner than that. Breakfast in bed, actually. Good idea, don't you think?'

'You just can't help yourself, can you?'

'No,' he answered. 'I think of you, sex comes too. It's like peaches and cream, cheese and crackers. Victoria and sex— inextricably linked.'

She giggled but a weird disappointment pressed heavy into her chest at the same time. It would only be the once and then he'd disappear from her life again. 'So this is the only reason you're calling me three times a day?'

In the resulting silence her discomfort grew. Because she *liked* talking to him. She liked laughing with him. But was all this merely a means to an end for him? He was putting in the spade work to get what little he actually wanted?

But she didn't want to sleep with him once and then lose him from her life for ever. She wanted more of *this*. It dawned on her that since the move to France, she'd been lonely. She wanted to laugh more—and she laughed when she talked with him.

'I want you to get this work done,' he finally answered, no smile in his voice this time.

Her work? *That* was what he cared about really? She stopped. Her work was for *Aurelie*. Victoria winced, so glad he couldn't see the mortification staining every inch of her skin red. Of course, he wanted his ex-girlfriend, the woman he'd been with almost three years, to have the wedding of her dreams. He was just passing time flirting with Victoria while keeping an eye that things were on track. A bit of fun, that was all. He didn't mean it—well, okay, he was sexually attracted. But that was all. He didn't want anything more. And his *primary* concern was for his ex. The one he'd liked enough to spend years with, not just one night.

Fair enough.

'Well,' she said, smiling brightly at the telephone so he wouldn't hear how hurt she was. 'I'd better get off and get it finished, then.'

Liam frowned as he slid his phone into the back pocket of his jeans. There was a vibe hurtling along the ether that he couldn't ignore. But she had to get her work done. He couldn't go see her—much as he wanted that breakfast in bed. He wanted Aurelie to have her nice cards and more than that he wanted Victoria to be paid and have her work noticed. He wanted what was best for Victoria.

Truth? He wanted this weekend to be over so he could go to her and finish what they'd started the other night.

She was right; his timing *was* lousy.

He paced. He only had a few days before he was due back on the water but he didn't want to leave until he'd had what he wanted.

He hated himself for that. She didn't want what he wanted. She didn't want him to cheapen whatever she thought this was. But lust *was* all this was, right? Nuclear-hot chemistry. The other night it had exploded. But he'd had to walk—to let her get her work done, to let her cool down from that kiss. Because he didn't want the regrets that a spontaneous, quick tumble would have brought.

Truthfully that insane, insatiable need had taken him by surprise. The overwhelming compulsion to bury himself inside her and stay there had been so sharp he'd run from it. Because Liam never *stayed* anywhere for long. He couldn't. Not for Victoria, not for anyone. She wanted and needed more than he had to offer. He ground his jaw, clenching his muscles— because that desire was still so incredibly strong.

And he'd seen her anxiety before he'd kissed her—the flash of self-consciousness, her admission that it wasn't going to be that good. Oliver had done that to her. He'd betrayed her by going off with another woman. Liam wanted to punch him, as Oliver had once punched him.

Oliver had let her down. Liam wanted to fix it and in that one small way he could. He could give her that relief, restore that confidence in her sensuality.

Bitterly he mocked himself. What, he thought he'd be doing her a *favour*?

He'd told her the truth. He was selfish. All he really wanted was her. Wanted to have her so bad he was almost certifiable.

He changed and went for a run to burn off the energy accruing inside, but he couldn't find his rhythm—couldn't shut his thoughts down. She'd been hurt. Not just by Oliver, but by her parents, her sister. No doubt her friends too. She didn't want to be hurt again.

He couldn't blame her for that.

All he could offer was one night. Nothing more. Was that fair to her?

No.

Calling her so often this week had been a mistake. He'd drop contact completely—go back to the stalemate of the last five years. Some things just weren't meant to be.

# CHAPTER FIVE

'GOOD,' THE ROTTWEILER disguised as the wedding planner said to Victoria.

Coming from her, the one word was effusive praise. Thank heavens. It was all Victoria could do not to collapse into the nearest chair and cry in relief.

She'd done it. She'd worked all through the night because she couldn't sleep for thinking about Liam anyway. Work had been a distraction. She'd focused on nothing but and she'd finished it.

He hadn't called again. No more scheduled work breaks and instructions to swing her arms around and flex her fingers to prevent cramp. He'd clocked off. He was probably busy catching up with other, *real* friends who'd arrived for the wedding now. Maybe he'd met another woman. That was fine. Of course it was. Excellent in fact. All she needed to do was get out of here as fast as possible.

'If you would like to, you're welcome to look at the set-up on your way out,' the wedding planner said. 'But, please, no pictures.'

'Of course.'

She couldn't resist a peek. There was no risk. Liam would be out chatting up some other woman, taking his mind off Aurelie's upcoming marriage. And she needed a walk. She'd been cooped up in her apartment for the last four days.

Outside she turned away from the more formal area where

the marquee was set, instead walking into the narrow alley-way that led to a small grotto.

Her heart leapt into her throat when she saw the figure ahead. She swallowed hard, but there was no denying the burst of excitement in her belly.

He walked towards her with that charismatic grace. As if everything was easy for him. She figured it actually was.

'You're helping?' she tried to ask brightly, as if his presence hadn't just sent her senses into overdrive.

He shook his head. 'Nothing for me to do. Everything is sewn up by that wedding planner from hell. She has a legion of minions and doesn't need another.'

Liam was no minion. But he was restless; she could almost see the energy sparking from him.

'I don't think you being here is a good idea,' he said roughly.

'I delivered the dinner seating plan and the last place names,' she said proudly, wanting him to know she'd done it.

'Right here, right now. You shouldn't be here,' he repeated, a frown spreading over his brow.

He didn't want to see her? He was angry with her?

With a muttered growl he took her hand and tugged, twisting her towards the other side of the path. 'They're testing the fountains—you're about to get really wet.'

Too late. As he spoke a whooshing noise all but drowned his words. Suddenly water showered in all directions.

'Oh, it's so pretty.' Victoria stared as light refracted in the droplets, creating rainbows in the air. She turned to smile at Liam.

One look and she froze.

She'd been spared the soaking. He hadn't.

His white tee bore the brunt and was now drenched on one side. The fabric had gone transparent and clung to his chest. Victoria didn't know where to look. Actually, she did. The chateau and the grounds weren't anywhere as majestic or enthralling any more. All she could see was Liam. Her mouth dried. Her cells shrieked for his touch.

She wanted to murmur his name. It was on the tip of her tongue. The desire to call him closer, to touch him, to tumble in this long alleyway—behind the ornate pillars and symmetrical archways. She wanted to steal the moment she'd always wondered about and explore the chemistry that had always drawn her so compulsively to him. Did it matter that his heart was elsewhere? Wasn't it his body she wanted? But something pulled inside her—stretching to a dull pain.

'Victoria.' A low warning.

She snapped out of it, lifting her hand to brush her hair back and take a moment to recover her equilibrium. 'What?'

'You really ought to go.'

'Am I bothering you?'

'You know you are. And you don't want what I'm offering.'

Actually she didn't know what she wanted any more. But it *was* something more than this. She was heartsore for all they didn't have. 'Why can't we just hang out together? Why can't we just walk through this beautiful garden and catch up like old acquaintances? Why can't we be friendly?'

'Are you that naive?' He glared at her.

'You can be friends with an ex-lover, one you were with on and off for three years,' she pointed out. It hurt. It was stupid, but it hurt. 'But you can't be friends with me? A woman you've kissed once?'

She caught the flare in his eyes as he strode towards her, but she was so taken by surprise at his speed she just stood there as he captured her face between his palms and planted his lips on hers.

Hard.

His body collided with hers a split second later—his taut, fit length sweeping against her so forcefully she grabbed for something to stop herself from falling backwards. She got two fistfuls of tee. No matter that the shirt was wet and the water cold, his skin beneath burned through. It fired her blood as much as the demands of his mouth on hers were.

She pushed back to balance, opening for him at the same time. He took total advantage, his tongue plundering and tasting in total dominance—overwhelming her with the intensity of his passion. But that intensity sparked her own—she found the strength to push back again, twirling her tongue around his, across his lips, into his mouth as she sought to explore him with equal rapaciousness. She felt the low rumble in his chest and he dropped one hand from her face to wind his arm around her waist in a grip that was gargantuan in its strength. She shifted, reaching up to curl her fingers into his hair, eager to clutch him closer and hold him as tight. His wet tee dampened her dress but their skin sizzled. She widened her legs so she could feel him more intimately against her. She loved the sensation of his denim-clad, granite-hard leg between hers and rubbed against him, suddenly wanting the fabric to disintegrate so there would only be sweat and steam and skin.

But as she rocked he suddenly let her go, lifting his hands as if there were a twenty-strong SWAT team aiming their guns on him.

'Now it's twice,' he growled, stepping back to put distance between them with an insulting speed. 'Two times too many. No, we can't be friends. Not until—' He broke off.

Until they'd had sex and this tension would be broken?

Breathless, Victoria watched him. His fury surprised her. His lazy tease had disappeared altogether. All that remained was one lean, hungry, angry man. One she suddenly, instinctively, knew she could push. 'You only want what you can handle?' she taunted, putting her hands on her hips at a provocative angle. 'What's with all these boundaries? Why do you have to be so in control?'

His biceps bunched as he fisted his hands and shoved them into his back pockets. He took in a deep breath, his chest expanding. He stood with his feet wide apart on the grass. His jeans emphasised the length of his legs, the strength, the absolute raw masculinity.

But as he exhaled that mask slid down again—smoothing out the lines of need that edged his mouth. Now it was the smile that returned.

'Women like it when I'm in control,' he drawled.

And that was so not true. Not for her.

That kiss had ignited something in her. Want, yes, but also, like him, anger. Her fury rose to meet his, because this desire was so strong it was irresistible.

*For her.*

Now his tease—something that usually made her smile—goaded her. Could he really step back so easily? She saw red—refusing to believe it. Anger propelled her to act like the vamp she'd never been.

'I think I'd like it best if you weren't in control at all.' Deliberately shameless, she stepped towards him, bunching a bit of her dress so more of her thigh was exposed.

The sudden flare in his eyes filled her with sexual confidence. He *did* want her. And she wanted him to want her *badly*.

His mouth compressed, his brows pulled together, his eyes were riveted on her.

'Victoria.' He spoke slowly, his voice spliced with a rough thread. 'Be careful what you wish for.'

Through his wet tee she could clearly see his nipples. Despite the summer heat they were diamond hard. She boldly looked lower to see how the front of his jeans was sitting. Stretched. Yeah, she'd felt that straining erection and she was sure it wasn't going down in a hurry.

She smiled.

He'd walked away so easily the other day. While she was grateful in some ways, she'd also been put out. How had he been able to *think*? How had he found the strength to make such a decision? She wasn't letting that happen again.

Wild excitement burned every one of her doubts to cinders.

She took another fateful step forward and fearlessly pressed her pelvis against his jeans, lifting her chin defiantly as she slowly circled against him. She was so taut with need, so tired of fighting it, there was no resisting the urge. She wanted what they'd started the other night. Hot sex?

Yes, please.

His hand clamped on her butt, holding her in place hard against him. She shivered at the fierce, close contact. His eyes hadn't left hers—his were dark, the pupils like black tunnels and she wanted to go the length.

His other hand slowly slid up the back of her thigh, his palm pressing firm but at the same time his fingers massaged her muscles—as if he couldn't help but caress. Hot, tight, yet softening inside, she gazed up at him. His expression seared as he stroked higher up her thigh, stealing up under her skirt—still not high enough. She wanted absolute intimacy. His erection dug into her stomach and twisted her tighter so she leaned right against him, letting him take her weight, letting him feel how pliant and willing she was.

He cupped the curve of her butt with both hands now—one outside her skirt, one underneath. She wanted him to slide his fingers inside her underwear, wanted him to tease her, take her. She'd lie with him on the sweet-smelling grass and satisfy this elemental longing. Here, now. They'd finish it.

But she didn't move more, didn't lift her mouth up to kiss him. She didn't sweep her hands over his chest. She was spellbound, lost in the glittering intensity of his eyes and the banked ferocity within them.

There was so *much* control in him. But it was close to tearing. She wanted it torn. The other day she'd been the one to break. It was his turn and she was waiting for it, holding his fierce gaze with a defiant dare in her own. Something rippled through him—surely not a tremble? A split second later he flinched, every muscle hardening. The spasm hit his hands too—his fingers pinched and he swore.

Victoria gasped but smiled as he thrust against her. Satisfaction surged as he bent his head—a kiss, completion, was only a sigh away.

'Victoria?' A row of trees over, the wedding planner's high-pitched call pierced. 'Has anyone seen the calligrapher? Is she still here?'

Once again Liam's fingers dug into her flesh. He thrust against her in another powerful move before stepping back and releasing her completely. She only just caught her balance.

'Lucky escape,' he ground out through gritted teeth.

Not lucky at all. 'Lia—'

'You want more than this,' he whispered harshly. 'But this is all there is.'

'Victoria?' The wedding planner sounded closer.

'I'm here. Just coming,' Victoria called out.

Well, she would have been. Instead she stood watching Liam stride away from her, from the chateau, his broad hand kneading the back of his neck as he went. Anger apparent in every line of his body.

A thin thread of satisfaction pulled her mouth into a frustrated curve. Yes, he might have wanted her to get Aurelie's work done. He might still hold a torch for Aurelie. But he still wanted *her*, Victoria. And he wanted her a lot.

Who was she kidding to think it had been anything more than sex? What drew them together was fire. Rampaging lust and hormones. Where, for whatever reason, their bodies were feverishly attracted.

It *was* just sex. And wasn't that all she wanted? Just sex. She didn't want another relationship. He most certainly didn't. It didn't fit with his lifestyle. He'd been right to offer the one night. He'd been honest.

She hadn't. She'd been confused. But things couldn't be clearer now.

Did she really want to spend the rest of her life wondering?

Was she going to pass up the chance to be with him—even for a short time—a second time?

This wasn't roses and rings and happy ever after. That wasn't in her plan. She wanted to build her company. And she wanted to be like any other normal woman in her twenties. She was free. If she wanted a fling, she could damn well have a fling. He was here for a few days. There'd be no anxiety about seeing him unexpectedly in the future. What better chance did she have of some fun? And of getting rid of this old 'what if' obsession.

Her blood zinged. High on the hit of sensual confidence and assertiveness, she went back into the chateau.

'Is there a problem?' She found the planner.

'Not at all, I wanted to know if you had some business cards on you. I might find them handy.'

Victoria's confidence multiplied more. 'Of course.' She gave the woman a stack, but she couldn't ignore the sizzling sensation in her blood. Not any more.

She went into the marquee, the tables already set for the wedding. She found the card that she'd had to write five times before getting it right—*Liam Wilson*—in that flourishing swirl. She flipped it over to the blank side. And in very ordinary writing, with a ballpoint pen she borrowed from one of the minions, she wrote a bald message.

# CHAPTER SIX

IN THE FOULEST mood imaginable, Liam pulled on his jacket. He'd actually tried to do the right thing. He'd left Victoria to get on with it. She didn't want complication—not even for a night.

Only she'd come onto him in the alleyway of the garden and torn his resolve to bits. She wanted to spend time with him. *Really*? What a horrific joke. Sure, he could text her. Tease her. Talk to her over the phone. But get him into the same airspace as her and all he wanted to do was kiss her. He couldn't see straight for wanting her. Lust in another league from anything he'd ever experienced.

He'd enjoyed his relationship with Aurelie. But in truth most of the time they'd been a couple, they'd been apart. Him competing in one ocean, her surfing in another. It had been convenient and easy and he'd always been able to walk away.

It had nearly killed him to walk away from Victoria in the garden this morning. He didn't like it. He didn't like feeling *tied*. Even if it was only a sexual bond.

He frowned at his reflection. Today his suit gave him a social veneer, but in reality he worked in a competitive, ruthless, isolated world. He was away for weeks, months at a time. The only relationship that could possibly survive that was with one very tough chick. Victoria wasn't anywhere near tough enough. He feared he'd tangle up her emotions. He knew he'd done that to Aurelie for a while—by taking what he wanted and not giving her enough. It eased his guilt, and pleased him, that she'd gone on to find what she needed with another, better man. Love—and that security and grounding.

Liam didn't do grounding. Liam did freedom—sailing fast over the water. He didn't want to feel as trapped as he had all his childhood. All he'd ever wanted to do was sail and keep on sailing. It wasn't a family gig. It wasn't a safe gig. And he didn't want to be dependent on anyone else. He liked to be alone. Just like his father. They were not family men. He wasn't having a kid only to ignore him the way his father had ignored him. And he would, because being on the water was the most important thing to him.

Victoria had always tried to give all of herself to everyone else—doing what she thought she had to to keep their affection. She had needs he couldn't meet. She'd be unfulfilled. And more importantly, she knew what she wanted now and she was going for it and he wasn't going to get in her way.

But he still wanted. And so did she. She'd wanted him back then—he'd seen it written all over her face. There was the irony. To anyone who'd bothered to look, her emotions were obvious. It was just that Oliver hadn't looked—not hard enough. Nor had her parents.

Oliver had cared more about himself than he did about her. And as a result her confidence had been crushed. She'd got less than she deserved.

But *Liam* too was so much less than she deserved. He couldn't give her the security he believed she still wanted. She'd been hurt already. Any kind of a relationship with him would see her hurt again.

But he could give her physical pleasure. He could show her. He ached all over wanting to give her that. He snorted at his own arrogance. So shallow. The best thing he'd done was shut it down and walk away.

Two hours later he watched Aurelie and Marcus exchange vows and wondered about Victoria's wedding. How had she looked on that day? His stomach cramped. He'd never been able to imagine it. He'd avoided all mention of it amongst his friends of the time, certainly avoided any pictures.

Now jealousy of that past wedding boiled in his gut. He really needed to sort his head out. He'd go back to the coast early and train hard.

He followed the other guests through to where the tables were set, the silverware gleaming in the candlelight. Her calligraphy marked each guest's place. It was overwhelmingly romantic. He sat and picked up the card bearing his name. Victoria's letters were pretty and polite and flourishing. He ran his thumb along the edge of the card and then flipped it over. He suddenly felt as if he'd been shot straight into the sun. What was written on the back was penned by the same hand, but the flourishing swirls were absent.

*One night. Tonight. Everything. Agreed? V.*

Victoria poured herself a glass of wine. So much for hitting the club scene and finding a social life. Or even a sex life. She didn't get dressed up, she stayed in her old shorts and work tee with a thin cotton robe over the top and sorted her desk. She had a new project, she'd get on with that—forget the past and take on the future. But she couldn't help wondering what Liam was thinking as he watched Aurelie say her vows to another man. Victoria's stomach twisted. How hard that must be. She shouldn't have left him that message. As if he'd want to see that at Aurelie's wedding? What had she been thinking?

And she'd not heard from him. What if someone at the table read it? They wouldn't understand it, right? Good thing she'd only left her initial, not her full name.

Mad with her idiocy and annoyingly one-track thoughts, she pulled her hair into a ponytail and gathered the materials needed for the two-day job that she had all of the next week to do. But she needed to keep busy tonight. She'd keep very, very busy.

Forcing concentration took huge effort. She took her watch off, put her phone in a drawer in the bathroom, put her favourite song on replay and wouldn't let herself move from her desk. For hours.

Eventually she settled into it. For this project she needed to be extra precise and neat. It was just what she needed.

The thud on her apartment door who-knew-how-long later killed her heart. Three seconds later it started beating back at a frenetic pace that had her breathless. She stood, glancing out of the window as she did. It was still reasonably light, not that late into the evening at all. So it wouldn't be Liam. The wedding party would only be starting.

Whoever it was pounded on her door again just as she got to it. She opened it, took one look at him and had to lean against the jamb because her legs went so weak. Tuxedos made any man look good; the effect on Liam was mind-blowing.

'It's early.' She sounded as if she hadn't spoken in years.

'You thought I'd stay there when you left me this?' He lifted his hand, flipping the place card in his fingers.

'I didn't mean for you to miss the party.'

He gazed at her, his expression dark. 'I'm not.'

'How was the wedding?' she asked, suddenly nervous about his answer.

'Beautiful.'

She bit the inside of her lip—anything could be read into the way he'd said that. And suddenly she needed to know exactly what he was feeling. 'Do you still love her?'

Liam put his hand flat against her belly and gave her a little push so she stepped backwards. He followed and then carefully closed the door behind him. Only then did he turn and face her. 'There's a part of me that will always love Aurelie.'

Victoria pressed her lips together, trying to stay strong and not let that stupid, unwonted hurt at his words show.

'She was as different from you as I could get,' he said. 'It should have been the perfect set-up. She was busy with her career, happy to let me get on with mine. We met up whenever our schedules let us. It was fun—and carefree. I thought it was all I needed and all she wanted. But she became unhappier, wanted more. Then one day she called to say she'd met Marcus. I wasn't heartbroken—in fact I was happy. We were more friends than we were lovers. And I'm happy to see her so happy. I'm not hurt.'

Victoria released the breath she'd been holding—the blockage in her throat eased. 'For what it's worth, I think she's crazy to marry someone else.'

Her words dropped between them—leaving a sudden silence in their wake. She bit her lip, holding back from admitting more.

'I couldn't watch you marry him.' His voice was so soft it was almost a slur.

Victoria's breathing quickened as she tried to hold back the emotional storm building inside her. This wasn't supposed to go this way. They should be in a tumble already. 'Because you knew I was making a mistake.' It wasn't because her marrying Oliver had hurt Liam. Not really.

'You both were. You weren't the right woman for Oliver.' Like a statue, he remained a few feet from her. But his soft words carried as clear as the sound of a glass shattering on a stone floor. 'Why didn't it work out?'

'You know why,' she said simply. 'That I even looked at you?'

'So why did you say yes?'

'How could I say no to him? How could I humiliate him in front of everyone? And I wanted to please him, to please all of them…' She swallowed. 'They cast Stella out. She became nothing to them. I didn't think I could cope with being nothing. Having no one.'

He stepped forward, his eyes not leaving her face. 'Would that have happened?'

It had happened—almost. While she wasn't as shunned by her parents as Stella was, it wasn't far off. The relationship was icy; they disapproved of her current choices. Blamed her.

'He was supposed to have been the safe bet,' she answered in a sad whisper. But he was human. As much as she.

'I'm sorry,' Liam said.

'Don't be.' She smiled. 'I learned lots. And I like this me better than the old me.' She had some backbone now. She had her plans.

'He was an idiot.' Liam's expression clouded. 'I'd never have done that to you. Never would.'

'No.' She actually managed a laugh. 'You'd never have married me in the first place. You'll never marry anyone.'

His lashes dropped. 'You're right.' He lifted his head and intently looked at her again. 'But I'd never cheat on you.'

She believed him. He had honour. All those years ago he had wanted, he had asked, but ultimately he had resisted. There was no real reason to resist now. She touched her tongue to her lips, her mouth dry. She wanted this conversation to be over. She wanted what she'd always wanted from him.

*Touch.*

He stepped closer still and she felt his magnetism pulling—urging her to move nearer too. But he still didn't reach for her.

'Why now?' he asked.

'I don't want to make the same mistake.' The mistake had been *not* saying yes to him.

'Are you sure?'

'You wouldn't be here if I wasn't.'

'I thought you didn't do one-night stands?'

'I can't fight it any more.' She lifted her shoulders. 'It's what I want.' She wanted to be released from the passion that imprisoned her—that made her think of nothing and no one else.

He looked at her—his gaze lifting to her hair and then down her body. That old smile tugged one corner of his mouth.

'What have you been doing?' He lifted a finger and pressed it against her forehead and then pulled it away and held it in front of her eyes. A sparkle of gold glinted on his finger.

She wiped her forehead herself and looked at her fingers, grimacing wryly when she saw more of the sparkles on her hand. 'I've been working on a poem for an anniversary. Using gold leaf.'

'What anniversary?'

'Fiftieth—the golden.'

'Wow.' He nodded.

'Yeah.' She smiled. 'It's a lovely poem too.'

'You're not tired from Aurelie's work?'

Of course she was.

His smile quirked. 'You're a gold-flecked angel.'

'I'm not that much of an angel.'

He traced the spots of gold on her face with his finger and then leant forward, pressing his lips to each marking. 'You're gilded.'

Victoria shivered and took a step back. She hadn't expected such tenderness and didn't know if she could handle it. She wanted fast, furious passion—care*free*, right? 'You're just feeling soppy because you've been to a wedding.' She reached for his belt buckle, her intention clear. 'Enough talking.'

'No.' He grabbed her wrists and pulled them away, locking them behind her back. It forced her chest right into his so she wasn't exactly disappointed. But why was he saying *no*?

His gold-flecked brown eyes drilled into hers. 'I've wanted this for a long time and even though we have only one night, I'm not going to have it over in five seconds. I'm not going to just strip you and screw you and walk out the door two minutes later.'

She swallowed, sure he could feel her heart pounding against him.

'I'm going to take my time and I'm going to savour every second I have. Don't plan on sleeping any tonight.'

Oh.

He didn't take his eyes off her and she couldn't drag hers away, not when his eyes were deepening so quickly—and inviting. 'Is that a problem?'

She shook her head, unable to make a sound.

He released her wrists, lifting his hand to cup her jaw. 'Why have you changed your mind?'

'I think I was wrong and you were right,' she whispered. 'This is…passion.' She chose her word carefully. 'And I think it needs to be dealt with.'

'You think you can deal with me?'

That old arrogance brought back her smile. 'I think for one night. Yes. I can deal with you.' She had to.

His eyes flicked to her hair. The way he looked at her made her so hot. She wasn't sure she was going to be able to go slow and savour; she thought she might incinerate first. She needed to cool off. And suddenly she was conscious of the ratty shorts and tee she had on—and the even rattier cotton robe she'd shrugged on as the evening cooled. 'I was going to shower.'

'Later,' he said, his voice husky.

His fingers traced over her skin—her jaw, down her neck—causing her to shiver even though she was hotter than she'd been in her life. She drew in a deep breath and shifted her feet—*so* restless.

'Slow,' he reminded her with a smile.

'I don't want slow.'

He kissed her neck, his teeth giving her a scrape before his tongue and lips soothed the sensitive spot. 'Yes, you do.'

Frankly she wasn't going to be able to do slow if he kept touching her like this. She was embarrassingly turned on already, suddenly desperate for him to be inside her. She wanted that intimacy—and that orgasm—right this second. She inhaled deeply and stepped back. 'Let me undress you.'

His eyes widened.

'I want to. I have to. Otherwise…' She trailed off.

'Okay,' he answered. 'If that's what you want.'

She wanted so many things, but doing this first might help her settle into it.

She started with his jacket, working one sleeve and then the other. He bent his head as she passed in front of him, briefly brushing a kiss on her jaw. She glanced up at him and smiled but said nothing. Slowly she undid the buttons on his shirt and opened it to reveal his chest. Sleek, hewn muscles, smooth strength. The kind of definition that was only built from daily training. And sweat.

Yeah, the guy was fit. So fine.

She hadn't realised she was holding her breath and she released it now in a harsh sigh. He was silent now too but his chest rose and fell a little faster than it had before. His belt was leather and soft and her fingers struggled to work the fastenings. But he didn't offer to help and she was glad. She wanted to do it all, discover it all.

She dropped to her haunches as she pulled his trousers down. He wore clinging black boxers beneath, fortunately made from that stretchy stuff as they were straining now. She slid her hands into the waistband. She pulled out the elastic, sweeping the boxers wide past his erection and down his muscled thighs. He stepped out of them. On her knees she glanced back up at him—practically agog at the magnificence of him.

'Now you're the one overdressed,' he said roughly.

She didn't care. She just wanted to put her mouth on him.

But he drew in a hissing breath and stepped forward, bending to haul her to her feet.

'My turn.' He didn't smile. He looked tense.

He pulled the belt of her robe right through until he'd tugged it completely free. She glanced at the length hanging in his hand. 'What do you plan to do with that?'

'I know how to tie knots.'

'Yeah.' She knew that; he'd had her in knots for a long time now.

But he tossed the belt to the side. 'This time, I want to feel your hands on me.'

But another time he wanted to tie her up?

'Ditto.' She glanced at the belt. 'But just so you know, I know how to tie some knots too.'

'I'm sure you do.' He stepped closer and took the hem of her tee in his hands. His fingers were trembling. She didn't think he could fake that.

In a second her shirt was over her head and had landed somewhere on the floor. She wasn't wearing a bra—often didn't at home. So now her painfully tight nipples were bared and screaming out for his touch.

He'd frozen—staring at her. She put her hands to the fastening of her shorts—that got him moving.

'No.' He put one hand over hers and pushed them out of the way.

He undid the button and slipped her shorts down. Then, so slowly, he slipped her thin knickers down too.

She stepped out of them both. For a fleeting moment she was surprised she wasn't more self-conscious. But how could she be when he was on his knees looking up at her like that? He reached out, putting strong hands on her legs—one just above each knee. She stilled, her legs parted.

'You're even more beautiful than—' He stopped, suddenly pressing close, his tongue swiping over her. She cried out and bent forward to put her hands on his shoulders for balance. Instinctively she pressed her hips close to him again.

It wouldn't take much for her to orgasm. Another touch? It was crazy how close she was just from being stripped by him. But suddenly she didn't want that—to come in a nanosecond. He was right to want to take this slow—to savour it. To indulge *fully* and finally complete what had been started so long ago.

But she wouldn't feel as if it was complete until—unless—he was right there with her, every step of the way.

She wanted him to feel this as strongly as she was.

'I want to come when you're inside me,' she said in a quavery voice. 'When you come too.'

His hands tightened on her legs as he lifted his chin, kissing her right there again. But then he stood, wrapping his arms around her and drawing her close.

'I'm not entering you until you've come.'

She blinked. 'What?'

'You heard.'

She snapped her spine and tilted her chin to look into his eyes. 'Well, I'm not coming until you're in me and on your way yourself.'

A smile stretched across his face. 'Gonna be a fun night, isn't it?'

She rose onto tiptoe and kissed him—openmouthed, wet, demanding. He shifted, widening his stance so he could keep them upright as she thrust against him, pushing her weight onto him. She could feel his erection slammed against her belly. She felt the way he kissed her back—as hot, as hungry, his hands sliding over her body, touching every part of her.

She smiled. So much for slow.

He lifted his head; his own smile was wicked. He kissed her again and his hands went to her breasts. She gasped at the touch. He didn't dive straight for her nipples, instead he cupped the full weight of her breasts, gently pushing, fingers circling. She felt the tug deep inside as he kissed her again. The guy had the most incredible sense of rhythm—sweet, carnal torment.

Suddenly she couldn't stand any more. Literally. He caught her as her knees sagged and he lifted her to her hideously narrow bed. She breathed out in relief, her legs parting, holding her arms out to him as he knelt over her.

But he didn't put his weight on her, didn't line up his pelvis with hers the way she really wanted. Instead he put his mouth

and hands to work in tandem again—repeatedly, rhythmically sweeping over her until she was hot and writhing and
so *ready*. She arched her hips, thrusting them against him
again and again.

'Liam,' she begged. '*Please*.'

He leaned back on his arms to look into her face. 'I've always wanted you,' he said, his expression strained. 'Always
wanted this.'

'Me too,' she confessed shamelessly. 'Please, please, *please*
get on with it.'

To her immense relief, he left her, efficiently scooping
his trousers from the floor and pulling a new pack of con-
doms from his pocket. A minute later she heard the snap as
he sheathed himself.

She lay back on the bed and spread her legs in welcome.
But he wrapped a hand around her ankle and started all over
again—kissing from her toes, all the way up the length of her
leg. It was torture. But it was bliss.

Why had she thought this wouldn't be a good idea? This
was the best idea she'd ever had. She writhed beneath him,
almost in tears, almost laughing, and totally furious that he
could still hold back from plunging into her. She rolled, deciding to take matters into her own hands—to mount him and
initiate the ride herself.

He let her on top—but he didn't let her slide onto him. Instead he laughed and caught her hips, using his insane, superior strength to keep her in place just above him. But still he
didn't penetrate.

'Tease,' she groaned.

'Not 'til you come first.'

She closed her eyes. 'Not without you inside me.'

He laughed. 'Then we're at a stalemate.' He bent his knees
and slid down the bed while lifting her so she remained in
place—now higher above him.

'You know how much I like to win,' he muttered, lifting

his hands to palm her breasts again. 'I'll do whatever it takes to win.'

He shifted a little more so he could kiss her right where she needed him to. His tongue swept into her.

She cried out, her head falling back at the extreme intimacy. 'Liam.'

'Come on me,' he muttered. He licked again and then fastened his lips around her clitoris and sucked.

Her thighs quivered and she pressed her fists onto her knees. He reached up, filling his hands with her breasts. She breathed hard, knowing there was no way she could beat him at this.

'If I come…' she panted.

'Yes.' He broke the rhythm of his tongue for only a split second to answer.

'If…' She couldn't get it out.

'Yes.' He manipulated her breasts more—perfectly in time to the sweeps of his lips and tongue.

'I…'

'Yes.'

'Oh—yes!' She shuddered as the orgasm hit. Unstoppable. Delightful. Her prolonged groan escaped through gritted teeth.

A satisfied sound rumbled from his throat as he kept tormenting her, so the waves of pleasure kept rippling through her in intense contractions.

She gasped, panting for breath. '*Please.*'

He released her and she slid, bumping her head on the wall as she tumbled to the side of him.

'Careful.' He pulled her into his arms, moving to slide her beneath him, but her stupid bed was too small.

They gave up on it, falling to the floor in a tight embrace. Victoria felt consumed by fire. Hooking her legs around his body. Her hands knotted in his short hair.

He looked down at her. His eyes gleamed. Wide, focused. *Desperate.*

A sense of power filled Victoria. 'Now,' she commanded.

Immediately he bore down on her, driving so deep it almost hurt. And it was so incredibly good she wanted more. She arched, urging. He pulled back and pushed into her again. Again. She grunted as she took the brunt of each powerful thrust.

'Okay?' he asked, his face creasing in agony as he paused.

'Don't stop,' she begged, grabbing his butt in her hands and squeezing to push him closer. 'More…' She groaned again. '*All.*'

He resumed his punishing, perfect rhythm. She wound her limbs round him and just hung on. She couldn't stop the feral moans as he ground into her, closer and closer with every pounding motion.

'Liam!' She screamed as she was tossed into the intense waves of pleasure. Her nails dug into his shoulders, her heels into his lower back.

He roared. His body stiffened, his hands gripping her hard and painfully tight as he shouted again as the tension mirrored in him was released just as violently.

A long moment later he lifted his head from where he was slumped over her. 'Don't go to sleep.'

In answer she tightened her grip on him so he couldn't lift away from her. She didn't think she'd ever sleep again. Every cell and nerve in her body was so wired she didn't think they'd ever calm enough for sleep to claim them. She was so hypersensitive she was afraid she might cry. She really didn't want to do that.

He lifted his head again and looked at her—nose to nose. 'I'm starving—you?'

His easy return to reality made her laugh. Relief swept through her as she relaxed. 'You didn't eat at the wedding?'

'Funnily enough I didn't feel like eating much after I got your message. Too tense. I couldn't wait to get out of there.'

His honesty kept her smile wide. 'Well, I'm sorry to disappoint you but there's nothing in the pantry.'

He rose up from the floor and walked over to the kitchenette area of her studio. He opened the one cupboard and sighed. 'That's because you don't have a pantry, you have a shelf. But—' he turned and winked at her '—you'll be amazed what I can conjure out of nothing.'

'Really?'

He nodded. 'I've come up with some desperate options in my time. Bet you've never had frozen-pea sandwiches the way I make 'em.'

'Nice.' She laughed but her heart tugged at the same time.

But he was laughing easily. 'Especially with stale bread.'

In the end he found some rice and cooked it up with the few vegetables he found lurking in her fridge. They had some almond biscuits for afters. It was an odd meal for one in the morning. She didn't want to sleep. Didn't want to miss a minute.

She watched him as he ate, wondered how many dinners he'd thrown together out of limited supplies in isolation. 'You don't get lonely when you're alone at sea for so long?'

'No. I've always been alone. That's the way it is.'

'But you wanted to join in that family Christmas.' She'd felt that longing in him. She'd recognised it because, if she was honest, it was echoed within herself.

'I was trying to be a good guest. Helpful.' He winked. 'And I wanted to be near you.'

It wasn't just her.

Liam picked up the belt from her robe and wound it round his hands, then unwound it. Now he'd refuelled, he was ready to have every inch of Victoria all over again. He'd glanced at the clock on the computer and felt a surge of panic. One night didn't seem so long at all this side of midnight.

'What are you planning to do with that?'

He smiled as he heard excitement tinge her not-quite-innocent question. 'Play with you.'

'Only if I get to do the same to you.'

'Sure. After me.' He turned to look at her.

Gold leaf still glittered on her body, but it was nothing on the glitter in her eyes.

She'd switched her lamp on to partially light the room. The beam from the bulb highlighted a patch on her thigh. He reckoned he'd start there.

'Why do you want to tie me up?' she asked as she offered her wrists for him to bind to the headboard of her bed. That she trusted him so implicitly gave him an immense kick of satisfaction. That she was so willing to be so physically intimate with him. Finally.

'I want to explore you without distraction,' he answered honestly. He wanted to caress every curve, every inch of her skin. 'It's hard to keep control when you have your hands on me.'

He wanted to give her pleasure again and again. To discover her body, her secrets. To understand what it was she liked. Never had he wanted to please a lover more. And that competitive part of him wanted to ensure he was the best she'd ever had.

She shifted—experimentally moving her legs. But she was smiling as he bent over her. 'So I nearly won, then?'

If he was honest, she'd won everything.

'You okay?' He checked again long minutes later as he finally did as she was begging and worked his fingers into her, his thumb circling over her most sensitive spot until she came wet, hot, screaming.

'I'm so doing this to you,' she panted.

'Soon.' He was pushing her over the edge again first.

It was over an hour later when he let her tether his wrists. She smiled at him with such wicked intent he was hard again in a second.

She swept her hands over him, looking at him as if he were something she'd wanted to toy with—and devour—since for ever. She bent over his body—kissing, caressing every bit of him with her hands, her lips, her hair. When she licked her lips and her gaze zeroed in on his erection he knew he was in trouble.

'Victoria.' Part of him wanted her to do it so much, but he also wanted to come inside her again.

But in the end he had no choice. She sucked him so hard, her hands working in tandem, there was no way he could hold back. No way he could resist diving headfirst into the generous, seductive attention she was gifting him.

She didn't untie him after—even though he was as limp as a dishrag. Dazed, he lifted his head with a huge effort as she slipped away from the bed.

'Victoria?'

A couple of minutes later she came back to him. She had a fountain pen in her hand.

'What are you doing?' he asked lazily.

'You're missing something all sailors have.' She carefully touched the nib of the pen to his chest.

'What's that?' He twitched at the tickling sensation.

'A tattoo.' She chuckled. 'A heart with "mother" or something across it.'

He flinched.

'Perhaps not "mother",' she said quietly and lifted the pen from him.

'It'd be okay,' he said, feigning ease. 'She died when I was very small.'

'I'm sorry.'

'It was a long time ago.' The pen tickled him some more.

'Did your father find anyone else?'

'No. He was a rough man. A stevedore who loaded and offloaded ships. He worked hard, drank hard. Frankly he stank. He didn't have a lot about him to attract another woman.' Except for the ones he paid for.

'So what did you do?'

'Found boats and sailed on them. As often as I could.'

He'd skipped school to sail. Until he'd become so good the schools had come to him wanting him to sail. Scholarships. Performance.

She ran a line down the side of his stomach. He flinched again because it tickled so much. She laughed softly as she dipped the pen in the well again and turned back to him. 'Your abs are amazing.'

He grimaced. 'I'm glad you appreciate them. They don't come easy.'

'Oh, I appreciate them.' She blew, drying the ink.

'Don't put that any lower,' he warned.

She laughed again. 'You don't want me to ink—'

'No, I do not.' He wondered what she'd written. But he wanted to feel her some more first. She clearly ached for more too, as suddenly she tossed the pen and straddled him.

'Release me.' He needed to hold her now—was desperate not just to cup her breasts and stroke her to ecstasy, but to embrace her. He wanted to hold her close. She still had gold leaf in spots over her skin and in her hair. His gilded, branded lover.

She slid off him and reached forward to untie the knots. On her way back down, she writhed her hips, teasing, freely expressing her enjoyment of him—of his touch, of his body. He shifted again—so his aching need was hard against her lush, wet heat. He arched up into her again and watched the burst of rapture on her face. He inhaled deeply, holding back the urge to dive into the mindless, exquisite release. Not yet.

She pushed on him, levering so she could ride him tighter. He rested his hands on her thighs, letting her. Until he felt her tiring—yet desperate.

'Liam.' Her call came, broken, needy.

He slid his hands higher, cupping her butt and supporting

her as he thrust upwards, maintaining her tempo, then pushing it further, faster.

She cried out—pleasure bursting in brief phrases and then moans as words could no longer be formed. He watched the deepening flush and glow of her skin, the red, tight nipples, even redder plump lips and the wild, big eyes.

This was the Victoria he'd wanted—the one he'd caught a glimpse of all those years ago. The lusty, pleasure-bent, hungry woman who'd take what she wanted. Not aiming to please him—but taking pleasure, enjoying herself. Able to give so much—yes. But also able to receive. The woman made for loving.

It satisfied him immensely that she was open, receiving pleasure from *him*. He arched, his spine stiffening as he realised how much he wanted to give her. Passion rushed in his ears as a piercing cry broke from her. He saw it as she shuddered, bearing down on him as the convulsions racked through her body. And he felt it as she collapsed forward, lax in his arms, blanketing him with her soft warmth.

He wrapped both arms around her, gripping her shoulders hard, his forearms pressing down on her back so she was squashed even tighter against him as he finally allowed himself to come.

He found he liked the tiny bed after all. The only way for them to fit on it was if they were locked together, either side-by-side or with one on top of the other.

Mid-morning he fell asleep like that. Still inside her.

# CHAPTER SEVEN

SWEAT HAD SMUDGED the ink—the words she'd drawn on him, mingled in a mess of blue on both their skins. Liam stood in the shower behind Victoria who had her eyes closed as she rinsed frothy shampoo from her hair. While she did, he scrubbed at the ink with the palm of his hand. He could still see the anchor on his hip.

Stupid to be so bugged by such a common, naval theme. A million guys out there had tattoos just like it. There was no underlying meaning in that symbol. Yet, impossibly, he felt bound—just by the play of last night.

He didn't want to be weighed down. He didn't want permanent ties. Nothing anchoring him—not any one place. Not any one person.

Suddenly a flannel-filled hand pushed his out of the way and tried to scour away the image.

'It's fine.' He grabbed her wrist, uncomfortable that she'd noticed his attempt to wash it away.

'It clearly bothers you.'

He automatically released her on hearing that cold edge to her voice. He made himself meet her eyes. 'We want different things.'

'Not so different.' An almost-smile twisted her lips. 'Your career is everything to you. So mine is to me. But they're not compatible. *We're* not compatible.'

Except physically. They were *so* compatible there. But that wasn't enough. 'I've stayed too long already.'

One night was all he'd offered her. All he *could* offer her. Yet here it was, late in the day already. He'd not been able to drag himself from her bed and body. The second night was already approaching.

'Yes.'

He hated that she agreed with him. Stupid to feel rejected all over again, as he had those years ago. Even though this was what they'd agreed—what *he'd* insisted on. 'We can't do more than this,' he repeated.

'No.' She glanced at the ink mark again. 'Some turps might help with that. Or nail-polish remover.'

'It's fine. It'll wear off.' Just as this gnawing ache to be near her would wear off.

This was the right decision. They did want different things, in different places. But he didn't like that remote look on her face. He drew her close under the streaming water and kissed her until she relaxed against him. Until she took him one last time.

He left the shower first, needing to recover alone, resenting the power of this pull towards her. He had to run.

Victoria wrapped a giant towel around her. She wanted him to leave. There was nothing she could do or say to make him change his mind and she didn't want to try. A reluctant boyfriend was not what she wanted. She didn't want a boyfriend at all. So it was fine.

When she emerged from the bathroom he was already dressed, lingering by the door, looking more uncomfortable than she'd ever seen him.

'It's okay, Liam,' she lied.

He tugged at his creased jacket. 'You know it was better than I'd ever believed it could be.'

She looked away. 'But not enough for either of us.' And she'd been a fool. She'd been wrong. This was more than sex.

So much more. But only for her. And it wasn't enough to change things for him.

'I'm sorry,' he said.

She put on an unconcerned smile. 'Don't be.'

She wouldn't embarrass them both by asking him to stay. She didn't want to ask him for something he couldn't—or didn't want to—give.

She didn't want him to feel bad, or, worse, pity her. She had more pride than that. She wasn't a pushover any more.

She'd had what she hadn't taken all those years ago. It was done. Finished. She'd get on with her business. She had a new priority in life. She was in control of her life. She was not going to wish or wonder 'what if?'. What was, was. And she'd make the most of every minute.

'It was great.' She forced herself to sound airy. 'But it's all I wanted too. It's time for you to go.'

She just held onto the smile until the door closed behind him. Only then did she release the painful, jagged breath. She looked around her apartment—suddenly it felt spacious without him in it. Anger slowly trickled into the huge gap he'd left behind. She was *not* changing her life for anyone else. Not trying to do anything and everything for someone else.

Never ever.

She had what she wanted—her independence. The strength to do what *she* wanted to do. And she wanted this. She would *love* this.

# CHAPTER EIGHT

THE EARLY MORNING sun streamed in through the window, the sky as brilliant and as clear as it had been the day before and the day before that. Liam rolled and buried his head under the pillow, totally over the relentless perfection of the weather. Why couldn't there be a storm to challenge him out in the boat? He had energy to release, adrenalin to be used. With a growl he thrust out of bed, tossing the pillow to the far corner of the big mattress. He rubbed his face; his eyes ached, his brain fogged. Yet his muscles leapt and twitched under his skin.

Never had he felt so unfulfilled. He'd sailed for hours this past week, but not even a marathon on the water soothed the inflammation scored deep into his heart. He'd scrubbed every inch of every boat in the shed. Then the shed itself. Even though it was someone else's job, he'd needed the activity—hoped the relentless grind would wear him out enough to sleep.

It didn't.

Nothing could exhaust him enough to stop thinking about *her*. And it wasn't the permanent hard-on causing the restless agony. It was the hurt in his heart. He missed more than her body. More than what they'd shared in bed those too few hours.

The inked image had long since washed away but it was as if the nib of that pen had been poisoned. Leaving him with an uncomfortable—invisible—scar. He didn't think it would ever ease.

Frustrated, he snapped at his crew as they trained. She had him questioning *everything*. What he was doing, what he wasn't doing, what he wanted in the future. Hell, he'd *never* thought too far into the future. He'd always lived for the next race, the next event. Loving the achievement—the solo endurance. The success—sporting and financial. And emotional.

He'd thought he had it so together. His life was perfectly set up.

To fail.

Because less than a week with her back in his life, here he was aching for all the things he'd sworn he'd *never* want. And the thing that hurt most of all was that she didn't want him. She didn't want his lifestyle. Didn't want anything other than what they'd shared.

Illogically—when he'd insisted the same—he wanted to know *why*. Why didn't she want him? He'd never known. She'd been attracted to him from the first moment she'd seen him— just as he'd been attracted to her. But she'd refused him— more than once she'd rejected him. And now, even once they'd shared that incredible night, she still rejected him. It burned his insides as if he'd swallowed a bottle of acid. She hadn't argued, hadn't fought. She'd just so civilly agreed.

Liam stopped winding up the coil of rope as it dawned on him—Victoria *always* agreed.

She always did what she thought the other person wanted. So how was he to know for sure that this goodbye was what *she'd* really wanted?

He shook his head at his fantasy. She'd been so business-like, so seemingly determined. Matching him in the 'career-comes-first' persona. She'd been legit, right?

But the idea took hold—hope took hold. Had she just been making it easy for him? Doing what someone else wanted the way she'd always done?

His heart thumped at the ridiculous eagerness spurting inside him. He was going to have a coronary if he didn't sort

himself out. And it was his own fault. He'd been an idiot—
too blind to see what was staring him in the face, too scared
to admit even to himself what he'd really like. If he'd given
them just a little more time, thought things through instead
of bolting—

He tossed the rope to the ground and pulled his phone from
his pocket. He wasn't spending another day avoiding the biggest challenge of his life.

Victoria couldn't believe the uplift in her business. It was absolutely as she wanted it—and keeping her busy. But being
the scribe who recorded the love notes of other people? Right
now it hurt.

But it also kept her faith alive. She'd survived betrayal and
divorce and isolation. She could survive this too. Other people
did. Other people went on to find happiness. And one night
was only one night, right? So she shouldn't be this hurt. Only
this wound was deeper than any other. It wasn't only the death
of that secret fantasy long locked away—it was the death of
the incredible reality of being with him. It had been so much
better than *she'd* ever believed it could be too. But she wasn't
thinking only of sex. She'd laughed with him, talked with him,
felt so content in his company, so inspired. It was so much
more than sexual. She was drawn to him on many levels. He
worked as hard as she. Was as determined as she. He helped
out—and she'd helped out too. They had so much to share.

Only he didn't want to. He didn't want her.

In the early evening she sat outdoors at a café in a trendier
part of town, glad to get out of the oppressive feeling of her
studio. She had a portfolio with her and a laptop to show pictures of some of her larger assignments. It was safer that way,
plus it got her a little 'Parisian café scene' fun.

Her prospective client was a guy wanting to do something
romantic for the woman in his life—a beautifully printed se-

ries of clues that were going to be part of an elaborate proposal. Lucky woman.

'Do you think she'll like it?' he leaned forward and asked for the fifth time.

'I think she'll love it. And I'd be honoured to do it for you.'

His entire face lit up. 'Merci. Perhaps if she says yes you could do the invitations. I like your work. I think she will too. It's unique.'

'Thank you.' Victoria felt the heat bloom in her cheeks, pleased she'd shown him her personal stationery portfolio as well.

'I must get going or she'll wonder where I am.' He stood and Victoria rose too, slinging her bag over her shoulder.

He stepped around the table and leaned forward to kiss her on each cheek in that polite, Parisian manner. 'I'll call you.'

'I'll look forward to it.' And she would. She smiled as she watched him walk down the street.

'Victoria!'

She turned, put a hand out to grip the back of the cane chair.

Liam was striding towards her. Looking icy. He swiftly got to where she stood superglued to the footpath. He was more tanned than usual, his eyes burnished. Gorgeous.

'It didn't take you long to move on.' He glared after the guy who'd just left her.

Coolly Victoria glared at *him*; the excitement that had burst into being only a second ago was instantly doused at the implication of his words. 'No.' She let the word hang ambiguously.

A muscle in Liam's jaw twitched. 'He's not your type.'

'Who is?'

He looked at her directly, eyes aflame. 'Me.'

She was furious. He was only interested because he'd seen her with another guy—someone he saw as a competitor. 'This was a business meeting, Liam,' she snapped. 'That guy's about to propose to his girlfriend of four years.'

'Oh.' He paused. 'Sorry, I—'

'Anyway, you've no right to comment on who I meet or talk to or sleep with, should I choose to,' Victoria interrupted. 'We had our one night. You left. It's over.'

'You wanted me to leave.'

'Yes.' She didn't want someone ruining her career prospects. She didn't want someone who wasn't going to be there most of the time. She didn't want someone who didn't love her. Not again. And she'd agreed never to see him again because it was what *he'd* wanted. *He* didn't want more.

He'd gone pale beneath his tan. 'I had no idea it was a business meeting. I misread the signs and thought—' He broke off and visibly regrouped. 'I'd never want to jeopardise your work,' he continued stiltedly. 'That's why I stayed away the week of the wedding. I knew you had to concentrate. Your business is amazing. You're talented. You're making it work and you deserve every success.' He backed up a pace. 'I'd never stand in the way of that.'

Unlike Oliver. Who'd been resentful. Who'd been as competitive.

'So you only called out because you thought that other guy was flirting with me?' She felt even more furious. Because that was it, wasn't it? The only time she got serious attention from guys was when there was more than one on the scene. 'You know, Oliver only wanted to marry me to keep me from finding someone else,' she said bitterly. 'Protecting his investment rather than looking at me.' He hadn't really loved her. Wanted her, yes, but more than that he'd wanted no one else to have her.

Liam's eyes widened—and a second later he frowned. Bigtime frown. 'You think I was that someone else?' He leaned closer. 'That my presence somehow forced his hand?'

Had Oliver sensed the attraction between her and Liam? He had to have. 'He hadn't planned that proposal. The ring was a family heirloom. He had access to it any time—it was in the safe in the house.'

'But you said yes.'

'Because they were all sitting there. Because they expected it. Because I wanted to please them, and him. Because I was a coward.'

Liam breathed in deep before stepping forward and taking her by the arm, drawing her away from the café and around the corner into a quieter side-street.

'I didn't come over because I saw you talking to that other guy in some random quirk of fate. I'm not supposed to be in Paris. I just abandoned my training and drove for hours to talk to you. I came to find you.'

This wasn't a chance meeting? Victoria stopped walking, so he did too. 'How did you know where I was?'

There was a long moment of silence. Victoria watched—fascinated—as colour slashed across his cheekbones. Don't-give-a-damn Liam was *blushing*?

'I put an app on your phone.'

She frowned. 'What kind of app?'

'I have the matching app on mine—our phones can track each other. It comes up on a map.'

'You basically bugged my phone?' With some kind of GPS tracking thing? 'That's a first-class stalker thing to do.'

'Yep.' He stared into the distance. Eventually he brought his gaze back to meet hers head-on. 'I didn't want to lose you again.'

Victoria's heart thundered. No. No, this couldn't be. She killed the hope making her heart skip double-Dutch style. 'Liam, I know you had to fight. You've competed against extreme odds to get to where you are. But I'm not some challenge. I won't be a prize.'

She didn't want to be a possession again—someone there to look good and support and not 'be' someone and something in her own right. She wanted to be valued for herself. Wanted. Supported in her own endeavours and not just the one supporting. She didn't want to be a sexualised object or fought over like two dogs did with a bone. Because in the end the bone wasn't of interest. The bone wasn't actually what was wanted.

'Is that how you think I see you? How I treat you?' He frowned. 'What am I to you? The bit of rough from your past? Am I not good enough for you? '

'How dare you?' she challenged, her voice low and raw as angry tears burned the back of her throat. 'You were the one who said we could only have one night. You were the one who said he couldn't give up his lifestyle for any woman.' She rolled her eyes.

'It's easier not to get emotionally involved when it's only one night,' he said stiffly.

'Well, we couldn't have emotional involvement, could we?' she said sarcastically.

He almost laughed at that; she saw the quirk to his mouth and the flash in his eyes. 'The less expectations, the better. I don't want to hurt anyone.'

'How considerate of you.'

'I like to think so.' A low purr, filled with that old arrogance.

She angled her head and pulled the strap of her bag more tightly to her shoulder. 'Of course,' she said conversationally, 'I wouldn't say that it was because you don't want to hurt anyone.'

'No?'

'I'd say it was because you don't want to be hurt yourself.'

'No.'

'No, you don't want to be hurt? Or no, I'm wrong?'

'You're wrong.'

'I've been wrong about many things, but I'm not wrong about this.' She cleared her throat. 'You're afraid of intimacy.'

He laughed outright at that.

'Not *sex*,' she sighed. 'IN.TIM.ACY. Letting someone in your life. Trusting someone. Being brave enough to rely on someone. You can't do that. And the work thing is just the excuse you give. You don't want to commit to anyone. You even admitted that once. And the reason is because you're too *scared*.' She snuck a breath, starting to get upset. 'But don't make excuses with me. Don't come back and bother me. Don't do that to me.'

'I bother you?'

Of course he bothered her. She hated him for it. For not loving her the way she wanted him to. But she could be okay with it, she could get over it, so long as he stayed *away*. 'All I've ever been is another prize for you to win. And once you've won, you're done—'

'You were *never* a prize to me,' he suddenly shouted. 'You were always—' He broke off, closing his eyes. 'Perfect.' His eyes flashed open again, serious and wide and riveted on her. 'You were the prettiest woman I'd ever seen. And the sexiest. The way you looked at me? And then I *really* saw you. Got to see and know the person you are. The way you did things for everyone. You cared so much for everyone. I wanted you to care for me. You were so lovely. You're still so lovely. Not a prize, but the most *precious* thing. And hell, yes, I feel scared around you—when you only have to look at me to pierce through to my bones. You have always mattered to me.' He paced away from her, then spun on his heel.

'I never wanted to care about what people thought of me. I already knew what they thought of me and where I came from.' He shook his head. 'But I knew that was irrelevant to what I wanted. I'm proud of the way I've made a success of my life. And I won't ever give that up—those wins are mine for ever. And I'll keep winning. But I knew I didn't fit in. Frankly I didn't care. Then I met Oliver and he didn't care at all about my background. No looks or comments. This from a guy who came from a background of such privilege—not just money, but *family*. He invited me to his home—the first real Christmas I'd ever had. Snow and everything—a fairy tale. And there was an angel there too. A porcelain doll with green eyes and blonde hair and her heart on her sleeve. Sweet, compassionate, caring. And when she looked at me? It wasn't disapproval or distrust that I saw. It was desire. Raw, adult desire.' He swallowed. 'I wanted her. I wanted everything she had to give. Like I've never wanted anything from any other person before.'

The pain in Victoria's chest spilled over. 'Did you want *her*? Or was she just a symbol of it all—the family, the Christmas—that whole scene that you'd never had?'

'I just wanted her. And I gave up what I'd found—that brotherly friendship—to try to have her.'

'No, you didn't. You didn't take what you could have taken. You said it yourself—you didn't seduce me. All you did was ask a question and I was too scared to answer it honestly.' She shook her head. 'I was supposed to be perfect,' she said sadly. 'I thought I'd lose everything. And then I lost everything anyway.' She sighed. 'So I'm not what you thought I was. I'm no angel. I'm not some perfect thing to be put on a pedestal. I make mistakes. I can be mean. I can't be perfect.' She couldn't live up to whatever image he had of her in his head. She'd only disappoint him.

'I know that,' he said. 'I know *you*. And I just want you all the more.'

Victoria drew a shaky breath. 'Other women had wanted you.'

'Yeah.' He smiled. 'Other women had. But you were different. You were genuine. You had a softness in you. You were so attuned to other people. So empathetic. So aware of how they were feeling. You care about how other people are feeling. You want people to be happy.'

'It's a weakness. I put off things that I wanted for fear of what other people might say or think or if they might treat me differently. You're so fearless. You don't give a damn.'

'I'm full of fear. And I do give a damn. Both are related to you.'

'This can't work,' she whispered. 'You said yourself relationships don't work with your lifestyle. And you can't change, you can't stop doing something that you love because of me. I couldn't live with that.'

'I'm not going to stop, I'm going to adjust. I want to set up a sailing school. I actually want to settle. If I'm with you. But I don't want to hold you back. I know you've held back because of other people in your life. I know you didn't do things because of your parents and what happened with your sister, and Oliver. I don't want you doing that because of me. But, Victoria, I love you. I've always loved you. I've found myself in tricky situations before—we can find a solution to this. But you have to tell me what *you* want. Don't say whatever you think I want to hear. Be honest. If you want me to leave, I'll leave. If you want me to stay, I can stay. Whatever, wherever you want.'

'I want to work.' She blinked back tears. She couldn't give up her job. She needed the stimulation, the security. But she also needed love. 'And I want to be with you. I want *you*. I love you too.'

His arms wrapped tight around her, pulling her in close. Noses bumped before lips touched and clung and her tears fell. He leaned back against the wall, taking her with him, so they both rested against the solid structure. The most incredible feeling of relief swept through her. Relief—and disbelief too.

'I understand you don't want to move.' He spoke fast, his warm breath stirring her hair. 'I have money. We'll get an apartment with a nice view of the river.'

Left Bank? She pressed her face against his tee before pulling back to shake her head and laugh—albeit a bit watery. 'I'd prefer an apartment with a view of the sea or the ocean. Whichever one.'

He frowned. 'But what about your work?'

'It's transportable,' she admitted. 'I just need a workspace with good light and an Internet connection and a post office nearby.' She looked at him. 'I don't want to lose you again either.'

'You never will.'

She curled her fingers into his tee. She nearly had lost him again. But he'd come after her. He'd held onto her.

His heart pounded against hers. She felt his tension, realised that he truly had been afraid. As vulnerable as she. She leaned closer into him and let him soothe her with the gentle strokes of his hand down her back, the light kisses he pressed into her hair.

'It's taken us so long to get here,' he said softly.

'I can't regret it. I won't. I don't. I'm not the girl I was when I first met you. I couldn't have handled you then. I can now.' She lifted her head and looked at him, brushed her fingers on his jaw. 'We weren't right for each other then.'

'You agree we are now?' He pulled her closer. 'I'm not letting you go again. Not ever.'

'Are you sure?'

'Don't doubt it.' He shook his head. 'There was always something about you. There was always just this. Just us. You make me want everything.'

He kissed her. Exquisite tension built between them—delicious torture, free of undercurrents and uncertainties. Nothing forgotten, but now, there was nothing forbidden, nothing hidden. Glorious desire surged as pure happiness filled her. She loved him. And he loved her.

She leaned closer, positively clinging. His hands clamped on her hips, an iron grip, stopping her instinctive circular sway against him.

'We need a room. Now.' He groaned, muttered a short swearword or three. 'I can't breathe for wanting you.'

She laughed, enjoying the heated agony in his eyes. 'Don't stop breathing.'

He frantically dug a hand into his pocket. 'I've got an app on my phone.'

She lifted her brows and teased, 'Another one?'

'Hotel finder.' He swiped and tapped at the screen. 'I'm locating the nearest.'

'Liam,' she chuckled. 'We're leaning against the wall of a hotel right here.'

'We are?' He glanced up at the flag hanging on the corner of the building. 'Thank God. Let's get in there.' He peeled away from the wall and took her hand in a death grip—but she was the one who led the way.

'Together.' She turned her head back to smile at him.

He stopped, tugging on her hand so she stopped too. He planted a kiss on her lips and then whispered, 'Finally and for always.'

# CHAPTER ONE

'No. No, no, no, no, no.' Vivi Grace shook her head at the woman who owned every minute of her existence.

'Too bad,' Gianetta growled, stretching out her hand, her fingers crab-snapping. 'No option. She's throwing one of her worst.'

No kidding. The current hissy fit would be heard three streets away and Vivi was only five feet from ground zero, her ears basically bleeding. Gritting back a helpless giggle, Vivi unclasped her bra and wriggled the straps out from the sleeves of her shirt. Good thing she stayed out back—she'd never be seen in public without boob containment. 'The things I do for you.' And for the spoilt brat who was the bane of her life.

'You're paid ridiculous amounts of money to do them.' Gia took the bra and glided across the room in her inimitable hovercraft style.

Vivi watched, grinning at the woman's *élan*. Impossible as it was, Gia was more mesmerising and unique than her million-dollar creations. But what she'd said was true and, not only did Vivi need the money, she was driven to nail every aspect of this job. It might be completely crazy at times, but she loved her work. And given her relative youth and inexperience, Vivi still felt compelled to prove herself. She had to be better than brilliant and she worked hard to be— twenty-four/three-sixty-five.

So if the brat wanted to wear Vivi's bra, she'd wear her

bra. Definitely one of the more mortifying things Vivi'd been asked to offer up in the last four years, but no real surprise. For the biggest events of the season—New York, Paris, London and this, Milan—she did whatever it took. Tonight Alannah Dixon, global supermodel *du jour*, would wear the ultimate haute couture design of Gianetta Forli, supreme fashion queen and Vivi's 'every-minute-you're-breathing' boss. It was the grande finale of the most fab collection and not a thing would go wrong. Not on Vivi's watch.

As Gia handed Alannah the bra Vivi was unable to stop herself from stating the obvious. 'You'll need to sew it or something, I'm way wider round the ribs.' She really shouldn't apologise. Only an eight-year-old starving orphan would be narrower.

'The point is you're fuller,' Gia muttered, already working a needle. 'The dress needs breasts.'

So why had Gia designed it for boobs when she'd known it would be ironing-board Alannah wearing it? Vivi bit back the bitchy thought. 'Got some stuffing?'

'Plenty.' Gia growled. 'You've lost weight, Alannah.'

'I couldn't help it,' Alannah whined as Gia deftly sewed a few last stitches into the fantasy frock. 'I couldn't eat last week.'

Vivi rolled her eyes. It was a guy. Alannah had lost her heart and her appetite with it. Again. She was master of the 'crush from afar', actors or musicians her favourite *objets de lust*, but when she actually met the guy in question, she was invariably disappointed in the reality. As a result, the world knew she was impossibly hard to please—which made her all the more attractive to many, *many* successful and overly assured men. Alannah the Unattainable.

If anyone bothered to think about it, they might call Vivi unattainable too. She didn't do crushes, flings or full-blown affairs. She didn't do anything. Definitely not during Milan Fashion Week. And she'd not eaten that much these last few days either, she'd been wired on nervous energy and a 'to do' list centuries long.

Braless and feeling as if she were bouncing all over the place, she stepped out to the main changing area to ensure everything else was going to plan. Some of the stylists saw her and immediately straightened and moved faster.

Good.

As Gia's personal secretary she had serious kudos. She was the person responsible for organising absolutely everything and everyone knew it. If anyone wanted to get to Gia, to impress Gia, even talk to Gia, they had to get through Vivi first. She was Girl Friday, Bouncer, Therapist, Exercise Buddy, Travel Agent, Punch Bag, Publicist, Chauffeur, Cook, Calendar, Cleaner, Censor, Enforcer, Enabler, Receptionist and more, all rolled into one.

Vivi turned away from the hordes of hairdressers and stylists, mentally preparing for the clean-up and post-show party mayhem. She rolled her shoulders, uncomfortable without her bra. Not physically, but because she worked hard to maintain her scary 'fail-me-and-you-die' persona. There was only success or failure and she ensured all staff and contractors knew it—from her attitude, speech and image. Her crisp white shirt and tailored black skirt reflected her all-business approach. Inoffensive, unobtrusive, efficient—it wasn't her job to look outrageous. Although just this second Vivi wished she'd worn some scarlet lace number that would've shown through the dress. But Gia knew Vivi always wore skin-coloured support under her starched exterior. She was nothing if not reliable.

Right now A-listers lined the front row, trying not to rip into the goody bags Vivi had ordered. She always had her pick of gifts to include; many companies sought an affiliation with Gia's label. Most were rejected. Only the elite were accepted—ensuring they became even more sought after. For another company, getting Gia's nod was like striking gold. Vivi didn't go to watch their glee, she stayed out back, clipboard, laptop and phone in hand—one eye on the security screens, one eye on the models before they went to Gia for final inspection, one eye on the technicians, one eye on the clean-up already. Yeah, she needed a lot of eyes, a few ears and several extra arms as well.

Quickly checking the nearest monitor, Vivi saw the models strutting evening-wear. One second 'til Alannah claimed centre-stage with her Vivi-bra boobs. She walked back to the private dressing room to get ready for the next phase. The monitor in there didn't capture audio but she could hear the applause thundering through the walls anyway. She paused from her manic paper-shuffling and smiled at the screen as Gia then appeared, owning the catwalk alongside Alannah, taking the adulation.

Vivi frequently pinched herself, still unable to believe she'd had the luck to land a job with Gia and then be promoted to such a coveted position. Hundreds would kill—or worse—for her job. She met amazing people, went to incredible places. But as the applause faded she sat on the leather sofa, more than a little tired. Her post-show crash was hitting too soon.

'Vivi!' Gia's strident tones echoed down the corridor. 'I need you.'

Naturally. Vivi inhaled deep, hoping for a hit of energy. Gianetta needed her for the most basic things. Not merely organisational skills and people management—being secretary to a creative genius meant hand-holding on a whole new level.

Other voices grew louder. A burst of Alannah giggles was underscored by deep male laughter. Great. Vivi frowned. Guests were coming already too? She glanced round for her jacket but it was nowhere to be seen and her bra was still sewn to Alannah's dress.

'We need drinks, Vivi!' Alannah sang. 'I've found a friend.'

Of course. Vivi shook her head. Time to forget about her boobs' bounceability. She lifted one of the already opened bottles and filled a couple of the flutes on the nearby tray, briefly wondering about Alannah's human appetite suppressant. Was he her usual elite A-list actor type, or an extremely wealthy benefactor? To be invited into the exclusive room meant he was *someone*. But still, he ought to have been vetted by security.

The door opened.

'Champagne?' Glasses in hand, she turned to offer one to the latest five-minute-flirt—and nearly fainted with shock.

Oh, no. Oh, definitely no, no, *no*.

Rigid—to stop her faint—she stared at the tall figure who'd stepped in after Alannah.

'Thanks.' Alannah pried one of the glasses from Vivi's clawed fingers.

Vivi didn't answer. Couldn't. She just kept on staring.

'This is Vivi. She does everything.' Sweeping past, Alannah didn't bother to tell Vivi her date's name—managing to compliment and insult Vivi at the same time. But Vivi didn't need Alannah to tell her who he was.

*Liam Wilson.*

Her long-time-ago lover. The one she'd worked relentlessly hard to forget about. *Entirely.* Yet faster than the burst of a champagne bubble, every memory, every sensation, every sigh, flooded back.

They'd run away together. A reckless, passionate impulse. She'd turned her back on everything—her family, her almost fiancé, her carefully planned future. And for what?

Her affair with Liam Wilson had changed the course of her life. Mostly for the better, right? But it had also brought heartbreak.

*He'd* broken her heart.

'Excuse me a moment,' Alannah purred, walking further into the room and pulling across a small screen that she'd get changed behind. Gia disappeared behind the screen too. Alannah was usually completely at ease with nudity, but never with a possible flirt in tow. She knew how to work mystery.

So Liam was Alannah's latest crush? That'd be right—

because Liam loved nothing more than a challenge. And that was fine. Of course. Because Vivi was so over him—light years over him. She'd not given him a thought in aeons.

But now he was right in front of her, a smile slowly curving his lips. Vivi remembered that smile and it hit her exactly as it had five years ago. Like the loud beat of a bass drum, one stroke set her heart on a new rhythm—led by him. But she wasn't listening to it this time, certainly not dancing.

She turned, looked at the glass in her hand, tempted to lift the thing and drain it—and then the rest of the bottle. But that would be telling and she wasn't letting him know how much his appearance had thrown her. Nor was she ever letting him know how badly he'd hurt her—not when he was here chasing someone else. Not when he was looking so, so...*fine*.

She turned back and offered him the glass. 'Champagne?' she repeated, pleased her voice sounded almost normal.

He was still looking right at her and his smile deepened. 'Thank you.'

The tips of his fingers brushed hers as he took the glass. She suppressed the shiver, turning to pour herself a glass with a slow, careful hand. She took a very small, very controlled sip. She drew a breath but her throat was totally dry—as if the liquid she'd just swallowed had evaporated. Actually it probably had, because she was unbearably hot.

*So hot.*

It would be rude not to look at him, right? Not to talk. Swallowing, she went back to staring.

Tall, dark—and, you got it, handsomer than any of those pretty guys who'd been strutting it down the catwalk all week—Liam Wilson exuded more masculinity than all of them put together. More rugged, more raw—nothing but muscle and determination, all but breathing fire. He was slightly thinner than when she'd last seen him and his hair might be longer, but his edges had hardened—leaving him leaner and, yeah, meaner. His smarts were still visible—splinter sharp in his gold-flecked brown eyes. More than intelligent, he'd been calculating. And, in the end, ruthless. Doubtless he still was.

Mr All or Nothing. The 'all' had been fierce intensity. The 'nothing' had meant absolute abandonment. He'd enticed her—claimed her completely. And then ditched her.

Well, that was okay. She'd moved on—higher, further than she'd ever imagined she would. So she had pride, right? Good defence. She'd argue the heat in her cheeks was because she'd been working hard.

'Hold still,' Gia snapped louder than the steel scissors she was using to free Alannah from the frock.

Neither Liam nor Vivi moved. But the amusement in his eyes deepened, as did the intensity of colour. Too gorgeous for any woman's good.

'Did you enjoy the show?' she asked, trying to suck back some cool. Failing.

'It was stunning.'

How had he come to Alannah's attention? Vivi didn't know what he did any more. Five years ago he'd been on the competitive sailing circuit. Teaching on the side, taking wealthy types like Oliver out, getting them some skills and himself money, status—building a reputation that led to demand. Alannah didn't seem the type to want to learn to sail.

But Liam had other talents. And he was clearly good at whatever he did now, given the fabric and fit of his suit. Bespoke. Emphasising the bold, beautiful body beneath.

Hot enough to combust, Vivi wrenched her gaze from him, hideously aware that beneath her white shirt her breasts were unfettered and right this second straining towards him.

*Stupid body.*

But it remembered. Everything. She'd had the hottest sex of her life with this guy—incandescent passion fraught with guilt. Three weeks of burning up bedroom after bedroom, barely surfacing to breathe and travel on. Intense. Insane.

Unsustainable.

Because it ought to have been forbidden. She'd broken all the rules and she knew it. Doubt had wormed its way into her heart. In the end the old cliché was true: lust was not enough. It was no foundation for anything solid to be built on. Even though she'd given him everything. Given up everything for him.

But he hadn't wanted it. All he'd wanted was—

'Don't move too fast—you'll wreck it.' Gia's words rang in the scorching room. Vivi snapped back to the present.

'Gia's work is incredible.' She produced a smile, determined to break the hot-ice moment and fill in the wait for the others to re-emerge.

'Yes, she's amazing.'

'As are the models, of course.' Vivi couldn't help an acidic tinge filtering through.

'Indeed,' he agreed, his voice deepening.

Of course. Back then she should have known he was nothing but a flirt, but she'd been so young—she'd believed in the happy-ever-after fairy tale. Fool.

'So, you're Vivi now?' he asked.

'Yes.' She lifted her chin. It had taken a long time and a lot of effort to become Vivi and she was proud of what she'd achieved.

He angled his head, watching her far too close for comfort. 'You'll always be Victoria to me.'

She froze at the friendly tease. 'Naturally you'd be unable to do something that I'd prefer. You've only ever done what *you* wanted to.' She covered the slight bite with a laugh and a superglued-on smile.

His smile also flashed wider, but his eyes sparked. 'Well, I'm still Liam. In case you'd forgotten my name.'

As if she could ever forget his name. As if she could ever forget his face, his mouth, his hands, his body and the way he used it…

She blinked and halted her thoughts. She'd been there, done

that, burned the tee shirt. She had self-control now. Grown up, mature, she wasn't the bowled-over idiot she'd been. And once bitten, she was now ninety-nine times shy of this guy. She should turn tail and run. She couldn't lose herself again.

Except she was no longer a coward. She was a highly paid, valued and skilled assistant to one of the world's most iconoclastic talents. And she wasn't going to let him get to her or cause trouble at a time that was far too important. And that was the point. She was being paid to be here and do a freaking awesome job. So here she'd stay. But she sure wished she could get her bra back on.

'It's been a while.' He offered another easy conversation starter with another too easy smile.

Okay, that was how they'd play it—like vaguely friendly, old acquaintances. 'I suppose,' she agreed, as if she'd not really noticed. As if she couldn't tell him down to the last minute.

He looked amused. 'You look different.' His attention lifted to her hair. 'And yet the same.' His lids fluttered as he swiftly looked down her body and back to her face. There hadn't been a blatant stare at her boobs, but she knew he noticed them—she felt it in their response.

'Still beautiful,' he added quietly.

Oh, hell. She wasn't going to let him seduce her with his soft-spoken, smiling wickedness—especially when she knew all it ever had been was words. No matter how sincere he could sound, there was no genuine emotion behind them.

'While you're looking as wolfish as ever.' She deliberately glanced at the screen Alannah was changing behind. 'You still love a challenge and a chase?'

He laughed. 'Possibly.'

There was no 'possible' about it.

'So you work for Gia?' he asked.

'Yes, I'm very fortunate.' Vivi maintained her composure. She hadn't spent the last few years working around models not to pick up a few points—like the ability to smile on demand no matter how you were feeling inside.

At that moment, Gia materialised, the steel scissors still in her hands. 'Tell me more about your plans,' she said to Liam.

Vivi leapt at the opportunity to duck behind the screen. Alannah was just pulling on a stunning minidress that should by rights be a tee shirt. She had no bra on either.

'It seems to be the look tonight.' Alannah winked.

Yeah, well, it was all right for Alannah—she was the definition of pert'n'petite.

'Where's my bra?' Vivi violently whispered.

'That ugly thing was a bra?' Alannah answered excruciatingly loudly. 'No idea.' She breezed out from the curtain to sing at the others. 'Comfort stop, won't be a sec.'

Vivi stayed hidden, hunting for her bra and acutely aware of the quiet—inaudible—murmuring between Gia and Liam. How had Liam met Gia? Victoria had control of the calendar; she knew everything Gia was up to, didn't she?

He had to be here for Alannah. He must be the guy the model reckoned was the love of her life. Vivi grimly hoped that the usual pattern was followed and the 'Unattainable' would eat him up and spit him out.

Finally she found remnants of her bra on the floor. Unlike the dress, no time and care had been taken to preserve it from the sharp shears. There was nothing for it but to go back out there and face him—headlights on full. Straightening her shoulders in pure defiance, she stepped out from the small screen.

'Vivi, hurry up.' Gia frowned.

She had no intention of hurrying anywhere with them. She still had work to do—thank heavens. 'Gia, I can't come with you now. I need to supervise the—'

'One of the others can do it.'

Oh, she had to be kidding. But Vivi recognised the hard light in Gia's eyes. The woman might be a genius but she was notoriously difficult when consumed by her latest idea. It seemed inspiration might have struck in the last ten seconds. Vivi kept her tones calm and sensible. 'All right, but I need to go by the hotel to—'

'There's no time for that,' Gia snapped. 'I need you with me now.'

No mistaking that tone. While Vivi was used to Gia's imperious orders, others were often shocked by her supersonic switch to demanding Diva-Of-Them-All. Vivi glanced at Liam and saw the slight tightening around his eyes. But he looked from Gia to her and his momentarily forbidding expression shattered as he turned on a smile.

Vivi turned away and drew breath. Great, so now she got to go to the glamorous after-party in the clothes she'd been wearing all day, without half her underwear, and in the presence of an ex-lover whom she'd never quite got out from under her skin. The one guy in front of whom, if she had to ever see him again, she'd want to look hotter than hot.

Well, doubtless she looked hot—her face felt as flamed as a tomato on a grill. Her frigidly efficient persona had melted and she was mortified. Given the field she worked in, maybe she should be less conservative sartorially, but her attire was part of her armour and at this moment she needed all the steel she could get her hands on. What she really needed was a chastity belt. She wasn't getting sucked under by the tsunami of sensual power that was Liam. Not again.

A bunch of paps loitered by the limo. Vivi put on her best secretary face and acted as bodyguard for Alannah. She'd long since learned the best way to ensure the photographers didn't bother taking a picture of her was to look as if she were on a mission and hold a clipboard or something. Tonight she clutched her bag to her chest.

Liam had also stepped ahead of the two stars and now held the car door for them—looking like a much more efficient bodyguard than she as she brought up the rear. Clearly amused, he looked right at her bag as if he knew exactly what it was she was really trying to hide. She got into the limo, painfully aware of him getting a face full of her butt as he waited to get in after her.

He took the seat opposite hers, the one next to Alannah. So she got to watch as he conquered the Unattainable? Okay, she didn't need the chastity belt, but a paper bag to stick her head in would be really welcome right about now. Because he *would* succeed where all others had failed. Wasn't that what Liam was all about? Winning what no one else could.

'So, what's so special about this boat you were telling me about?' Gia picked up on the conversation she'd been having with Liam while Vivi had been bra-hunting behind the screen. 'Sell it to me.' She went into bottom-line businesswoman mode.

'Everything. Sleek lines, luxurious fabric, simple design. You get comfort but elite performance. The speed over the water is unlike anything in its class. I think you'll find it an exceptionally good fit.' Liam didn't do plain business-speak. The way he spoke evoked the sensuality of the design he was discussing. It was obviously still boats for him, then. Still that 'freedom' that was so important to him and that he could never find on land. Glancing at Gia, Vivi could see his effect in action. He always spoke with that smile in his voice, with the kind of confidence that had everyone leaning forward and listening.

'Will you take me out on it?' Alannah asked with one of her coquettish giggles.

'I'd love nothing more.'

Goosebumps feathered over Vivi's hot and cold skin. She was hyper-aware of him sitting so close, but she point blank refused to look at him. She studied the plain fabric of her skirt instead. Once she'd had the freedom to touch him when and how she liked. And she'd liked—too much. But it wasn't just the possibility of touch making her squirmy; he managed to attack all her other senses too—most especially with that scent.

Vivi wasn't wearing perfume, nor were Gia or Alannah. The models used nothing to stain the delicate fabrics used, nothing that would interfere with the understated scent in the catwalk salon—Gia's shows were carefully designed multi-sensory experiences. So that subtle scent in the car wasn't coming from anyone but Liam.

Musky, masculine, delectable.

Once he'd smelt of sea and sun, even in mid-winter. Now that was masked with a splash of something expensive—and every bit as devastating.

'I think it could work,' Gia said. 'I want to see it. We can go from there.'

Vivi's muscles screamed with tension. Liam and Gia were working some deal? It was Vivi's job to have all potential business partners screened by Gia's financial advisers. She could have had this nixed had she been aware of it. Because no way on this earth did she want to have to work with Liam on anything. She was getting through this car ride and then leaving him and Alannah to it. She just did *not* want to know.

'We're looking at using Liam's new boat for a one-off fashion shoot.' Gia coolly confirmed the worst. 'You arrange it, Vivi.'

Vivi glanced at him, stiffening as she encountered his watchful eyes. He had an annoyingly amused look on his face, as if he suspected how much she *didn't* want to arrange it. As if he knew she wanted to tell him to go jump off one of his precious boats. But she didn't tell him. Instead she pulled on her tough-nut, impervious-to-stress persona.

'Of course.' She smiled. What Gia wanted, Vivi did. She was professional and she had no problem working with someone equally professional. She'd calmly navigate these waters with Liam's own secretary. 'No doubt you have an assistant I can liaise with, Liam?'

'Not here,' he answered with a roguish drawl and a deliberately *un*apologetic shrug. 'I'm afraid you're going to have to *liaise* directly with me.'

# CHAPTER TWO

THE EXTRAVAGANT HOTEL in Milan had more bouncers roaming the rooms than the fashion magazines had models. There were roped-off areas within roped-off areas—screens protecting the most rich and famous from the merely rich and famous. And, in the central, most holy, V.V.V.V.I.P part of the place stood Liam Wilson.

He didn't let it go to his head. He was only here because of mystery, reputation and mutual benefit. Because the world's most sought-after designer was happy to work with him and her pet, the world's latest 'It' model, was happy to use him. He wasn't afraid of using contacts to get ahead either—not in the professional sense. But this wasn't just about business. This was personal too.

He'd wanted to catch up with Victoria Rutherford—the woman now named Vivi Grace. He'd known she'd be somewhere behind the scenes at the show tonight but, even so, finally seeing her again had taken him by complete surprise. It was that gloriously sexy, uptight outfit. He'd had to freeze as if it were a game of musical statues to stop from hitting on her as he had five years ago. In less than a second the urge had bitten all over again. Red hot, rampaging lust.

*Rot.* He gritted his teeth. He did *not* still find her attractive. It was merely her braless state. Finding real curves in this particular environment was heady stuff. Plus, he'd been single—i.e. sex-starved—these last few months. He'd been working vicious hours. His juices were flowing because he smelt business success in the air... Oh, he could come up with a hundred excuses for the instant rock-hard reaction he'd felt.

But he couldn't help looking at her. Drinking her in. She had the same beautiful curves—swollen breasts, slim waist, sweet hips. Her white shirt and black skirt were clearly intended to give off the uber-efficient, frigid school-mistress stereotype, but they totally failed. The knee-length skirt simply emphasised the legs on show beneath and made a man itch to slide the hem higher to see the thighs Liam already knew were supple, strong and yet soft. The fabric curved tight over her hips, giving her a slim roundedness that was so much more attractive to him than the bony frame of the supposed supermodel.

On her feet were the instruments of torture that were uniform in this industry—the highest of heels. He'd no idea how she could walk in them but he liked how they brought her face nearer to his. Not quite eye to eye but tantalisingly not far from mouth to mouth. They were a superficial sign of change—so different from the slip-on things she'd worn that winter. Her hair was different too. Gone were the long waves of blonde. In their place was a sharp-edged cut just to her chin. Very French. He'd seen the style a lot. On Victoria it looked good, but so different from the style she'd had those years ago. A veneer of sophistication had replaced sweet innocence. She'd topped off this change with her new name. *Vivi*.

But none of those changes wiped the image he had of her in his head—with her naked and able only to breathe through the moments beyond climax. The most beautiful woman he'd ever known.

And he'd known plenty in the last five years.

Yet none had left the same impression. None had left this residual irritation—like a barb beneath his skin. None had led to another moment of madness—the one that had brought him here. Liam tried to rein in the energy building in him—the

very, very red blood pulsing round his body. Victoria Rutherford.

Too hot to handle. Too hot to last.

For a moment his mind was so fogged with tumultuous
memories he couldn't speak. It could have been an hour ago
when she'd been soft, warm, willing and he'd lost himself in
her. He'd not meant to get that physical that quick once they'd
walked out on everything. But she'd stunned him with her
sweetness and he'd been unable to resist. Taking what she'd
offered. Stupidly, he'd become more jealous of Oliver than
he'd been before. She'd drilled him open until he'd never felt
so unsure in his life. He'd asked her stupid, insecure questions, needing to know that what was between them was better. But whatever had brought them together eroded—again
more quickly than he'd imagined it could.

She'd left and he didn't just lose his heart. But everything
he'd achieved.

Business contacts, work, his world. She'd no idea how much
it had cost him. No idea what he'd brought himself up from
only to be dumped in an even worse place. He'd had to start
all over again—from below the line he'd started. Because he
then had the reputation, the ostracism, to overcome. He'd betrayed someone who should have been like a brother to him.
But Liam had never had a brother. Never had anything anyone
could call a family. And that was the way it would stay—no
long-term lover, certainly no marriage. Career came first and
always would. It was the one constant in his life and what gave
him greatest satisfaction.

Which wasn't to say he didn't like sex. Usually he pursued
plenty of it—and won. Now he had the money and status that
came with success, he won even more. Which gave him more
reason to doubt a woman's motivation. Because back in the
day when all he'd had to offer was himself, it hadn't been what
she'd wanted. It hadn't been *him* at all. Victoria Rutherford

had used him all those years ago and he'd suffered through hell because of it.

He took another sip of his drink and told his imagination to settle and his pulse to slow. It wasn't that she'd broken his heart. It had been a *crush*. He'd been tempted by the forbidden and by hormone-fuelled fantasy. And he'd recovered what he'd lost. He'd worked round the clock. He'd had to leave the UK and try Europe—doing anything and everything. Clawing his way back up the ladder. In truth, he'd probably done better than he would have had he stayed, because he'd had to reach round for other business opportunities. It had cost him hours and hours of sheer graft, struggle and sweat but he'd done it. Single-handed. And single he would remain. Always. He'd never risk his security again.

So, for now he'd sort out this photo shoot deal with the designer. It was a win-win proposition and the old bird already knew it. He could handle a few meetings with Victoria. He'd pull a satisfactory outcome from this lame burst of curiosity. But right now that curiosity bit harder. Liam looked across the room to where she stood in the corner, yapping into her mobile phone. He pegged it as defensive—a way of disengaging from the scene in the room and the threat of a scene with him.

Too bad. He started walking. Because it was time for the kind of scene Victoria had once loathed.

A frisson of awareness skittered down Vivi's spine. She turned and watched Liam walk nearer. He watched her in a way that set her teeth on edge. Compelling, confident he'd get her attention. Of course he bloody would. He got everyone's attention. She'd done some quick research as soon as she'd got Gia ensconced centre stage in the room with her favourite drink on tap. Liam hadn't hidden the way she had. So now she knew—he headed a luxury boat-building firm based on the Italian coast. He'd turned the ancient, once-family-owned company around. In only a few short years he'd pulled them out of the red and into the utterly desirable. He'd fended off an aggressive take-over threat from a far bigger rival and come out on top. He had people queuing for orders and celebs calling in favours to get in first—almost as many as Gia. Vivi knew to have achieved that much in such a short time meant he'd worked every hour there was. He simply had to have a team with him now.

'Are you sure you want to organise this shoot yourself?' she said the second he got within earshot, a bright smile pinned to her lips. 'You wouldn't prefer to have an assistant work out the fine details with me?'

'The thought of dealing directly with me really does bother you.' He stopped walking an inch over a socially acceptable distance from her.

'Of course it doesn't.' She maintained her smile through gritted teeth and resisted the urge to take a step back. 'I'm just surprised you have the *time to waste* on something small like this.' She less than subtly emphasised the 'time to waste'. That was what he'd said to her in the heat of one of their many arguments in the last few days they were together.

*I don't have the time to waste on this.*

*On you.*

'It's a very precious boat and has yet to be revealed to anyone,' he said lazily, not taking his eyes from her face. 'It's under tight security until the Genoa show in a couple of weeks. This is my absolute priority.'

'You don't think you're leaving it a little late to get promo shots?'

He laughed. 'I already have promo shots. But when you get the chance to have the world's most popular designer and her model work with you, you take it.'

'Yes,' Vivi mused, her bitch-claws flashing out. 'You were always good at taking every chance you got.'

'It is a skill of mine. And I'll continue to take full advantage of every chance I get until I have all that I want.'

'And what do you want?' She stared right back at him, refusing to think that there'd been any subtle suggestion in his tone. 'Global domination?'

'Why not?'

'Why indeed?' she answered lightly. 'All the money, the travel—'

'Don't forget the women.' His smile was lazy but his eyes were sharp.

'Oh, how could I forget the women? So you have everything you desire—fame, fortune, fawning minions?'

'Minions?' He chuckled. 'Is that what you are?'

Anger flashed—white-hot, rapid—but she controlled it, using everything she had to preserve an almost unruffled exterior. 'I'm no minion.' Certainly not his. 'I'm the puppeteer. I organised this party—this whole decadent circus was on my instruction.'

'Really?'

Something about that answer set her on edge—as if he was indulging her. She was proud of who she'd become, what she'd done. 'Absolutely. You know—' she stood taller '—I really ought to thank you. This job, my life—' she waved a hand at the opulent room '—all because I walked out. My leaving home, leaving you—it was the best thing I ever did.' She lifted her chin, emphasising her bravado. Masking the tendril of fear that was uncurling in her stomach—fear that one chink of her armour had loosened from one little *look*.

There was a moment of silence.

'Well.' He paused again. 'Congratulations.'

Caution niggled—something in his tone alerting her. His face had shuttered again, his lashes lowered, hiding the warmth in his eyes.

'I want you to meet with me first thing in the morning,' he said.

'That's not possible.' She smiled an insincere apology.

Thank goodness she was having a few days off. She'd arrange his shoot once she got back. 'I have—'

'But Gia promised you'd take care of everything and meet every single one of my demands.' His shoulders lifted and his eyes widened as if in total innocence.

Vivi mentally counted to five. Because she recognised the single-minded obstinacy beneath his good-humoured façade. She couldn't let him muck up her rep with Gia and she suspected he would. 'As long as every single one of your demands is *professional*, then of course I will.' She smiled. For Gia.

'You think my demands might not be professional?' he leaned in to murmur.

She angled her head back, aware she exposed her neck as she did—ignoring the secret flare of desire within for him to kiss her vulnerable skin. 'I think the professional and the personal are intertwined for you.'

'Oh?'

He moved forward and she backed up a pace before thinking better of it and locking her knees tight. 'Nothing matters to you more than the professional and you're more than happy to use the personal to get there.'

She ignored the battling urges within her—flee-or-fornicate. Crass it might be, but those had always been her only options when it came to Liam. But she was doing neither tonight. She was in *control*. She'd never been in control of her feelings around Liam before, but she'd grown up plenty since then.

'Then it's just as well you're still so eager to please, isn't it?' He angled his head bringing him to a way more personal than professional distance—a kiss distance. 'How ironic that the girl who was so determined to achieve independence has become the ultimate in slave.'

She blinked. 'Excuse me?'

'Running around after your boss. Never saying no. Definitely a *slave*.'

Oh, that was rude. But worse was her melting reaction to the way he lingered over that last insulting word. The dreadful thing was she'd felt enslaved all those years ago—so in love she was all but bound to him. Being that enthralled was what she'd run from. Especially when that depth of emotion had never been reciprocated. She fought harder to hide the electrical current running red-hot between them now. 'I'll *never* be your slave.'

'No?' He lifted his hand and brushed the back of his finger along the edge of her tightly clenched jaw before he stepped away. 'Seven-thirty tomorrow morning. My hotel.'

Liam walked away before he did something really stupid— like pushing her back to the wall and kissing the sass out of her. Since when did Victoria Rutherford talk back like that? Since when did she deny what was so obvious between them? She'd never been able to before.

And *he'd* been unable to help stepping closer just then. Drawn like an idiot moth. Again. And she'd admitted that she'd used him—that what had happened had been the best thing for her. Just as he'd suspected. All she'd really wanted was to get out of that small village and the life her parents had mapped for her. He'd been the convenient taxi driver— one that gave her a few thrills along the way. Now she was Ms Independent and so happy about it?

She'd got more than some lip with her sophistication. She'd got bite. And frankly, she made him want to bite back. His teeth were already sharpened, thanks to the driving attraction that had surged back within a second of seeing her again. But here she was acting all uninterested? All cool and calm and unaffected? Little liar. He'd read the signs—he'd heard the husky edge in her voice, seen her flush and the tension in her body. Sexual tension. Well, he wasn't letting her deny it. She wasn't rewriting history. That attraction had been insane. It still was. Those hormones still crazy powerful—but not un-controllable. At least, not for him.

And he'd prove it.

He smiled as he raided a tray of hors d'oeuvres. But it was another appetite he was planning to sate. He hadn't felt driven to prove a point in a long time. But this was irresistible. He'd play. He'd take such delight in teasing. And in less than a week he'd have Victoria Rutherford begging him to bite her.

Vivi tried not to watch him from across the room but she was viciously aware of him laughing with Alannah and Gia and everyone else having a jolly good time.

She *wasn't* anyone's slave. She was paid a mint and she deserved to be. Gia was lucky to have her. But for once she didn't want to stay sober and sensible and on the sidelines. She stepped forward, grabbing a glass of champagne from a tray being carried straight past her. She'd participate, she'd prove how she belonged right in the heart of this society.

She took a sip and heard a laugh from nearby. She turned. Nico, one of Gia's fave photographers, was watching her. 'You're in a strange mood tonight, Vivi.' He stepped closer.

'You think?' She took another deep sip of the champagne. She was infuriated with Liam for showing up. As for stand-ing that bit too close, speaking that bit too soft—as if it were yesterday that they'd been shagging as if there were no tomor-row? There hadn't been a tomorrow, of course. There hadn't been anything for him but blind lust and she wasn't falling into that trap again.

Nico nodded, his gaze roaming over her. 'You have an aura about you.'

'An aura?'

'A lot of energy.' He looked her up and down again.

'There's definitely something in the air tonight.' Nico looked surprised. 'You really do look different. More liber-ated.'

'That would be my lack of bra,' she said bluntly. 'Alannah used it in the show and now it's shredded.'

'Alannah seems to be interested in another of your possessions at the moment.'

Her *possession*? Vivi followed Nico's gaze and looked over to where Alannah was hanging on Liam's every word. 'She can do what she wants with that.' Vivi determinedly turned back to Nico. 'He's not mine.'

'Vivi.' Nico looked amused. 'You forget I record expressions for a living. I understand every flicker of emotion on someone's face. My trigger finger knows when to snap that flash of pure, personal honesty. You *own* that guy.'

'As if.' Vivi damped down the violent surge of feminine satisfaction at the possibility. It was ludicrous. 'You don't understand emotion—you deal with blank canvasses and give the *illusion* of emotion with make-up, staging and lighting.'

'Vivi—' Nico put his hand on his chest '—you wound me.'

'It's true. And then you tweak the fantasy pictures even more on the computer.' She teased with a smile. 'You're not a photographer, you're a two-bit magician using sleight of hand and trickery to deceive the eye.'

Nico laughed with relish. 'Definitely a blazing aura. I wonder just what—or *who*—it is that's set you on fire tonight.'

'I've already told you.' Vivi shrugged. 'It's the lack of bra.'

'When stripped, Victoria's a completely different person,' Liam drawled behind her.

Vivi stiffened and turned.

'*Victoria*?' Nico laughed again. 'Who *is* this woman?'

Liam stepped between her and Nico. 'The one I want to talk to.'

Brows sky-high, Nico lifted his champagne flute in a silent toast and slinked away.

'That was classy,' Vivi admonished Liam lightly, but her fingers were so tight around her glass it was a wonder it didn't shatter. 'What if he was my boyfriend?'

'He'd have stayed,' Liam answered in a 'duh' tone. 'Anyway, it's obvious he's not. The cow-eyes he was giving me...' He grinned, unabashed.

Everyone in the room was sending that look to Liam. It was grossly unfair of him to be more attractive than all the models in the room. And all the models were looking at him as if he were the predator they hoped to be prey for. They preened and posed, but to no avail. Liam didn't seem to notice them, certainly didn't do the same. He'd no need to conform to some code of coolness. He wasn't afraid to throw his head back and laugh freely. In short, he was so comfortable in his own skin he drew everyone towards him. Which infuriated her—because he affected her most of all.

'What did you want to talk about?' she asked, trying to regain her legendary efficiency.

'I had another thought about the shoot.'

'We can discuss it at the meeting you scheduled first thing tomorrow.'

But he grabbed her wrist as she turned away—his large hand wrapping around her, branding her skin.

'Don't tell me you've clocked off for the night? Rumour has it you never stop working. But...' he leaned closer '...I'm happy to go personal if you'd prefer.'

She hoped he couldn't feel her frantic pulse. She rolled her eyes. 'See? Some things don't change.'

'Such as?'

'Leopards, spots...'

'Hmm.' He nodded. 'Nor do the laws of physics, right? Magnetic attraction.'

Vivi smiled sweetly. 'And let's not forget repulsion.'

He laughed. This time it was a warm burst of infectiousness that lingered a long time after he'd fallen silent. He let her go. Yet she didn't step away. Didn't want to. Because there was something about him that called to her—that sensuality, yes. But also that sense of *fun*. So very inviting.

'You're even more arrogant.' She shook her head.

'I wasn't arrogant,' he denied oh-so innocently. 'I was a callow youth caught in the throes of his first love affair.'

'First?' She choked—one quarter outraged, three quarters amused.

His eyes twinkled. 'The first that counted.'

She let her brows shoot to the ceiling. 'Have *any* counted?'

'You've changed,' he mused. 'You talk back.'

Hell, yeah, she did. 'Well, I am five years older.'

'Wiser.' He nodded. 'More experienced.' A whisper of a wink. 'And at pains to point out how perfect your life is now.'

'Because it is.' It was. And, yes, she wanted him to know it.

His eyebrows did a dance then. 'There's always room for improvement.' His voice dropped. 'A tweak here and there.'

What kind of 'tweaks' was he thinking of when he spoke in such a wicked way? 'Are you flirting with me?'

He spread his hands wide, his shoulders lifting an inch. 'You have a problem with that?'

'We now have a business relationship.'

'What's with all this emphasis on boundaries? You were happy to ignore other kinds of relationships five years ago.'

Oh, that was low. 'Well, you can flirt all you like, but I'm not playing.'

'No?' He laughed. 'You challenging me? Don't you remember I find those hard to resist?'

She swallowed. 'You're saying you haven't changed? You're not older and wiser and more experienced?'

'Two out of three isn't bad.' He shrugged.

'No prizes for guessing the two,' she snapped back.

He smiled—easy, amused. 'I can't wait to catch up more at our meeting tomorrow. Seeing you first thing was always a pleasure.'

She suppressed a shiver but there was no hiding the attraction was still there. That chemistry. She had to mentally grip

every muscle and *not* move. Not preen or lean towards him.
Not lick her lips. Not shift her legs apart.

There was a moment where she just stood before him—her
gaze locked in his, her thoughts chaotic. Then, thankfully, he
stepped back. She watched him walk away. Then she forced
her eyelids to shut and she pivoted—like an owl, to stare in
another direction. To her surprise Alannah was standing beside her.

'What'd you do to get him to look at you like that?' Alannah's mouth was hanging open.

For a moment Vivi panicked that the diva model was
going to have some kind of petulant fit. But then she realised
Alannah was serious—as if genuinely amazed. Vivi grimaced.
Was it so far-fetched that a guy might think she was attractive?
Well, yeah, this would be the first time in history that a guy
had looked at her when Alannah or any of the other models
were anywhere in the vicinity.

'I tied him up and whipped him,' Vivi quipped, wishing—
just for this second—that she really could.

'He's submissive?' Alannah's eyes went watermelon wide.

The idea of Liam being submissive to anyone was totally
laughable.

'Um…' Vivi felt a shift in the atmosphere as Alannah gazed
at her with a weird intensity.

'Oh… My…' A nodding Alannah looked her up and down
and spoke in a theatrical whisper. 'I can see it now. It makes
total sense. You're a domme.' She paused and actually fanned
her face with her fingers. 'Wow. You know I can be submissive too. I love it when a lover makes me beg.'

'Uhhh…' Was Alannah for real?

Alannah giggled so hard she all but doubled over. 'You
should see the look on your face.'

Vivi groaned. 'You're a brat.'

'But such a good one. Dontcha wanna whip me?'

'Go away. I was kidding.'

'Oh, I don't think so,' Alannah teased. 'But honestly, Vivi, you should take the boots off and do whatever he tells you to. Let him take the reins—and the whip.' She winked and sashayed away.

Uh huh. Tried that once already and look where that had got her. Pain so wasn't her thing.

Back in her hotel room she sat at the desk programming appointments and updating Gia's schedule. Except Liam's image kept sliding into her mind.

*Damn.*

She'd not thought about him in years. She'd done a brilliantly good job of training her brain not to dwell on men at all. She knew what they were about. And a guy wasn't part of her life at this point in time. She was all about work this week, this month…this whole year.

She didn't need a lover and was decades off marriage and kids. Because she'd learned that what *she* wanted was never of importance in a relationship. She always came in second. Always had to be the one to sacrifice and put her wishes behind his. That had been how it was with Oliver. Liam was supposed to have been different, but he'd turned out to be the worst. The few guys she'd dated since had just added a few ditto marks to her scoresheet. So she wasn't going there for ages yet—not when she had an amazing career to make the most of.

She'd do this meeting, set up this shoot, prove herself to be the professional she was. But as she slipped into bed and switched out the light she had to sternly remind herself. She would not remember. She would *not*.

# CHAPTER THREE

HIS LIPS BRUSHED hers. Gentle. The barest rub, back and forth. She tilted her chin and heard approval rumble deep in his throat. The kiss deepened immediately. She opened and he took what she offered—claiming her with his tongue, caressing the roof of her mouth. Startled, she shivered. So quickly seduced.

She'd already been seduced. She'd been his from the first moment she'd seen him in the guest bathroom when she'd been in nothing but a towel and he'd been all steam, strength, sex—and fun. Such fun. That kiss had started with a smile, an intimacy she'd been unable to resist.

With her lips parted, her mouth his to own, his hands roamed, moving in time with the tease of his tongue. He swept a broad palm down her spine, pulling her closer to him while at the same time pushing her against the cool, concrete wall behind her. His other hand teased, feathering strokes against her hip, up her side, feeling out the soft swell of her breast. His thumb scraped over her nipple. This time the moan of approval was hers. She arched into him, rising on tiptoe to get closer.

She wanted more. Needed so much more.

Vivi opened her eyes and stared at the dim ceiling. It was more than a dream. It was a memory.

That first kiss had been outside some motorway services restaurant. She'd been excited but slightly scared at the same time. She'd never kissed anyone but Oliver before. Liam was taller. Broader. Stronger. Liam was more everything.

He'd pressed her up against that wall of the building for what had to have been hours. Until some blushing security guard had interrupted and asked them to move along.

They'd moved to the nearest hotel.

Finally unleashed, the simmering passion between them had meant there was nothing else they could do. They didn't leave that room for three days. Then it was further south only as far as they could be bothered before falling into bed in another hotel. A few more days. Another hotel. Slowly travelling, hungrily seeking that physical satisfaction.

Frustrated, Vivi threw back the sheet, got out of bed and got some chilled water from the minibar. Her memories were fantasy enhanced, right? Dreams highlighted, magnified... It hadn't been all that fabulous. Five years was a long time. She was over it.

But now five years didn't feel like long enough.

She got to sleep ten minutes before her alarm rang. Thank heavens Gia had taken the day off from her usual schedule. The last thing Vivi felt like was managing her as well as Liam.

She stood beneath a cool shower spray and gave herself the pep talk. She *could* handle him—she'd handled way worse with ease. She'd meet him, arrange things beautifully with an utterly businesslike manner. No more laughing and almost flirting. This had to be a quick, efficient strike. It'd all be over in half an hour or less. And she'd be sure to arrange things that meant she didn't have to see him again. Ever. Piece of cake.

Liam's hotel was only a short walk from hers but she took a taxi. She didn't want to be in the least bit flushed when she met him again. Nothing like the blushing schoolgirl she'd been last night.

He was in the hotel restaurant in loose chinos, a white cotton tee and an amused smile—the kind a cat circling a broken-winged bird would wear.

'You want to eat?' he asked.

'No, thanks, but some orange juice would be great.'

As she took her seat he ordered for her. Oh, Lord, the guy was temptation enough without suddenly switching to Italian and sounding all seductive first thing in the morning.

He caught her staring and raised an eyebrow. 'So how does this work?' he asked.

'Basically, you tell me what you want and I arrange it.' She ignored the widening smile on his mouth. 'Gia instructed me to do whatever it takes for this to happen.'

'Whatever it takes?'

She sighed. 'Your little mind's still in the gutter.'

'But I've got the rest of me out.'

'I never thought the rest of you was in it,' she said simply. 'Now tell me what you want.'

His smile slowly widened again. 'So, this is what you do all day? Arrange things for Gia?'

'That is my job.'

'It must be exhausting.' He sat back as the waiter served them both a glass of fresh juice. 'What are the perks? You obviously don't get to wear her designs.' He gave her fresh white shirt and black skirt combo a cursory glance—clearly uninspired.

Good. That was the point. But she couldn't stop a little defence seeping out. 'Men wear suits—why not women?'

'In a creative industry?'

'It's not my job to be creative. I need to be efficient.'

'Why not both?'

She shook her head. 'Around Gia I need to be unobtrusive.'

He laughed. 'Doesn't matter what you wear, darling, you can never fade into the background.'

He was doing it again. Making her laugh. Paying her attention. Making her feel warm and alive and so easily attracted to him.

'So your life is nothing but work? No boyfriend?' he asked.

Her eyes narrowed. It was tempting to say there was. To invent a wildly passionate lover. To be as in love as it was possible to be. To be *safe*. But her wayward body dominated. Answering while she was still mulling her options—her head slowly shaking.

'Don't tell me you've been living like a puritan all these years?' He chuckled. 'You still feel guilty about what happened?'

She sharply glanced at him. He'd known she felt guilty?

His smile softened at her expression. 'You were such a "good girl", Victoria. You'd never gone against your parents' wishes.'

'I went against everyone's expectations that day,' she pointed out with a touch of heat. She hadn't been that much of a child.

'True. But that's nothing to feel guilty about.' He paused. 'You didn't cheat on him.'

No? Where was the line? Just by looking at Liam she'd been all but cheating.

He shook his head. 'You broke up with him before anything happened with me. You'd already said no to me before you broke up with him.'

But then it hadn't taken her long to change her mind. How had this happened? She'd been in his company less than five minutes and already they were talking past and *personal*. 'Don't worry, what happened between us hasn't scarred me for life or anything.' Vivi laughed lightly. 'I'm so over it.'

'So you've had other boyfriends since me.'

'Of course.' Not a lie this time.

'But nothing serious?'

She didn't have to answer that.

'And no boyfriend now?'

She ran her fingers over the cool glass. 'Not during the show season.'

'What, you put relationships on hold for that?'

'Of course. I can't be bothered with a man moaning about being neglected.'

He chuckled. 'Neglected? I can't imagine you ever neglecting a lover—you were always so generous...'

She chose to ignore *that* reference. 'Well, *you* know how it is, Liam—people tend to feel ignored when their partner is wholly focused on work. I find it's easier to be single at the busiest times.'

'I would have thought a true partner would understand when his lover has a huge crunch on at work. Wouldn't he be supportive? Offer an end-of-the-day massage?'

'Is that what your girlfriend does for you?' Vivi smiled, oh, *so* sweetly.

He chuckled. 'No, I'm every bit as single as you. I've had girlfriends but it never seems to work for long. I guess long-term relationships don't fit with my personality.' He sounded careless.

'It's not that you're having too much fun enjoying the *variety* in your high-flying lifestyle?'

'I know you love to think the worst of me, but I'm actually not a slut.'

'What?' She paused for effect. 'You mean you don't sleep your way to what you want?'

He bridled. 'Aren't you getting a little desperate to score a point?'

'No point scoring, just an honest assessment. Isn't it an extension of networking and schmoozing?'

'I guess it could be but I think you've been hanging around the Hollywood types too much. You know, most of the people I need to network with are guys,' he said dryly. 'And you know I'm not gay.'

'So you're telling me you don't all get together at lap bars and do your deals amongst breasts and legs?'

'You're really trying to have the lowest opinion of me, aren't you?' He looked way too amused. 'Why so determined to talk yourself into disliking me? Dreaming up the worst dirt your mind can dredge? Sorry, darling, but I'm not going to help you out. Fact is I'm an all right guy. That's not to say I don't have sex, but it's always good and it's always with a woman who's as happy about it as I am.'

'I'm sure she is,' Vivi ground out poisonously.

'And naturally, any man lucky enough to date you would be very, *very* happy,' he added.

She bit back a bitchy retort. She really needed to steer them back to business.

'Or are you holding out for Mr Right?' he asked with a laugh.

'There's no such thing,' she growled, provoked. 'No hero on the white charger. No love of your life.' No grand passion. There was companionship and good sex. Neither of which she had time for right now.

'No.' He said it with such finality and, even though she believed it herself, she was somehow wounded.

'Shall we get back to business?' Vivi forced herself to back away from the boggy territory they'd wandered into. 'We have a limited time frame. Alannah has a shoot in Venice today and tomorrow. Gia was supposed to be having a few days at a spa.' And Vivi had been longing for three days' solid sleep.

'You can get Gia into the spa a few days later and I have a plane that can get Alannah from Venice as soon as she's done.'

'You want Alannah that much?'

His gaze lifted. 'I want her in the pictures for my company.'

No man just wanted Alannah on paper.

Liam openly laughed. 'I don't think I'm her type anyway. She was looking at me very oddly last night.'

'You mean not in the usual total adoring way you're used to? Women just fall at your feet, don't they? Well, men just fall at hers. So perhaps she's the perfect challenge for you.' She glanced at him to see his reaction.

A smile played around his mouth. 'She's not a challenge for me.'

'Oh, please. Every man on the planet sees her as the ultimate score.'

'Not me. As far as I can see there's no discernible personality there.'

'It's there. She just hides it.' Vivi reckoned she had to, in order for her to survive the insanity of her life. 'So you only like women you see as a challenge?' It was all about the challenge.

'Not a challenge to get into bed. I like a woman who challenges me on every level. Physically, intellectually.'

'Emotionally?' she mocked. 'You'll never get me to believe that, Liam.'

He kept looking at her so long she grew uncomfortable with the silence.

'Maybe Alannah looked at you funny because I told her you like me to tie you up and whip you.' She cleared her throat and sat back, waiting for the explosion.

But he didn't blink. 'Well in one way you did. I was only a toy for you.' His eyes met hers. 'You used me.'

'Excuse me?' Vivi's temperature rose so she worked hard to keep her tone calm. '*You* used *me*. You wanted in. You wanted acceptance.'

'Stealing you away from your family and almost-fiancé was hardly going to gain me acceptance,' he said, equally cool. 'I was some kind of escapist fantasy—the bit of rough. But once reality hit, you couldn't wait to get away. You used me, Victoria. Not the other way round.' He leaned over the table. 'You wanted to escape the nice middle-class prison you were in. You didn't want to marry Oliver but you felt trapped. I was your escape route. Nothing more.'

How could he possibly think she'd used him like that? 'You've no idea how hard it was for me to walk out of that house and go with you. I walked away from everything.'

'Which was exactly what you wanted.' Obstinately he stuck to his warped view of what had happened.

'How would you know what I wanted?' He'd never asked her. 'You weren't interested in anything I wanted to do. You just expected me to fall in with your plans. I was supposed to sit on the beach or something while you were out sailing. It was all about *your* dreams. You had no clue what mine were and you didn't want to know.' She didn't want this—to go over what had gone wrong. 'Look, I'll rebook Gia's spa and get her to Genoa and rework Alannah's schedule. Given your inability to stay on track with any kind of serious planning this morning, and given the pressure on *my* precious time, I'm going to leave now and will keep you updated with plans via email.' She stood up from the table and looked at him. 'Anything else you need from me right now?'

'Just one thing,' he answered blandly, following her out of the restaurant.

Vivi kept walking. 'What is it?'

'A kiss goodbye.'

What? She lurched to a standstill and turned, scraping up a laugh. 'That's not appropriate in a professional relationship.'

'Yeah, well, this relationship was never going to be professional.' He stepped closer. 'You're going to have to get over that.'

She opened her mouth but he put his finger on her lips.

'A kiss makes for a better goodbye than harsh words, don't you think?'

Five years ago goodbye had been a doozy of an argument. He'd got wild with her and she equally so. She'd never been so angry in her life. He'd made her lose control of her emotions in more ways than one. She'd lost him. She'd already lost her family. And she'd kept all her emotions under control since.

'You can't reheat old soup.' She tried to ignore the sensations of his finger on her mouth as she spoke.

'You think? Don't things taste better when the flavours

have had time to infuse or ferment? Isn't that the difference between grape juice and wine?'

She didn't need to get drunk on Liam again. 'You're incorrigible.'

'But you know I'm right.'

'No.'

'Then prove me wrong.'

'You can't tease me into this.'

'No?'

'Public displays of affection are tacky.'

'This isn't affection.'

'Then what is it?'

He moved so fast she didn't stand a chance. His hand dropped from her mouth and slid round her waist, pulling her close against him. His head dropped.

His lips didn't brush, they bruised. But only for a moment—they softened almost immediately, caressing, then the pressure increased again. He teased—always such a tease. And then he lifted just a fraction. She knew he was going to pull away.

No. That wasn't enough. She reached up and stopped him stepping back. She kissed him.

He met her again, his arms swiftly coming tight around her, and she clung right back. Her mouth parted, her tongue seeking greater intimacy—to stroke and torment as good as she was getting. Memory and reality slammed together.

She felt the rumble deep in his chest. He pulled her tighter into his heat. She felt him hot and hard. Her heart ripped open. No one had ever made her feel like this. Not just lust—not just turned on. But *touched*. Somehow he woke something so deep within her, something she'd never been aware of until him. And he made her want more. Always more. She wanted everything.

*No.*

She pushed back, her breathing choppy—wildly waving a hand in the air, seeking some stability. He reached out and held her hand hard—allowing her the distance but supporting her at the same time because he knew just how close she was to stumbling. Falling. For him.

Oh, no.

'That shouldn't have happened,' she said firmly.

For once he wasn't smiling, his chin was lifted, determination written in the intensity of his eyes. 'You wanted it as much as I did. You wanted more. You want me.'

She did. But she shook her head. 'This can't happen, Liam. I can't let this happen.'

# CHAPTER FOUR

LIAM STARED SIGHTLESSLY at the designs on his screen, unable to stop thinking about Victoria. He'd had his victory, right? He'd teased her. Traded barbs. And it had happened—he'd drawn her in. He'd kissed her. But even better, *she'd* kissed him back. She couldn't deny their explosive chemistry. And she hadn't. So he'd proved the point, right? But the second he'd taken that success, she'd stolen it back with her decree—she couldn't 'let this happen'.

Why not? The need to know drove into him. But his need to follow through did more than dominate. The desire to have her—to win—consumed. He didn't want her to 'let it happen' either. He didn't want her in passive mode. That was what bugged him most—her lack of honesty. She hadn't just 'let' that kiss happen. She'd pulled him close—*taken* for one hot moment. And now he wanted it all—it was pure chemistry. Undeniable and so strong. He wanted her to push for all of him. Not to be the one pleasing, the one offering, or 'letting', but the one taking. He wanted her to admit it—to ask. To demand.

And he'd answer the only way he could.

'No, we have to have that fabric sample by Tuesday morning at the latest. Needless to say, if we don't receive it by that time we won't be looking at your supplier again.' Vivi, on the warpath, ended the call and immediately placed another. Typing with one hand while texting with another and talking on her earpiece to someone else altogether. Clients were melting down at the prospect of Gia extending her time in Italy; one reporter was psychotic over her not being back in London in time for some interview.

'Could she do an interview on Skype?'

'Gianetta doesn't Skype. You'll have to reschedule.'

Liam's last-minute photo shoot had caused an almighty headache but Gia seemed determined for it to go ahead, meaning Vivi was busier than ever on the day she should have had as a break. Usually being busy was good. But being busy for something Liam-related? Not so much. It meant she thought about him *all* the time. Most especially in the too few hours she'd had to snatch sleep. Memories stole into her mind—like wicked little elves breaking into a locked garden to frolic and play and torment. She remembered the slide of his hands, the steel of his body, the intensity of his expression...

She tossed, turned. Gave up.

Maybe she should hit the nearest open-all-hours sex-aids store and grab a vibrator? But she was in Italy and had no idea where or how to find one. Besides, she already knew the thing wouldn't work it for her. She wanted hot, real touch.

With just one look, one smile, she'd been bitten again. Just as she had five years before. But their affair couldn't be repeated. She'd not just walked away from her family, she'd lost *herself.* That was a huge part of what she'd run from in the end. Looking back, she knew she'd been sheltered. Her relationship with Oliver had been sweet—in truth a little cloying. With Liam it'd been fevered, uncontrolled passion. But he'd been right the other day. She'd felt guilt and it had worsened as those weeks passed. Leaving Oliver for Liam made her conscience burn—unnecessarily maybe—but it had. Worse had been her *need* of Liam. Conflicted—insecure—her emotions flailed and never found the foothold she'd needed. Not from him. She'd never get it from him.

The 'goodbye' kiss the other morning told her. She couldn't

touch him again. She had to turn her back on temptation. He'd always be too much for her to handle. She'd fought too hard to make something of her life. She wasn't losing it for another short-lived affair. So she forced focus. Sent him a very brief, businesslike email explaining the shoot details she'd arranged.

His reply came back within ten minutes. For twenty more she stared at it, her blood heating, until finally she picked up her phone.

'You can't call me "darling" in an email,' she said as soon as he answered.

'Why not?' he asked innocently. She could hear the wicked smile in the words.

'It could be considered sexual harassment.'

He snorted. 'Doesn't everyone in the fashion industry call each other darling?'

'Not me.'

'Why? You give them a frosty look and scare them off?' He chuckled. 'Is this the phone equivalent of that?'

'Yes,' she said firmly.

'Hmm,' he murmured. 'Am I allowed to sign off my emails with a kiss? A little "x" like they all do?'

'Not me,' she repeated, regretting calling him now because the wretch always seemed to make her smile. To make her take a step closer.

'Of course not. I'm thinking you're more triple "x", right?'

'Liam, *you* are my ex,' she said pointedly. 'And you're staying that way.'

'It didn't feel over the other morning,' he answered softly. 'Is it sexual harassment to say I'm looking forward to seeing you again?'

She gritted her teeth. 'I guess not.'

'I think sexual harassment would be something much worse than a "darling",' he added thoughtfully. 'Explicit suggestions…instructions maybe.'

She closed her eyes, her flush blooming, her body five

steps ahead of her brain even though her brain was on over-time—sending images that were way worse than triple X-rated. He wasn't saying anything bad. Not really. It was all in the *way* he said it.

'I *am* looking forward to seeing you again,' he repeated in that deceptively soft, dangerous voice. 'Watching you come… here. Watching you work. And seeing you satisfied when all is done.'

In the echo of his words all kinds of explicit suggestions—instructions—filled her head. And she wanted them. She did. She'd always wanted him. She wanted what they'd had. She wanted more. She probably always would. But she could resist. She *would*.

'You're not going to answer back?' he prompted.

'No.' She forced herself to say it to him.

Practice made perfect, right?

'You really need me to go with you?' she asked Gia later that day, trying to hide the high-pitched 'please say no' edge in her voice.

'Of course.' Gia barely grunted her reply.

Twenty-four hours later Vivi landed in Genoa with Gia, Alannah and a couple of male models, Nico, a pair of stylists and scores of bags.

The coastal city was beautiful, but the boats in the marina were mind-blowing. Vivi was used to excess. Working for Gia, she met pop stars and actors, oil barons and media moguls—all of whom loved to have pretty models surrounding them. So she'd seen some fancy boats and apartments in her time. But this was something else again. But they were whisked past far too quickly for her to really appreciate them, and taken to a large shed on the furthest side of the facility. They went through another round of security and were finally allowed in. Liam's boats were locked away, carefully hidden from view.

He was waiting for them. Vivi tried to stay at the back of

the group. Tried to stay busy helping one stylist manage her bags. But she couldn't resist looking as he relentlessly watched her *coming* nearer towards him. His eyes were dark. The longer cut of his hair didn't soften him any, or make him look casual. He looked like a pirate. She tried to stop the slither of her body towards him, it was so unfair of him to be so irresistible. She'd never seen him sailing all those years ago. It'd been winter, Christmas. He'd been covered up until she'd stripped him in that hotel room. But now? All bronzed and in shorts and boatshoes and standing easily along the wooden deck of that beautiful cruiser? There was too much skin on show, too much *man*. He looked every inch the warrior who knew how to fight, how to seduce, how to win.

She turned away. Gia was in raptures. The boat 'in the flesh' was even more marvellous than she'd expected. Nico was an over-the-top nightmare, already barking orders and deciding on angles. Vivi hadn't even noticed the boat. Now she forced herself to pay attention.

She stepped onboard, drawing breath as she did. He'd designed this? She carefully gazed around, stared at the boat and then him. He'd been so competitive. So ruthless in achieving what he wanted. She'd have thought he'd be all function over form. But this was beautiful. Elegant. Simple. Every feature well thought out, sleek and stylish. No wonder he'd become so successful so quickly. He deserved to be. She felt a bubble of pride. Astonished, she realised she was pleased for him—and she couldn't hold back her smile.

He looked at her, his eyes mirroring her smile. 'You're surprised.'

Reluctantly she nodded. 'Don't be offended. There was a lot I didn't know about you back then.' She had a feeling there was still a lot—back then she'd been too self-absorbed to realise it.

He nodded briefly. 'You need a hand with those bags?'

'No, I have it covered, thanks.'

But she didn't. Nico was bellowing orders, as was Gia.

Alannah was tired and demanding caffeine. Vivi needed thirty extra helpers to carry all the gear to where it was needed. She glanced at Liam, who was standing too close and watching with a far too amused look on his face.

'Can't those pretty boys help, or are they scared of breaking a fingernail?' he asked.

She refused to laugh. 'They're getting their make-up done.'

'Ah, well. Since I'm handsome enough without make-up…' He stepped forward and took a heavy bag in each hand. 'You tell me where to put them.'

Well, she wasn't a total idiot. If he wanted to help, he could help. And she? She'd…try really hard not to watch too closely as his muscles worked, not stare at his butt as he bent down, not feel the itch in her fingers to touch. And not dwell on just how handsome he was without make-up. Without anything.

Dear heaven, she was going to need so much help not to do those things.

It took over an hour for Alannah's hair, face and body to be made-up—slightly less for the two male models, and slightly more for Nico to decide on how he wanted them draped in his first scene.

Finally they got to taking some pictures—meaning Vivi could have a moment to step back and organise refreshments. Good thing—she didn't want to watch everyone start sweating as they took in Alannah posing in a teensy bikini.

'You want some help?' Liam caught up with her as she stepped off the boat.

She sent him a suspicious glance. 'You don't want to go watch the models writhe on your deck?'

He shook his head.

Oh, she didn't believe him. 'You'd really rather do the coffee run with me?'

'I'd rather writhe on my deck with you, but sadly that isn't an option.'

She choked back both her blush and a laugh. 'We need to be quick.'

'Do we?' he asked idly. 'Shame.'

Oh, he was naughty. So much naughtier than he'd been all those years ago. And even more irresistible. 'You're appalling.'

'I'm not as bad as you,' he argued mildly. 'Here's you spending your life doing everything to keep everyone else happy. When do you do what you want? Take what you want? You've got the give, where's the take?'

He might sound as if he were teasing, but she got the less-than-subtle criticism. 'This is what I want. I have everything I need.'

'Everything?' His brows arched and he waggled an admonishing finger at her. 'No boyfriend. No orgasm.' His expression reckoned she was missing out big-time.

She rolled her eyes. 'What was I thinking?' she played along, sarcasm dripping. 'Of course, no life is complete without sex.'

'You said it.'

She sent him one of her stern-secretary looks. 'I do not need a man to have an orgasm.'

'Oh, my.' His laughter rumbled. '*So* independent now.'

'That's right,' she said loftily, walking down to the doorway to collect the coffees she'd ordered to be delivered. 'From meek and mild to self-sufficient and successful.'

'And sassy,' he noted. 'But still someone else's slave,' he called after her.

'Secretary,' she corrected, giving him a kill-shot look over her shoulder.

'Same thing.' He shrugged it off.

'Insult me all you like—it's not going to work.'

He grinned and stepped in front of her to take the tray for her from the delivery boy. Easily dealing with the transaction in flawless Italian for her. At least it sounded flawless.

It sounded gorgeous.

'Where did you go?' he asked as they walked back to take it to the others. 'After we split?'

For a moment she tensed, then consciously relaxed. Why not talk about it? They were adults now, right? They could hold a conversation about the past without getting worked up—neither flirting nor fighting.

'London.' She gestured for him to put the coffee down until the current crop of pics had been taken. 'I had no money, no skills, three quarters of a degree, nowhere to live.' She'd fought hard to get a foot in the door. She hadn't had the time to think about him. Not ever think about him. But she was proud of what she'd achieved.

'What about your parents?' He frowned. 'You didn't go back to them?'

'Why would I do that?' she asked. After the way they'd spoken to her—making their opinion of her crystal clear? After what had happened to Stella, she'd known what she was in for when she'd walked out of that door with Liam. When her sister had left home as a teen, all record of her existence had been obliterated. Her parents were unforgiving. No memory of Victoria would remain in their home.

'But…' He picked up a coffee but didn't take a sip. 'You see them now?'

She hesitated. 'I send them a Christmas card.' Because there was that tiny part of her that ached.

'Do they send you one back?'

She didn't answer.

'You're kidding.' He looked appalled. 'They really did it, then? Cast you out? They don't even acknowledge *Christmas*?'

'Well…' Vivi shifted uncomfortably '…I don't put a return address on the envelope.'

Liam paused, then his left eyebrow lifted. 'You haven't told them where you live? Or what you do? Or anything?'

Vivi unnecessarily brushed her fingers through her bob,

knowing it would fall perfectly back into place. Hooray for working with the world's best hairstylists.

'You haven't given them a chance?' he pushed.

'What was the point? I know exactly what would happen. Look at Stella.' She was too scared. If they didn't have her address, she wouldn't hope for contact. She couldn't be disappointed.

'Right.' He nodded. 'Well, what about her? Have you tried to get in touch with her?' His voice raised enough for Nico to turn and frown at them.

Vivi took a step back from the others and sent Liam a frown of her own.

'I thought about it.' But she hadn't wanted to come begging. She'd wanted to succeed on her own first. And she had. Then she'd made some friends at work. They'd become her family. And why would Stella want to get in touch with her? She'd walked away and never looked back. Never once thought to call her little sister.

'But you never did?' Liam had an intent, almost disapproving, solemn look on his face. 'You're so unforgiving.'

Vivi folded her arms across her chest. 'No, I'm not.'

'You are.'

'Stella never once tried to get in touch with me. My parents told me that if I left, not to bother coming back.' Hell, hadn't Liam heard that? Her mother had shouted it so loud half the world must have.

'You've never said anything awful in the heat of the moment?' Liam asked quietly.

There was a silence and she sent him a look. Then sighed. 'Trust me. I know they're not interested. They're the ones who are unforgiving. When Stella left, I saw what they did to her stuff. Why would I do that to myself? Why would I knock on the door only to have it slammed in my face?'

'So you're afraid,' he said softly.

'No. I'm just not stupid. Besides, I don't have the time. I'm too busy—'

'Doing everything for Gia.'

That again? 'Gianetta's been more of a friend to me than anyone in my family ever has,' Vivi pointed out. 'And believe me, I understand that the relationship I have with Gia is a business one. If I annoy her, I'm out the door.' She knew what she had to do to survive. And survive she would.

'Okay.' He blew out a big breath and then cleared his throat. 'So what do you do for Christmas?'

Oh. She couldn't help the guilty grin. 'I work. What about you?'

'I work.'

She laughed. So not surprised. That Christmas they'd had together had kind of killed the spirit. When you had people screaming at you, it didn't make things festive.

'Can you two be quiet, please?' Nico glowered at them.

Vivi bit back her smile and went to ensure the lunch caterers were going to make it past security. It seemed the monsters needed feeding.

An hour later she was exhausted—having checked and double-checked that all the special orders were fulfilled. She'd lost sight of Liam for a while, presumed he'd gone to do some work somewhere. She wished she could escape for a bit too. The constant demands from the 'talent' were wearing.

'Hey, have this.' Liam appeared at her side and offered her a steaming cup.

'Oh, thanks.' She took a careful sip and smiled as the flavour hit her taste buds—peppermint tea? She couldn't believe he'd found some. What surprised her even more was that he remembered it was the only tea she drank—that he'd noticed she'd not had any of the coffee. He'd sat up with her that night she'd been making Christmas decorations for Oliver's mother. He'd kept her laughing. He'd teased her about the tea. He'd offered…more than he should have.

'Not everything changes, right?' He stood beside her, dangerously intimate.

'No,' she said ruefully. 'I guess not.'

Another hour went by. Another change of bikini for Alannah, new trunks for the men, more adjustments with the lighting and the spray-on mist-to-look-like-sweat. Vivi fetched, carried, stood—all with Liam at her side making amusing comments and general chat. Until Nico was fully engaged with another set-up.

'I thought you'd gone back to Oliver,' Liam said quietly.

She went completely cold. 'Oh, no.' She shook her head. 'No.'

Liam turned away from the models, angling so he could see her face. 'Do you wish you'd said yes to him that day?'

'No.' She didn't hesitate. 'He wasn't right for me either.' She braved looking at his face as she said that last.

He looked thoughtful. 'I saw him recently.'

'*Oliver*?'

'Yeah.' Liam grinned at her squawk. 'He bought one of my boats.'

'Oh. Great.' Vivi swallowed back her shock. 'He's well? And happy?'

Liam nodded. 'Married and climbing his way to the top of an investment bank. Exactly on the track he'd always wanted to be on.'

Yeah, it was that same life plan. Just with a different woman.

'So he's done okay through the recession?' Vivi shook her head at her own stupidity. 'Of course he has—he's bought one of your boats.'

And he was happy. That was good. She wouldn't have been happy with him and she knew she'd have made him unhappy too. 'I'm glad he's doing well,' she said, meaning it. But she was thrown that Oliver and Liam were still...*friends*? Well, she supposed it figured. Mates before dates, right? Then she remembered. 'I'd forgotten you'd gone to work for his family friend…' She frowned, confused. 'But when did you move to Italy?'

Liam had straightened up and faced back towards the models. 'I never worked for the friend.'

'Yes, you did.' She turned towards him to read his face. 'That's why you were there that Christmas. How you got the visa to come to England. Oliver got you that job. You were starting in the new year—you were going to Cowes.' Oliver's family had pulled strings to get Liam a job with a close contact in the yachting industry there. She'd thought it would be okay—truth be told she hadn't thought about it at all.

'They rescinded the job offer. I found other work.'

Her blood ran cold. 'When?' She fought the churning sensation in her gut. 'When did they rescind the offer?'

'A couple of days after we left.'

'But—' She broke off, oddly breathless. 'You'd signed a contract.'

'They found some loophole. What was I going to do—fight it?' He laughed.

But it wasn't funny. She stared at him, a horrible hurt feeling inside. 'You never told me.'

Liam kept looking beyond her, at the scene Nico and Gia had staged. 'I hadn't seen him for years until he came to buy the boat. He asked after you.' Liam sighed. 'He wondered how you were getting on.'

Had Oliver thought she and Liam were still together? 'What did you say?'

'I didn't. I thought you'd gone back to him, remember? I was totally thrown when I found out the wife he'd been going on about wasn't you. Turned out neither of us knew a thing about you. Then I did a couple of searches, but it seemed you'd vanished.'

So Liam had then searched for her? Why?

'How did you hide?' he asked.

She grasped onto that—trying to keep the conversation light, trying not to dig deeper into something that seemed a lot like a giant can of worms. 'With all this social media it's supposedly easy to track anyone down. From the fifteen kids in your first ever class at school to the three hundred in your uni lecture hall. You can find anyone and everyone with a quick Facebook look, right? Unless you consciously change. I shortened my name. Shut down all my accounts. Cut my hair. Became someone new.'

'Vivi.'

She nodded. 'It took a while, but I became the person I wanted to be.' She'd worked in a stationery store to start with but wanted to get into design. She'd loved drawing and doing graphic design on the computer. But it wasn't for her to do fashion at university. That was a hobby, not a career, her father had lectured. Doing French hadn't exactly been much of a career option either. But she could type and organise and she'd picked up computer systems quickly. She learned to get what she needed from other people simply because she had to. 'I got an admin job in Gia's office.'

'And then you showed them what you could really do.'

'I worked so hard,' she said. *How* she'd worked. 'And it's been worth it.'

'So you've proved yourself?' He gazed at her.

'For *myself*. Not anyone else.' She frowned. 'When was it you saw Oliver?'

'A couple of months ago.'

Her heart thudded. 'So, is that why…?'

'I never liked how it ended between us. I thought it'd be interesting to see what had become of you since then.'

*Interesting.* 'So you're combining business with something personal. Looking up an old flame? This is merely curiosity?' It was silly but somehow it hurt. What was he going to do now—report back to Oliver and the others?

He stepped closer, turning to face her again. 'I don't think this is *merely* anything.'

'Vivi, where the hell is the bag with the power strips?' Nico's shout echoed around them.

Vivi tore her attention from Liam, turned away. And tried to stay away while she processed what she now knew of the past. Liam losing the job offer and never telling her. He must have been so worried—she'd known he didn't have money, didn't have a family… He didn't have much of anything.

And she'd shouted at him. She'd left him.

Eight hours later she was so, so tired. The shoot was taking for ever. She walked off the boat, walked down the back of the boatshed where it was dark. She could hear Nico ordering Alannah about, Gia adding her views. The stylists flitted around like moths. A cast of thousands—and Vivi was supposed to be the one at the back ensuring every single one of them was happy and had all they needed.

Too bad. Right now she needed a break. From Gia's demands. From Alannah's. From Liam.

From the way he watched her. From the way he made her feel—so hungry, so yearning, so turned on all the time. It was insane. She sank into a pile of sail bags in the furthest corner she could find. Her body ached from tension and sleeplessness. She'd steal a few minutes. Five. Then she'd be ready to handle them all again. Handle him.

Liam grimly stopped himself hunting round for Victoria. He didn't need to stalk her. But fifteen minutes later she hadn't come back to the spot where she'd been watching the shoot. He wanted it to be over. He wanted to be alone with her. Truth? That was all he'd wanted. He didn't give a toss about publicity photos and magazine spreads.

He'd been a fool to think it was a stint of celibacy that had made him so hot the first night he'd seen her again. No woman had ever had the effect she had on him. The minute he'd found out Oliver had no clue where she was, that no one knew anything about her… He'd needed to find her.

Ten minutes later he couldn't cope with her absence any more. He went searching. He found her right at the far corner of the boatshed, curled up in a pile of gear, sound asleep but looking horribly uncomfortable with her head at that angle.

Very carefully, quietly, he bent down. Holding his breath, he gently lifted her and slid in beside her, pulling her back to rest against him. He gazed down at her pretty but pale face. She hadn't stirred. Which meant she had to be exhausted.

She worked too hard.

That was something he understood. He'd been working too hard for too long as well. He'd been obsessed with building a company, a basis for a future. Security. She had too. They'd viciously fought that last day—her wants versus his. But it turned out they were incredibly similar.

He'd not realised how much she'd sacrificed and risked to go with him. She'd not understood how desperate he was for money. He'd not told her about the email rescinding the job offer—it had landed in his email account two days after they'd left Oliver's family home. It had meant he had nothing to offer her. He'd felt utterly useless and absolutely determined all at the same time. He'd been so desperate to secure something for his future. For theirs.

But he'd been too proud to admit it all to her. And she'd got angry with him—that he was expecting her to just 'fall in'. He'd thought she was full of bravado that last day when she'd yelled that she didn't need him or anyone and she'd prove it. He hadn't believed her. He'd thought she'd gone back home. Back to her stifling parents. Back to Oliver.

But he'd been wrong. And she had proved it. Changed her name, her look. Built a career. Worked incredibly hard. Turned her back on everything.

He frowned. You couldn't turn your back on everything for ever.

And at heart Vivi Grace was still Victoria Rutherford—generous, caring torment who spent her life pleasing others. He'd tried to tell himself it was just sex that drew him to her. But it wasn't lust filling him now. There were so many more, conflicting, emotions. Amusement, annoyance, *concern*. He'd thought he had this figured out. Now he didn't know what he was going to do with her.

Well, he did. Kissing her the other morning had brought it home. He wanted her. But what he wanted, even more than that, was for her to want it. For her to ask.

Just once. To complete their history.

Vivi wasn't just warm and comfortable, she was lax and hot. She breathed in deep, the scent filling her lungs. Salt air, strong man. She opened her eyes and gasped. He wasn't just with her, he was beneath her—encircling her. His arms were around her, his chest below her cheek.

She looked up at him, trying to read his beautiful eyes. They were dark, but lit by that fire. The sharp planes of his jaw roughened by short stubble. She wanted to stroke it with her fingertips to feel it; she wanted to touch her lips to his.

There was nothing she wanted more than his kiss.

'Something you want?' His voice was so low, she felt it more than heard it.

She said nothing. He knew already.

'Victoria?'

She lived in London. He lived in Italy. She didn't want a relationship. Nor did he. This time she was certain of where this would go, when it would end. With such firm parameters, she'd be okay, right? This would bring closure. She'd expunge the remnants of that lust, reveal it really wasn't that good, and she could prove she had control of her emotions. Able to enjoy a moment.

It could only be a moment.

'Something you want?' he repeated.

'Kiss me,' she breathed.

'Nico?' Alannah's piercing voice shattered the moment just as she lifted her chin to press her lips to his.

'I'm just finding Vivi.' Nico's voice sounded way too near.

Vivi turned her head so quick she almost got whiplash. Nico was a few feet away, his camera in his hands. 'Gia needs you,' he said.

'Of course,' Vivi said.

But she couldn't move—Liam's arms were too tight around her. She looked back at him as she heard Nico walk away. Liam's expression hadn't changed—still trained on her. Still hot. Still determined. And she liked it.

It seemed some things didn't change.

# CHAPTER FIVE

GIA, THE MODELS, Nico left.

Liam didn't.

Vivi was usually the last away from a shoot, the one to ensure all had been done. She was aware of him silently working beside her. Carrying things to the truck for the stylists. Until they too left.

'You need to get back to your hotel.' He finally broke the silence between them. 'I'll give you a lift.'

'Thank you.'

He didn't speak on the drive. Nor did she. At the hotel she got out of the car, hyper aware that he did too—that he tossed the keys to the valet, that he was right by her side as she walked through the reception and to the elevator. That he took the key card to her room from her and opened the door.

'I owe you a kiss,' he said, standing just back from the doorway.

Stepping through the doorway, she turned her head to look him in the eye. 'Then you'd better come in.'

To her amazement a tinge of colour slashed his cheekbones.

She walked on, suddenly smiling. Suddenly sure. She wouldn't say no tonight, didn't want to. Denying what she so badly wanted wasn't going to protect her. Walking away in the morning wouldn't hurt as it had before. Last time there'd been shattered dreams—she'd grown up quickly, painfully. This was merely fun, right? The kind of fling she knew she could handle. She turned in the centre of the room—a half-metre from the bed—and faced him.

He kept walking until he was right in front of her. She lifted her chin and waited. Slowly, too slowly, he pressed his lips to hers. The touch was too careful, too light—but her body went incandescent anyway.

'Anything else you'd like from me?' he breathed.

She gazed into his fire-lit eyes and down his beautiful body. 'One night.'

'Doing what?'

'Everything.'

This time the kiss wasn't light—but it was still full of care. Steeped in passion. She clung to him—he to her. Hands clutched, caressed, swept—pulling bodies closer, stroking. Needing.

'You mind taking off your clothes?' He tore his lips from her neck and gasped. 'I'm likely to rip them if I try to do it.'

She sent him an amused glance.

'It's not funny. I'm serious.'

'Oh, in that case.' She stepped back and slowly undid each button of her white blouse.

'A bra today,' he mused, his eyes twinkling. 'I wondered.'

'You didn't wonder. You already knew. You've been staring at my chest most of the day,' she said tartly, letting her shirt fall to the floor.

'It's not because of your breasts that I'm here.'

'No?'

He shook his head. 'It's your legs.'

She chuckled.

'You mind taking the skirt off?'

She complied. Quickly as she watched the fire in his eyes burn brighter.

'Actually,' he amended, 'it's everything about you.' He backed her up against the bed. 'Always was.'

He kissed her. Vivi leaned into him, curling her arms

around his neck and giving into it. All was unleashed. She'd always been so carried away in her passion for him. Stunned by the sensations he'd made her feel. How could it be like this again? How so quickly?

'It's been a while.' She pushed him away for a second so she could breathe. Regroup. Focus. Narrow-eyed, she frowned at him. 'Why aren't you naked?'

His laugh had a desperate edge. He rubbed his fingertips over his forehead. 'It's been a while for me too. I need to keep myself in check somehow.'

'No constant stream of girlfriends?'

He hesitated. 'Not constant. None constant. Long term not my thing. Never will be.'

She didn't doubt it. She knew he was reminding her of that line in the sand. And she had to accept it. There was no changing him. And she didn't want to, right? She only wanted this one night too. Now she understood he'd been emotionally alone for a long time—and he only wanted fun. Well, so did she.

'What do you want me to do?' he quietly asked.

She picked up on the subtle meaning—he was giving her the chance to change her mind. She didn't want to think about the past any more. Or the future. Instead she focused on the present. On the present that he was to her. 'I want you naked. Take your tee shirt off.'

He removed it immediately. Suddenly she felt confident. A confidence she'd never had all those years ago. Back then she'd just been overwhelmed. This time it was going to be different. Maybe he was right. This time she'd take all she needed from him. Do everything she wanted to. After all, it was only sex.

She reached for his shorts, deftly undid them and shoved them—together with his boxers—down to his knees.

'And now?' He stood there, all bared magnificence.

'Touch me.'

He stepped out of the clothes and reached for her. And as

he caressed her she caressed him. Running fingers over the body she'd once known so briefly, but so well. Still knew. Still admired…adored. She glanced back to his face, touched light fingertips to the smile that always melted her. He stepped closer, feathering kisses down her neck, to her breasts, his hands leading the way—tender, savouring, tormenting, until she was hot, restless, breathless.

'Liam?'

'Anything.'

She whispered, her confidence growing still. And he answered in action—quick, devastating action.

'We need to…' He broke away for a moment and found his shorts, swiftly fitting the protection. Then his hands returned to her—sought out her sensitive parts. He listened, but too soon she couldn't speak. It didn't matter. He seemed to remember her as if it were yesterday. What she liked. What she *really* liked. What she discovered that she now adored.

She shivered and tried to slip away from his touch as she got too hot, too quick. 'I don't want to come without you. I want you to be in me.'

He laughed, again that edge of desperation. 'Be over too soon.'

His fingers trailed more, teasing until she was sighing and rocking and escalating towards the peak way, way too quickly.

So now she needed to do more than speak; she had to *seize* control. Before she'd always lost control. Always been swept away. She shoved, her hands slapping on his chest. To her delight he fell back, letting her straddle him.

'You gonna break out your whip now?' he teased.

She laughed but then shook her head. 'No pain,' she whispered. 'I don't want this to hurt.'

His laughing expression sobered completely. 'No.' Suddenly he moved, sitting up, his sky-high erection solid between them, rubbing against her in a way that had her squirming to lift and slide straight onto him.

But it was the kiss that killed her. He thrust his fingers into her hair, cradling the back of her head in his broad palm, holding her in place as he kissed her in a way she'd never been kissed before. Not just passionate, not just deep.

But somehow almost desperate—as if he were pouring a part of himself into her. She felt it raining down inside her, filling the gaps with warmth and sweetness.

*Giving.*

Oh, dear Lord, she couldn't cope with this. She wanted this to be *sex*. Hot, sweaty, wild sex. She didn't want something that seemed so much more.

Trembling, she wrenched her mouth away. That was too savage, too tender, too much. How could it be even more intense than it had been before?

She pushed away, slipping onto the middle of the big mattress. There had to be a way she could control this better, could put this into the purely sexual box she needed it to be in. She bent her head, trying to cope with the yearning of her body. And heard the hiss of his indrawn breath.

Smiling, she leaned further forward onto her fists, sending him a glance over her shoulder and registered with pleasure the way his fiery gaze travelled down the length of her—to the part of herself she'd exposed.

Yeah, that was what he wanted.

She bent further, presenting herself to him, pressing her face into the pillow, her knees apart, her hips rotating in bold invitation.

'Oh, wow,' he growled. His hands lifted, smoothing over the curves of her butt as if he couldn't resist touching.

And that was what *she* wanted. Nothing but sex. To be nothing but the receptive female. To feel a mate's strength pound into her. All animal. Hot, satisfying. Over.

She waited, feeling him move into position. She groaned as she felt the strength of his thighs lock against hers. She quivered, her body shaking already in a precursor of ultimate pleasure.

He leaned forward, his hands sliding up from her hips now—up the length of her spine. He slid one hand around her ribs, boldly sweeping, and tweaked her nipple, while his other hand continued up her spine to massage the base of her neck. She angled her head as his fingers worked, she arched her rear up higher, rocking back and forth against the hot, hard erection he was holding back just out of her.

He gave her nipple another tweak, half laughing as she moaned. But then he slid that hand lower—his hand spread wide, firm down her stomach. Down, down, to the part of her that was burning, ready for him.

One touch was all it took to make her beg. 'Oh, please,' she sobbed. 'Please, please, please.'

He thrust hard inside her. The force pushed her face harder into the pillow, muffling her scream. Her fists tightened as she tried to absorb the pleasure as he growled and then rocked into her, again, then again. Oh, he was good. How could she have forgotten just how good? How had she ever thought anyone or anything could ever match up to this? This was the *ultimate* pleasure for her.

His fingers toyed, teasing over her too sensitive nub until she was bucking like a wild pony. But his other hand clamped onto her shoulder, holding her in place so he could continue to thrust into her with brute strength, such masculine force, she thought she was going to break apart with the pleasure.

She closed her eyes, her face locked hot against the feather-filled pillow. She could hardly breathe. But it was good. He couldn't see into her eyes and take everything from her. Not all her secrets. She just wanted the sex. Wanted the orgasm.

His fingers tightened on her skin. She relished the slight pain—recognising how close he was to losing control. She wanted that. She wanted it to be a raw, physical, *fast* explosion. She groaned again and again as he pushed her higher, further until she was so close she—

'*Damn it.*' He pulled out.

'What—?' She fell forward, bereft.

But he deftly flipped her onto her back. Her lax legs fell apart and in seconds he'd covered her. His chest to hers, his pelvis to hers, his nose to hers. His eyes boring into hers. 'What do you want? Tell me what you want.'

'You can't figure it out?' she growled at him.

He shook his head. 'You're offering, giving. Don't just offer—*take.*'

'You didn't like that?'

'Of course I did,' he roared through gritted teeth. 'You make it so easy to take from you. But what do *you* want?'

So excited, so exposed, so needy, she was pushed beyond limits—beyond self-preservation. 'You!' she breathlessly screamed, her eyes watering. 'I just want *you.* All of you.'

He didn't move for a moment. Didn't answer.

Then he lowered his mouth that last inch and kissed her. Another kiss of the kind before—the one she'd been unable to bear. Explicitly sensual, yes, but also warm and sweet. *Loving.* And as he kissed her he thrust—slid—straight back inside. So deep, so full, so right.

He didn't stop kissing her—his tongue stroking, the rhythm matching that of his hips. He hadn't just settled over her, he'd sealed them together. So nearly satisfied, she wound her arms tightly around him, her hands spread wide over his muscles, her fingers digging into his tight, flexing butt. She could feel the power of him, but she could also feel the slight trembling, the oversensitive spasms of *his* body as well as those of her own. The sensations battered her defences, his grip on her body—her heart—too strong.

She screamed in his mouth, her body clamping around his. Finally, finally, finally he pushed her over the edge—and caught her. And she clung as if he were her life raft. As she convulsed and cried his name over and over, he lifted his head, gazing down at her with absolute satisfaction in his eyes, a beautiful smile on his lips, before he let out a glorious growl of release of his own.

Vivi collapsed in his embrace. She'd drowned again.

# CHAPTER SIX

SOMETHING WAS SCREECHING in Liam's ear. Loud, electronic, incessant.

'Is that your phone?' Aghast, Liam sat bolt upright in bed, rubbing the gritty feeling from his eyes.

He blinked in time to see Victoria's wincing nod as she swiped up the gadget to answer. 'Hi, Gia. Of course. I'll be there in three.' She ended the call and grimaced. 'I must have slept through.'

Liam reached out and grabbed her wrist, stopping her slide from the bed. He didn't want her to leave. 'Be where?' he asked, an ominous feeling in his gut.

'In Reception, waiting for her to turn up.'

'To do *what* at this hour?'

'She likes to keep fit. She runs for forty-five minutes every day.'

Liam didn't let her go as he glanced at the illuminated numbers on the clock on the bedside table. 'You're kidding. She wants you to go running with her *now*?' At three in the morning?

She freed her wrist with a sharp twist and stepped away from the bed.

'Gia doesn't like the paparazzi taking pics of her exercising so she goes out when the world is asleep.'

Liam's heart started thudding as if he'd been running for two hours already. 'Why doesn't she use the hotel gym?'

'She prefers to exercise outdoors. Fresh air. Like many people.'

'Why doesn't she take a bodyguard? Why does it have to be you?' He frowned, concern obliterating the remnants of his sleepiness. 'It's not safe for the two of you to be out running in the dark streets at this time of night.'

But Victoria chuckled. 'She does take a bodyguard. But she likes to talk to me. She gives me instructions.'

'So what, you're taking dictation while you're out jogging?' Appalled, he watched her pull running shorts from her case. 'You're prepared for this?'

'We run most mornings.' She tossed the shorts and sports-singlet on the bed and walked through to the bathroom.

'But you worked so late.' And she'd got to sleep so *much* later. He slid out of bed to follow, watching as she efficiently flicked on the shower. Part of him wanted to step in after her so he could soap her up. Most of him wanted her to come back to bed. *Now*.

'It's the way she works.' She lathered the soap. 'She doesn't need a lot of sleep.'

'What about you? Don't you need sleep?'

'I can sleep later.' She swiped soapy bubbles around her body.

'But you won't.' He frowned and pulled a towel from the rail for her. 'You're too busy organising Gia's life and running errands and keeping Alannah out of trouble.'

'It's good for me to keep fit too.'

'It's not good for anyone to have their sleep interrupted like this. This is the middle of the night. This is bad for your body clock.' And bad for every single one of his internal organs. He didn't want her to go.

She rinsed off and plucked the towel from his fingers. 'My body clock is just fine.'

His blood was running cold; he gritted his teeth but it didn't stop the chills spreading down his spine. He didn't want her to walk out on him. He didn't want to lose what he'd just found. He wanted her to stay. He'd do whatever he had to to make her stay. 'We only got to sleep half an hour ago, you know.'

Oh, Victoria knew. He'd asked her again and again what she wanted. And she'd told, she'd taken. She'd indulged so many fantasies. Only now she had so many more. And, man, she wished he'd pick up a towel to put around his hips. He was distraction incarnate. She bent to jam her feet into trainers and tie her laces and avoid looking at him. Then she made it to the door.

But he was waiting there for her.

His hands swept over her body—one around her waist, one sneakily slipping up her thigh. She couldn't resist another look at him. He was as hard as iron.

'You're panting already,' he drawled in her ear. 'How are you going to run for forty-five when you're already as breathless as this?'

'Don't tease.' She leaned against the door for support, letting herself enjoy this last touch.

'I'm not teasing.' His grin proved him a liar. 'I'm seriously concerned for your welfare.'

'I—' Her phone chimed again. She glanced at the screen but didn't take the call. 'I'll tell her I was in the elevator and didn't have reception.'

The last thing she wanted to do was go running and listen to all the things Gia wanted her to do today. Not to mention do all the soothing, calming talk if the boss was panicking about something. Which no doubt she would be. Because she always was. But Vivi had to go.

'Victoria.' He settled both hands on her waist. Firmly. His smile fading. 'No job is worth this.'

She narrowed her eyes. 'This one is.'

'Really?'

'I'm Gia's longest serving assistant. We have trust. I'm not letting her down.'

'You have trust? What would happen if you didn't go?'

Vivi didn't answer. She didn't want to think about that.

'I don't care how much she pays you, she's asking too much.'

'You can't accuse me of being a workaholic.' She deflected the argument back on him. 'You're way worse than me.'

'I *had* to work. There were people relying on me. Pulling a company back from the brink is almost harder than building one from scratch.'

'You don't think I *have* to work?' Her temper flared. 'I'm the one who ended up alone in London with no money, no friends, no family. I got this job on my own and I'm damn well going to keep it. And what makes you think I can't cope with working as hard as you?'

'Of course you can.' He let out a frustrated growl. 'I admit I worked like a dog. Most of the time I still do. Every bit the same kind of crazy hours as you. But there's a crucial difference. This company is *mine*. It's all my effort. It's *my* baby. I'm in control of it.'

'So working for someone else isn't as good?' she snapped. 'Is that what you're saying?'

His frown was quick, so was his attempt to explain. 'You're a talented person. You had design ideas of your own back then. Maybe you should be doing more for yourself.'

More? More like what? 'This may be hard for your feeble brain to compute,' she said crossly, 'but I find it rewarding to support another person.'

'*Exactly.*' He leaned forward. 'And it seems to me you've ended up in the *exact* same position you were in five years ago. Running around doing everything anyone asked of you. Doing everything for other people and not for yourself. Not taking care of yourself. Answer me this—do you really want to go?'

'It's not about what I want.'

He looked frustrated. 'You're already regressing? Unable to say what you really want? Too scared of Gia's disapproval?'

'I have *responsibilities*.'

'Unreasonable ones.' He looked furious. 'If you go, I won't be here when you get back. And I won't come back.'

Vivi froze. 'Is that a threat?' She glared up at him. 'Because *that's* unreasonable.'

Just who did he think he was? She couldn't give up her life again. And that was what this would be. If she refused Gia now, she'd be sacked on the spot.

'Can you put what you want first?' he asked. 'Not what I want. Not Gia. But you.'

'No, this is only about what *you* want. You say I can ask you anything? You only mean sexually. You still don't *listen*. You don't respect what I do. What I want.'

He still only wanted to win. To be the one she chose. And for what?

Of course she wanted to remain locked in his embrace. But she wanted more. *Already* she wanted more. Being intimate with him only worsened her attraction to him. He was like a drug. Her absolute addiction. Addictions were never a good thing. Too much led to bad. And here it was already—the request to bow to his will. And the thing was—he *didn't* want more. He'd made that crystal clear.

He'd stilled, his hands at his sides. Fisted. 'You said one night.'

'Yeah, and my night is over. The day has begun.' And she really needed to get moving—away from him. She needed to get on the first plane back to London.

'Whereas my night has a few hours left.' He stepped back into her space. His fingers skimmed the edge of her shorts.

She couldn't hide her instinctive shiver—not just from his touch, but the determination, the intensity in his eyes.

'Victoria,' he asked softly. 'How long do you think you can last?'

She stiffened—he knew, didn't he? How much his touch affected her. This was a deliberate attempt to seduce her. Too bad. Because she'd lasted *years* and she *wouldn't* be bowled by him again. 'It was only sex, Liam.' And she'd had other sex. Good sex even.

His eyes narrowed. 'Only the best sex of your life.'

'All right, yes. The best. That satisfy you?' She paused, admitting the truth hurt. But it was true. It had always been there, had never gone away, never died. It had only taken one look, one fraction of a second, to burst back to life stronger than ever. But it was all he wanted and it wasn't enough. 'It's lust. It's purely chemical. For some reason my body thinks yours is the best one on the planet to procreate with. But *you're* not the best person for me. You're not Mr Right. We want different things.' She shored up her defence—reminded herself of what she'd worked so hard for. 'We're both career driven, we live in separate countries. I can't give up my life again. And you wouldn't want me to. You've said it yourself—you don't want more. This has to stop. I can't let this happen again.'

When she'd been with him, it had been as if the rest of the world could crumble around them. Such a cliché. He'd been her escape. But he'd also been her prison. In the end she'd needed to be free of that too. The intensity still frightened her.

He stepped back, looking oddly pale under the dim light from the bedside table. 'You regret it.'

'I think…' She hesitated again. 'Yes.'

'This life you got going isn't that great,' he said. 'Not when you have to go on freaking training runs at three in the morning. But you can't say no. You're afraid to stand up for yourself for fear of rejection.'

'There's a major point of difference you're missing. Gia *pays* me.'

'You're still scared of her. Of disapproval.'

'I *choose* to work for her. You're as hot-headed as ever, like some bulldozer barging into a situation and not getting the subtleties. Doing and getting what only *you* want regardless of the impact on anyone else. Did you know Gia was due a holiday after Milan? Your demands ruined it.'

'Gia is a machine who never needs rest,' Liam scoffed. 'The person who missed out on the break was *you*. And you can't ask her for it because you're completely afraid. You're still too scared to be honest.'

'Oh, I can be *honest*. But you can't seem to *listen*. Here's some honesty for you. I want you out of my room. Out of my life.' She couldn't cope with him—with the power of her emotions. Not when it wasn't reciprocated. When for him it was just sex and for her it was *everything*.

She heard his indrawn breath, felt his muscles brace as he lifted his chin. She swore as her phone beeped again. She opened the door. 'I have to go.'

She had to run.

# CHAPTER SEVEN

FROM VICTORIA'S HOTEL room Liam watched the rising sun compete with the streetlights. He'd not been able to think of anything but Victoria for days. Even in the few moments when true concentration claimed him, she snuck in somehow. He'd wonder what she'd think of a new design feature. Whether she'd smile if he repeated the lame joke a salesman had told him. Her opinion mattered. It always had. He'd been boyishly nervous about her seeing how he'd refitted that boat. He, who never had wanted to impress anyone, had wanted to impress her. And what had she done once she'd got inside his prized shed?

Fallen asleep.

A rueful smile crossed his lips. She'd been so tired. So tense. So wary.

Because of him.

Five years ago he'd doubted he could live up to her—his youthful ideal. He didn't think she'd understood the dire situation he'd come from. He'd clawed his way up—scholarships, the dreaded networking. Using every skill he'd had to gain some kind of footing. Then he'd met her and thrown it all away. Landing them both in the worst position either had been in.

On the road with her, he'd *had* to get some kind of security behind him because he knew relationships didn't work when life was impoverished. It wasn't so much dog-eat-dog, but an isolated hand-to-mouth existence. No one had energy to spare for caring.

He hadn't wanted her to experience that. He'd wanted to protect, care, provide for her in the way that she should have been provided for. That she was used to. But all he'd done was cast her adrift and leave her alone to face exactly those kinds of trials.

Him too. He'd had to start from an even worse position—he'd killed his 'team player' rep. He'd broken the unspoken honour of fraternity by betraying Oliver. The shame he'd felt when he'd got that email rescinding the job offer—the realisation he had nothing to offer her. Nothing that she'd want for long.

And now? Now—for all the success he had, the money and the success she had—it still wasn't going to work.

Because he still wasn't enough.

In all his life he had never felt so alone—not even when his father had left for hours, days at a time, or when he'd spent months sailing alone at sea, when he'd spoken out and betrayed his best friend…none of that was worse than this moment.

He'd moved on from his past. But now he'd lost the most precious *possibilities* for the future.

He bowed his head, hating how ripped apart he felt. How stupidly vulnerable he'd allowed himself to get so quickly. No one central to his life had stayed with him—neither mother, father, nor the girl he'd once thought he loved.

Now he knew he loved her. He loved the strong woman she'd become—the generous, loyal, smart, beautiful woman. Because tonight, what had started as something of a game—a challenge—had become something so serious. So much more. For him.

He'd opened up to her. He'd offered her all he actually had to give—himself. Not just his body, but his support, his humour, what compassion he had…whatever else there was in him to be wanted. He'd wanted to give it all.

And he'd wanted her to take all of him. To embrace him.
And she had—for one moment he'd been what she wanted.
And it had felt so good he'd wanted her to hold on tight. He'd
wanted to be her first choice. He wanted everything.

He'd pushed. Asking too much, too soon. *He'd* been the
one to regress—to the insecure, needy youth he'd once been.
Selfish. And, yes, unreasonable.

So she'd pushed him away. She didn't want what he had to
offer. He didn't blame her for that. He was just going to have
to learn to live with it. Again.

He still believed she deserved more to her life—for all the
fabulousness of her career. She shouldn't remain so isolated
from her home, her history, her family. The wistfulness in her
eyes when she spoke of them told him that. So did her need to
be integrated into a community—to be necessary—that was
why she'd made herself so indispensable in her work.

How much of an idiot he'd been no longer mattered. All he
wanted was for her to be happy. Maybe, from a distance, he
could help her reconnect.

But he had to leave now—because that was also what she
wanted. And, frankly, he couldn't stay to face her rejection
again. She'd said no and she was right; it was time he *listened* to her.

So Liam did as she'd asked. He dressed. He left.

He didn't look back.

# CHAPTER EIGHT

VIVI WASN'T PAYING attention to Gia as they jogged. She clutched her phone so she could leave herself voice messages if Gia gave orders. But she was half hoping for a message or something from Liam. There was nothing, of course.

Her whole body ached but she mentally beat herself up all the more. Why had she lost it like that with him? Why'd she have to get so melodramatic and scream at him? Why couldn't she just chill out and go a few more rounds with him? Have a whole night fling and take it for what it was? Sex that good wasn't easy to find…

But she was deluding herself and she knew it. She wanted so much more from him. Always had. Always would.

Her nerves shrieked as she swiped her card to get into the room. But before she stepped in she knew. She sensed the void. For once he'd done as she'd asked. He'd listened. He'd left.

She couldn't feel hurt by that—it was what she'd wanted, right? And he'd got what he wanted too. But all that emotion she'd thought she'd felt in those kisses? In that connection? To her it had felt as if he'd stopped them from having sex. He'd switched it totally. He'd made love to her—making her love him. He'd opened up to her, offered so much to her. And he'd held her as if he never, ever wanted to let her go.

But it seemed all that had only been her imagination.

\* \* \*

A week later, back in London, winter had arrived early and Vivi felt the chill to her bones. Gia was on a bender—she'd been hit with inspiration after the boat shoot and wanted to design a whole range with a nautical theme in time for the following spring. Vivi couldn't bear it. When Gia was in full-on create mode she shut everything else down, leaving Vivi to deal with every inquiry, every problem. So her hours were worse than ever and the ache in her soul worsened with every sleepless second. Nights were interrupted not just with the runs with Gia, but with memories of Liam—the building of an ache so great she didn't see how it could be eased. And the more tired she became, the worse it got, the less she could sleep.

Finally one morning after a run that had gone on way too long, she glared at the bland monotony of her wardrobe, then turned her back on it. She stomped into work in ancient jeans and a huge jumper and went straight to the room where samples were kept. She found a scarlet shirt that was almost large enough. Gia wouldn't stand for her wearing another designer's outfits. Then she marched into Gia's design room without knocking.

Gia lifted her head and stared frigidly.

Too bad. Vivi tossed the dictation machine she'd had couriered that morning onto Gia's desk. 'If you need to make notes for me, the bodyguard will hold this. I'm not getting up at three any more. I need my beauty sleep.' She totally snapped.

Gia just kept staring at her. 'Anything else you'd like to address while you're here?' she asked, her face completely impassive.

Vivi barely thought about it before biting the bullet. 'I need another assistant to work on the new online distribution project. It's getting too much for me to handle alone. Plus I need to take the next few days off work. Sorry for the short notice but I missed my holiday for the Genoa shoot and I need the time now.' She needed to go and sort her head out. Get away completely, lick her wounds in private. Come back refreshed and ready to take her career to the next level—on her own terms.

If Gia didn't like that, if Gia sacked her, then she'd just find work somewhere else. She had a name—a rep in the industry that she'd worked so hard to build. It was time to call on it. Only now, now she'd had a second to breathe… She held it in and waited for the bomb to blow.

But Gia just blinked. 'All right.'

Vivi blinked back. 'Really?'

Gia actually laughed. 'Really.'

'Okay.' Vivi breathed out, then turned and walked across the room before Gia changed her mind.

'The red looks good on you,' Gia said as Vivi got to the door. 'I've been wondering when you were going to get as bossy with me as you are with everyone else,' she added.

Now Vivi chuckled. 'Not bossy.' She paused, lifting her chin. 'Just…balanced.'

'Bossy. But I like it.' Gia's eyes went slightly glassy. 'And I really do like that red… Can you get me some—?'

Vivi held up her hand. She'd won a point here and she wasn't conceding it the next second. She was going on in her new, fully sorted style. 'I'll get someone else to come in and take notes. I'm away the next few days, remember?'

Gia's eyes snapped back into focus and she laughed. 'Okay. But no more than four days—I can't cope longer without you.'

Four days was longer than Vivi had had off in one stretch in the last four years. But she grinned at Gia's genuine appeal—at the realisation that her incredibly demanding boss did actually recognise that Vivi was great at her job. But she also deserved more.

Back in her own office she drew a deep breath. If she could manage Gia, she could figure out the rest of her life, right? She could take it on.

'Can you sign for these, please, Vivi? They're both on your

sig. only.' The receptionist looked nervous as she came to the door. Yeah, Vivi had been grumpy these last few days. So she smiled sweetly and signed. 'Thank you.'

Two parcels. She picked up the top one—the smaller. It was addressed to her, with 'private and confidential' typewritten on the front of it. Inside was another packet—with only her name on the front. This packet she unwrapped slowly, her heart thudding. Because she recognised her mother's delicately perfect handwriting. She'd never really appreciated how beautiful it was before.

Inside was a whole bunch of envelopes, bound together with a rubber band. Her name on each envelope, but no address. She opened the top one. At first she couldn't read the words, she was too nervous. Goosebumps rippled down her arms and she sat in her chair, her legs wobbly. The letter was signed from them both.

Her parents were in touch with Stella? Her parents wanted to get in touch with her?

And inside all those envelopes were all the letters her mother had written over the years and never known where to send them. The Christmas cards. The birthday cards. All kept. All written. Some short messages. Some longer.

Vivi's heart beat so violently it was a wonder it didn't burst from her chest. How had they got her address? This was marked so clearly—to Gia's private bag. Someone had known to address it to Vivi not Victoria.

Liam had been right. She was afraid. She'd run from her problems and she'd never stopped running, never turned to face them. It was beyond time she did.

She put the letters to the side. She'd read them later—she needed to regroup now.

The next was a parcel from Nico. She frowned. She didn't want to see the prints from the Genoa shoot, but he'd addressed this packet to her personally with a private note scrawled across the corner in his hand.

*Thought you might like this. Snapped it the other day when you were snoozing.*

It wasn't just a print. He'd blown it up and framed it. In the black and white portrait, she was curled against Liam's chest. He—like she—was oblivious to the photographer. Liam was looking down at her, his arms cradling her. It was the second after she'd woken. The second she'd looked into his eyes. That perfect moment just before he'd encouraged her, when all emotion flowed simply and purely. Wordlessly. So incredibly obvious.

It was what Nico was revered for—capturing the essence. No Photoshop magic needed here. No wonder the guy won every award there was.

She'd no doubt that the shots of Alannah on the boat were magnificent, but none could be as beautiful as this. This was art. And what was most important was there for anyone to see. Love written all over her face. And on Liam's?

That intensity, yes. But also, in his beautiful eyes, that slight strain of vulnerability.

Pain shafted through her. She wanted to believe in that image so badly. All those years ago he'd been the one to help her through the night when she'd been insanely making Christmas decorations. Because he'd wanted that one thing? He'd wanted to win her from Oliver?

Or had it been more than that? He'd come from nothing, from no family, no love. She'd never really understood how neglected he'd been—on so many levels. He'd worked hard to fit in—using his humour, his sporting ability. But he'd fallen for her. He'd wanted her. He'd given up everything he'd gained in his pursuit of her.

That humbled Vivi now—hurt her—as she realised he'd wanted to help her again. This time knowing there was nothing more. Putting her parents in touch with her was a gesture of generosity—of compassion, caring. The only way left to him to show it. Because she'd pushed him away. She'd rejected him. Once more they'd failed to communicate properly.

He'd listened. But she?

She'd not been honest. She'd not done as he'd challenged her to—she'd not asked for what she'd truly wanted. And she could have.

Vivi stood. She'd go and see her parents. Yes she would. She'd meet Stella. She'd sort out her past. But there was something else she had to do first. She had to lay claim to her future.

Eighteen hours later she locked her wobbly knees as she knocked on the door, clutching the parcel under her arm. Back in Italy, hoping like crazy he was in his office.

A woman opened the door. She wore shorts. Incredibly stylish shorts that showed off incredibly slim and toned legs. Vivi tried not to panic and asked in painful Italian to see Liam.

'He's not here.' The woman answered in English.

Vivi blinked, her blood chilling. 'Where is he?'

'London.'

'London?' Vivi felt faint, then frustration kicked in. 'When did he go to London?'

The pretty woman looked at her oddly and then called to another worker out of Vivi's sight.

'When did he go?' Vivi repeated, her tone rising. Why had he gone to London? Her heart leapt but she tried to jump on it. He wouldn't have gone to see her. It would be for business. That was it.

'He goes later today.' The man had come to the door.

'Then where is he now? Is he at the airport?' Had she just crossed paths with him in some mean twist of fate?

The Italians exchanged another glance.

'I think he's in his rooms,' said the man. 'If you'll follow me.'

Of course she'd follow. After the mad packing, the long flight, the crazy taxi ride...

'Liam?' The guy broke into a string of super-quick Italian.

But Vivi stepped past him and her guide went quiet.

Liam looked up, leapt to his feet. Then froze.

The Italian disappeared, shutting the door behind him.

'Victoria?' Liam's face shuttered the second he said her name. So carefully bland.

'Yeah.' Vivi swallowed and walked further into the room, tightening her grip on the packet in her hands. She noticed the bag on the floor near the door. It was small. Just a short trip, then? 'Am I stopping you from getting somewhere?'

A very faint smile tweaked the corner of his mouth. 'No. It doesn't matter.'

Okay. She breathed out. She'd never felt so nervous in her life. Not even in that moment when Oliver had asked her to marry him in front of everyone, when she'd been so terrified of the reaction and so unsure which way to go.

This was a million times worse. Because this time she knew exactly what she wanted, exactly how much it mattered.

It meant everything.

'I got sent a parcel,' she began. 'Actually I got two.'

His brows flicked.

'You told them my address, didn't you?'

He said nothing. Didn't ask who she meant but she knew he understood exactly.

'I know it was you,' she said, managing a smile. 'There's no one else it could have been.'

He rubbed his lip with his index finger. 'What was in the parcel?'

Her eyes filled before she could get the words out. 'All the letters they've written to me over the years and never been able to send.'

'Have you been to see them?'

She shook her head.

He jerked. 'Don't you think—?'

'I had to see you first,' she interrupted roughly. 'I needed to see you.'

He froze, his gaze riveted to her.

Vivi stepped forward. 'The second parcel was from Nico.' She cleared her throat and pulled the portrait from its bubble wrap and put it on the desk between them. 'Did he show it to you?'

Liam slowly lowered his gaze to look at the picture. Vivi watched his face, saw the flicker of a muscle in his jaw before that rigid control took over again. He looked at the picture for a long time.

Finally Vivi took that last step forward. 'I don't want a picture,' she said, suddenly feeling liberated at putting it all on the line. Her heart thundered and chills feathered over her skin but adrenalin pushed her on. Finally saying what she really wanted—and knowing that at this moment he was *listening* so intently. 'I can handle people in a business sense. But you were right—I wasn't asking for anything for my personal life. I was avoiding anything very personal. But not any more. Not after…the other night. I've contacted my parents. I was scared but I offered the olive branch and I think it's going to be okay.' She breathed in deep. 'And then there's you.'

'Are you offering me an olive branch?'

'No. For you…' she paused to draw in some steel '…I'm fighting.'

'Fighting me?'

'If I have to.' She walked around the desk.

He leaned away slightly, letting the desk take some of his weight as he regarded her. 'I was an idiot,' she said. 'I'm sorry I lost my temper.'

The smallest smile appeared on his lips. 'I was glad you weren't afraid to with me.'

'I was afraid,' she admitted softly. 'That's why I sent you away.'

'It hurt.' He barely moved as he spoke.

'I'm sorry.'

'No.' He shook his head. 'I deserved it. You accused me of not listening to you. And you were right, I didn't. Not back then. Back then I was too busy trying to figure solutions on my own. It was what I was used to and I was too proud to let you in. I'm sorry about that. But last week I should have. Then you put the words in my mouth—that I wouldn't want more from you—'

'Words you'd once said.'

'But it's not only women who're allowed to change their minds.' The corner of his mouth curved. 'And honestly, for me it wasn't a change of mind, it was more a recognition of what's been true all along.'

Vivi's heart was almost bursting from its speed. 'What is it that's true?'

'That I love you. I realised I'd never actually told you. But I do.'

'I never believed you felt for me as strongly.' Her eyes filled again, this time the tears spilled.

'How could I *not*?' He jammed his hands into his pockets. 'I fell so hard. I gave up everything for you.'

'So did I.'

'I know that now.'

And she'd just thought he'd done it because it was a challenge. And that once he'd had what he wanted he'd got bored. She hadn't ever realised he'd been as flipped out by it as she'd been. That he'd lost as much as she.

She glanced at the picture and then looked back at him. 'I'm still scared, Liam, but I'm not going to let that stop me from asking for what I want any more. And I'm asking for you to come over here.'

'I can't.'

'No?' Her heart smashed.

A small, rueful smile softened his mouth. 'You know what will happen if we touch.'

'Well…' She bit her lip, relaxing a smidge as she saw that smile. 'I was kind of counting on that.'

'We're not making the same mistake as we did then. We touch now, it'll be all on. We have to talk this through first.'

'What more do you need to know?' She gazed at him. 'I love you. I've always loved you. And it totally scares me.'

His rigid stance melted; in a step he was there, his arms around her. 'Okay,' he muttered into her hair. 'There's nothing to be scared of now.'

He kissed her. Kissed her the way he'd kissed her the other night. With all the love in the world, until her toes curled in the crazy high heels she'd worn specially to get tall enough to see eye to eye with him. And she kissed him back—as fervently, deeply, sweetly.

'I can't let you go now.' He groaned. 'You know I was going to London this afternoon.'

She knotted her fingers into his shirt, keeping him close, and failed to answer coolly. 'Your assistant mentioned it.'

'I was coming after you. I've never felt so bad. Hurt. Furious with myself. I realised I'd never been honest with you either. I'd never let you in the way I should have. I never told you…so many things I should have. Especially that I was in love with you.' He pulled her closer into his heat, a pained expression on his face. 'I should have opened up to you all those years ago. I should have come after you.'

'No. We weren't ready. Way too young. I had baggage to get over. I had to grow a spine.' She smiled. 'And you had a business to build. It's better now.'

He bent, resting his forehead on hers. 'I love you. Always have.'

A feeling of utter contentment seeped into her bones, but as she leaned against him reality—logistics—bothered the bliss. 'How are we going to make this work?' she voiced her fears. 'We failed so badly last time.'

'No.' He framed her face with his hands, tilting her so she

had to meet his gaze head on. 'Failure is making the same mistake twice. The first time wasn't failure. It was merely a mistake.'

'Merely?'

'Merely.' His eyes twinkled. 'We won't fail now. So long as you ask, I listen.'

'And vice versa.' She nibbled on her lip, clutching his shirt more tightly. She never wanted to leave him but there was no choice. 'We can make distance work.'

'No,' he said softly. 'I've had enough nights without you already. I've done what I can with the business here, now I'm ready to sell it on. I'm ready for the next project. That will be wherever you are.'

Shocked, she dropped her hand and stepped back. 'You can't sell your business.'

'I can.' He chuckled, capturing her by the waist and moving in close again. 'Darling, I'm bored. I need a new challenge.' His eyes sharpened. 'And, no, I will never get bored with you.'

That wasn't what she was worried about. 'Your career matters. I won't let you sacrifice anything for me. You'll resent me.'

'This isn't a sacrifice. I came looking for you and as soon as I saw you again, spoke to you again—it was all over. It just took me a bit to get my head around. I'm never losing you again. You're what matters most in my life. This time I need to give us the chance. This time I can. I can't afford not to.'

'But your business—'

'What is it that matters to you—the financial security I have or me?'

She stared at him—at the vulnerability in his eyes, the same that had been caught in that portrait. It was real. Now she understood—part of him was as afraid as she. 'You.' She tightened her arms around his neck. 'You, you, you.'

She felt the tension ebb from his body—and another kind of hardness steal in.

'Then if you don't mind risking it with an entrepreneur, you'll be fine. I'm ready for new challenges. Business challenges. Family challenges.' He grinned. 'Trust me, Vivi.'

'Vivi?'

'That's who you are—my Victoria, my Vivi. My life.'

She smiled, glowing inside. Knowing, believing that he loved her the way she loved him. Suddenly she saw that the overwhelming passion wasn't going to drown her. Their bond was so much more than sexual, it had humour, support, substance. Being with him would enhance her life, not diminish possibilities, but expand them. He'd never stifle her. And she'd never hold him back either.

'If you like,' he muttered, 'I'll even come with you on your three-a.m. runs with Gia.'

'Actually, there's no need.' She grinned, feeling a sense of strength and pride rippling through her. 'I stood up to her. Handed her a dictation machine and told her to go with the bodyguard.'

Liam laughed and kissed her. 'How'd she take it?'

'She basically high-fived me.' Vivi giggled. 'But you know, there's still a problem.'

He looked concerned. 'What's that?'

'My body's used to a really tough workout in the early hours of the morning. I'm going to need some kind of activity to replace that run…something really, really energetic…'

He bent, sweeping her into his arms, that wicked smile on his mouth. 'You know, I think I can come up with something that might wear you out…'

'When can you come up with it?'

'Oh, it's up now.'

She chuckled at the lame innuendo, delighted in being carried off by the one true love of her life.

Long, quiet moments later he gazed into her eyes—his own free of tension, alight with love and passion.

'It was only ever you,' he promised.

'And you,' she answered.
Finally. Always.
*For ever.*

\* \* \* \* \*

# A MOST SUITABLE
# WIFE
## JESSICA STEELE

**Jessica Steele** lives in a friendly Worcestershire village with her super husband, Peter. They are owned by a gorgeous Staffordshire bull terrier called Florence, who is boisterous and manic, but also adorable. It was Peter who first prompted Jessica to try writing and, after her first rejection, encouraged her to keep on trying. Luckily, with the exception of Uruguay, she has so far managed to research inside all the countries in which she has set her books—travelling to places as far apart as Siberia and Egypt. Her thanks go to Peter for his help and encouragement.

# CHAPTER ONE

TAYE let herself back into the apartment and wandered into the sitting room. Looking around at the smart furniture and fittings, she recalled the poky bed-sit she had lived in for most of the three years previously, and knew that she just could not bear to go back to that way of living.

Not only could she not, but, with the rent of this apartment being very much more than she could afford on her own now that Paula had left, Taye determined that she would *not* give up the apartment unless she absolutely had to.

To that end, and after a very great deal of thought, she had just taken the first steps in getting someone to pay half of the rent. She did so hope that someone would see the advert and apply soon.

Unfortunately, because Paula, while giving her the name and address of the letting agent, had taken the lease with her, Taye felt on very rocky ground with regard to her own tenancy agreement. The fact was, although Taye had looked high and low for the lease, she had been unable to find it, and so was unsure of her actual tenancy position.

The lease was in Paula's name and while Paula had said that provided the rent was paid on time—quarterly in advance—she was sure the agents would not care who was living there or who paid the rent, Taye was not so certain.

She would have liked a sight of the lease before Paula

had left, if only to have some idea if there was any restriction on sub-letting. Because it seemed to Taye to be fairly obvious that a lease would not be worth as much as the paper it was written on if the tenant went ahead their own merry way.

But she had a feeling that any approach to the agent to check might see Wally, Warner and Quayle saying that there was a 'no flat-share sub-let' clause—and that caused Taye to hesitate to approach them. Yes, she knew that she should approach them. That she ought to go and see them and explain that Paula Neale had left the area. Fear that they might say that she would have to leave too, caused Taye to hold back. Should they be even likely to enquire into her suitability to be a tenant—her financial suitability that was—they would know straight away that by no chance could she pay the high rent required on her own.

Burying her head in the sand it might be but, bearing in mind that she had been Paula's sub-tenant, Taye preferred to look on it from Paula's viewpoint: that as long as the rent was paid they would not care who lived there provided they were respectable and paid the rent when due.

All the same, when considering her options—pay up or leave—Taye knew she did not want to leave and go back to the way she had up until three months ago been living.

Which left the only answer—she must get someone else to pay half the rent the way she had paid half the rent to Paula. And how to go about that? Advertise.

The only problem with that was that Taye felt she could hardly advertise in the paper. Without question she suspected that any agent worthy of the name would keep their eyes on the 'To Let' column of the local paper.

Which meant— Her thoughts were interrupted when someone rapped smartly on the wood panelling of the door. Anticipating it would be one of her neighbouring apartment dwellers, Taye went to answer it.

But, although she thought she had met all of the other tenants in the building in the time she had been there, she would swear she had never caught so much as a glimpse of the tall dark-haired man who stood there before her.

'How did you get in?' she questioned abruptly when for what seemed like ageless seconds the man just stared arrogantly back at her.

She thought she was going to have to whistle for an answer. Then Rex Bagnall, who had a flat on the next floor, rushed by. 'Forget my head...' he said in passing, making it obvious he had just gone out but had dashed back for something he had forgotten—and that answered her question. The man who had knocked at her door had slipped in as Rex had gone out.

Then suddenly it clicked. 'You've come about the flat?' she exclaimed.

For long silent minutes the stern-faced man studied her, and she began to think she was going to have to run for any answer to her questions. But then finally, his tones clipped, 'I have,' he replied.

Oh, grief! She had been thinking in terms of a female to flat-share with! She could not say either that she was very taken with this grim-expressioned mid-thirties-looking man, but she supposed even if she had no intention of renting half the flat to him that there were certain courtesies to be observed.

'That was quick,' she remarked pleasantly. 'I've only just returned from putting the ad in the newsagent's window.' She might have gone on to say that she had been looking for someone of the female gender but Rex Bagnall was back again, dashing along the communal hallway. Not wanting him to hear any of her business, 'Come in,' she invited the unsuccessful candidate.

He followed her into her hall, but so seemed to dominate it that she quickly led the way to the sitting room. She turned, the light was better there, and she observed he was broad-shouldered and casually, if expensively, dressed. He could see her better too, his glance flicking momentarily to her white-blonde hair.

'I—er...' she began, faltered and, began again. 'I know I didn't say so, but I was rather anticipating a female.'

'A female?' he enquired loftily—causing her to wish she knew more about the Sex Discrimination Act and if it came into force in a situation like this.

'Have you shared a flat with a female before?' she asked, feeling a trifle hot under the collar. 'I mean, I don't mean to be personal or anything but...' She hesitated, hoping he would help her out, but clearly he was not going to and she found she was saying, 'Perhaps it won't be suitable for you.'

He looked back at her, unspeaking for a second or two. Then deigned to reply, 'Perhaps I'd better take a look around.'

And such was his air of confidence that, albeit reluctantly, Taye, with the exception of her own bedroom, found she was showing him around the apartment. 'This, obviously, is the sitting room,' she began, and went on to show him the dining room, followed by the bathroom and kitchen and utility room. 'That's my bedroom,' she said, indicating her bedroom door in passing. 'And this is the other bedroom.'

'The one for your—tenant?'

'That's right,' she replied, glad, when he had silently

and without comment inspected everywhere else, to hear
him say something at last.

He went into what had been Paula's bedroom and
glanced around. Taye left him to it. She returned to the
sitting room and was preparing to tell him that she would
let him know—it seemed more polite than to straight
away tell him, No chance. He was some minutes before
he joined her in the sitting room—obviously he had been
looking his fill and weighing everything up.

'I see you have a garden,' he remarked, going over to
the sitting room window and looking out.

'It's shared by all of us,' she replied. 'The agents send
someone to tidy up now and again but it doesn't require
too much maintenance. Now, about—'

'Your name?' he cut in. 'I can't go around calling you
Mrs de Winter the whole time.'

Her lips twitched. Somehow, when she wasn't sure she
even liked the man, his dry comment caught at her sense
of humour. He all too plainly was referring to the Mrs
de Winter in Daphne du Maurier's *Rebecca*. The Mrs de
Winter who all through the book had never been given
a first name.

'Taye,' she replied, in the face of his unsmiling look
controlling her urge to smile. 'Tayce, actually, but I'm
called Taye.' She felt a bit foolish all at once, it suddenly
seeming stupid to go on to tell him that her younger
brother had not been able to manage Tayce when he had
been small, and how Taye had just kind of stuck. 'Taye
Trafford,' she completed briefly. Only then did it dawn
on her that she should have asked his name the minute
he had stepped over the threshold. 'And you are?'

'Magnus—Ashthorpe,' he supplied.

'Well, Mr Ashthorpe—'

'I'll take it,' he butted in decisively.

That took her aback somewhat. 'Oh, I don't think…'

'Naturally there are matters to discuss.' He took over the interview, if interview it be.

Well, it wouldn't hurt to discuss it a little, she supposed. At least she could be civilised. 'Would you like coffee?' she offered.

'Black, no sugar,' he accepted, and she was glad to escape to the kitchen.

No way did she want him for a fellow tenant! No way! Yet, as she busied herself with coffee, cups and saucers, she began to realise that she must not be too hasty here. What if no one else applied? The rent was quite steep after all. Yes, but she might well have a whole horde of people interested in a flat-share. Look how quickly he had seen her ad. That card could not have been in the local newsagent's window above ten minutes, she was sure.

'Coffee!' she announced brightly, taking the tray into the sitting room, setting in down and inviting him to take a seat. She placed a cup and saucer down on the low table near him, and, taking the seat opposite, thought it about time to let him know who was doing the interviewing here. 'The flat—the flat-share—it's for yourself?' she enquired. He stared into her wide blue eyes as though thinking it an odd question. 'I mean—you're not married or anything?' she ploughed on. And when he looked unsmiling back, as if to ask what the devil that had to do with her, 'I only advertised for one person. I wouldn't consider a married couple,' she stated bluntly. She was beginning to regret giving him coffee. She would not mind at all if he left now.

'I'm not married,' he enlightened her.

She looked at him. He was quite good-looking, she observed. No doubt he was more interested in playing the field than in making any long-term commitment. 'This is a fairly quiet building,' she felt she ought to warn him. 'We—um—don't go in for riotous parties.' He took that on board without comment, and she began to wonder why she had bothered mentioning it, because she was growing more and more certain that there was no way she was going to have him as a fellow flat-share. He had not touched his coffee—she could hardly stand up and tell him she would let him know. 'The—er—rent would not be a problem?' she enquired. 'It's paid quarterly— thirteen weeks—and in advance.' From his clothes she would have thought he was used to paying for the best, but she had to talk about something. 'I—er—the landlord prefers the rent to be paid on the old quarter days to fall in line with his quarter-day ground rent payments. He owns the building but not the land on which it's built,' she added, but, conscious that she was talking just for the sake of it, she skidded to an abrupt stop.

Magnus Ashthorpe surveyed her coolly before stating, 'I think I'll be able to scrape my share together.' Which, despite his good clothes, gave her the impression that he was in pretty much the same financial state that she was. Her clothes, limited though they were, were of good quality too.

'Er—what sort of work do you do?' she asked, but as he reached for his coffee she noticed a smear of paint on his index finger: the sort of smudgy mark one got when touching paintwork to see if it was dry.

She saw his eyes follow hers, saw him examine the paint smudge himself. 'I'm an artist,' he revealed, looking across at her.

'Magnus Ashthorpe,' she murmured half to herself. She had never heard of him, but it might embarrass him were she to say so, and she had no wish to hurt his feelings. 'You're—um—quite successful?' she asked instead.

'I get by,' he replied modestly.

'You wouldn't be able to paint here,' she said swiftly, latching on to a tailor-made excuse to turn him down. 'The landlord wouldn't care to—'

'I'm allowed the attic where I'm now living. That serves well as a studio,' Magnus Ashthorpe interrupted her.

'Ah,' she murmured. And, feeling desperate to take charge again, 'Where *are* you living at present?' she asked.

'With a friend,' he answered promptly.

'You're—um…' Heavens, this interviewing business was all uphill. 'You're—er—in a—relationship that—er…' She couldn't finish. By the sound of it he was in a relationship that was falling apart. But she just could not ask about it.

Grey eyes continued to appraise her, but briefly his hard expression seemed to soften marginally, as if he had gleaned something of her sensitivity. But any impression she had of a warmer side to the man was gone in an instant. And his voice was cool when he let her know she could not be more wrong if she thought he would tie himself down to any sort of one-to-one relationship.

'Nick Knight and I have been friends for years. He let me move in a year back, but now he wants to move his girlfriend in.' He shrugged. 'While I prefer not to play gooseberry, Nick prefers to have his spare room back.'

'But you'll continue to work from his attic?'

He nodded, and Taye started to feel better. While she had no intention of offering the flat-share to him, if he had a studio—be it just an attic—then at least he had somewhere he could use as a base if this Nick Knight wanted him to leave sooner rather than later.

Magnus Ashthorpe had finished his coffee, Taye noticed. She got to her feet. 'I'm not awfully sure…' she began, to let him down gently.

'You'll want to see other applicants, of course,' he butted in smoothly.

'Well, I have arranged for the flat-share to be advertised all next week and to include next weekend,' she replied. 'And—um—there will be a question of references,' she brought out from an unthought nowhere.

For answer Magnus Ashthorpe went over to the telephone notepad and in a speedy hand wrote down something and tore the sheet of paper from the pad. 'My mobile number,' he said, handing the paper to her. 'I've also noted the name of my previous landlady. Should you want to take up a reference, I'm sure Mrs Sturgess will be pleased to answer any questions you may have about me.'

Since he was not going to be her co-tenant, Taye did not think she would need the piece of paper, but she took it from him anyhow. 'I'll—um—see you out,' she said, and smiled. It cost nothing and she was unlikely to see him ever again. 'Goodbye,' she said. They shook hands.

She closed the door behind him and went swiftly to the dining room. Standing well back from the window, she saw him emerge from the building. But she need not have worried that he might look up and see her lurking near the dining room window—he was already busy in conversation with someone he had called on his mobile phone. No doubt telling his friend Nick Knight that he had found a place!

Taye went back to the sitting room, the feel of his hand on hers still there. He had a wonderful handshake. Still the same, she knew she would not be phoning this Mrs Sturgess for a reference.

Taye purposely stayed in all of that Saturday and the whole of Sunday, and frequently watched from the dining room window for callers. But callers there were none. She had thought there was a huge demand for accommodation to rent, but apparently no one was interested in renting at such a high rent.

And that was worrying. She had not lived in what was termed the 'garden flat' all that long herself, but already she loved it. She had moved to London three years ago after one gigantic fall-out with her mother. But only now was she in any sort of position to pay half of the rent herself. To find all of the rent would be an impossibility.

Taye had a good job, and was well paid, but she just had to keep something back for those calls from her mother. Despite her mother all but throwing her out, it had not stopped her parent from requiring financial assistance from time to time.

Worriedly, knowing that she did not want to go back to the bed-sit existence she had known before her promotion and pay rise, and prior to Paula Neale's invite to move in and share expenses, Taye thought back to how her life had changed—for the better.

There had always been rows at home—even before her father had decided after one row too many that enough was enough and that they would all be happier, himself included, if he moved out.

His financial ability had made the move viable only when his father had died and he had come into a fund which he had been able to assign during her lifetime to his money-loving wife. The fact that Taye's father had no illusions about her mother's spendthrift ways was borne out by the fact that he had made sure that the fund was paid out to her monthly and not in the lump sum she had demanded.

Taye had been fourteen, her brother Hadleigh five years younger when, nine years ago now, their father had packed his bags and left. She loved him, she missed him, and she had been unhappy to see him go. But perhaps they would all be free of the daily rows and constant carping. Perhaps with him no longer there, the rows would stop.

Wrong! Without her father there for her mother to vent her spleen on, Taye had become her mother's target. Though if being daily harangued by Greta Trafford for some over-exaggerated misdemeanour kept the sharpness of her tongue from Taye's nine-year-old brother, then Taye had supposed she could put up with it. What would happen to Hadleigh, though, when she eventually went off to university Taye had not wanted to dwell on.

Then she had discovered that she need not have worried about it, because when she reached the age of sixteen she discovered that her mother had other plans for her.

'University!' she had exclaimed when Taye had begun talking of staying on at school, and of taking her 'A' levels. 'You can forget that, young lady. You can leave school as soon as you can, get a job and start bringing some money in.'

'But—it's all planned!' Taye remembered protesting.

'I've just unplanned it!' Greta Trafford had snapped viperously.

'But Daddy said…'

'Daddy isn't here! Daddy,' her mother mocked, 'was delighted to shelve his responsibilities. Daddy—'

'But—'

'Don't you interrupt me!' Greta Trafford threatened. 'And you can "but" all you want. You're still not going.'

And that Taye had had to accept. But while she had struggled to get over her disappointment and upset at the loss of her dream, she'd known she was going to have to hide how she was feeling from her father. He had been so keen for her to go to university that all she could do was to let him think that she had gone off the idea.

She might have had to accept her mother's assertion that there was no money to spare, but what Taye would not accept was that her father had shelved his responsibilities. He had maybe given up the occupation that had provided them with a very high standard of living, so that his income was nowhere near what it had been. But now working on a farm and living in a tiny cottage that went with the job, his needs small, she knew that in addition to the fund he had assigned for their upkeep, he still sent money to his former home when he could.

It was not enough. Nor was it ever going to be enough. Even when he had been a high earner it had not been enough. Money went through her mother's hands like water. She did not know the meaning of the word thrift. If she saw something she wanted, then nothing would do but that she must have it—regardless of which member of her family ultimately paid.

As bidden, Taye had left school and, having inherited her father's head for figures, she had got a job with a firm of accountants. Her mother had insisted that she hand over her salary to her each month. But by then Taye had started to think for herself. There were things Hadleigh needed for his school work, his school trips, and he was growing faster than they could keep up with. Taye held back as much of her salary as she could get away with, and it was she who kept him kitted out in shoes and any other major essential.

Taye had been ready to leave home years before the

actual crunch came. It was only for the sake of Hadleigh that she had stayed, for he had been a shy, gentle boy.

Taye had reached nineteen and Hadleigh fourteen when Hadleigh, after a row where their mother had gone in for her favourite pastime of deviating from the truth, with the first signs of asserting himself had told Taye, 'You should leave home, Taye.' And when she had shaken her head, 'I'll be all right,' he had assured her. 'And it won't be for much longer. I shall go to university—and I won't come back.'

Perhaps a trace of his words had still been lingering in Taye's head when she journeyed home from work one Friday a year later. She had anticipated that Hadleigh would be grinning from ear to ear at the brand-new bicycle she had saved hard for and had arranged to be delivered on his fifteenth birthday. But she had arrived home to discover her mother had somehow managed to exchange the bicycle she had chosen for a much inferior second-hand one—and had pocketed the difference.

'How *could* you?' Taye had gasped, totally appalled.

'How could I not?' her mother had replied airily. 'The bicycle I got him is perfectly adequate.'

'I wanted him to have something new, something special!' Taye had protested. 'You had no right…'

'No right! Don't you talk to me about rights! What about my rights?'

'It wasn't your money, it was mine. It was dishonest of you to—'

'*Dishonest!*' Her mother's voice had risen an octave—which was always a signal for Taye to back down. Only this time she would not back down. She was incensed at what her money-grubbing mother had done.

So, 'Yes, dishonest,' she had challenged, and it had gone on and on from there, with Taye for once in her

life refusing to buckle under the tirade of venom her
mother hurled at her.

And, seeing that for the first time she was not going
to get the better of her daughter, Greta Trafford had re-
sorted to telling her to follow in her father's footsteps
and to pack her bags and leave.

And Taye, like her father, had suddenly had enough.
'I will,' she had retorted, and did. Though it was true she
did almost weaken when she went in to say goodbye to
Hadleigh. 'Will you be all right?' she asked him.

'You bet,' he said, and gave her a brave grin, and,
having witnessed most of the row before he'd disappeared, 'You can't stay. Not now,' he had told her.

Taye had gone to London and had been fortunate to
find a room to rent, and more fortunate to soon find a
job. A job in finance that she became particularly good
at. When her salary improved, she found a better, if still
poky, bed-sit.

She had by then written to both Hadleigh and her
mother, telling them where she was now living. She also
wrote to her father, playing down the row that had seen
her leave home. Her mother was the first to reply—the
electricity bill was more than she had expected. Since
Taye had used some of the electricity—even though she
had been at home contributing when she had used it—
her mother would be obliged to receive her cheque at her
earliest convenience.

Her mother's 'requests' for money continued over the
next three years. Which was why—having many times
shared a lunch table with Paula Neale in the firm's can-
teen, and having commented that she would not mind
moving from 'bed-sit land'—when Paula one day said
she had half a flat to let if she was interested, and men-

tioned the rent required, instead of leaping at the chance, Taye had to consider it very carefully.

Could she really afford it? Could she not? She was twenty-three, for goodness' sake, Hadleigh coming up to eighteen. And their mother had this time promised he should go to university. Was she to wait until he was at university, Taye wondered, or dared she take the plunge now? It had been late February then, and Hadleigh would go to university in October. Taye—while keeping her fingers crossed that nothing calamitous in the way of unforeseen expenditure was heading her way—plunged.

And here she was now and it was calamitous—though this time that calamity did not stem from her mother but was because, unless she could find someone to share, Taye could see she was in a whole heap of financial trouble. But, so far, no one except for one Magnus Ashthorpe had shown an interest. And, as an interested party, he was the one party she did not want.

All that week Taye hurried home ready to greet the influx of potential flat-share candidates. Julian Coombs, the son of the owner of Julian Coombs Comestibles, where she worked, asked her out, but she declined. She had been out with Julian a few times. He was nice, pleasant and uncomplicated. But she did not want to be absent should anyone see her card in the newsagent's window and call.

But she might just as well have gone out with Julian because each evening she retired to her bed having seen not one single solitary applicant.

She toyed with the idea of inviting Hadleigh to come and stay at the weekend. But he worked most weekends waiting at tables in a smart restaurant about five miles from Pemberton. It was, he said, within easy cycling distance of Pemberton, the village on the outskirts of Hertfordshire

where he and their mother lived. And, besides Hadleigh not
wishing to miss a chance to earn a little money for himself,
Pemberton was not the easiest place to get back to by public
transport on a Sunday.

So Taye stayed home and almost took root by the dining room window. Much good did it do. Plenty of people
passed by but, apart from other residents in the building,
no one came near the door.

And early on Monday evening Taye knew that it was
decision time. By now the newsagent would have taken
her card out of his window, and she could see no point
in advertising again. Clearly the rent required was more
than most people wanted to pay. In the nine days since
she had placed that card in the newsagent's she had received only one reply. So far as she could see, with the
rent due on quarter day in a few weeks' time she had to
either give up the apartment—and heaven alone knew
what she was going to do if they demanded a quarter's
rent in lieu of notice—or she had to consider sharing the
flat with a male of the species; a male who, for that matter, she was not even sure she could like.

Oh, she didn't want to leave, she didn't! How could
she give up the apartment? It was tranquil here, peaceful
here. And with the advantage of the small enclosed garden—a wonderful place to sit out in on warm summer
evenings, perhaps with a glass of wine, perhaps chatting
to one of her fellow flat dwellers. Perhaps, at weekends,
to sit under the old apple tree halfway down the garden.
There was a glitzy tinsel Christmassy kind of star lodged
in that tree—it had been there, Paula had told her, since
January, when a gust of wind had blown it there from
who knew where. And Taye loved that too. She was in
London, but it felt just like being in the country.

On impulse she went into the kitchen and found the

piece of paper with Magnus Ashthorpe's phone number on it. She should have thrown it away, but with no other applicant in sight she rather supposed it must be meant that she had not scrapped it. Not that she intended to ring him. She would see what sort of a reference this Mrs Sturgess gave him.

'Hello?' answered what sounded like a mature and genteel voice when she had dialled.

'Is that Mrs Sturgess?' Taye enquired.

'Claudia Sturgess speaking,' that lady confirmed.

'Oh, good evening. I'm sorry to bother you,' Taye said in a rush, 'but a man named Magnus Ashthorpe said I might contact you with regard to a reference.'

'Oh, yes, Magnus—er—Ashthorpe,' Claudia Sturgess answered, and suddenly seemed in the best of humours. 'What would you like to know about him?'

'Well, he has applied to rent some accommodation,' Taye replied, it somehow sticking in her throat to confess it was shared accommodation—which she freely admitted was ridiculous. How was she to find out whether or not he was some potential mass murderer if she didn't give the right information and ask the right questions? Giving herself a mental shake, Taye decided she had been reading too many thrillers just lately, and jumped in, 'I wonder how long you have known him and if you consider him trustworthy?'

'Oh, my dear, I've known him for years! Went to school with his mother,' Mrs Sturgess informed her with what sounded like a cross between a giggle and a chuckle. 'May I know your name?' she in turn enquired.

'Taye Trafford.' Taye saw no reason to not tell her. But, hurrying on, 'Do you think he would make a—um—good tenant?'

'First class, Miss Trafford,' Mrs Sturgess replied without the smallest hesitation. 'Or is it Mrs?'

'Miss,' Taye replied. 'You—can vouch for him, then?'

'Absolutely. He's one of the nicest men I know,' she went on glowingly. 'In fact, having had him living with me one time, I'd go as far as to say that if he doesn't get the accommodation you have on offer, I would welcome him back here to live.' Taye reckoned you could not have a better reference than that. 'Where is this accommodation?' Claudia Sturgess wanted to know. 'London?' she guessed.

'Yes,' Taye confirmed. 'He, in your opinion, is trustworthy, then?'

'Totally,' Mrs Sturgess replied, all lightness gone from her tone, her voice at once most sincere. 'He is one of the most trustworthy men I have ever come across. I would trust him with my life.'

'Thank you very much,' Taye said, and, realising that she could not have a better reference than that, she thanked her politely again and put down the phone.

Yet, having been sincerely assured by this woman who had been at school with his mother that Magnus Ashthorpe was totally trustworthy, still Taye hesitated. Even though she knew that mixed flat-shares went on all over the place, she somehow felt reluctant to have him so close. And, if she didn't make that call to him, well, it was not as if he was desperate for somewhere to rent, was it? By the sound of it, Mrs Sturgess, his mother's friend, would have him back living with her like a shot. Presumably, though, he did not want to return there.

Taye thought of her own mother's friend, the hardbitten Larissa Gilbert. Would she want to go and live with the thin-lipped Larissa? No way.

The decision seemed to be made.

Taye picked up the phone and dialed, half hoping Magnus Ashthorpe had his mobile switched off. He hadn't, but he was already taking a call. She waited a long five minutes and then, aware that she had no option unless she was to go on the apartment-hunting trail her-self—the much smaller apartment hunt; she could not bear the thought of returning to a bed-sit—she had to make that call.

She redialled—it was picked up at the fourth ring. 'Pen...' he began, and then changed it to, 'Hello.'

She guessed his previous caller was probably someone called Penny, and he thought it was she ringing back from his previous call. Sorry to disappoint. 'Hello,' Taye replied, and began to feel more comfortable to know he had got a woman-friend. 'It's Taye Trafford.' He said nothing. Not one solitary word. And she swiftly recalled how he had barely spoken when he had come to view the apartment. Perhaps that was what Mrs Sturgess liked about him—that he was not forever chattering on. 'About the flat-share,' Taye resumed.

'Yes?'

She found his monosyllabic reply annoying and started to have second thoughts. 'There isn't a garage,' she drew out of nowhere, even at the eleventh hour, as it were, attempting, when she really needed him, to put him off. 'Well, there is, but the owner is abroad and has a lot of his belongings stored in it.'

'That won't be a problem.'

'You don't have a car?'

'I find public transport quite useful,' he replied, and, assuming too much in her opinion, 'I'll move in tomor-row,' he announced.

Her mouth fell open in shock. Of all the... 'I'll try to

get off work early—' she began, and was interrupted for her pains.

'You work?' he questioned shortly. 'You have a job?'

She did not care for his tone. 'Of course I have a job!' she exclaimed. They were on the brink of a row—and he hadn't even moved in yet! 'It's how I pay the rent!' she added pithily.

'Huh!' he grunted. It sounded a derogatory grunt to her. But before she could ask him what the Dickens that 'huh' meant, something else struck her.

'You can pay rent in advance?' she queried, everything in her going against asking him for the money but realism having to be faced. 'I shall need the whole quarter's rent before quarter day, the twenty-fourth of June.'

'I'll give you the cash when I see you tomorrow,' he replied crisply.

'A cheque will do as well,' she calmed down a little to inform him—she could bank his cheque on Wednesday, that would still give it plenty of time to clear before quarter day.

'If that's it—' he began.

'One other thing,' she butted in quickly. Again he was silent, and she felt forced to continue. 'Er—naturally I'd expect you to respect my privacy.'

'You mean when you bring your men-friends home?' he questioned tersely. What was it with this man? She had not meant that. Thank goodness there was a lock on the bathroom door. 'Naturally,' he went on when she seemed stumped for an answer, 'you'll afford me the same privacy?'

'When you bring your women-friends back?' she queried tautly.

'Until tomorrow,' he said, and cut the call.

Slowly Taye replaced her telephone. Somehow she just could not see the arrangement working. But, for better or worse, it seemed she had just got herself a tenant.

# CHAPTER TWO

MAGNUS ASHTHORPE moved into the garden flat on Tuesday evening. On Wednesday Taye banked the cash he had given her. It exasperated her that he had given her cash. It was almost as if Magnus Ashthorpe did not have a bank account! But, since he seemed to think she would feel happier with the cash than with a cheque, she supposed she should not complain. It was just that thirteen weeks of half the rent in cash was such an awful lot of money to be carrying around.

He had been up and about before her that morning—and she was an early riser. Surprisingly, with the stranger sleeping in the next room, she had slept much better than she had envisaged. She had gone to bed wary and wondering if she should prop a chair under the door handle. Then she recalled the glowing reference Claudia Sturgess had given him, her 'I've known him for years', her 'He's one of the nicest men I know', her comment that she would trust him with her life—and Taye, as it were, bit the bullet, and decided that to place a chair under her bedroom door handle was no way to start out.

By Friday she had started to relax at having a male flat-share. Given that he was rather taciturn of manner, he was quiet and clean. And, apart from the fact that his eyesight appeared a shade faulty when it came to clearing up a few toast crumbs from the work surfaces, Taye felt she had not done too badly to take her one and only applicant. Another point in his favour—he was seldom ever there. He arose early, went out early, and came home late. He was, she decided, one very busy painter.

She frequently worked late herself, but, having accepted a dinner invitation with Julian Coombs that evening, Taye hurried home from her office to shower and change. She found her flat-share had beaten her to it.

For once, having let himself in with the spare keys Paula had left behind, he was home early. Taye could hear the shower running as she went in and walked by the bathroom. It was not a problem; he did not spend anywhere near the length of time in there that Paula had.

Taye went into her bedroom and, Julian having mentioned the smart establishment where they would be dining, extracted a smart dress from her wardrobe. Up until the age of fourteen she had been used to the best of clothes. Habits formed up until the time her father had left home were ingrained deeper than she had known, and she had discovered that she would rather wait until she could afford something with a touch of quality than buy two of something inferior. That was not to say that if a cheaper item looked good, she might not buy it.

She glanced at her watch just as she heard the bathroom door open. Oh, good! Taye left her room in time to see a robe-clad Magnus Ashthorpe leaving the bathroom.

She almost disappeared back into her room but, Get used to it, she instructed herself, he lives here. 'Finished in there?' she asked brightly.

'It's all yours,' he answered, and went to his room, leaving her to it.

A quick shower, a light application of make-up and Taye was seated before her dressing table mirror wondering whether to wear her straight white-blonde hair up or down. Down, she decided. It was Friday night; she had worked hard all week. Time to party.

Well, she qualified, Julian being more earnest than frolicsome, time to unwind. Dressed in a straight dress of heavy silk with fragile shoulder straps, Taye left her room.

To her surprise she found Magnus taking his ease in the sitting room, reading his evening paper. A small 'Oh!' escaped her before she could stop it. He must have heard it because, unspeaking, he lowered his paper, and she somehow felt obliged to explain, 'I didn't expect you to still be here.'

'Here is where I live,' he reminded her coolly, and while she felt a touch embarrassed, and a touch annoyed at one and the same time, she saw his glance skim over her silky shoulders, bare apart from the thin straps of her dress, down over her slender but curving in the right places form, then dropping to what Paula had called her 'glorious legs'. Clearly, though, he was not impressed by what he saw, because his expression seemed to tighten when bluntly he challenged, 'You have a date?'

Any embarrassment she had felt disappeared as her annoyance surged. As if it had anything to do with him if she had a date or not!

But this was no way to go on. She was stuck with him until the end of September at least. With difficulty she swallowed down her ire, her glance flicking over his fresh shirt and lounge suit. 'You don't actually appear dressed for staying in,' she replied. She smiled. He stared at her upturned mouth, his gaze lingering for a second before suddenly his grey eyes moved up to her lovely blue eyes. His eyes hardened; he did not smile.

With no idea what to make of him she went into the kitchen to wait until Julian called. She knew quite a few men whom she thought she could regard as friends. They were an eclectic mix at Julian Coombs Comestibles and she got on well with all of them. But this man, this Magnus Ashthorpe, was something else again! He might be totally trustworthy, and Claudia Sturgess might think he would make a first-class tenant but, Taye owned, changing her mind about not having done too badly to have him as a fellow tenant, right now she was finding him extremely hard work.

Thankfully Julian arrived ten minutes before the appointed time, so she did not have to hang about in the kitchen over-long. She went to the intercom to check that it was Julian ringing the bell, and while releasing the outer door catch she turned to her flat-share and civilly informed him that she did not think she would be late.

Like he cared! He looked unblinking back at her. And suddenly she was remembering their conversation about privacy. 'Er—will you be bringing anyone back?' she enquired nicely—like *she* cared!

For a moment she thought he was going to let her whistle for an answer. But then, dryly, he replied, 'We'll go to hers.'

Her lips twitched. What was it about this man? He had not intended to amuse her with his 'go to hers' but, when she did not particularly like him half of the time, he seemed to have the oddest ability to make her want to laugh.

Julian tapping lightly on the door did away with any further speculation. She went and let him in and, as a courtesy—one of them should make an effort to make this flat-share work—she took Julian into the sitting room and introduced him to Magnus.

It pleased her to discover that there was nothing wrong with Magnus's manners when there was a third person

present. He shook hands with Julian and in the few
minutes before she and Julian went out to Julian's car
exchanged politenesses and showed that he was not lack-
ing when it came to social graces.

'I imagined your new flat-mate to be somewhere in his
early twenties,' Julian opined as they drove along. 'He—
Magnus—he's quite sophisticated, isn't he? You know,
he's got that sort of confident air about him.'

'I suppose he has. I've not really thought about it.'

'You're getting along all right?' Julian asked.

Taye wasn't truly sure that they were 'getting along
all right', but diplomatically replied, 'I don't see very
much of him. I think he has a date tonight, so I may not
see him again before morning.' And probably not then if
he stays out all night up to no good at 'hers'.

'Her' was probably Pen—Penelope, Penny—Taye
mused, and then forgot about the pair of them, or tried
to, as she gave herself over to enjoying her evening.
Julian was three years older than her. He was pleasant
and charming, good, undemanding company, and she
liked him very much. He was easy to get along with and
seemed to agree with everything she said.

So much so that, when she caught herself thinking that
she would not mind too much hearing if he had an op-
posing view, she began to wonder for one panicky moment if she had inherited some of her mother's traits and
would turn into some cantankerous woman who liked to
argue purely for the sake of it.

Taye felt better when she thought of the many times
her mother had thrown at her that, while she had inherited
Greta Trafford's beauty—her mother's words, not
Taye's—she had inherited nothing else of her but was in
temperament totally her father's daughter.

'Shall we have coffee here?' Julian asked. 'Or we

could go back to my place? I make a splendid cup of coffee.'

Julian had a flat about fifteen minutes away from where she lived. And Taye had once been back to his flat for coffee. They had kissed a little, she recalled, and it had been quite enjoyable getting some practice in. But she never had been too free with her kisses and, while finding Julian physically attractive, he was not so attractive that she lost sight of what was right for her. To make love with him had not been right then. Who knew? It might be at some future date. But for now that time had not arrived.

'Coffee here, shall we? Do you mind?'

'Yes, I mind,' Julian replied, but, as ever the nice person he truly was, 'But anything you say,' he added, and grinned.

Most oddly, though, she did not feel like asking him in when he stopped his car outside her building. 'I won't ask you in,' she said, adding quickly for an excuse, 'Magnus may have changed his mind and decided to do a bit of—er—entertaining at home, and until I get to know him better I shouldn't like to embarrass him.' The idea that arrogant Magnus Ashthorpe would ever be embarrassed about anything was laughable, but Julian accepted her excuse.

'Come out with me tomorrow?' he asked. 'We could…'

'I'd rather planned to visit my father tomorrow,' she found she was inventing on the spot.

Julian swallowed any disappointment. 'He lives in Warwickshire, doesn't he? I think I remember you mentioning it one time. I'll drive you down, if you like?'

'I couldn't let you,' she answered quickly. 'It will be no trouble for my father to pick me up from the station.

I'd better go in,' she said in a rush—and just had to wonder what had got into her that, when she quite enjoyed Julian's company, she should put him off. And why when, as they left the car and he walked to the outer door with her, he went to take her in his arms, as he had a few times before, she should experience a feeling of not wanting to be kissed.

And what was even more odd was that an image of Magnus Ashthorpe should at that moment spring to mind. 'Goodnight, Julian. I've had a lovely time,' she said.

And, mentally sticking her tongue out at that Magnus Ashthorpe image, she stretched up and kissed Julian— though quickly pulled back when she felt his arms begin to tighten about her. He let her go and she went indoors, still pondering what was going on in her psyche.

To her surprise there was a light on in the sitting room when she went in. 'I didn't expect to see you back,' she recovered to say pleasantly to Magnus, who used the remote and switched off the television. 'Don't do that on my account,' she hurriedly bade him.

'It had just finished. Have a good time?' he thought to ask. She liked him better like this.

'Julian's excellent company. I'm about to make a drink. Would you like one?' Perhaps they could set about creating some kind of flat-sharing harmony, some flat-sharing give and take.

'Thank you,' he accepted, but followed her into the kitchen.

'Did you have a nice time?' she kept up the politeness to enquire.

'So-so,' he replied, and Taye suspected Penny was on her way out. Her lips twitched at the touch of whimsy that came to her that the Penny was about to be dropped.

'Thoughts of Julian make you smile?' Magnus interrupted her trend—and suddenly he sounded quite grim.

'I told you—he's very good company,' she reminded
him. Grief, this man was never the same two minutes
together!

'I seem to know his name from somewhere?'

'You've probably heard of his father—Julian Coombs
of Julian Coombs Comestibles. They're big in—'

'I know them,' he cut in. 'Quite financially sound,
from what I hear.'

She did not know how he, an artist, got to hear these
things, but, working quite high up with the Finance
Director, she knew that Magnus had heard quite rightly.
'They're flourishing,' she agreed.

Magnus looked at her speculatively for long moments.
'So the son isn't exactly on his uppers?' he commented
at last.

And Taye at once resented the inference she saw in
his comment; as if he considered she would not be going
out with Julian were he not loaded. 'Julian will one day
inherit a fortune,' she said stiffly, in the interests of com-
patibility doing her best not to fall out with the man facing her.

'And you're serious about him?'

Taye felt her hackles rising. She had near enough had
it with one Magnus Ashthorpe, and no way was she ready
to discuss her love life with him, thank you very much!
'I might be!' she retorted, her fine blue eyes flashing.

Hard grey eyes looked hostilely back. Then at that moment the kettle snicked off. 'Forget the drink!' he ordered
curtly, and, turning about, left her staring blankly after
him. Just what had that been all about?

By morning, trying not to think of the longest three
months of her life stretching out in front of her, Taye

resolved once again to do her best to get some sort of amicability going. To that end, up early and in the kitchen before him, she overcame the thought that if he wanted a drink he could jolly well make it himself.

'Coffee?' she offered when he joined her, having only just made a fresh pot.

'Thanks,' he accepted. No smile, just a hard stare. And, as if taking up from where they had left it last night, 'How long have you known Julian Junior?' he questioned, not the smallest sign of humour in his expression.

Julian Junior! Taye's decision to try and get some amicability going began to flounder. She could have mentioned that she and Julian worked at the same place, but did not feel inclined to do so. Though she did give herself top marks that she answered Magnus Ashthorpe at all. 'Ages,' she replied briefly—and received another of his hard-eyed looks. Resisting the temptation to slam his coffee down on the counter top next to him, Taye controlled her spurt of annoyance and informed him evenly, 'I shall be away overnight. I'm—'

'Julian Coombs?' he barked before she could finish.

To the devil with him. This kitchen just was not big enough for the two of them. Carefully she placed his mug of coffee down near him. 'Actually, no,' she replied with hard-won control. 'Not Julian. His name is Alden. He's—'

But, making cutting her off mid-speech into an art form, Magnus Ashthorpe did it again. 'Just how many lovers do you run at one and the same time?' he snarled.

This time it was she who went without her drink. 'That's none of your business!' she erupted hotly—and got out of there before she gave in to the temptation to hit him.

She was on Paddington railway station before she had cooled down sufficiently to be able to think of something other than the abrasive manner of her flat-share. Oh, why did he have to be the only one to reply to her advert? Just about anyone else would have been preferable.

Taye pushed thoughts of Magnus Ashthorpe out of her mind and took out her phone and rang her father. 'Hello, it's me, Taye,' she said when he answered.

'Hello, love. I was just thinking about you,' he said, and she could hear the smile in his voice. 'Any chance of you coming to see me some time soon? I—er—need to see you about—something.'

She felt pleased that her father wanted to see her, but was intrigued about the 'something' he needed to see her about. 'As it happens, I'm on Paddington Station as we speak,' she answered with a smile.

'Great!' he said enthusiastically. 'I'll pick you up in Leamington. Eleven o'clock?'

Her father was on the platform waiting for her when her train pulled in. And Taye, having searched and wondered and speculated all through the train journey to Royal Leamington Spa, was utterly flabbergasted when, not waiting until they arrived at his cottage, he revealed what that 'something' was.

Though she supposed she rather invited it when, as they got into his ramshackle car, she more or less straight away asked, 'You needed to see me about something?'

'If you hadn't managed to come here, I was going to try to come to you.' And, straight on the heels of that, after only the smallest hesitation, 'I've met someone,' he announced as in his ancient car they trundled out of town and towards a rural area.

'You've met someone?' Taye asked, not with him for the moment. Then, as it began to sink in, 'A girl? I mean, a woman?'

'Hilary's forty-seven,' Alden Trafford replied. 'Do you mind, Taye?'

Taye was more winded than minding. 'But… No,' she said then. 'Just give me a minute to…' Her voice tailed away. She turned to give him a sideways look. He was fifty-one and, given that he was virtually penniless—her mother would see to that—quite an attractive man. 'Er— is it serious?' Taye asked, getting her head back together.

'I'm going to ask your mother for a divorce,' he replied, and Taye reckoned he could not get much more serious than that. Her mother would create blue murder!

'Oh, dear,' Taye murmured faintly.

'I'm sorry, Taye. Unfortunately you'll not be able to get through this without some of your mother's bitterness spilling over onto you in some way. But you're living away from home now, and it won't be all that long before Hadleigh goes off to university. And, while I want to be fair to you both, I want to be fair to Hilary too.'

'Of course. Don't worry about us. Um—have you known—Hilary—long?'

'Three years. But it's only since New Year—we were both at a friend's house—that things have—er—hmm— blossomed between us,' he answered, with an embarrassed kind of cough. 'Anyhow, I want to marry her, and your mother and I have been separated long enough now to make a divorce between us a quite simple procedure.'

Taye smiled; what else could she do? The divorce might be a simple formality, but the fall-out it engendered would not be.

'Will I meet Hilary this weekend?' she asked.

'I rang her after your call. I asked her to pop round this afternoon and have a cup of tea with us.'

Taye took to Hilary within a very short time of meeting her. Hilary was a widow, worked as a schoolteacher, was short and a little on the plump side—and it was obvious from the way Alden Trafford's face lit up when he saw her that this woman meant everything to him.

And, as Taye adjusted to this new state of affairs, she could only be glad for him. He had had it tough for long enough. Prior to him leaving their home he had worked in high finance. But, feeling stale in the work he had been doing, he had changed employers—but had not cared for some of their accounting procedures. When he had started asking pertinent questions he had found himself out of a job. He had been unable to find other work and, after a year during which his savings had dwindled, his wife had seemed to much prefer her room to his company—and then his father had died—and he had moved out.

When Taye returned to London early on Sunday evening it was not without a few worries gnawing away at her. That she had taken to Hilary Wyatt caused Taye to feel a little disloyal to her mother. But there was no denying that she and Hilary had liked each other. And, seeing how much Hilary meant to her father and soon realising that he wanted to spend as much time as he could with the woman he hoped to make his wife, Taye had invited her to stay on to dinner.

They were suited, her father and Hilary, but all hell was going to break loose when her mother heard about it. After thinking about it, Taye's father had decided he would do his present wife the courtesy of telling her in person. In his view, though he considered he owed her very little, it did not seem right to let her find out via the auspices of his lawyer.

Taye let herself into the apartment she now shared with Magnus Ashthorpe, and saw he was speaking with someone on his mobile phone. 'I'll come over next week,' he was saying warmly. 'No, no.' He was obviously answering something said on the other end.

Taye decided to take her overnight bag into her bedroom and so leave Magnus to finish his call in private—although for that matter he was quite capable of walking to his own bedroom and taking his phone with him.

Taye had reached her bedroom door when, 'Leave it with me, Elspeth,' she heard him say. 'I'll deal with it.'

So, Pen-Penny was out? Goodbye, Penelope—hello, Elspeth!

When she thought she had given him enough time to finish his call, though to be on the safe side Taye opened her bedroom door a crack and listened, she left her room. Soon, she suspicioned, when her mother knew about the divorce, there would be enough unpleasantness around without inviting more from anywhere else.

That being so, she decided to ignore the spat she'd had with Magnus yesterday morning. Pinning a pleasant look on her face, she popped her head around the sitting room door. 'I'm making a pot of tea if you're interested?'

'Thanks,' he accepted, and buried his head in his newspaper.

Waitress service! Now, now, don't get cranky. She made the tea and took it through to the other room. He lowered his paper as she poured some tea and placed his down on the small table next to him.

'Good weekend?' she enquired, attempting to build bridges.

'Average,' he replied. 'You?'

She thought about it. Yes, given that she had been a touch shaken by her father's news, it had been a good weekend, a happy weekend. 'Lovely,' she replied, a smile in her eyes as she thought about it.

'Hmph!' Magnus grunted sourly, causing her to want

to give up. The man was insufferable! 'And does dear Julian know about dear Alden?' he had the nerve to ask.

Does dear Penelope know about dear Elspeth? From somewhere Taye found a smile. 'Well, they've never actually met,' she replied, keeping her tone as pleasant as she could in the circumstances. 'But Julian did very kindly offer to save me a train journey and drive me to meet him.'

'My stars, there's no end to your brass-necked—'

Taye, having roused him to anger—without any idea why—found tremendous delight in cutting in on what he was saying for a change. 'Naturally I refused—'

Her delight was short lived. 'Even you baulked at entertaining two lovers at one and the same time!' He cut her off aggressively—and insultingly.

She'd had it with him! Oh, how she'd had it with him! 'For your information,' she hissed furiously, 'Alden Trafford is my father!' And, unable to bear being in the same room with this unbearable man any longer, she sprang up from her chair, tears of she knew not what— anger, hurt—spurting to her eyes. She made it as far as the sitting room door before he caught up with her, and with a hand on her left arm he halted her and turned her round to face him.

He looked down into her shining mutinous eyes. Taye looked belligerently back at him. 'Oh, hell!' he muttered, his hand dropping away from her.

'If that was an apology, I don't think much of it!' she snapped, and, feeling better now that the threat of tears had subsided, 'You're an insulting, insufferable, diabolical pig!' she laid into him. 'And if it wasn't for the fact that I've got your rent and that no one else has applied, I'd kick you out right now!'

He stared at her. And then he laughed. To her astonishment, he actually laughed! His lips parted, showing a superb set of teeth, and his head tilted back and he gave a short bark of laughter.

Rebelliously she continued to look hostilely at him. Then all at once she started to see the funny side of it too. She was five feet nine, and slender with it. He was well over six feet, broad-shouldered and with plenty of muscle. The idea of physically setting about kicking him out *was* laughable. 'Well,' she mumbled lamely, but could not control that, when she had been absolutely furious with him, she could not now stop her mouth from picking up at the corners.

'Come and finish your tea,' he persuaded, 'and tell me all about your weekend.'

Persuaded was the right word. Because, when she was determined cats and dogs would sprout feathers before she would sit sipping tea with him again, she found she was returning with him to take the chair she had so rapidly bolted from.

Though to her mind, as he went and took the seat opposite, there was very little of her time spent with her father that she wanted to tell him about. The fact that her father wanted a divorce from her mother was something that had to be conveyed to her mother before it became general knowledge.

'You had a lovely time, you said?' Magnus prompted. 'What did you do?'

'Not very much. It was just lovely being with him, relaxing. You know, generally unwinding.'

'Where do your parents live?'

Taye, a rather private person when she thought about it, could see no harm in him knowing a little of her family. 'My mother lives on the outskirts of Hertfordshire, my father in Warwickshire.'

'Your parents are divorced?'

Not yet! 'Separated,' she supplied, and, feeling she was being ever so slightly grilled here, was about to ask him about his parents when he picked up from that one word that matters were far from amicable with her parents.

'And never the twain shall meet?'

'Something like that,' she murmured. But, to her astonishment, heard herself confiding, 'Though I think my father intends to call on my mother fairly soon.'

'He wants a reconciliation?'

Like blazes! Her parents may have been close at one time, but they were poles apart now, and both liking it that way. Taye shook her head, her lips sealed. 'How about your parents?'

Abruptly any sign of good humour left him. 'What about them?' he asked shortly.

And she was just a little bit fed up with Mr Blow Hot, Blow Cold Magnus Ashthorpe. Though tenacious if nothing else, and always believing that fair was fair and she had after all told him about her parents, 'Are they still married?' she asked. 'I take it they were married?' she asked sweetly.

He didn't think that funny, she observed, as a sudden glint came into his eyes. 'My father was killed in an accident when I was fifteen.'

'I'm sorry.' The apology had come instinctively. 'Have you any brothers or sisters?' she enquired gently—and wondered as his expression hardened what she had done now.

'That's none of your business!' he retorted bluntly.

Taye stood up and this time he did nothing to prevent her from leaving. 'I made the tea,' she said pointedly. 'It wouldn't hurt you to wash the cups and saucers.' With that she put her nose in the air and stormed out. It wasn't a brilliant exit line, but it was the best she could think of on the spur of the moment.

Thankfully she saw little of him the next day. And on Tuesday she woke up and made herself think not long now before she got rid of him. From where she was viewing it, though, July and August, not to mention September, were going to stretch out endlessly.

She worked late on Wednesday, but found, Magnus home before her, that there was a mild thawing of hostilities in that, making tea for himself, he actually offered her a cup. 'Good day at work?' he enquired when, choosing to drink her tea in the kitchen, she pulled out a chair and he followed suit.

'Not bad,' she answered, not trusting him—he was as changeable as the wind.

'Where do you work?' he wanted to know. He had been living under the same roof for a week and only now he wanted to make overtures of friendship? He could take a running jump.

'Julian Coombs Comestibles,' she answered briefly.

'Which is where you met Julian Coombs Junior?'

Again Taye had an uncanny feeling that she was being given the third degree. But she'd had some of this merchant before, with his draw-her-out tactics and then, when she started asking questions in return, slapping her down.

'True,' she answered warily.

'How long have you been going out with him?' Magnus asked crisply.

She expected the big freeze any moment now. 'Long enough,' she replied.

He let that pass, but, 'What do you do there—at Coombs Comestibles?' he wanted to know.

He could not possibly be interested. But, perhaps *he* wanted to build a few bridges this time. She gave him the benefit of the doubt. 'I work for the Finance Director,' she conceded a little.

'You're an accountant?'

She shook her head. 'I don't have any qualifications. I just sort of seem to have a head that's happy absorbing numbers,' she answered modestly, aware that she was quite well thought of at Julian Coombs Comestibles. 'I seem to have inherited my father's aptitude for figure work,' she expanded, then decided, for all Magnus Ashthorpe appeared to look interested, that she had said quite sufficient.

'Your father's a mathematician?'

'He did at one time work in the upper echelons of complicated calculations, but he's a farm hand now,' she replied. 'Though he still keeps his hand in with accountancy,' she added, and explained, 'Only last weekend he was saying how he'd taken a look at his employer's figure-work to help out, and now seems to be doing more paperwork than anything else.'

'And he's happy with that?'

Taye thought back to last weekend. She had never seen him look more contented. 'Oh, yes,' she said. But, getting to her feet, 'And now I'd better dash. Julian's picking me up in half an hour.'

She looked at Magnus, mentally daring him to make some snide remark about her 'lover'. And it was true, he did look as though he was about to lob some acid remark her way.

She braced herself. But when it came, it was a dry, 'I'll see to the cups and saucers, then, shall I?'

Taye left him, only just holding down a laugh. She reached her room and discovered she was smiling anyway. What was it about the man? Never, ever had she come across such a one. He could make her angry, furious, bring her to the brink of tears and, in a split second, he could make her want to laugh.

What it was she could not tell, and in the end she gave up trying to puzzle it out and started to get ready to go for a light meal with Julian. There was a new pizza parlour he had heard of and thought they might like to give it a try.

Taye left her office at the end of her working week knowing that she should go to Pemberton and see her brother and mother. The thing was, though, that she had an idea that her father was planning to make the trip to Pemberton this weekend. And, on balance, Taye thought she would not be doing her father any favours by being there. She knew in advance that he was in for an uncomfortable time, and such was his sensitivity he would by far prefer that she was not around as a witness.

Which meant, of course, that she would really have to make that visit the following weekend. It would not be a very pleasant weekend; she knew that in advance too. All she could hope was that in the days between her father's visit and her own her mother would have had time to cool down.

Magnus was first home. It was the greyish sort of day that sometimes happened in June. Taye suspected the light in his attic studio must have defeated him. Artists needed plenty of good light—didn't they?

He was in the shower. She saw no harm in making them both a cup of tea while she waited. She dropped her bag and bits of shopping down and had just set the kettle to boil when a phone rang. It was not her phone. She looked about and saw Magnus's phone on one of the work surfaces. She went over and looked down at it.

'Elspeth' she read, and as Taye saw it she had two—no, three choices. She could take the phone to the bathroom to him. No, thank you. She could ignore it. Or she could answer it. Oh, he'd just love that wouldn't he? Her having a cosy chat with his girlfriend!

Taye chose the middle option and ignored it, and, changing her mind about tea, went to get out of her office clothes. Wearing a light satin kimono, her father's Christmas gift, she got out the trousers and top she intended to wear for her date with Julian that night. She pinned her hair up so it shouldn't get soaked in the shower, and then heard the bathroom door open.

Believing she had given Magnus time to get clear, she left her room—and met him, robe clad. His hair was pushed back, damp and black, and she glanced down and found she was thinking what nice legs he had. Then all at once she was so tongue-tied by the idiocy of that thought that she could not think to say good evening. She switched her gaze abruptly upwards. Magnus was not saying anything either, but seemed taken by her white-blonde hair all bundled up any old how on top of her head.

Then his faintly amused grey eyes had transferred to her blue eyes, and, not liking to be an object of fun, Taye found her voice and blurted out, 'Elspeth rang.'

My word, had she said the wrong thing! On the instant his expression darkened. 'You spoke to her?' he grated, outraged in a moment. 'You answered my phone!' he snarled. 'You—'

Taye was not far behind when it came to instant fury. 'Would I dare?' She cut through what he was about to say. 'It lit up!' she hurled at him. 'And I can read!'

With that, she pushed past him and went fuming into the bathroom. My heavens, what a man! He was a monster! Thank goodness she had a whole three months in which to take her time and find herself a more congenial flat-mate. Oh, she could hardly wait to give Magnus Ashthorpe his marching orders!

Taye fastened her thoughts on that and started to feel better suddenly—she did so look forward to telling him goodbye. In fact she had never looked forward to anything so much. Oh, what pleasure, oh what joy. She did not know how she would be able to wait to wish him good riddance as she slammed the door shut after him!

# CHAPTER THREE

WHEN Taye left for her office on the following Monday, the end of the June to September quarter seemed to be light years away. They were, as usual, busy in her department, which meant that she worked late. That did not particularly bother her. She had nothing she wanted to rush home for. She had made the decision to not try to be friendly with Magnus Ashthorpe any more. What was the point? It always ended up with them snapping and snarling away at each other. It reminded her of being back in her old home in Pemberton with all that bad feeling—no wonder her father had left home!

Her sense of humour came along and tripped her up at that point. She wasn't married to the wretched man. And whoever it was who would eventually marry Magnus Ashthorpe, she was more than welcome to him. She wouldn't take him on for a gold-lined pension!

Taye arrived at her building and let herself in through the main outer door, checked the post table in the hall as she passed—nothing for her—and mentally prepared herself to do battle with *him* if he was in one of his sour moods. But, with any luck, the object of her non-affections would be out.

Squaring her shoulders in case, she inserted her key in the apartment door and went in from the hall into the sitting room—and had the shock of her life! For there, a coffee and a plate of sandwiches in from of him, sat her brother! And sitting opposite was a relaxed looking Magnus Ashthorpe.

'Hadleigh!' she gasped, as he left his chair and came over to greet her. 'What are you doing here?'

Her surprises for the day were apparently not over. 'Magnus let me in,' he answered. 'And when time went on and we didn't know what time you'd be home, Magnus made me some sandwiches.'

'You...' She turned to her loathsome flat-share, her mouth falling open in shock. 'Er—thank you, Magnus,' she managed, her thoughts flying in every direction. What was Hadleigh doing here? And what had he and Magnus been talking about? 'Well, I'm always pleased to see you, Hadleigh,' she told him, urging him to sit down and finish his sandwiches. *Magnus* had made them for him!

She took a close inspection of her brother and from what she knew of him thought, from the look of strain in his eyes, the uptight look of him, that something was badly amiss. Had Magnus spotted that too? Had he actually, on learning Hadleigh was her brother, by inviting him in and sitting him down, thought to help him through whatever was troubling him? But that was not the Magnus she knew. Or, remembering his 'Oh, hell' when he must have spotted she was on the brink of tears that time—his fault, of course—was he more sensitive than she had given him credit for?

But there was no time to go into that now, time only, without giving away family confidences, to find out what was upsetting her brother. 'Does Mother know you've popped up to see me?' she asked casually, knowing full well that whatever it was that troubled him, her mother's hand would be in it somewhere.

'Nope!' Hadleigh answered tautly, and Taye wished Magnus would make himself scarce so that she could have a private talk with Hadleigh.

But, was he moving? Was he blazes! She started to

feel annoyed with him, then wondered how she could feel that way when he, observing her brother was all tension, had endeavoured to get him to unwind.

'I'll just go and make myself a drink then we can have a chat,' she said, with a smile to her brother and a big hint to Magnus Ashthorpe.

Much good did it do her! He continued to sit there. And, while she was more interested in talking to Hadleigh than in making a drink, she was left having to go into the kitchen and leaving Magnus there with him.

For a further surprise, however, she had barely switched the kettle on when Magnus followed her in. 'I'll do that,' he volunteered, and she was so taken aback that she forgot entirely about Hadleigh for a moment.

'You will?' she replied faintly.

'That's one very stewed up young man in there—I think he needs his big sister's support until he gets himself more together.'

She stared at Magnus and admitted she had never suspected this sensitive, more intuitive side in him. 'Has he—er—said—anything to you?'

Magnus gave her a sardonic look that was more in keeping with the man she thought she knew. 'He hasn't let any family skeletons out of the cupboard if that's what you're asking. Though he did mention that your father had paid a visit yesterday. But you told me yourself that he intended to call on your mother.' Magnus paused. 'Has your father's visit anything to do with it, do you suppose?'

Taye gave a small sigh. 'Just about everything, I imagine.' And, having said that much, 'My father told me last Saturday that he intends to divorce my mother. He would have called yesterday to acquaint her with his intention.'

Magnus studied her for a few moments. 'It upsets you that your parents are divorcing?'

'I'm more concerned about my brother,' Taye replied, and left Magnus to return to the sitting room. Not sure how much private time she had before Magnus joined them, 'How's Mother?' she asked for starters.

'I'm not going back,' he said mulishly. Which answered her question precisely. Her mother was in fine shrewish form, and Hadleigh was getting the backlash from their father's visit. 'Dad came yesterday,' Hadleigh went on. 'He wants a divorce—and she's playing all hell!'

Hadleigh was usually much more respectful when speaking of his mother, so Taye could only guess that their mother had gone all the way over the top this time. 'Are you upset that Dad's getting a divorce?' Taye asked gently.

'He should have divorced her years ago!' Hadleigh sniffed. 'I'm not going back. I'm not,' he repeated.

Taye had to make a hurried decision. 'You don't have to.' Not tonight at any rate. 'I can make you a bed up on the sofa.'

'Did you know? About the divorce?'

'I popped down to see Dad last weekend,' Taye admitted.

'He's got a lady-friend,' Hadleigh stated. 'Mother went ape! If it was me I wouldn't have told her, but you know Dad. Tell the truth and shame the devil.'

'I'd better give her a ring and let her know where you are.'

'Huh! You think she'll be worried about me?' Hadleigh asked cynically, and Taye could not believe this change in her sweet and shy brother! Not until, that was, he added in a still shocked voice, 'She was positively gloating when she told me I could forget all about university. That she was cancelling everything and that I could go and get myself a full-time job, starting as of now.'

Taye stared at him in disbelief. Then she started to get angry. Her mother had determined that *she* could not go to university, thereby robbing her of her chance; she was *not* going to do the same with Hadleigh.

But, in the face of him being so upset—and she could quite see why—Taye saw no point in distressing him further by going into a rant. 'She didn't mean it.' She tried to soothe him down. 'She was upset at—'

'She meant it.'

'I'll ring—' Taye began, about to say she would ring her immediate boss—there being nothing for it but that she would take a day off work tomorrow and go back with him.

'I'm not going back,' he said stubbornly. And, while Taye was thinking, We'll see... 'I like Magnus, by the way. Are you and he—er—an item?'

'No. Good heavens, no. We just go halves on the rent, that's all.' Her brother liked him—but then Hadleigh was still in shock! 'I'd better go and see where my coffee's got to,' she said, realising that since Magnus *was* paying half the rent she had better have a word with him about her brother staying the night. Hadleigh had endured enough, with all his thoughts, hopes and dreams of university disappearing, without any more tension being created if Magnus objected to him staying.

Magnus was still in the kitchen when she went in. 'Found out what the problem is?' he enquired, and she realised he had deliberately stayed out of the way.

She nodded, but did not elucidate. 'The thing is, Pemberton—the village where Hadleigh lives—is a

Dickens of a place to get to by public transport most times, more especially weekends, and…' with a glance to her watch '…at this time of night.' She paused for breath. 'Have you any objection if he sleeps on the sofa here tonight?'

'He's a tall lad.'

'It's a three- or four-seater.'

'Finished your chat?'

'For the moment,' Taye replied.

'How old is he?'

She did not know what that had to do with anything. 'Eighteen—just,' she answered, trying to keep up with this man's brain.

And still hadn't caught up when, 'Then we won't be breaking any licensing laws,' he stated. She blinked, and received another surprise, not to say shock, when Magnus added, 'That young man's wound up so tight he's going to fracture at any minute. All right with you if I take him for a pint?'

Her head jerked back and Taye could only look at the tall dark-haired Magnus in astonishment. What was more likely to have Hadleigh unwinding, as young as he was, than a beer in some pub?

'Oh, Magnus,' she said shakily. But, suddenly recalling how easily he could turn, 'You won't get all—stroppy—over nothing with him, will you?'

For a minute, as a hard light entered his eyes, she thought he was going to revert to the sour brute she was more familiar with. But whatever thoughts had come to him, he for once overcame them. 'I give you my word—I'll save all my spleen only for you,' he promised nicely.

Hadleigh, who in his weekend job as a waiter had downed the odd pint or two after his work, was all for the idea of going to some bar with Magnus. Taye waited until they had gone and then rang her mother's number.

Greta Trafford was not home, though Taye knew in advance that she was not out looking for Hadleigh. When the answer machine kicked in, Taye said, 'Hello. It's Taye. Hadleigh's with me.' She debated briefly about telling her she would be coming with him tomorrow when he returned, but decided to leave it at that. Then she went to turn the sofa into a bed.

Taye could not get to sleep that night for thinking about everything. Even knowing her mother as she did, she could barely credit that she could be this mean. Particularly as she had known that Hadleigh, from a very young age, had been way above average intelligence, his recent school work classed as academically outstanding.

Knowing that the more she thought about it the more het up she was becoming—not conducive to sleep—Taye channelled her thoughts elsewhere. And what about Magnus, her brute of a flat-share? His behaviour that evening had been faultless! Albeit he had promised to save all his spleen only for her, he had behaved impeccably the whole time Hadleigh had been around. He had even made him some sandwiches too!

They had not stayed out very long, but Hadleigh had seemed much brighter when they had returned. Magnus had wished them both goodnight and had left them to it. And, observing Hadleigh, she had judged that her emotionally drained brother needed sleep more than he needed her impressing on him the need to return to Pemberton tomorrow.

She would go with him, of course. Her mother could be pretty vicious when she got started; Hadleigh wasn't up to handling that. Taye was not so sure that she could handle it very much better herself.

Perhaps she should arrange to have more than one day away from the office. It was for certain she was not going to leave Pemberton until everything was sorted out in Hadleigh's favour.

She would ring Julian Coombs Comestibles first thing in the morning and—Taye's thoughts broke off mid-thought. The rent on the flat was due this week. She had the cheque already made out and had intended to call in at the agents during her lunch hour the next day to pay. She had already rehearsed what to say to whoever was on the desk: that this was the quarter's rent for Paula Neale at this address. Taye had then planned to make a hasty retreat before anyone could start asking questions.

She could, she supposed, post her cheque with a note to the effect that Paula Neale was away or indisposed and had asked her to send a cheque, but... Taye eventually dropped off to sleep not liking that particular idea very much. It sounded sort of—fishy—somehow. Yet it was important that the rent was paid on time and that everything went smoothly. Various other ideas floated into her head but, probably because by then she was so tired, most of them seemed half baked.

After a few hours' sleep she was up extra early. She slipped on her delicate blue satin kimono over her night-dress and padded quietly to take a look round the sitting room door. Hadleigh was sound away. She left him to his peaceful world and went silently to the kitchen.

She had made a pot of tea and was sitting pensively sipping a cup when a robe-clad Magnus strolled into the kitchen.

'Couldn't sleep?' he enquired.

She could have asked him the same question. He was an habitual early riser, but that morning they were both astir extra early. 'I've a few things to sort out today,' she replied. 'There's tea in the pot.'

Magnus poured himself a cup and brought it over to the table and pulled out a chair. 'You're not going in to work,' he stated, as if it were a fact.

'I'll phone in later and ask for a couple of days off my holiday entitlement,' she replied. And just had to say, 'Thank you for looking after my brother the way you did when he arrived yesterday. He was in a bit of a state, and you were very kind.'

'Kind is my middle name,' he replied, poker-faced, and she had to laugh. He knew as well as she that, up until Hadleigh's arrival, he had been more swinish than kind. 'So what's so heavy that you're going to have to take two days off work to sort it?' he did not refrain from asking.

'Didn't Hadleigh tell you?' she countered.

'I had no need to pry,' Magnus replied. 'But when he started to open up I saw I could either stop him, and let him stew with what was eating him up, or be prepared to listen if he felt so over-burdened that he needed to get it out of his system.'

'How much did he tell you?'

Magnus shrugged. 'Basically that you'd had a raw deal when your mother scuppered your hopes of going to university, and how she has stated she intends to do the same for him. Which seemed to me something of a pity,' Magnus observed, 'because it became clear to me, once we started talking of other things, that Hadleigh is extremely intelligent.'

'He is,' Taye said earnestly. 'Oh, it's not just me that thinks so. You've just said… And, depending on his A level results in August, which are predicted to be close to outstanding, he has been assured of a place at Oxford.'

Magnus was silent for a moment or two. 'But your mother says he is not going?'

'He is going!' Taye replied, the light of battle in her eyes. And found she was explaining, 'Way back, before my father lost his job for speaking up about some bad business accounting he'd come across, we never—um—had to think about money. My mother—' Taye broke off, trying to think up some excuse for the way her mother behaved. 'My mother has always been used to having money. When they split up my father made over his quite considerable fund, inherited from his father, to her, but…' But what? What, kindly, could she say? 'But she's had—um—trouble adjusting—um—financially.'

Magnus, his eyes alert, sharp, took that in, and then enquired, 'What sort of work does your mother do?'

Taye stared at him as if he was mad. Work? Her mother? 'Work?'

'Her career?'

'She—doesn't have one,' Taye replied, having searched for some defence for her mother's preferred idleness without much luck. 'Anyhow, I'll go back with Hadleigh today and see to—er—matters.'

Still looking at Magnus, she thought she saw a warmer kind of light in the grey eyes that regarded her. 'Two days,' he said quietly. 'It's going to take you two days? Sounds as if you're anticipating a few problems?'

Was she ever! 'I might be back tonight.' She tried to inject a lighter note. 'Anyhow, getting my mother to see that Hadleigh must have his chance is only one of my problems.' Taye attempted to get the conversation away from what was very personal to her and her family. But only to find she had slipped up and was then left trying to hold back from revealing something that she had wanted to avoid him knowing anything about.

'What other problems do you have?' he asked, as she—too late—had somehow known that he would.

She wriggled and sought but could not come up with any other problem than the one that was staring her in the face. 'The quarter's rent is due to be paid this week,' she said, meaning to explain that, had she been in London, she would have popped a cheque into the agents in her lunch hour.

Only she did not get the chance. 'You haven't got it!' he accused, that hard-eyed expression she was more familiar with there again. 'You've not only spent the cash I gave you for my share, you've also—'

'*No, I have not!*' she exclaimed hotly, indignantly. Honestly, this man! 'I have a cheque already made out!' she spat furiously. Oh, wouldn't she like to punch his head! 'How *dare* you accuse me of stealing that money you gave me!' She steamed on at top speed, too furiously to be able to sit still—too furiously, as she shot to her feet, to stop and think what she was saying. 'For your information,' she raged—how dared he accuse her of stealing his money?—'I intended to call at Wally, Warner and Quayle in my lunch hour today and hand over the cheque for Paula Neale's rent, and—' She came skidding to a halt, her temper rapidly cooling as, on the instant, she heard what, unthinkingly, she had just said.

Magnus was on his feet too, glaring at her. 'Paula Neale?' He barked the question toughly, as she would have known he would had she paused to think about it. But she had not stopped to think, and now she was sinking into a giant hole of her own making—and she had not the smallest idea of how to get out of it. 'Who the hell is Paula Neale?' he demanded.

'It's nothing to do with you,' Taye answered defiantly.

'Like hell it isn't!' he retorted, an unrelenting look about him that she did not care much for.

'You made me mad!' she said, by way of non-explanation.

'So—give?' he insisted darkly.

'You'll—shop me if I tell you.'

'My patience is wearing thin,' he warned her icily. Oh, go to hell, she fumed! 'Shop you?' Magnus questioned ruthlessly.

Taye sighed. Hadleigh could wake up and come meandering in at any time. She did not want him blundering in to the middle of a storming row. 'Report me,' she explained reluctantly.

'To Wally, Warner and Quayle?' As she had guessed—known—he picked things up quickly. 'Just what have you been up to?' he wanted to know.

Taye had visions of being thrown out of the apartment on her ear—it was all the extra she needed to go with the unpleasant hours she anticipated ahead when she saw her mother. 'Well, if you must know,' she began belligerently—she might be down but she wasn't out—'the tenancy—um—here is not actually in my name.' Oh, my word, his expression had darkened, and it had been pretty dark before. He looked positively barbaric as hands at his sides bunched, almost as if he would physically set about her. 'B-but Paula said, thought, it would be all right to—um—sub-let.'

'Paula?' he barked.

Telling herself that she was not afraid of him, Taye nevertheless did not see any reason to delay answering—she had already told him Paula's name, for goodness' sake.

'Paula Neale,' Taye said quickly, and, not certain that he wouldn't yet set about her if she didn't hurry up with

some answers, 'Paula's the actual tenant. I paid my rent
to her—she'd already paid it up to this week. Anyhow,
the lease is in her name. And—and although I've never
actually seen the lease—Paula must have taken it with
her when she went.. and—' Taye broke off—Magnus had
gone from looking evilly murderous to now looking absolutely dumbstruck. He was still staring at her speechless when Taye feebly tried to regain her thread. 'And—
er—Paula got a job out of London and went—'

'Went?' he interrupted tersely.

'Left,' Taye explained, starting to get annoyed again.
Confession was supposed to be good for the soul, but she
wasn't feeling any better for being made to explain, or
by his interruptions. 'She…'

'When did she leave?' he insisted.

Taye threw him an exasperated look. 'About a month
before I advertised. I love it here but I realised I couldn't
afford to stay here on my own—it's a struggle as it is.
But Paula couldn't see any reason not to sub-let. Couldn't
have done. I'm her sub-tenant after all.' Taye was starting
to feel a shade pink, and did not go a bundle on this
confession business. 'Anyhow,' she finished in a rush, 'I
sort of got to thinking, Well, I do really love it here, but
that perhaps the agents might not be too happy about me
sub-letting from Paula and—er—then—um—sub-letting
to you, and—'

'My being here being against the terms of the tenancy
agreement, you mean?' he butted in, quite mildly, Taye
realized, in the face of how chin-thumpingly angry he
had seemed before.

'Sort of. Though most of the time I feel sure it is perfectly all right,' she assured him hurriedly. 'It's just that
there's this small question mark I have that makes me
wonder if the agents will be—well, a bit sticky about it.

If…um—' She broke off as just at that moment her brother wandered in.

But, while she was praying that Magnus would not make a fuss in front of him, he was asking Hadleigh, 'How did you sleep?'

'Like a log,' Hadleigh answered, and, turning to his sister, showing that his sleep had done him quite a lot of good, 'I suppose I'd better go back home.'

'I'll come with you if you like,' Taye said lightly, and caught Magnus looking at her, his expression inscrutable. He knew she was going back with her brother whether Hadleigh wanted her with him or not.

But Hadleigh appeared delighted. 'Will you?' he asked, his face beaming.

'Make yourself a fresh pot of tea while I go and get showered,' she said, filling the kettle and setting it to boil for him as she spoke. She turned to Magnus, 'Er—unless you wanted to shower first?' she asked, grateful that, so far, he wasn't kicking up a fuss.

'After you,' he allowed, though followed her out of the kitchen and caught up with her by her bedroom door. 'If it will make things easier, I can drop your cheque into the agents for you.'

Her beautiful blue eyes widened. 'Would you?' she gasped.

'Quarter's rent for Paula Neale, I think you said.'

'You won't say anything—about…?' she began panickily.

He smiled then, and it was truly a terrific smile, a sincere smile. 'I like living here too,' he replied. Her insides went all funny.

His smile stayed with her while Taye stood under the shower. Had she really…? Had he…? Would he tell…? No. Somehow, she trusted him. She did not know why.

He could be quite, quite awful sometimes. But yet she could not believe that any man with such a sincere genuine smile would turn around and, as it were, stab her in the back.

She and Hadleigh were in Pemberton, going up the drive of her old home, when she began to worry had she been right to trust Magnus Ashthorpe? It was too late then, she knew, to wish she had not told him anything. Though once Paula's name had slipped out he had not given her a chance to do anything other than tell him the rest of it. And, in one way, it was a relief to not have to guard her every word any more.

She had handed over her cheque a few minutes before she and Hadleigh had left. 'You won't...?'

'I won't,' Magnus had replied, had shaken hands with her brother, made some light comment about seeing her when he saw her, and that had been it.

Taye had telephoned her place of employment from the railway station; it had been too early to do so before. She had apologised for the short notice, but explained she had a domestic matter to deal with. 'Anything I can do to help?' her immediate boss had asked, and she had thought how typical that was of the true gentlemen she worked for. They were up to their eyes with work, and yet Victor Richards's first question had been could he help.

'No—no,' she had answered. 'I'll get in as soon as I can.' She did not have to say she would work late to catch up, she was sure he would know that.

She and Hadleigh entered the large imposing residence and one look at her mother's vinegary expression was sufficient to tell Taye that she would be lucky if she cracked her hard exterior in under three days, let alone two.

'Hello, Mother,' Taye greeted her as Hadleigh sloped off to his room.

'How gracious of you to honour us with a visit,' Greta Trafford said by way of welcome.

'You know why I'm here.'

'You could have saved yourself a journey.'

'Hadleigh *is* going to Oxford.'

'And I'm going to the moon. Though first—' as a car was heard pulling up outside '—Larissa and I have a shopping trip arranged. *Do* make yourself at home.' With that, her mother picked up her handbag and went out to greet her friend.

Taye metaphorically dug her heels in. Her mother, despite noticing her overnight bag, would probably not expect her to still be there by the time she got back. Did Taye have news for her!

But it was the following morning before she was able to sit down with her mother and work something out. And by then, if she had not known before, Taye knew why she so loved living in the London apartment. This house, with its elegant fittings, its lush carpets, was a bleak and a cold house, a house without any personal warmth. The night had stretched endlessly; two nights there would be more than was to be endured.

'About Oxford,' she began, breakfast, such as it was, cleared away, her mother's cleaner busy upstairs, and nothing else to occupy her parent just then.

'"That sweet city with her dreaming spires,"' her mother quoted, as if she had no idea to what her daughter was alluding.

'That's the one,' Taye replied, staying calm with difficulty. 'Hadleigh has been assured of a place...'

'Too bad he won't be taking it. Though some other

student whose mother has money to burn will probably be grateful to have his place.'

'You haven't done anything about... You haven't written and said he's not interested?' Taye questioned hotly.

'Not yet,' her mother replied with saccharine sweetness, letting Taye know that it was only a matter of time before she did so.

'He has to go!' Taye stated vehemently.

Greta Trafford shrugged. 'Since you feel so very determined about it, then I suggest you arrange to pay for him.'

'Me?' Taye exclaimed, startled.

'His student loan won't go very far—and he's not getting a penny from me!'

'But...'

'At his age he should be working. Paying for his keep.'

'He works weekends!' Taye protested, knowing without having to ask that their mother would expect him to hand over his earnings, and would not baulk from taking them. 'Hadleigh's bright! He's got a brilliant future in front of him. He...'

Her mother stifled a delicate yawn, and Taye knew then that all the talking in the world was not going to get her mother to change her mind.

But he was going to have his chance. He was. 'I'll pay,' she said firmly. 'Don't do anything—just leave things as they are.'

'*You'll* pay?'

'It was what you suggested.'

'I didn't know you had any money!' Greta Trafford perked up, looking interested for the first time.

Sorry to disappoint. 'I don't have any. I'll have to see about getting a bank loan,' Taye replied. 'Only please don't tell Hadleigh that.'

'You think he's too proud to take your money?'

He must get that from my father, Taye thought acidly, though knew better than to say so. Not that she thought she might bruise her mother's sensitivities—she had few. It was just that Taye did not want to be the cause of her mother being spiteful to Hadleigh over anything she said.

'May I have your promise that, provided it doesn't cost you anything, Hadleigh can go to university?' she asked instead.

Her mother took her time about answering, but eventually agreed. 'I shall be poorer in pocket—you do appreciate that,' she added—and Taye saw in that comment a very big hint that she might be called upon to help out.

Hadleigh went with her to the railway station, which took a two-mile walk, a bus ride for the next four miles, and then another shorter walk. But he was clearly overjoyed. Greta Trafford had magnanimously told him she had reconsidered—and he was bubbling over with relief.

'I don't know what it was you said to Mother, but whatever it was, thanks, Taye.'

'Play as well as work when you get to Oxford,' she replied, having read of students who suffered breakdowns from over-studying.

'I shall do my best.' He grinned, and it was wonderful to her to see his confidence growing by the minute.

It was only when she was in the train on her way back to London that, though fiercely certain that Hadleigh should have his chance, she began to wonder if she had been just a little rash is saying that she would finance him. In terms of money, her outgoings just about kept pace with her incomings. Would the bank play ball?

Surely they would? In almost every post there was some outfit offering to lend money. She would work out her finances and see where she could make savings and then hope her bank manager would feel like being generous.

Meantime she was oh, so glad to be away from that house in Pemberton. The atmosphere there was just so—so unpleasant.

Taye thought of the apartment she shared with Magnus Ashthorpe. Then thought of Magnus himself who, in truth, had been in her mind quite a lot these last two days. She found she was very much looking forward to getting back. Though that was because, after her old home in Pemberton, she loved the flat so well. So well she could not wait to get there. It had nothing to do with the fact that Magnus would be there—of that she was totally certain.

# CHAPTER FOUR

THE apartment was empty when Taye got in. She presumed Magnus was out on some commission. But he arrived shortly after her and, to make her feel much more cheerful, seemed to have retained his mild manner. It was a relief, she owned. She just did not want to have to cope with his former aggressiveness.

'Everything sorted?' he asked when he saw her, his eyes searching her face.

She smiled and decided if he could only stay in this kind of mood she could quite grow to like her flat-mate. 'Yes, thanks,' she replied. 'Busy?' she enquired as he came to take his ease on the sofa opposite. He was business suited and, she had to admit, looked rather good.

'Doing my bit,' he replied smoothly.

'You've been painting today?' she asked.

'Have to pay my share of the rent,' he answered easily.

But if by mentioning the rent he thought to open up a discussion about the property they both rented, then Taye realised she was not yet ready to do so. 'You've never painted in that suit,' she challenged. The cut of it alone was just reeking 'expensive', and that was before she took into account the fine wool material.

'I've been to see a prospective client,' he replied. And, with a smile that held nothing but charm, 'You thought artists went around the whole time in paint-stained jeans and moth-eaten sweaters?'

She could not say she had given the matter very much thought. 'You leave your—work clothes—at your studio?'

66

His smile became a grin. 'I didn't think you'd like the smell,' he said—and she just had to laugh.

'Just how successful are you?' she then felt able to ask him.

'I get by,' he replied, and from that she sort of gathered that, for all his expensive suit, he, like herself, sometimes found it a struggle to manage.

She might have said something in empathy with him, only just then the phone rang. She was nearest. She picked it up. It was Julian.

'I stopped by your desk; you weren't there! Mr Richards said you were having a couple of days off?' he queried straight off, and in the sort of tone that suggested he thought she should have acquainted him with such details in advance.

Taye was not so very sure how she felt about his proprietorial attitude and, had Magnus not been there—tuned in to her every word—she might well have made some gentle comment to that effect. But Magnus, showing no sign of intending to leave, *was* there, and she was left explaining, 'I've just got back from paying my mother a visit.'

'Come out with me tonight?' he asked. 'We could…'

She liked Julian, but if he was starting to think that she was his girlfriend on a permanent kind of basis, she wasn't sure that that was what she wanted. 'I've a few things I need to do tonight,' she prevaricated, very conscious of Magnus just sitting there.

'Tomorrow, then?'

She started to feel embarrassed, for herself *and* for Julian. 'I'm free Friday evening if—'

'I'll pick you up. Around seven-thirty?' he promptly accepted.

Taye put down the phone after the call, and owned to feeling a familiar resentment towards her flat-mate. He could have made himself scarce! Had the call been for him, had it been Elspeth, then she would have left him to take his call in private, Taye felt sure.

She looked across at him, but not only was he totally unconcerned that, without saying a word her expression was making her feelings known, he, to her amazement, actually questioned, 'Julian?'

She nodded, and abruptly decided to go and take a shower. During which time she cooled down sufficiently to face that she had grown upset over nothing. Had it been Paula sitting there on the sofa, she would not have expected her to have got up and disappeared.

Feeling a touch shame-faced, she returned to the sitting room. Magnus had his head buried in the newspaper he must have brought in with him. 'I'm sorry I was a bit sniffy earlier,' she said. He slowly lowered his paper and looked at her. She at once felt a fool. 'Shall I make some tea?' she asked quickly.

She saw good humour light his eyes. 'You apologise so beautifully,' he said.

'I've never lived with a man before,' she explained awkwardly. 'Shared a flat-share with a man, I mean. It—it just—it's just a bit of an adjustment to make, that's all.'

'For both of us,' he agreed pleasantly. And suggested, 'Why don't I just sit here and read my paper in the time-honoured way, while you go and bring me a nice cup of tea.'

Doormat? Taye stared at him, in two minds. Then considered how, quite astonishingly, he had made her brother something to eat when he had seen how weighed down and stressed he was, and she reckoned that to make Magnus a drink, and deliver it while he sat there reading his paper, was the least she owed him.

'Anything to eat?' she asked in her best waitress fashion. His mouth picked up at the corners as he shook his head.

Taye went into the kitchen, hardly able to credit that they were getting on so well. When she thought of what a taciturn brute he had been up until Hadleigh had come looking for her, she could hardly credit the change in him.

Perhaps, though, recalling his 'For both of us' just now, he had never lived with a female flat-share before and had initially, as they got used to each other a little, felt a shade awkward about doing so, about making that adjustment too.

She could hardly credit that either. On the face of it he was a sophisticated man. She would have assumed it would take a lot to faze him. It certainly did not bother him to wander around in just his robe. Though, of course, he only wandered from bedroom to bathroom and back again so dressed, and maybe first thing in the morning to the kitchen. But she had witnessed in him an unsuspected sensitivity, so perhaps his adjustment was every bit as great as hers.

Taye took the tray into the sitting room, and as Magnus put down his newspaper and accepted the tea she had poured him she thought that now—now that he knew the facts about the tenancy and wasn't being uptight about it—perhaps they could move forward with much more openness and honesty.

'Er—everything went off all right when you paid the rent in at Wally, Warner and Quayle?' she began, on her new-found spirit of '*glasnost*', a subject which until then she had been at pains to steer clear of.

'I thought you'd never ask,' he replied suavely. Her lips twitched; he hadn't missed her attempts to keep off the subject, then? 'It went without a hitch,' he assured her.

'They didn't notice the signature on the cheque?'

'If they did they probably assumed it was someone paying Miss Neale some funds they owed her.' He paused, then thought to enquire, 'It was *Miss* Neale, I suppose?'

'Oh, yes. Paula isn't married,' Taye replied, and, feeling more comfortable with Magnus, more how their flat-share was meant to be. 'There was someone, but—' She broke off. It was not her business to gossip about her former flat-mate.

'But?' Magnus asked, doing his best too, she realised, to get this flat-mate relationship on a much more friendly basis than it had been.

'Well,' Taye began, 'I don't think Paula would mind me saying that she had been going out with someone for quite a while. And then they started to drift apart.'

'You mean they broke up?' he demanded, rather than asked. But he must have realised he was slipping back into old habits, because he smiled a self-deprecating smile and asked nicely, 'How long ago would that be?'

'It would be around the time Paula asked if I'd like to share. I never ever met Graeme, but Paula used to mention him quite often—and then didn't. And the next thing she had given in her notice at Coombs Comestibles, where we both worked, and had taken a job with some hotel chain on their overseas circuit.' Taye gave him a smile. 'And that's where you came in.'

'And this Graeme—he never came looking for her?'

Magnus asked, surprising her a little because she had thought what she had said had brought them up to date.

'Not so far as I know,' she replied. 'I mean he could have rung Paula on her mobile, for all I know, but I never took a call from him here.'

'Who was he? Any idea?' Magnus asked casually.

Taye shook her head. 'As I said, I've never met him. I've an idea he was something to do with Penhaligon Security—you know, the electronic security equipment people. But that's by the way.'

'So it is,' Magnus agreed. 'I'm here now, not Miss Paula Neale. Do you think she's likely to come back?'

Taye shook her head. 'I'm fairly certain she won't. She said life had got pretty much samey around here and that she wanted to go away and start off fresh somewhere.' Taye smiled as she assured him, 'Your tenancy here is safe, if that's what worries you…' She had never seen anyone looking less worried, but you never knew.

'My sub-tenancy, you mean.'

She felt a touch pink around the gills. 'Er—Mrs Sturgess gave you a terrific reference, by the way,' Taye rapidly took him away from the sub-tenancy subject. He gave the merest inclination of his head. 'But then,' she went on as he took a draught from his teacup, 'she said she had been at school with your mother—' she broke off when he briefly choked on his tea '—so she's probably more like an aunt to you.'

'In the main she has been very kind.' He recovered, and sent Taye a winning smile.

'Her super reference got you half this apartment, at any rate,' Taye replied. And, having opened up with him, felt able to confess, 'Though, to be honest, you were the only applicant. But then the—' She had been about to go on to say that the high rent required must have put other would-be applicants off when something in his expression arrested her. 'What?' she queried, and discovered that he had some confessing of his own to do.

Though he did not seem to look on it as a confession when, entirely untroubled, he openly owned, 'I expect I was the only applicant because I didn't waste any time removing your ad card from the newsagent's window.'

Taye stared at him thunderstruck. 'You did what?' she exclaimed, hardly able to believe her ears. She had waited in that particular weekend! Had watched the road from the dining room window for would-be fellow tenants! Only no other fellow tenant had been around because the flat-share had no longer been advertised! 'When did you?' she gasped.

'When I left here after viewing the apartment,' he answered, completely unabashed.

'Straight away?'

'Within minutes,' he replied, and, that winning smile there again, 'Well, you wouldn't want to share with just any Bill, Jack or Tony, would you?'

'Chance would be a fine thing!' she retorted, still feeling stunned.

'Now you've gone all huffy!' he complained.

In truth she was not feeling all that friendly. She stood up. 'Oh—read your paper!' she instructed snappily. But as she left the room she was certain she heard a smothered laugh coming from behind that raised broadsheet.

In actual fact, when she calmed down a minute or two later and got to thinking about it, she had to laugh too. Though, of course, she would never let him know of it. But she supposed it was funny and, now that it was a *fait accompli,* she rather thought it was better the devil she knew than the one she didn't. And anyhow, if she kicked him out now, what was to stop him from trotting along to Wally, Warner and Quayle and, to coin a phrase, blowing the whistle on her?

Taye wasn't sure she was too happy about having that particular sword dangling over her. But, remembering his kindness to her much troubled brother, she did not truly believe that he would now 'shop' her. Though since, at the moment, they appeared to be ticking over quite nicely, she saw no reason to give him his marching orders. In any event, now that she had paid their quarter's rent, she did not have the means to return to him that which he had paid, so how could she now tell him to go?

She saw little of him for the rest of the week. She stayed late at the office on Thursday and was ready for her bed when she arrived home. She was late on Friday too, and they clashed with bathroom times. 'Provided you're quick, you can have first shower,' he condescended.

For no reason his lofty manner irked her. 'You're out tonight?' she asked snappily. Elspeth? Not that she was that interested anyway, Taye decided sniffily.

'Why should you have all the fun?' he countered, but then asked sharply, 'Are you bringing Coombs back here?'

Taye looked at him, neither liking his question nor his tone. 'Unless you intend to bring your date back!' she retorted. But—and she didn't know what it was about this man, but even in the middle of a spat he could winkle out her sense of humour—'I tell you what, we'll "go to his",' she compromised. Her lips quirked upwards. Her flat-share's did not.

'I've changed my mind—I'll go first,' he grated. And, while she took off at speed, he beat her by a split second and slammed the bathroom door shut between them.

She heard the shower start up, heard him singing—and could have throttled him.

She was right about Julian becoming too proprietorial, Taye discovered later that evening. She could not quite put her finger on what it was: just the warm glance here, or the touch of his hand to her hand, to her arm. She liked him so much and did not want to hurt him. She did not even think that she wanted to stop going out with him—and confessed to being more than a bit mixed up. But as he was driving her home Julian suggested that it was about time that she met his parents ice formed round her feet.

'Some time,' she hedged, having seen his father from a distance at her place of work. She knew she should tell Julian No way, but still did not want to hurt his feelings.

They kissed on parting—he amorously, she starting to panic. She was not sure she enjoyed kissing him any more. Mixed up? Was she ever!

'Shall I see you tomorrow?' he asked as she backed away. 'I can come round early and—'

'I'm doing something with my family tomorrow,' she lied, knowing only that she did not want their relationship to change. Knowing that if it did, she was going to have to stop seeing him. Yet still not wishing to hurt him.

'Sunday's out too, I suppose?'

'I'll see you at the office Monday,' she said brightly, and went indoors feeling fairly flustered. When she walked into the sitting-room it was to see Magnus sitting there nursing what looked like a Scotch. 'You're home early!' she exclaimed in surprise.

'She decided to wash her hair.' Like she would believe that! 'You're looking a little pink-cheeked?' Magnus observed.

She didn't doubt it. 'There's no answer to that,' she replied.

'You've been back to his place,' he accused, his tone suddenly curt.

'No, I haven't!' she denied hotly. 'Not that it's any business of yours anyway.'

'Temper, temper!' he admonished, mocking all at once. But on noticing she looked a little upset, 'What did he do?' he questioned, all mockery gone. But, when she did not reply, 'And do I have to kill him?'

That brought a smile to her lips, but she shook her head. 'He didn't do anything. It's—more me than him.' And, even though it did not seem right to be talking about Julian like this, there was something about Magnus that made her confide, 'I sense—feel—that he, Julian, is getting a bit serious—I'm not sure how to handle it.'

Magnus chewed over what she had said. 'You don't want to marry a rich man?' he teased.

'He didn't ask.'

'You wouldn't consider a poor man?'

'If you're offering—forget it!' Taye retorted, but, as she guessed had been his aim, when he burst out laughing she joined in. 'Goodnight,' she said, and went to bed feeling happier than when she had come in a few minutes earlier.

She decided when she got up on Saturday morning that she would ask Magnus to forget what she had said to him about Julian getting serious. She pattered to the kitchen, knowing she had been wrong to mention it to him—even if it had started to dawn on her that it would be better if she did not go out with Julian again.

Her opportunity to say anything at all to Magnus, however, was scant, when he stepped briefly into the kitchen and, with overnight bag in hand, told her he was off for the weekend.

Something inside of her seemed to plummet, and even as she smiled and wished him, 'Have a good time,' she somehow felt flattened.

That weekend turned out to be one of the longest weekends of her life. The weather had turned sunny, warm and beautiful. But it did nothing to improve her suddenly restless humour. With her chores for the day completed she picked up the book she was currently reading and went and sat outside in the garden. But for once even gazing at the beautiful old apple tree with that twinkling, unshakable and unreachable star stuck in its boughs could not cheer her.

Taye gave up wondering what in thunder was the matter with her. She certainly wasn't the least bit bothered that Magnus Ashthorpe was tom-catting somewhere. She hoped it stayed fine for him—wherever he was!

She tried to get absorbed in her book, but only to have visions of his face float too frequently into her mind. She wondered, sourly, who he was turning on the charm for this weekend—and, impatient with herself, got up and went indoors. She made a snack meal that she was not particularly interested in eating. And, with constant mental interruptions from her absent flat-mate, gave herself up to serious thought on her lack of finances and her promise to financially assist her brother—her mother, actually, because Taye did not want Hadleigh to know about it.

In her view her mother was being most unfair. It was not as if her husband had walked out and left her financially high and dry! She not only had the house, mortgage-free, and all of its paid-for contents, but she also had a substantial monthly sum paid into her bank account as arranged by Alden Trafford. It was not by any means a small amount.

But Taye wondered, not for the first time, would any bank, on the strength of her earnings, allow her to have a loan? And, if they did, bearing in mind her monthly expenditure, how on earth was she going to be able to repay it?

Realising that there was little point in going to the bank until she had figured out how she was going to make repayments on the loan, Taye pulled matters this way and that, and every way she could think of. But, at the end of some very in-depth thinking, she knew that to take on a loan in her present circumstances was just not on. And yet Hadleigh was going to have his chance. About that she was adamant.

Taye considered the possibility of approaching her father, but guessed he lived a pretty much hand-to-mouth existence as it was. He'd had a miserable time of it with her mother but now had the chance of happiness with Hilary. Her father was a proud man and, while he would believe there was sufficient arriving in her mother's bank to fund Hadliegh's years at university, Taye knew in advance he would put Hadleigh in front of his own happiness. He would find the money for his son even if it meant leaving himself penniless and, in his pride, unable to live on his new wife's income. Which in effect he would see as Hilary paying to educate his son. He would, Taye just knew, cancel all idea of marrying Hilary.

Taye considered the possibility of taking an extra job. Perhaps evening and weekend work. Against that, though, she quickly saw, was the fact that she very often worked late in the evening at Julian Coombs Comestibles. And also, if there was some special meeting on, it was not unknown for her to go in on a Saturday too.

All of which meant that if her brother was to have his education—and he was, there was no question about that—then, regrettably, the only answer she could see was that she was going to have to move into somewhere less expensive! With a tremendous bout of reluctance, Taye had to face full on that there just was not anything else that she could do.

The weekend at that point became even more bleak. She did not want to leave. She *loved* it here! She tugged again at her dilemma—but still could not see so much as a glimmer of any other way out.

Taye went to bed that night, her decision made. But, since the rent was paid until the end of September, and Hadleigh would not start at Oxford until the beginning of October, she had close on three months before she would need to take some positive action. Well, say two months, before she gave the agents a month's notice and started looking for—she sighed hopelessly—some relatively inexpensive bed-sit.

Having spent a fractured night plagued with the knowledge that she would have to call and see Wally, Warner and Quayle at some point, Taye left her bed on Sunday morning without enthusiasm. At some point too she was going to have to tell Magnus that by the next quarter day, the twenty-ninth of September, he would have to find somewhere else to live.

When Magnus did not return on Sunday night, Taye went to bed feeling quite disgruntled. By the look of it, he wouldn't care anyway that she was giving up the apartment. All too clearly he had no trouble finding somewhere else to rest his head!

Julian came to see her at her desk on Monday. 'Fancy having a bite somewhere tonight?' he asked. 'I'm off to our Edinburgh office tomorrow for a couple of days.'

'Umm… Do you mind if we leave it a while?' she replied, and felt upset that he looked upset.

'Fine,' he said quietly and, having quite a busy job himself, went back to his own office.

Taye had a feeling that she had not handled that very well, and was in the middle of wondering how better she could have handled it when she received a call from a man she knew vaguely from a party she and Julian had been to not so long ago.

'Damien Fraser,' he introduced himself. 'We met at Sandy Stevenson's party. I expect you've forgotten me, but…'

'Of course I remember you, Damien,' she answered pleasantly. Tall, blond, affluent and, if she remembered rightly, going around with a very attractive brunette. 'What can I do for you?'

'Have dinner with me?'

'Have…' Her mouth fell open; she hadn't been expecting that.

'You and Julian Coombs aren't an item?' he asked. 'I'm not stepping on his toes?'

'Er…' she hedged. They were not an item, and she knew now indelibly, without actually knowing how she knew, that they were never going to be an item. 'Er— no,' she said. 'But aren't you going steady with…?'

'She dumped me,' he said, sounding so remarkably cheerful about it that either, as she suspected, he had done the dumping or he was not particularly bothered.

Taye decided that she quite liked him. Especially since he was allowing his ex-girlfriend her pride by letting it be known that she had dumped him. But Taye was not sure that she wanted to go out with him just the same. He was somehow just a touch brash for her tastes. And anyhow, she had not yet broken with Julian.

'Dinner?' Damien urged.

'I'm not sure of my immediate plans,' she demurred. 'If you'd like to give me your phone number, I'll get back to you.'

Without a moment's hesitation he gave her his home and business phone numbers, included his mobile phone number, added, 'Don't keep me waiting too long, Taye,' and then said goodbye.

Taye supposed it was quite pleasant to know that someone wanted to take her out. But when she went home that night she had no idea when, or even if, she would ever ring any of the numbers Damien Fraser had given her.

She let herself into the apartment, musing she would make herself a tasty Spanish omelette and… She discovered that Magnus was not home. All at once she did not feel very hungry.

Her heart oddly lifted when around eight o'clock she heard his key in the lock. Good grief, as if she cared if he never came home! 'The wanderer returns!' she commented when, tall, all male and good-looking with it, he strolled in, weekend bag in hand.

He stopped in his tracks—she supposed she had sounded far more acid than she had meant to. 'What did I do?' he asked.

She knew she had earned that, but affected to be off-hand. 'You tell me.' Quickly she countermanded that. 'No, don't. What you get up to when you're away from here is absolutely nothing to do with me.'

'You're right,' he retorted crisply. 'It isn't.' He paused then, though, and, his glance suddenly speculative, 'Though for a moment there I got the impression you were a wee bit—jealous.'

Taye stared at him in astonishment. 'Oh, please!' she exclaimed in disgust, and picked up her book that was never going to get read at this rate. He went to his room and she read the same line ten times as she fumed at the ridiculous notion that she was in any way jealous.

She tried to read, heard the shower running, and decided to make a warm drink and take it, and herself, off to bed. She was still in the kitchen when a robe-clad Magnus Ashthorpe appeared and decided to make toast. What he put on his toast was up to him, but, not wanting to go to bed as if they were no longer on speaking terms, 'Don't forget to wipe up your toast crumbs,' she offered, quite pleasantly.

'What?'

As if he did not know what she was talking about! 'You have a habit of leaving breadcrumbs littered about,' she reminded him evenly.

'I do?'

'I was—suggesting—you clean up after yourself.'

'Well, that's a new experience!'

She wasn't with him. 'What is?'

'Being bossed about by a woman.'

'I wasn't bossing!' she informed him heatedly. 'I was merely…' She felt exasperated suddenly. 'If you want to encourage mice that's up to you!' she told him shortly.

He smiled. He looked at her and actually smiled as, silkily, he replied, 'I'm so glad I came back.'

Taye went to bed without her warm drink. She huffed out of the kitchen, leaving her beaker on the counter-top—she would rather die of thirst than go back for it. And he, the sarcastic brute, did not bother to knock on her door to either tell her about it or bring it in.

Taye was still smarting over his 'jealous' remark when

she was sitting at her desk the next morning. As if! Ridiculous. Totally ridiculous! But, no matter how she dismissed the notion, it still niggled away at her.

Which was perhaps why, when in the late afternoon Damien Fraser again rang, and suggested she may have lost his phone numbers, and when he again asked her out, she said yes. And, what was more, she gave him her address so he should call for her that night.

She was not sure, five minutes after putting down the phone, that it was such a bright thing to have done. But by then it was too late. She had still not done anything about Julian, and it normally just was not her way to date one man while going out with another.

Taye was in her room getting ready to go out with Damien that night when she paused to consider that nothing seemed normal any more. She was in the middle of wondering when the start of 'not normal' had begun— was it before Hadleigh's crestfallen visit, or before…?— when she thought she heard the sound of the door buzzer.

She glanced at her watch. If that was Damien, he was around fifteen minutes ahead of time! She was almost ready. She applied a finishing touch of lipstick, drew a comb through her hair and made it to the sitting room in time to see Magnus bringing Damien in.

'I'm early,' Damien apologised, looking at her as if he thought she was as good to look at as he remembered. 'I wasn't sure I knew the way here—I didn't want to be late.'

She smiled. There was not much else she could do. But at least Magnus Ashthorpe could put that in his 'jealous' hat and eat it. Did she look jealous? Huh! Damien was somewhere in his late twenties, he dressed well and, she supposed some would say, was quite a catch. Good for the non-jealous ego, if nothing else.

She set about introducing the two. 'Damien—my flat-share, Magnus Ashthorpe—Damien Fraser,' she completed. Though it appeared they had already done the honours themselves.

'I was just saying to Magnus that I seem to know his face from somewhere,' Damien commented.

'Magnus is an artist,' Taye supplied.

'Perhaps we've met at some function or other,' Damien remarked.

'Perhaps,' Magnus agreed, but Taye got an impression that he thought it unlikely.

'I own Fraser Future Investments.' Damien seemed to think he should say what work he did. 'We're doing extremely well,' he announced without modesty.

'I'm sure,' Magnus murmured urbanely.

'Shall we go?' Taye jumped in, sending a smile to her escort.

At the start of the evening she had quite a pleasant time. But as the evening wore on Taye formed the view, from his comments and the unexpected leading remark Damien made, that he was more forward than Julian. But she smiled and chatted while being unable to refrain from comparing that while Julian was probably in the same financial bracket he was much less boastful about it.

Strangely Magnus kept popping into her head, and she could not help but think that while he was nowhere near as affluent—by comparison probably on his uppers—there was still something genteel about him. Sophisticated, yes; genteel, yes; sensitive... Good grief! Forget the wretched man.

'Let's go on to a nightclub?' Damien suggested with a wide smile that held none of the charm of her flat-share's. 'I know a super club,' Damien enthused. And, with a not so surreptitious lingering glance to her bosom, 'Or if you'd rather we could go back to my place, listen to some music and—'

'Actually,' Taye cut in, feeling decidedly uncomfortable, 'tomorrow's a work day.' Thank goodness. 'I think I'd better go home, if you wouldn't mind.' She knew that home was where she was headed whether he minded or whether he didn't.

'Oh, no!' he exclaimed, giving her the full horrified treatment.

'Oh, yes! I have a busy day tomorrow,' Taye stated pleasantly, but firmly, adding a smile.

He took the hint. 'Perhaps we can do this again on Friday?' he suggested. 'No work Saturday.'

Perhaps we can't! She had dipped her toe in a different pond. It felt alien. She knew it would not get any better. Whether he took her silence for agreement she did not know, but he drove her home without further objection.

Though did think to ask, as he drew up at her door, 'Will your flat-mate still be up?'

She would get him out of bed if he wasn't. 'He's usually working on something in the sitting room long after I've gone to bed,' she invented, having no idea what Magnus did once she had closed her bedroom door. But there was no way she was going to offer Damien the coffee he was all too obviously angling for. 'Thank you for a lovely evening,' she trotted out as a prelude to making her escape.

'Friday?' he asked.

'I'm sorry. I've a family thing on this weekend,' she excused, hoping he and Julian would never get around to comparing notes.

'How about—?'

'I really must go.' She cut him off, reaching for the car door handle.

Only as she reached for the door Damien reached for her and pulled her back. 'Don't I get a little reward?' he asked, in what she assumed he thought was his sexy voice. And before she could tell him not a chance, he had grabbed her in a suffocating hold.

She gave him an almighty shove for his trouble, and was fortunately able to evade his mouth, his kiss landing somewhere to the side of her head. *'Don't!'* she yelled angrily, bunching her hands and giving him another hefty shove. She did not want to be kissed by him, or by Julian, or by anybody else for that matter. Weirdly—even as she was pushing Damien forcefully away—she thought of Magnus.

Weird was not the word for it, in her opinion, though in times of stress who could account for what went through one's mind?

'I read it wrong, didn't I?' Damien said by way of apology as he let go his hold.

You can say that again! She followed through her earlier intention of getting out of the car. 'Goodnight,' she managed civilly, and left him sitting there. She had closed the outer door of her building behind her before she heard him start his car engine.

She owned to be feeling upset, which, under the circumstances, she considered was not surprising. She recalled his brute force and shuddered at how she would have fared had she been daft enough to go back to his place. No wonder she had thought of Magnus earlier. He had been yards away. Perhaps if she'd had to scream, and had screamed loud enough, he would have come to her aid.

Having been able to analyse why Magnus had sprung

to her mind when she was realising that she did not want Damien's kisses, or Julian's either, Taye let herself into the apartment.

She still felt a little shaken from the way Damien Fraser had grabbed her. What she just did not need as she walked into the sitting room was to have Magnus Ashthorpe blast at her, 'Playing the field?'

She knew what he meant. Julian one night, Damien another. But she was rattled. 'I'm not giving myself to just any man, that's for sure!' she snapped.

'Huh! Saving yourself for your future husband?' Magnus jibed scornfully—and her already out of sorts disposition fractured completely and her temper went rocketing.

'It's what we virgins do!' she hurled at him, and sorely wanted to hit him.

His look was totally sceptical. 'At least that's what you're going to claim when you sell yourself to—'

'Don't be disgusting!' she erupted hotly. But, having cut him off, she knew she was losing it. Her voice was all shaky and she was close to tears. She swallowed hard. Opened her mouth to give him an earful—only then something in her seemed to crumble. Taye made a dive for her bedroom.

Had she hoped, however, to have some space, some time alone in which to get herself back together, then she soon discovered that she did not stand a chance. Because Magnus, with barely little pause, must have taken off after her. He was in her bedroom with her at any rate before she had time to close the door.

'Clear off!' she yelled, still swallowing hard.

'Aw, don't cry. Please, Taye, don't cry,' he urged, and came to her and made to take her into his arms.

'Don't you come near me!' she hissed fiercely, tears

glinting on her lashes. 'I thought you were genteel, sensitive—but you're a—a pig!'

'It's true,' he agreed. 'And you hate me.'

'And I...' He had done it again! He had made her laugh! There was no sense to it. She did hate him. At that very moment she hated him like fury—but he still had the power to make her laugh at the most unexpected of moments. She turned her back on him. 'I'm all right now,' she mumbled, letting him know that she was not going to break down in floods of tears so he could go away.

She heard him move; but not away from her. He came closer, and turned her to face him. 'What brought this on?' he asked gently, one hand coming beneath her chin to tilt her head up so he should see into her eyes.

'You don't think you had anything to do with it?'

Magnus smiled that smile she had once seen as sincere, that smile that would charm the birds from the trees. 'I'm a pig; we've established that,' he agreed. 'But I think, on reflection, you were upset about something when you came in.' A sudden glint came to his eyes. 'What did Fraser do?' he questioned toughly.

She did not want to tell him but, tenderly almost, Magnus all at once gathered her into his arms. And suddenly, as he held her gently cradled in his arms—arms that somehow seemed to be far more comfortable than any other man's hold—she found she was telling him, 'Damien didn't do anything so very bad. And I suppose it must be more me than him—my discovering that I didn't like him as much as I thought I did.'

'He's not going in your little black book, then?' Magnus coaxed.

'Poor man,' she said, feeling a bit shame-faced now she thought about it. 'Though when he made one or two leading comments I should have seen that he'd expect a kiss goodnight.'

'Did he get one?' Magnus asked, his arms tightening a little as he held her.

Taye shook her head. 'I think I might have thumped him. I can't be sure.'

'That should have cooled his ardour.'

'He let me go, anyway,' she agreed. 'But I was still upset when I came in—only to have you accuse me of selling myself to the highest bidder!' He had not actually said that, but she was sure he would have done had she not cut him off.

'Pig's too fine a name for me,' he said nicely.

'Oh, you…' she mumbled, and was astonished at the thrill that shot through her, and how good it felt when Magnus gently dropped a kiss on the tip of her dainty nose.

He was still gently cradling her when he asked, 'Do I take it you won't be seeing Fraser of Fraser Future Investments again?'

She had to smile. She had dashed to her room feeling anything but like smiling, but here she was… 'True,' she answered, sobering. 'That's one more off my list.'

'List?'

'The list of wealthy eligibles you seem certain I have.'

'You'll probably end up marrying some poor man and having half a dozen babies who will keep you poor—' Magnus broke off as she shook her head.

'I'd rather stay single than marry a poor man,' she told him seriously.

'That bad?' he enquired.

And all at once, and slightly to her own amazement, she found she was confiding, 'My father came from monied people and earned a top salary. But it—the money—

all sort of disappeared around the time he lost his job. But even before that I grew up in a household where any love my parents had for each other was soured over money. When the money started to run out—it became intolerable.' Taye shuddered in his hold. 'The rows were constant—that's not going to happen to me.'

'You think it might?' he asked seriously.

She gave a shrug of her shoulders. 'Apparently, while I feature my mother physically, according to her I'm my father through and through. But that still makes me my parents' daughter—I'm not risking it.'

'They've damaged you, haven't they?' he said softly. 'Between them they—'

'I don't know about that,' Taye cut in quickly.

'You don't think, aware of all the pitfalls, that you won't take extra care to not end up being the same?'

'I'll take jolly good care; that's a given,' she answered. 'I still won't be risking that pauper—and the parcel of offspring you seem to think goes with it.'

'You're forgetting one thing, though,' he said.

'And that is?' She did not think she had forgotten anything. The idea of ending up like her parents had been— the endless bickering, the daily explosions into furious rows, her mother's voice raised to near screaming pitch, the rows, oh, the endless rows, before her father had left home—that sort of life was just not to be considered.

'You have forgotten, little Taye, that you are a person in your own right. You are not your mother who, when I look at you, must be beautiful on the outside, and nor are you your father who, when I talk to you, I know must have an inner goodness.'

'You think I have an inner goodness?'

'You have an outer beauty that is matched by your inner self,' Magnus assured her warmly.

'Oh, Magnus,' she whispered, and felt near to tears again. 'I think that's the nicest thing anyone has ever said to me.'

She was still feeling much moved by what he had said when his head came down and very gently he slowly, unhurriedly, laid his lips over hers.

And when he eventually pulled back, Taye felt utterly incapable of speech.

Which made it just as well that Magnus had no such problem. 'Go to bed, sweetheart,' he told her. 'But remember and keep it in mind that whatever has happened in your past you must not let it cloud your future. You are your own person—and a very nice person at that.'

Taye was still standing there spellbound when, his arms falling away from her, Magnus stepped back, seemed to look at her as if to check she would be all right, and then left her.

Left her staring after him. She remembered his kiss, long and lingering—and unthreatening. He had kissed her, and she had not objected. How could she? His kiss was the most wonderful kiss she had ever known.

He had held her in his arms, and she had never imagined such an incredibly comfortable hold. He thought her beautiful too, inside and out.

Without question he must obviously be seeing her with his artist's eyes. But his kiss, his hold, his sensitivity... Taye went to bed knowing that she would not sleep. But, strangely, she did. Somehow she felt at peace within herself—and with him.

# CHAPTER FIVE

TAYE was not at peace with herself the following day. While it was a fact she did wake up with a smile on her face, once she began analysing the happenings of the previous evening, after her date with Damien Fraser, she began to feel more than a touch edgy.

She thought about Magnus's kiss, his wonderful kiss, and any peace she had known was, in the light of morning, shattered. They were flat-mates, she and Magnus, and that was all that they were. They were not kissing flat-mates, nor did she want them to be.

She got out of bed, but did not go straight to take her shower. But stood at her door for several hesitating seconds. Then she heard the distinctive sound of the door into the main hall closing and locking. Magnus was up bright and early, and away about his business.

Still Taye did not move, but remembered again his kiss, how comfortable his arms. For all his kiss had lingered, it had been unhurried and she had at no time felt threatened. It had been a giving kiss, not a taking kiss. He'd asked for nothing but to comfort her and she...

Taye was at her office before it came to her that she had been pretty much mesmerised by the feel of Magnus Ashthorpe's well-shaped mouth over hers. Had she not been so mesmerised, who knew? She might well have responded!

Shaken by that realisation, she was horror-struck when she thought of what Magnus's reaction would have been had she held on to him and kissed him back. She felt hot all over just thinking of what *his* realisation would have been that she misread what his unthreatening kiss meant. Which she now saw had only been to take away the unpleasant experience she'd had with Damien Fraser.

Such thoughts haunted her through most of that day. As a consequence she felt awkward about going back to the apartment she shared with him.

In no hurry to go home, she decided to put in an extra hour or two at her desk. Which made it nearer eight than seven when she got in. But only to discover she need not have bothered trying to keep out of his way. Magnus did not come home at all that night. And that—peeved her.

So much so that when she bumped into him in the kitchen the next evening, she had moved from any feeling of awkwardness to a feeling of hostility with him.

'Hello,' she managed.

'Good day?' he enquired coolly.

'Fair,' she replied.

It was about the sum total of their conversation that night. She did not feel much like talking to him—he, likewise, clearly could not be bothered.

Treating the place like some hotel, she fumed when she went, early, to bed. It wouldn't take much for her to tell him in the morning that come the end of September he would have to find some other 'hotel' to rent.

By Friday Taye was starting to feel a wee bit ashamed of herself. What was the matter with her, for goodness' sake? She had been behaving downright cranky. While it was true Magnus had not exactly been doing cartwheels of joy across the kitchen floor last night, he had every right to treat the place as a hotel if he wanted to. He had scraped together the rent, which made it now his home. Home was his base, and with the likes of Elspeth, not to mention Pen—or Penny—Penelope—around, well, for heaven's sake, you only had to take in the virile look of the man to know that there would be occasions when he might find the call of a different place to rest his head of more interest.

Taye frowned, felt something akin to sickness in the pit of her stomach, and realised she needed something to eat. Before she could leave her desk, though, a colleague she was friendly with rang through on the internal phone to invite her to an impromptu kind of party she had just decided to throw on the following evening.

'You've probably got a date, so no need to say yes or no now. But if he's really dishy, bring him too.'

Taye had to smile. But no sooner had she cleared that call than a call came through on an external line. It was Damien Fraser. 'How do you feel about a nightclub to-night?' he asked warmly.

I'd rather glue my feet to the floor! 'I'm—er—seeing someone tonight,' she replied, and could not help wondering why she was trying to spare his feelings.

Silence for a moment. 'How about Saturday?'

You would have thought he'd give up! 'I'm sorry Damien, I—um—it doesn't feel right to me to go out with you when I'm seeing someone else.'

'I don't mind,' he declared at once. She couldn't think of a reply to that, but guessed he must have cottoned on. 'You still have my phone numbers?'

She was glad to have said goodbye to him, but only to realise that as if by auto-suggestion—call it what you will—in telling him she was seeing someone else that night she had conjured up Julian.

It was Julian's first day back since his Edinburgh trip, and she had hoped that when she had asked him to 'leave it a while' he might leave it longer than this. 'I wonder how you feel about having a break from London this weekend?' he asked. 'We could go tonight after work. There's an MG rally in—'

'Oh, I don't think so, Julian,' she cut in quickly, gently.

'You could have your own room,' he urged, and, to make her smile, 'If you absolutely insist.'

'You're a gem, Julian. But do you mind if I say no?'

'Yes, I mind,' he replied, but smiled too, and bent and dropped a kiss on her cheek. 'Would *you* mind if I went without you?'

Taye went home that night knowing for certain that, much though she did not want to hurt Julian, she was going to have to tell him that she would not go out with him again. The very fact that he had asked if she would mind if he went to the rally alone, as if they were joined at the hip or something, told her she had better tell him before too long. She did not look forward to doing it.

Neither did she look forward to going back to the apartment after work. If Magnus was in the same taciturn frame of mind tonight, they were in for a very jolly weekend! That was, should her flat-mate deign to delight the apartment with his presence that weekend. For all she knew he would be taking his weekend bag and 'delighting' some other abode—some other female—with his company.

At that point Taye brought herself up short. She had already run the gamut of his 'treating the place like some hotel'. It was where he lived, for goodness' sake. He was perfectly entitled to tote his weekend bag wherever he wished. And, not forgetting by any means that he had not come home on Wednesday night, perfectly entitled to take his overnight bag with him in the week too if he wanted to.

They were busy at the office which meant she was late

leaving. But Taye eventually went home, having determined that since she and Magnus were stuck with each other she must make more of an effort.

To that end, she breezed into the apartment, into the sitting room, and, Magnus home first, smiled when she saw him, long legs stretched out in front of him, reading his paper.

''Lo, Magnus,' she greeted him brightly, and, heading for the kitchen, 'Fancy a cup of tea?'

Silence. She kept on walking. 'I'll join you in a pot,' he finally accepted as she reached the kitchen door.

She felt cheered, happy suddenly. She put her bag down, set the kettle to boil, washed her hands at the kitchen sink and proceeded to load a tray. Once the tea was made she carried the tray into the sitting room.

'Read your paper,' she instructed when he lowered it. 'You don't have to—'

'And if I want to?'

She hid a smile. 'Are you out tonight?' she asked, handing him a cup of tea.

He put his paper to one side. 'I thought I'd stay home,' he answered.

'Obviously saving your strength!' was out before she could stop it. Magnus looked at her, one eyebrow slightly aloft, causing her to feel slightly pink. 'Sorry.' She apologised for her remark.

His expression stayed pleasant; she took it as a sign she was forgiven. 'You?' he asked. 'Are you home—or out on the tiles?'

Her on the tiles! He could talk! 'I had a couple of offers,' she confessed, not to let the side down. 'You know how it is.'

He nodded, but, after the grumpy brute he had been the night before, was charm personified when he replied,

'I'm surprised there were only two. Which one did you accept?'

'Neither.'

'Ah!' Magnus murmured. 'Fraser Future Investments blotted his copybook on Tuesday and you've decided not to give him a second chance. But—Julian Coombs?' he left it there, though after a moment queried, 'Backing off, Taye?'

She bit her bottom lip worriedly. 'I don't want to hurt him.'

For a second she thought she espied a kind of warmth in the grey eyes that studied her. But his expression was steady as he advised, 'Then end it. End it sooner rather than later.'

She had already decided to do so, but thought to change the subject. 'That's enough about my love-life. Or lack of it,' she added with a light laugh. And was about to go on to ask about his work, a subject that strangely had never come up, when Magnus spoke first.

'Is it true?' he asked.

'Is what true?' she replied, mystified.

'Your—lack of love-life.'

She stared at him. 'My lack...' Suddenly it clicked what he was referring to. 'I've—had my moments,' she said defensively—and saw him smile.

'But,' he went on, determined, it seemed, to be answered, 'you've never actually—tiptoed through the tulips?'

The cheek of the man! Though, since it was she who had brought up the fact that she was a virgin in the first place, perhaps he, this time, could be forgiven. 'No, I haven't,' she admitted. 'And, no,' she hurried on, 'before you ask, I don't have a hang-up about—about such matters.'

Magnus looked into her lovely blue eyes, his expression softening. 'You're sure?' he asked. 'Most girls start experimenting early...'

'I'm not most girls,' she cut him off.

'I think I'm beginning to discover that,' he remarked quietly.

'And I don't think I feel very comfortable with this conversation.'

'There—and I thought we could tell each other everything,' he mocked.

She wanted to laugh, but wouldn't. Sometimes she didn't know whether to hit him or kiss him. Kiss him? Weird—where had that notion strayed in from? 'I've never seen any of your work,' she said abruptly.

'How about that for a quick change of topic?' he commented, and she had the weirdest notion that he was trying to avoid discussing his work. Weird—it was her day for weird!

'Have you any of your paintings here?' she pressed.

'You wouldn't want them cluttering up the place.'

'I suppose it takes ages for the paint to dry,' she lobbed back. He wasn't the only one who could be determined to stick with the subject.

'Depends which medium you use,' he informed her.

'Which one do you use?' He gave her a look she read as saying For goodness sake shut up. 'Indulge me?' she requested lightly.

'Oils, mainly,' he decided to yield.

'What subject matter?'

'You really do have the bit between your teeth!'

'Landscapes?' she suggested.

'Portraits,' he answered, and, should she be feeling smug, he changed the topic this time—to talk of something she had absolutely no wish to talk about. 'I didn't mean to kiss you the other night,' he said, quite out of the blue.

It could have been, she reflected, that Magnus had been feeling awkward too ever since that kiss, but she doubted it had preyed on his mind as much as it had on hers. 'Pfff—I never gave it another thought,' she answered off-handedly, on the basis that if you are going to tell a lie, make it a whopper! 'I was going to make myself a snack. Have you eaten?' she asked, getting to her feet and re-loading the tray.

Taye took herself off to bed early that night. Magnus had already eaten and required nothing, and, truth be told, she never knew what subject of conversation he would start on next. Perhaps it was because, prior to sharing with him, she had never gone in for such open sort of conversations but, recalling the personal matters that had come up for discussion, she felt that enough was enough for one night.

Which in her view made it peculiar that, when Saturday mornings were usually a chance for her to have a lie-in, she should feel the urge to get up and get to the kitchen, lest Magnus decided to go off early somewhere, as was not unknown.

She decided tea first, then shower, and padded off to the kitchen and had the kettle boiling when, showered and dressed, Magnus strolled in, his eyes on her white-blonde hair.

'You look very fetching with your hair all messed up like that,' he commented, his eyes on her all-over-the-place hair. She felt a little pink, very self-conscious, and pushed straightening fingers through her hair, then tightened her satin kimono at the waist. 'Sorry,' he apologised, observing her blush. 'I didn't mean to embarrass you.'

'This—um—flat-share business takes a bit of getting used to,' she mumbled, and turned from him to pour boiling water into the teapot.

'It doesn't worry you, though?' he asked. She set the kettle down, and, turning to face him, had never seen him more serious.

'Given that you're a surly brute sometimes—though I'll admit not so bad now as when you first came here— I'm not at all worried.'

His glance remained steady on her, as if he was satisfying himself that she was speaking the truth. Then, 'Good,' he said, and asked, 'What are your plans for today?'

For one heart-sprinting moment she thought he was asking her out. Common sense nailed that one on the head. He was a worldly-wise man; his tastes would lie with worldly-wise women. 'Oh, there's a party I'll probably go to tonight—one of my colleagues from work,' she explained. 'Apart from that, there's washing, ironing, some shopping, some cleaning thrown in,' she answered lightly. 'A bit of this, a bit of that. You?' she asked.

'Mainly that,' he replied, which told her precisely nothing.

'You could help with the cleaning if you like?' she said generously.

'I don't suppose it's every day you get such an offer turned down, but I'll give that one a miss, if you don't mind.'

She had to smile. 'I didn't really think you'd agree— I just wanted to see the whites of your eyes.'

Magnus gave her a playful tap on the nose, took a step closer, and she had the strangest notion that he was about to embrace her. But instead he took a hasty look at the kitchen clock and, remarking, 'I'm going to be late!' did not stop for a cup of tea, but went.

No sooner had the outer hall door closed than Taye was hurrying to the dining room. It was from her vantage point by the window that she saw him swing out of the building and, overnight bag in hand, go striding down the street.

Disappointment hit her like some dark cloud. Even while she was telling herself that she did not care one iota that he would not be coming home tonight, and probably not tomorrow night either, she could not deny feeling quite ridiculously down about it.

And it was ridiculous. She should not give a button, but she did. She recalled how her heart had hurried up its beat when she had thought him on the point of asking her out. And Taye faced then that, having started off quite disliking the man, she now not only liked him but was quite attracted to him.

And that would never do! They were flat-mates, and that was all. Flat-mates who happened to be of the opposite sex. Attraction just did not come into it. So Taye told herself as she cleaned, dusted and attended to laundry.

Perhaps it was just as well that, come late September, they would go their separate ways. She had been on the point of telling him that morning that she would be giving up the tenancy; not that it was hers to give up, in actual fact. There had been an excellent opening when they had been discussing their mixed flat-share, but either the moment had got away from her—or she had been reluctant to end their joint tenancy.

Reluctant to end their tenancy! Taye backtracked on that thought. Well, it was not that she was reluctant to end *their* joint tenancy, dope. It was just that going back to live in a bed-sit had no appeal whatsoever. That was the only thing she was reluctant about.

Taye managed to keep herself fully occupied during the day. After completing her domestic chores she went shopping for a few groceries, checking the post on the main hall table on her way out. Nothing for her—and who was Mr M. A. Penhaligon? she wondered of the parchment envelope reposing there. She did not think there was a new tenant; perhaps Rex Bagnall or the Davieses had someone staying?

Penhaligon was not a name she came across very often. In fact she had only come across it before in connection with Penhaligon Security, where she thought Paula's ex worked. She opened the main door into the street and as thoughts of Magnus started to intrude so the name Penhaligon went from her mind.

By early evening, her weekend chores completed, Taye began to feel restless. Somehow she just could not seem to settle. She decided to give Hadleigh a call. She might just catch him before he pedalled off to his restaurant job. She worried about him pedalling the five miles home in the dark late at night, but her mother had pursuits other than those of going to pick up her son, so bicycle power it had to be.

'Hello, Mother,' Taye greeted her pleasantly. 'Um— everything all right?'

'And if it's not?'

And if it's not what are you going to do about it? was what her mother meant. 'Going somewhere nice?' Taye asked, keeping her tone pleasant. There was no question of her mother staying home on a Saturday night.

'Larissa is having a dinner party. I'm in the middle of getting ready.'

In other words, state your business and hang up. 'Is Hadleigh there?'

'Oh, he went ages ago!'

'He's already left?'

'He's working extra hours today.'

There seemed little more to say. Soon her mother would grow impatient and would bluntly ask her why she had called. Taye inwardly sighed; she had given up wanting a warmer relationship with her parent. You could only bang your head against a brick wall for so long.

'I'll see you soon,' she said.

'I'll look forward to it.' They didn't come any more insincere than her mother!

Feeling more down than ever suddenly, Taye did not feel very good company just then, and decided against going to the party.

Around eight she took herself off to indulge in a long hot soak in the bath. To lie there getting prune-fingered was a luxury. Conscious as she was not to hog the bathroom, it was usually a quick shower and out. But tonight she had the apartment to herself; she just did not want to think about Magnus and where he might be.

Which was obviously at some female's house or apartment; he would not be able to afford to live it up at some fancy hotel somewhere. All Taye sniffily hoped was that Elspeth, or whoever, was the domesticated sort who believed in fifty-fifty and made him vacuum the place through tomorrow before he left. Or, before whenever he left. It had been a Monday night before he had come home once, she easily recalled.

But she was not going to think about him. Deliberately, and not for the first time, she turned her thoughts away from the man she shared the apartment with. The bathwater was going cold. Should she heat it up or get out?

Such major decisions were suddenly and abruptly swiped from her mind when she thought she heard the sound of a door closing. She began to pull herself up, her head cocked to one side listening, when, to render her horrified—not to say bereft of speech—the bathroom door opened and Magnus came in!

For stunned moments—it could have been seconds—they stared at each other, Magnus equally dumbstruck as his glance took in her white-blonde hair, pinned all any old how to the top of her head, her naked and wet shiny body, and her beautifully rounded breasts with their hardened pink tips now that she had chilled a little. Taye was still half lying there as his gaze travelled down her body.

Then with a flurry of arms she struggled to sit up and double over to hide herself from his view. 'I didn't—' she managed hoarsely.

'I thought—' he began.

And at the sound of his voice Taye suddenly came to life. '*Get out!*' she screeched, and was glad he did not stay to argue but, turning smartly about, was already on his way.

Shaken and distressed, Taye felt in one giant turmoil. Oh, how dreadful! She suddenly saw herself as he must have seen her—naked, her breasts on view, her belly, her... In a flurry, as though hoping to escape the picture she must have made, Taye quickly got out of the bath.

She felt aflame from top to toe, and did not know how she was ever going to face him. Hastily she towelled herself dry, then wondered just why she was hurrying. She was in no rush to see him again.

Donning the fresh nightdress she had brought in with her, but still feeling too hot all over to bother with her kimono, Taye cleaned the bath and tidied up after her. Then, knowing she could delay no longer, but hoping to avoid seeing Magnus, she shrugged into her kimono, opened the bathroom door—and bolted to her bedroom.

Though any feeling of relief she might have experienced to have made it that far without seeing him was short lived, when all at once there came a light tapping on her door! It was on the tip of her tongue to yell at him to go away. But her feelings of being upset were all at once mingling with a most peculiar but not to be denied urge to see him.

Despite that, she was still not feeling very friendly towards him when she went to the door and yanked it open. 'Yes?' she demanded.

Magnus eyed her, his grey eyes steady on her crimson face. 'Did anyone ever tell you you have truly a most beautiful body?' he had the utter nerve to pleasantly enquire.

Her mouth fell open from the sheer audacity of the man. On the instant her embarrassed colour faded. 'I was expecting a profuse apology at the very least!' she exploded. But, as she stood glaring hostilely at him, Taye suddenly caught a gleam of devilment in his eyes, and she knew she was not going to like what he said next, and that was before he said it.

'I should like to say that I'm very sorry that I'm—um—the only one to have ever seen you—er—knickerless,' he began, 'but I'm not.'

She hated him. He was making her laugh—she could feel it bubbling up. And she did not want to laugh. 'You're outrageous, Ashthorpe!' she snapped, while wondering if to make her laugh was his way of easing what for her had been mightily mortifying.

'Pose for me?' he asked nicely, and she realised he had no personal interest in her body but was again seeing her with his artist's eye.

'I thought you only did portraits?' she stayed there to query. 'I presume you weren't thinking of painting my portrait?'

'I was thinking, in your case, I could quite enjoy painting nudes,' he answered charmingly, and she was hard put to it not to laugh.

Her lips did actually start to twitch. She turned sideways to him, but, since she had formed an opinion that he missed little, she doubted he had missed that he had reached her sense of humour.

'Goodnight, Mr Ashthorpe,' she bade him.

'Goodnight, fair maid,' he answered. She closed her door on him. She had a smile on her face.

When later she climbed into bed and put out the light she still had a smile on her face. Magnus was home; all was right with her world.

It was her curiosity—why had Magnus come back last night?—that had Taye getting out of bed on Sunday morning hoping that he was up and about. He was, and had already been out to collect his choice of Sunday newspapers.

'Tea?' she called, on popping her head round the sitting room door. He was deeply absorbed in newsprint.

'Just had one, thanks,' he refused.

Taye went and made herself a drink and returned to the sitting room, wanting to talk while at the same time not wanting to interrupt his time of relaxation.

Magnus, however, settled it when, having finished the section that had been holding his interest, he put his paper to one side, looked across to where she was sitting, and asked, 'So, what do you want to talk about?'

'Am I so transparent?'

'I have a crystal ball,' he replied solemnly.

'It's a pity you didn't use it last night when you came

barging in—' She broke off, colouring, dismayed that she, not him, had brought the subject up. She took a steadying breath. 'Go on, say it!' she invited sharply.

'As in—how was I to know you hadn't gone to your party? As in—you usually lock the bathroom door. And how was I to know you were in there as naked as the—?'

'I didn't lock it,' she butted in quickly. 'I—er—kind of got the idea you wouldn't be home last night.'

Magnus looked interested. 'What gave you that idea?'

The fact that you went out carrying an overnight bag was something of a whacking clue. But she could hardly tell him she had been peeking behind the curtains. Or could she? 'I saw you with your overnight bag.' She decided on honesty.

Magnus looked at her for a few silent moments, but, to save her any more blushes, refrained from asking how she had managed to do that. Then, giving an exaggerated sigh, 'Can't a man take his dirty washing home to his mother without you making capital out of it?'

'Your mother lives near here?' Taye asked in surprise.

'She has to live somewhere.'

'We have a washing machine here.'

'I couldn't take advantage.'

'I wasn't offering!' Taye exclaimed. Sometimes he was more than outrageous. 'What are you doing living here when you have a mother living locally?' she went on to challenge.

'Love her dearly though I do, I haven't lived in my old home since I left to go to university,' Magnus informed her. And asked, 'Could you go back to your old home to live—to live with your mother?'

'Point taken,' Taye replied, and wished she had the same loving relationship it sounded as though Magnus had with his mother. 'So, what about Elspeth?' It seemed only fair that, since Magnus knew all about Julian and Damien, she should know something about his friends of the opposite sex, in this case Penelope and Elspeth. 'What about your lady-friends?' came blurting out before she could stop it.

Magnus stared at her in some surprise; she supposed it had come out sounding a bit blunt. 'You're not proposing I should take them my dirty laundry?'

Again she was torn between murder and humour. She gave him a speaking look. 'You know all about Damien and Julian,' she said reproachfully.

'You're not suggesting I kiss and tell, I hope?'

She supposed she was, really. 'Perish the thought!' she exclaimed warmly. 'I was just attempting to get us more flat-matey,' she excused, and could have hit him when he burst out laughing.

'I'm not really into girly confidences,' he told her. And, before she could get offended, 'If you've nothing else planned, I'll take you out for lunch.'

'You can't afford it,' she said without thinking.

'I didn't suggest I'd take you to Claridges,' he replied.

'Tell you what,' she countered, realising she would quite like to go out to lunch with him, 'I'll take you for a pie and a pint if you like.'

He looked at her warmly, a new kind of light in his eyes that she could not understand. 'Accepted,' he said quietly, then seemed to collect himself, and, glancing from her to the window, 'What do you know? Sunshine,' he remarked casually. 'I think I'll read my papers out in the garden. Give me a shout when you want to go.'

Taye later spent a good ten minutes checking through her wardrobe for something smart to wear. Absurd, she freely owned. Who dressed up to go down to the pub?

At ten past twelve, dressed in cotton trousers and a loose but fairly smart top, she went out into the garden—where Magnus was in conversation with Jane and Huw Davies, the couple from the top floor apartment, who had decided to take advantage of the sunny weather too.

'Ready to go?' Magnus queried on seeing her, getting to his feet.

They spent a few minutes in friendly conversation with their fellow tenants, then went back indoors. Taye waited while Magnus went to wash the newsprint off his hands, and had to own that never before had she felt this flutter—a sort of breathless excitement—at the thought of going down to the pub with someone.

Though in actual fact they had not made it as far as the sitting room door when the telephone started to ring. 'For you?' she queried, with a glance to the tall and good looking male by her side.

'Leave it?' he replied. Plainly, if Elspeth was going to ring him he considered she would do so on his mobile.

'It might be Hadleigh,' Taye said, going over to the phone, thinking that perhaps her mother may have mentioned to him that she had phoned last night. 'Hello?' she queried, on picking up the phone.

'Taye?'

Just that one word, that one abrupt sound of her name, and Taye knew that it was her mother. 'Hello, Mother,' she replied, while wondering how much her parent wanted this time. Feeling very conscious that Magnus was within earshot, she strove hard to keep her tone light. 'What can I do for you?' she asked pleasantly, and momentarily forgot all about Magnus at her mother's reply.

'It's your brother.'

'What's wrong with him?' Taye asked sharply.

'Nothing except that he's turned idle and deliberately awkward!' Greta Trafford replied waspishly.

Taye knew her brother, knew all of his goodnesses along with his few human failings. And idle and deliberately awkward was something he definitely was not.

'What do you mean, idle?' she asked bluntly, forgetful in that moment that Magnus was in earshot.

'He has decided not to go to work this lunchtime.'

'That's not Hadleigh!' Taye exclaimed. 'No way is that Hadleigh!' And, sensing her mother's devious hand in this somewhere, she almost bluntly asked what her mother had done to upset him. But Taye knew that to challenge was not the way to handle her mother. 'Something must have upset him.'

'I suppose it must have,' Greta Trafford agreed. 'He's in his room now, writing to the powers that be to tell them to not hold his Oxford place for him.'

'He's doing *what?*' Taye asked faintly.

'He has this peculiar idea that you can't afford to finance him. That—'

'You *told* him!' Taye accused. 'When I particularly asked you not to, you told him I intended to get a bank loan to fund him! How could you?' she demanded, starting to grow incensed. 'You know how sensitive, how proud—'

'Who do you think you're talking to?' her mother cut her off. And, to show she was not in the mood to hear any more of it, without more ado she put down the phone.

Taye was so angry she dialled the number straight back. 'I'd like to speak to Hadleigh, please,' she said, with what control she could find. And had the phone put down on her again. Angry and extremely upset, Taye put down her own phone—only then suddenly becoming aware of Magnus standing there watching her.

'Trouble?' he asked, just that one word, and Taye was much too agitated to dissemble.

'I need to get to Pemberton,' she replied, her brain racing. How to get there? It had to be before Hadleigh posted his letter. It had to be today.

Magnus did not argue. Did not say What about lunch? But, as though having gleaned all that he needed to know from what he had overheard, and as if recalling how she had said how difficult it was to get there at weekends, 'I'll take you,' he promptly offered.

Taye blinked at that. 'You haven't got a car!' she reminded him.

But even as she spoke Magnus was heading out of the door. 'I'll borrow one,' he said, and was gone.

And Taye was so concerned about her brother she was extremely grateful. She did not care what sort of a car he borrowed from one of his probably equally hard-up friends. Be it a clapped-out box on four wheels, as long as it got them to Pemberton before Hadleigh posted that letter that would ruin his chances she would be just so terribly grateful.

And grateful too that Magnus had not stopped to ask the whys and wherefores, to argue or to reason, but, on seeing her distress, had acted. Now that was what you called a wonderful kind of flat-mate.

## CHAPTER SIX

TAYE was not left to fret over her brother for very long before Magnus was back. She was agitated enough to not move from her position at the dining room window, but was standing in front of it, looking up and down the road watching for Magnus, when a long, sleek and up-to-the-minute car glided to a halt outside.

At first she did not believe it could be Magnus, and her eyes widened in surprise to see that it was indeed him who got out from behind the steering wheel. All too plainly, while not too flush himself, her flat-share knew at least one person who was not as impecunious as he.

It was odd, Taye considered as she hurried out into the main hall so as not to waste another moment—and especially odd when she was feeling so het-up about Hadleigh—that she should absently notice that the hall table was clear. Obviously Mr M. A. Penhaligon had collected his mail. He could not be staying with the Davieses, surely, or they would have invited him to spend time in the garden with them earlier.

Just then, however, Magnus put his key in the outer door, and as Taye at the same time reached it Mr M. A. Penhaligon, whoever he was, went out from her mind.

'Let's go,' Magnus encouraged, and, feeling choked suddenly, Taye had nothing to say until she was beside him on the genuine leather seats. 'Some car!' she commented, trying to not think of her brother and how the postbox in the village was but a short bike ride away.

111

'It sometimes pays to have friends with a few pennies,' Magnus replied.

More than a few pennies, she would have said. 'You've driven this car before,' she observed.

'What makes you say that?'

Taye wasn't sure. 'You're handling it so effortlessly,' she replied.

'A car like this doesn't require a lot of handling.' Magnus shrugged.

There was silence in the car for a while, and her worries about Hadleigh were back. 'Your friend... He didn't mind lending you his car?' she asked, wanting to talk about anything to take her mind off the problem that awaited her in Pemberton.

'He doesn't know.'

'You stole it?' she cried in alarm.

'Not at all. He's—er.. away,' Magnus explained.

'Where did you get the key remote?'

'You were a detective in your former life, yes?'

'Where?' she insisted. She *was* desperate to get to Pemberton, but no so desperate that she could accept Magnus being charged with auto theft.

'His girlfriend gave it to me. Satisfied?'

'Would that be the same girlfriend who moved in when you moved out?'

'I see you're all there with your lemon drops,' Magnus replied lightly. Taye said nothing, but waited. And was rewarded when he relented. 'Actually, yes. Mick left his car keys behind when he—'

'I thought you said his name was Nick?'

'What *is* this?' Magnus asked shortly.

'I'm sorry,' she at once apologised. 'I suppose I'm trying to focus on anything but that which awaits when we get there.'

'The problem obviously concerns your brother.'

As he had noted 'obviously', there seemed little point in pretending otherwise. Particularly since Magnus had gone out of his way to borrow a car to help her.

'Hadleigh's on the point of withdrawing his university application. I need to get to him to try and make him see reason.'

'You think he'll listen?'

Taye wished she knew. 'He's proud, and as stubborn as blazes,' she replied.

'Would you like me to have a crack at him?' Magnus offered.

'Oh, no!' Taye exclaimed at once. 'This is my problem. I'll sort it. Please don't...'

'Pride must run in the family,' he commented, but thankfully, as though accepting that she wanted to keep away from the subject of what awaited her at the end of their journey, he said no more.

And all was silent in the vehicle for some while until, having mentally marshalled her arguments to Hadleigh to the limits of exhaustion anyway, Taye sought for something else to pin her thoughts on.

'How long has your friend been away?' she enquired casually.

'Ages. A month or more at least.'

That surprised her! 'Would that be before or after you came to flat-share with me?' she asked, and realised that Magnus had seen straight away where she was heading.

'He moved his girlfriend in and was then called away. And, no, his girlfriend did not go with him.'

'Which means, if she's not working, she is there during the day while you are working in your attic studio,' Taye reasoned. And, on a sudden thought, 'If he's away, your friend Nick-Mick Knight, which makes you no longer an unwanted third, why did you have to leave at all?'

'Precisely because he is away.' He was watching his driving. 'He's the jealous sort. Good friend though he is, he wouldn't want me sleeping there.'

'But it's okay for you to continue to work there?'

'Apart from the utter disloyalty to a friend you appear to think I'm capable of, you're suggesting I might take advantage at some time during the day?'

Taye was beginning to wish she had never got started on this. But something—and she was sure *she* was not the jealous sort, so piffle to that—something did not seem able to let it go. 'So far as I'm aware, hanky-panky is not a reserved night-time occupation,' she commented loftily.

And had Magnus glance her way, his glance speculative, before he answered mildly, 'But then, dear Taye, so far as *I* am aware, you are not the most qualified to know anything at all about hanky-panky, are you?'

He'd got her there. Taye decided to let the subject drop. What with one thing and another, she accepted that her head was more than a little on the fidget just then, her thinking perhaps a little muddled. But in any event she was certain her fidgeting at it had nothing to do with jealousy. For crying out loud, why would she be jealous?

She had more important things to worry about, that was for sure. Hadleigh was back in her head. Oh, he could not let this chance go by. He just could not. He had to have his chance at Oxford; he just had to.

How could their mother have told him about her intention to fund him? Taye fretted. It had been a foregone conclusion that he would dig his proud heels in. A foregone conclusion that he would refuse to allow her to finance him.

'We turn left just up ahead.' She suddenly found her voice as she recognised where they were. And later, as they pulled up on the drive of her substantial, but cold old home, 'I'm so grateful to you for borrowing this car and bringing me here, Magnus…'

'But?' he queried, able to read her without any problem, she realised.

'But I need to have what might be quite a lengthy private talk to Hadleigh.'

'You'd like me to stay in the car?'

'Not at all. Though would you mind if I deserted you and…?'

'Fate worse than death—left me with your dragon mother?'

'She's not such a terrible dragon.' Fingers crossed, Taye felt honourbound to defend her more often than not disagreeable mother.

'You do what you have to do,' Magnus invited. 'I'll fit in.'

Something stirred in Taye for him then. 'Oh, Magnus,' she said softly, and just had to lean over and kiss him. 'Sorry.' She backed away instantly, for all it had been nothing like the lingering kiss he had given her that time.

'Your emotions are all over the place just now,' Magnus excused, to her relief. 'Come on—you won't feel better until it's done.'

That was true. And she had to admit to be feeling all upset inside as she took Magnus into the house and introduced him to her elegant but today icy parent.

'Your car, Mr Ashthorpe?' she enquired of the expensive automobile parked outside the drawing room window.

'Magnus borrowed it when I said I wanted to come here,' Taye butted in.

Greta Trafford took that as foreseen. 'I knew it was too much to hope that my daughter would throw in her lot with anyone other than some penniless artist!' she commented offensively.

'Mother!' Taye cried, appalled. 'Magnus, I…' She turned to him, horrified—but only to see that, far from looking offended, as he clearly had a right to be, Magnus appeared more amused than anything.

'Why not go and find Hadleigh?' he suggested pleasantly.

'You…' She hesitated, such a protective feeling for him coming over her—almost as if she wanted to guard him against her mother.

'Go,' he instructed.

Taye turned to glance at her mother, and would normally have asked some polite kind of, Is Hadleigh in his room? question, but, after her mother's dreadful remark just now, Taye felt that even that politeness would stick in her throat. Without another word, hoping her brother was still in the house, she went looking for him.

She found him in his room. He was lying on his bed, staring unhappily at the ceiling. 'Taye!' he exclaimed when he saw her, and sat up smartly. 'Mother rang you!' he at once realised. 'She shouldn't have.' And, plainly knowing why his sister was there, 'I'm not going,' he declared mulishly.

'Oh, love!' she cried, going over and sitting on his bed beside him. 'You can't give up this splendid opportunity…'

'It's impossible,' he muttered glumly.

But just then, to prove to Taye that, whatever the circumstances, he still desperately wanted to take his university place, she spotted a letter propped up on his desk beneath the window. Had he been prepared to abandon all hope, that letter would be reposing in the postbox by now.

'It is not impossible,' she countered. 'There's no—'

'I'm not taking your money,' he cut in emphatically.

'I've already earmarked the money for you,' she told him, feeling more than a touch desperate.

'It's not on, Taye,' he replied, shaking his head. And, obviously having used some of the intelligence she knew he had, 'I've thought it all through, and there is no way I'm going to allow you to finance me.'

'But—'

'No. Save your breath,' he cut in. 'I appreciate your offer, I truly do. But it won't stay at just that, will it?'

'It will, and it will only be for a few years, and—'

'And during those years Mother will still be on to you for help when the electricity bill or the phone bill comes in—or any other bill she hasn't put the money aside for. She's already hinted that she would expect me to send money home from any work I'm able to get in Oxford—and she's not above asking for some of my student loan. Which, with her constant harping on, apart from having to repay any money I've borrowed, would see me up to my eyes in debt years after I've got my degree—with no guarantee that I'll be able to get a halfway decent job afterwards to start repaying it.'

'I'll help. You know I—'

'No.' She had never known him so decisive. 'It's marvellous of you to offer, but, since I have no intention of saddling myself with debt for years and years to come—and I know in advance Mother will expect me to give her financial support when I start on the first rung of my career—I'm not saddling you with years and years of debt either.'

It was a long speech for him, her shy brother. But it

showed Taye the maturity of his thinking. She wished then that, bearing in mind the not unsubstantial allowance their mother received by their father's arrangement, she and her brother had the strength to tell their mother no when she demanded as her right financial aid from them too.

But, a kind of emotional blackmail though it was, Taye knew she, and Hadleigh too, were unable to turn a deaf ear to their mother's 'requests' for help with some bill or other.

'Hadleigh, listen to me…' Taye began.

Fifteen minutes later, having tried and tried anyhow to get through to him how very important this decision was to his whole life, she had to face that it was to no avail. He would have none of it; there was no way he would agree to her subsidising him. And in the end, while he remained resolutely determined that she was not going to finance his time at Oxford, Taye saw that her only hope of getting him to change his mind lay in her trying to think up something that would be more acceptable to him than, as he put it, that she should beggar herself on his behalf.

'I'll think of something,' she told him urgently, panicking madly with not the smallest idea of what that something might be. 'Just promise me you won't post that letter until I've had a chance to think.'

'There is no way,' he stated. 'If there was a way I could go without being a burden to you, I'd leap at it. But there isn't. You know it and I know it.'

'But there's no need to send that letter yet,' she argued. 'You've five or six weeks yet before you get your exam results. So there's no earthly reason for you to do anything until then.'

Hadleigh did not look convinced, but to her relief did

see the logic of her argument. 'I'll hold off until I've got my A level results,' he promised at last. And, while Taye would have preferred a promise that he would accept his Oxford place when offered, at least with his promise not to send that letter just yet she had some time to try and think up something.

'And you'll phone me first, before you do anything at all? Promise?' Taye asked.

'Persistent to the last,' he commented, but smiled as he said, 'I promise.'

'Good. Now, come and say hello to Magnus. He borrowed a car to drive me down.'

'Oh, Taye, I've put you and Magnus to so much trouble.'

'That's what sisters are for,' she told him lightly.

'And flat-mates,' he took up as they left his room.

Her mother was alone in the drawing room when they went in. 'Where's Magnus?' Taye asked, with a hasty glance to the drawing room window. Relief sped in. The car was still there. For a moment or two she had thought that he'd had enough of her mother and had decided to return to London—alone.

'He's in the garden. Apparently the colours of the mixed geraniums are quite spectacular.'

'He's an artist,' Hadleigh exclaimed warmly.

'You did mention,' his mother replied dryly, causing Taye to wonder if Hadleigh had been singing her flat-share's praises since he had been taken for a pint by him a couple of weeks ago, when he'd been so upset.

'I'll go and see him,' Taye murmured, and escaped into the grounds of the house.

She saw Magnus before he saw her—and her heart turned over. She did not need to analyse the sudden rush of feeling for him that crashed in with a mighty roar—

but accepted what had been there in front of her a short while ago when, sitting in the car, he had bade her, 'You do what you have to do. I'll fit in.' and she had just had to kiss him. She accepted then what that protective feeling she had experienced had all been about for this man who had no need of anyone's protection. She was totally and irrevocably in love with him!

Feeling utterly all at sea from her discovery, Taye just then realised that while Magnus might not have seen her, he knew she was there. 'Everything fixed?' he asked, and that was before he turned around.

Taye went forward, still catching her breath but hoping to hide the love in her eyes, hoping that her voice would sound normal. 'Hadleigh has written a letter that will end his chances if he posts it. I've managed to get him to promise not to send it for a while.' She smiled at Magnus. 'Er—how did it go with you?'

'Me?' he asked, as if he had no idea what she was talking about.

'Was my mother too awful?' she asked, the time gone for pretence.

'Thoroughly awful,' he replied pleasantly—she had guessed as much; why else would he seek refuge in the garden? 'How old did you say you were when you left home?'

She did not remember having said. 'Twenty. Three years ago,' she answered honestly, and loved him yet more when he forbore to say he wondered how she had managed to stay until she was twenty.

'Ready to go back?' he asked instead.

'When you are,' she replied, not wanting to inflict any more of her mother's acid on him.

Not that they saw Greta Trafford again. She had left the drawing room when they went in, in favour of her bedroom. Taye knew she would not wish to be disturbed. Hadleigh came out to the drive with them and admired the car, but grinned at Magnus as he commented, 'By contrast, I'd better get out my bike. I do some waiting work in a restaurant,' he explained to Magnus. 'I rather let them down at lunchtime.'

'Did you let them know you wouldn't be in?' Magnus asked.

'Oh, yes. I wouldn't just not turn up.'

'Then I'm sure they'll forgive you.' Magnus too grinned. 'If you go now I'm also sure they'll let you help with a bit of dishwashing.'

Hadleigh's grin had widened as the two shook hands, the man she loved and the brother she loved, and Magnus opened the passenger door for her. 'You haven't eaten!' Taye exclaimed as the car gently rolled its way back down the drive. 'I promised you a pie and a pint! I'm sorry,' she apologised at once. 'I forgot all about it when my mother phoned. Would you like to stop somewhere on the way…?'

'You haven't eaten either.'

'I'm not hungry. But you…'

'We'll get something when we get home,' Magnus suggested, and that sounded so pretty wonderful to her— home, their home—that she temporarily forgot that she should be setting her mind to other things. For one, how on earth was she to get Hadleigh to take his place at university when he was so stubbornly refusing to let her chip in financially?

But if that ever present problem had been sidelined under the mammoth discovery that the man by her side held her whole heart, the problem had not been sidelined by that man, she realised.

For barely had they driven another mile than he was asking, 'Feeling better now?'

'Less panicky, do you mean?'

'Does your mother always wind you up?'

Taye had not really thought about it, but she had suddenly given her first loyalty to this man she loved, and wanted only to be truthful with him. 'I rather think she does,' she admitted.

'Then it's just as well that you're living with a penniless artist,' he said nicely, and when she glanced at him, looking for a sting, she saw none. And she loved him some more that he was only trying to lighten what had been a tense time for her. That he was as good as saying that he was on her side.

Her thoughts alternated between him and Hadleigh for the rest of that drive. With Magnus sitting next to her, sitting this close, it was so heady she was having the utmost difficulty in concentrating for any length of time solely on her brother.

She concluded she must abandon serious thought until she was on her own, Magnus not there. Then she would try to work something out. Though what escaped her.

'Something on toast? Or shall I see what's in the freezer?' she enquired when, five minutes after arriving home, they met in the kitchen.

'Would your mother really allow you to take out a bank loan to fund Hadleigh?' he asked, which was no sort of an answer in Taye's opinion.

Though, since he had been within earshot when she had grown angry enough not to care who heard her side of that telephone conversation when her mother had rung, Taye supposed she could not blame him for asking the question he had. The only wonder was that he had waited this long to put it. Though, as he had observed in the car, her emotions had been all over the place, so perhaps that was why he had left it until now.

'Oh, yes.' She answered his question. 'I'm afraid she would.'

Magnus nodded at that, but went on to ask another question, one which she just had not given thought to. 'So why, when you had asked her to not tell him what you proposed to do, would she deliberately make sure that he knew?'

Taye stared at Magnus. 'I—don't know,' she answered slowly, while she hurriedly searched round for a reason that she had not previously so much as considered. She had thought it might be all part and parcel of her mother not being happy unless she was upsetting someone. But, apart from the satisfaction she would gain from seeing them all jump through hoops, what else would she gain? 'Not unless she's anxious not to lose the amount Hadleigh puts into the coffers now. But she knows that I'll help out if she gets into any sort of financial difficulty.'

'You do so now?' he asked.

He was too shrewd by far, in her opinion. 'Er—not so much,' she prevaricated. 'Anyhow, my father has seen to it that she has a splendid allowance.'

'But it's never enough?'

It would never be enough. Taye knew that as fact. Were that allowance to be doubled then Greta Trafford would still want more. 'I don't suppose it's any too easy for her,' Taye replied, her loyalty stretched, but feeling a shade uncomfortable at the thought of running her mother down. Even to Magnus, the man she loved.

Whether he noticed that she was not feeling too comfortable with the subject she did not know, but he abruptly left the matter of her mother and her grasping ways to enquire, 'What about your father?'

Taye blinked, not at all with him. 'What about my father?'

'Are you going to ring him?'

'What about?'

'This latest development.'

'I can't do that!' she gasped, horrified at the very idea.

'Why not?'

She stared at Magnus. He did not understand. 'Because I can't.'

Magnus stared back at her, all male and logical. 'He sounds an honourable man…' he began.

'He *is* an honourable man!' Taye flew. Love Magnus though she did, she was not going to sanction anyone thinking less of her father. But, in the face of Magnus calmly observing her, taking in the twin spots of colour in her cheeks, she calmed down a little to explain. 'He will have to know that Hadleigh has decided to not accept any university place offered…'

'Like you had to decide not to,' Magnus put in, his expression gentle.

She found his gentle look unnerving, and guessed then that her emotions must still be to some degree all over the place. 'I knew long before I was eighteen that university was out,' she said quickly.

'What did your father have to say about that?' Magnus insisted, and she could only look at him and wonder at his 'dog with a bone' tenacity to find out her father's involvement in the decision making when it came to his two offspring.

'If you must know—' she replied, more sharply than she meant—not that it appeared to bother Magnus how sharply she spoke, because he stayed in there, leaning

against one of the kitchen units as he waited for her answer. 'If you must know,' she repeated, 'I let my father
believe I'd gone off the idea of going to university.'

'You lied to him?'

'Oh, shut up,' she mumbled. But, after some silent
seconds, felt forced to admit, 'Yes, I suppose I did. But
what else was I to do? He had given my mother the house
and every penny he could spare. He didn't have anything
else to give.'

'And your mother wanted you earning, not studying.'
It was not a question; it was a statement.

'How did you get to be so perceptive? I thought you
were an artist not some wised-up brainbox!'

'You'd be amazed what we artists see,' he informed
her. But was apparently still not ready to let go what she
guessed was his opinion that her father should be told
when he went on, 'So—you're not going to tell your
father that his son, too, is going to be denied his chance—
and why?'

'I can't!' she exclaimed warmly, and, suddenly not
wanting to fall out with Magnus, 'Don't you see? It is
precisely because my father is an honourable man that I
cannot tell him.' And, realising that perhaps she should
explain, 'My father has met someone—a very nice lady.
She's a teacher,' Taye began. 'His years with my mother
were not happy years. In fact, knowing him as I do, I can
only now wonder that he tolerated living at home for as
long as he did. But now he is about to find happiness
with Hilary. Only I know in advance that, were I to tell
him that financial hardship is the reason for Hadleigh
turning his back on a university education, my father
would straight away cancel all his plans to remarry.'

'Because?'

'Because he would see any further financial help he

was able to give us as depriving his new wife of what is rightfully hers. Or, worse, he would see his new and salary-earning wife as making a financial contribution to something that is his responsibility alone. And he would not be able to accept that.'

'But he would accept you impoverishing yourself to take out a bank loan?'

He wouldn't know. 'I wouldn't tell him!' Taye exclaimed. 'He'd have a fit if—' She broke off. There was a sudden stillness about Magnus that caused her to know that his perceptive artist's brain had just seen something else. 'What…?' she began.

'Presumably, until your mother's phone call today, you were all set to go for that bank loan?'

'I may still go that route if I can think up some way to convince Hadleigh that I'm—er—not, to use your word, "impoverishing" myself. He's so proud—'

'I don't mean to be prying,' Magnus cut her off, 'but…'

'You've done nothing but pry ever since we got home!' she protested.

'We're flat-mates; we can share everything,' he explained, and she had to smile. Though she was not smiling a moment later, and nor was he when, 'Forgive me for knowing that, financially, you struggle to keep your head above water…' he said, managing to look as though, with the bit once more between his teeth, it would be just the same if she forgave him or didn't. 'But how did you anticipate repaying any loan your bank made you?'

No! No, she did not want to tell him! She loved him— loved him so much she could not bear to live apart from him. She wanted to stay living with him. Yet she knew if she were able to carry through her original plan that she was going to have to live elsewhere.

She looked away from him, her glance absently taking in the stove. 'You haven't eaten!' she said in a diverting rush. 'You've missed lunch, and—'

'How, Taye?' He refused to be diverted. 'I imagine that would be one of the first questions your bank would ask before considering making you any sort of a loan. How are you going to repay it?'

She opened her mouth to tell him, and could not. She closed it again. But he was waiting. She had intended to tell him anyway. Only she had not faced then that he had stolen her heart.

'I...' Her voice was suddenly all husky...guiltily, painfully, in love with him husky. 'I was going to—move into somewhere smaller—somewhere cheaper,' she managed to drag out from between reluctant lips.

Magnus eyed her solemnly for long, tortuous seconds. 'You were going to leave here? Leave this apartment?'

'I didn't want to. You know how I love it here,' she said. 'But I couldn't see I had any other choice.'

'I see,' Magnus commented tautly. But a tough note had entered his tones as he determinedly challenged, 'Do I assume, as the other half of this flat-share, that you intended to tell me about it some time?' Oh, crumbs. 'Or was I just expected to come home one evening and find you'd done a flit, bag and baggage gone?'

'No!' she exclaimed. 'I would have told you...'

'When?' he demanded. 'Before or after...?'

'Don't! Oh, don't Magnus,' she pleaded. 'I wanted to tell you, only—' she broke off. How could she tell him that she had not been able to mention it because she had been too busy falling in love with him—only she had not known about that herself then? 'Oh, please don't...' she cried huskily, and, unable to look at him, stared down at the floor.

And the next she knew, whether because of something in her look or maybe in her tone she neither knew nor cared just then, Magnus had left his position by the kitchen units and had come over to her. And his voice was all soft and bone-meltingly gentle when he gathered her into his arms in an empathy of the moment and sympathetically breathed, 'Poor little love, you've been on an emotional merry-go-round all day. You've had enough, haven't you?' he murmured. 'You've got as much grief as you can handle without me badgering away at you.'

'I was going to t-tell you.'

'Shh, and let me give you a hug.'

In seventh heaven, she leaned against him. Soon he would take his arms from around her—and she wanted to savour every delicious moment.

She put her arms around his waist, and felt him drop a light comforting kiss to the top of her head. Her arms, of their own volition, it seemed to her, tightened about him, and she raised her head and looked up into warm grey eyes.

'Don't look at me like that unless you mean it,' he murmured.

'Look at you how?' she answered huskily, just the fact of looking into his warm and gentle gaze sending any thinking power haywire.

'As though you want to be—kissed,' he replied, but made no move to release her from his hold.

She smiled a dreamy kind of smile. 'I think I might like to be kissed,' she invited softly, her dreamy smile deepening as she added, 'If memory serves, you do it so nicely.'

He gave a low laugh, and his head came down. He did not wait for a second invitation, but tenderly placed his mouth over hers.

'Ooh,' she whispered, when he drew back to look into her eyes once more. 'That was so nice—do you think I could have another?'

'I don't think…' he began, his eyes searching her face. Then a kind of groan escaped him, and the next Taye knew was that she was being drawn closer up against him, and his kiss this time, as well as giving, was taking.

'Magnus!' She sighed his name.

'Magnus, no?' he enquired.

She kissed him, stretched up and, with her body leaning against him, kissed him. 'What do you think?' she asked shyly.

He looked into her lovely blue eyes, his eyes showing delight. He kissed her—with growing warmth. And Taye, her heart pounding against her ribs, responded fully.

For how long they stood in the kitchen, their bodies pressed up against each other as they kissed, and held, and kissed, gave and took, and then kissed some more, Taye could not have said. All she knew was that to be in his arms like this was bliss—pure bliss.

When next Magnus pulled back she saw a fire there in his wonderful grey eyes that, feeling slightly incredulous, she realised she was responsible for lighting.

She guessed that her eyes must be showing pretty much that same fire, because as Magnus looked tenderly down at her, kissed first one corner of her mouth and then the other, he smiled, and said, 'I think, Miss Trafford, that, in answer to your question, we would both be more comfortable elsewhere.'

Taye was ready to agree with whatever he suggested. And she guessed he must have read that in her eyes too. Because when next his mouth sought hers, he at the same time lifted her up in his arms—and kissed her all the way to her bedroom.

He did not set her down again until he was standing next to her bed. Gently then he kissed her, his tongue teasing at her slightly parted lips.

'Oh, Magnus!' she cried, and gripped on to him tightly.

'Sweet Taye,' he murmured, his hands gently exploring beneath the fine material of her loose top. With breath-holding torture, as his hands searched unhurriedly upwards, she clung on to him. And gave a gasp of pure wanting when finally those caressing hands took possession of her full and throbbing breasts. 'You can say no any time you want to,' he thought to gently state, perhaps bearing in mind her inexperience.

'What a diabolical suggestion,' she whispered, and loved him some more when he laughed a low, tender laugh.

Again they kissed, and the fire inside her began to burn out of control when, her bra somehow undone, Taye felt the warmth of his hands on the creamy skin of her breasts, cupping and moulding.

'I want to get close to you,' she murmured shyly, for her words sounded forward in her ears.

'Do what feels right for you,' he instructed softly.

'May I unbutton your shirt?'

'I would love you to unbutton my shirt,' he replied lightly. And her heart swelled with her love for him. But her fingers were shaky as they neared the buttons. 'Nervous, darling?' Magnus asked, his hands leaving her breasts to take hold of her hands.

'A—bit,' she owned, her heart melting at that endearment. She knew, though, that she had no need to be nervous. To make love with Julian had not been right for her—because she did not love Julian. But she loved Magnus with her whole heart, and to make love with him was right for her.

'Am I going too fast for you?'

She shook her head, and, to prove it, set about unbuttoning his shirt. Magnus helped her. And—removed it. 'Oh!' she whispered huskily, and just had to gaze at his magnificent broad chest. Just had to touch him. Touch the dark hair, his skin, his nipples. She felt his spontaneous movement and, her eyes wide, she looked up. 'I'm sorry,' she apologised. And asked, 'Do you mind me—er—exploring you like this?'

'Sweet love,' he replied. 'It's all new to you, isn't it?' But, to show that he did not mind in the least, he hauled her into his arms once more, and all was silent as they kissed, and held, and kissed.

Taye, without panic, became aware that Magnus was removing her top. Then removing her bra. She was still not panicking when, in next to no time, they were both standing naked down to the waist. Why would she panic? She loved him, he was her love.

But as Magnus looked down, so instinctively her hands shot to cover her breasts. He smiled gently, his eyes tender with understanding. But, drawing her to him, he kissed her with such a growing passion that she forgot all about modestly hiding her intimate self from him and wrapped her arms around him—her naked breasts pressed up against his naked chest as she tried to get closer, yet closer to him.

And this time when he relaxed his hold and looked down to her breasts her hands stayed where they were, resting on his shoulders. 'You're exquisite,' he breathed, and just had to bend his head to salute in turn each hardened pink tip of her breasts, his lips lingering to pleasure and tease. A thrill of pure desire swept through her.

But when she found that, without apparent haste, Magnus had moved her, moved with her, until they were both lying on her bed, unwanted nerves returned and began to bite with a vengeance.

She wanted to make love with Magnus. It felt so right to make love with him. And yet... A gasp left her as with gentle seeking hands his fingers strayed inside her trousers, investigating parts of her where no man had trespassed before.

'Magnus!' she cried out.

His hand stilled. 'I didn't mean *now!*' he groaned.

'What?' She barely knew where she was, and had no idea what he was talking about.

'I said you could say no at any time, but I didn't mean for you to say no at this late stage,' he enlightened her, having picked up, from the way she had cried his name, it seemed, that at almost the point of no return she was unsure. 'You know I want you?' he asked gruffly.

Yes, she knew that. She was not so innocent that she did not know that. She wanted him too—but she also wanted, needed, him to tell her that he loved her—even if it wasn't true. Which, of course, it wasn't.

'You're saying no now, right?' he asked, a note of strain there in his voice somewhere.

Tell me you love me! Just one word of love, that was all she would ask. But no word of love had been spoken. 'This—this isn't right,' she said chokily. 'I'm—confused,' she confessed. Wasn't that the truth!

She wanted to make love with him, was quite desperate to know his body, to love him with her body—and knew, weakly, that should he care to he could so easily persuade her that it *was* right.

But Magnus was not into persuading, apparently. As though the feel of her warm belly beneath his touch burned his skin, he yanked his hand away and sat up, his back to her so he should not see her uncovered breasts.

And, as if needing to focus his thoughts on something other than her, until a few minutes ago, eager and waiting, wanting body, 'I'd better go and take that car back!' he grunted, and, grabbing up his shirt as he went, he strode urgently from her room.

# CHAPTER SEVEN

MAGNUS did not come home that night. And Taye felt that she loved and hated him at one and the same time. Not that she was ready to see him again yet; the way she felt now she did not know if she would ever be ready to see him again. But jealousy scourged her; just who was he spending the night with?

She tried to think that after he had returned the car he had borrowed he had gone on to his mother's home. But the name Elspeth, Elspeth, Elspeth insisted on hammering away in her head.

Taye tried to think of Hadleigh and what she must do about his refusal to accept her help. But all too soon she found she was again thinking of Magnus—and his lips on hers.

His kisses were sensational, his caresses so tender. He could have been hers, she his, for a short while. She felt so mixed up she did not know whether she was glad or sorry that their lovemaking had ended when it had. Indeed, now that she had space to think about it, she could barely remember how she had caused their love-making to come to such an abrupt end.

She had loved his endearments, she recalled. The way he had murmured her name, called her 'darling'. Had she truly heard him call her 'sweet love'? It was all such heady stuff, she could no longer be sure. But what she was sure of was that, though he may have called her 'sweet love', no other word of love had left his lips.

Perhaps all women wanted to be told that they were

loved that first time. She did not know. All she knew was that he had not told her he loved her. And he did not love her. And he never would. And he had probably spent the night with Elspeth—and Taye hated him.

She felt bleary-eyed when she went in to work the next day, but was too busy to dwell overlong on that which really mattered to her—how was she going to face Magnus again, and what was she going to do about her brother?

Julian Coombs stopped by her desk during the afternoon. 'Good weekend?' she asked, finding a smile, glad she had managed to remember he had been at some rally or other.

'It would have been better with you there,' he answered. She made no comment—she just wasn't up to this. 'Doing anything tonight?' he asked.

'I'm a bit up to my eyes at the moment,' she hedged.

'I've got to go to our Edinburgh branch again tomorrow. But I'll be back Friday,' he said, and pressed, 'Come out with me Friday?'

Taye knew then that this could not go on, though she was loath to say what she must at the office. 'I—rather wanted a word with you,' she brought out, after an internal struggle, only to see him start to look a little wary.

'I rather wanted a word with you too,' he said solemnly.

Please say the word you wanted is that you've met somebody else, that you're just being kind and want to dump me as nicely as you can. Oh, please do. 'I'll see you on Friday, then,' she agreed, knowing that the office was just not the place for either of them to bid the other a social farewell.

Magnus tried to get to toehold within a very short space of Julian leaving her desk. She pushed Magnus out of her thoughts and made valiant efforts to concentrate solely on her work.

But when the time came to go home she fell to wondering if he would be there when she got there. Did she want to see him? Well, of course she wanted to see him; she loved the wretched man. But… Taye decided to work an extra hour or so.

But a half-hour later she could stay away no longer, and cleared her desk ready for a fresh start in the morning.

Her heart started to hurry up its beat the nearer she got to the apartment she shared with him. She tried turning her thoughts away from him. Now, what on earth was she going to do about Hadleigh?

Taye was no nearer to finding an answer to that problem when from the top of the street where the apartment was situated she saw someone standing outside of her building. He was vaguely familiar. It was… Surely not! Her feet went from walking to hurrying. 'Dad!' she exclaimed when she was near enough for him to hear her. He had never been to the flat before. 'What are you doing here?'

'Trying to get in,' he answered dryly.

She grinned. 'Come in,' she invited, unlocking the outer door. She guessed before she opened the flat door that Magnus was not home yet—if indeed he intended coming home. Otherwise he would have answered the intercom and, as he had with Hadleigh, he would have asked her father in.

'Nice place,' Alden Trafford approved as Taye took him into the sitting room.

Taye sensed he had not come to town merely to admire where she now lived. 'Take a seat. I'll make some tea,' she said, her thoughts darting all over the place.

In normal circumstances her father would have phoned in advance if he intended paying her a call, she felt sure. So she could only imagine something out of the norm had taken place. She did so hope that everything was all right with him and Hilary and that he had not hit some snag with his divorce.

'What's up, Dad?' she asked as she handed him a cup of tea.

He did not preamble but came straight out and told her, 'I had lunch with your brother today.' And, while Taye was still blinking at that, 'Oh, love. I got it all wrong, didn't I? And you're the one who had to pay.'

He sounded so upset Taye could not bear it. 'I'm fine,' she assured him, having no idea what had caused him to be so grief-stricken.

'You should have told me,' he mourned. 'I should have pressed you further. Blindly, when I full well know your mother could lie for England, I believed every word she told me. Believed what you told me. But I should never have left you with her. I see that now. I just thought then, and when I know her so well too, that she was the better person to look after you. I thought I was doing what was best for you.'

Taye knew that. How could he have taken her and Hadleigh with him when he had split from her mother? He had barely had a roof over his own head back then. But she still could not make much sense of why he had come, or what it was he was saying. Though, from what he had said so far, Taye saw her mother at the root of his visit somewhere. 'This has something to do with my mother?' she asked—and, oh, my word if she did!

'Your mother rang me last night to inform me that Hadleigh had decided not to go to Oxford.'

'Oh, she didn't! Oh, I'm so sorry. I didn't want to worry you or—' Taye began fretfully.

'Then you should have!' Alden Trafford cut in severely. But lost his severe look to say more gently, 'I'm your father, Taye. It's my place to be worried when things go wrong.'

'But you're getting married, and I didn't want—'

'I think I know you well enough now to know why you have done what you have. But, had you come to me, I could have sorted everything out.'

'You could?' she asked, respecting him, but doubting he could sort this one out. But how much did he know? Did he know why Hadleigh had made the decision he had?

'I could,' her father confirmed. 'And you needn't be scared of telling me too much. I know everything.'

Taye stared at him, uncertain still. 'You and Hilary... This—um...'

'This will make not the slightest difference to our plans,' Alden Trafford assured her. 'And I know what you intended to do for Hadleigh—had he let you.'

'He told you?'

'I know he turned stubborn when his mother told him you intended to go around barefoot in order to secure a loan—and how he refused to let you do it.'

'Barefoot's a bit of an exaggeration,' Taye said with a smile, hurrying on, when her father did not return her smile, 'I just wanted to do whatever I could to help.'

'And I appreciate that. Taye. But it's not your place to do that; it's mine. And,' he said heavily, 'it has all been taken care of.'

Taye stared at her father. His needs were small, but so was his income. She doubted that there was anything over for much else. 'Mother shouldn't have phoned you…' she began, but only to be contradicted.

'Somebody should, and it wouldn't have been you. And, after speaking to Hadleigh today, it's a foregone conclusion that he wasn't going to ring.'

'Don't worry, Dad. I'll see he gets his chance somehow,' she said, starting to get seriously worried.

'You don't have to. I've told you, everything has been taken care of.'

'It—has?'

'Your mother said when she rang last night that Hadleigh had decided against university. That said, she went on to stress how, being a six-footer like me, and big with it, he takes a man size in all his clothes and shoes and she just couldn't keep up. And I,' he said, shaking his head, 'almost swallowed it. In fact it wasn't until I was relating all this to Hilary that I realised that what Greta had said had a very familiar ring. It was, in fact, an almost word-for-word playback of the telephone call I had from her when you were sixteen and I discussed with her about you going to university when you were old enough.' He looked at her sorrowfully then. 'The decision not to go was your mother's, not yours, wasn't it?' he asked.

In the face of such a point blank question, Taye could not lie to him. 'We couldn't afford for me to go,' she mumbled.

And looked at her father, staggered, when he said bluntly, 'Yes, we could,' and went on to explain, 'A month after you were born I set up a fund especially so that, should we reach hard times—though Lord knows I never expected to—there would be a pot of money available to pay for your education. I set up the same sort of fund when Hadleigh was born.'

'I never knew that!' Taye exclaimed in awe.

'Foolishly, I see now, I didn't want my children to concern themselves about money. But hindsight's a wonderful thing—it's now plain to me that I should have told you. I was, in fact, going to tell Hadleigh. I thought I'd wait until he rang to tell me his A level results, and tell him then. Anyhow, that's by the way now. When things went rocky for me financially I had to move to freeze that education fund. But there would still have been enough when you reached eighteen to see you didn't have to worry about money. I'm afraid, my dear, that all your mother wanted was the money that was set aside for your further education.'

'Oh!' Taye gasped, knowing without question that her mother had had that money, and spent it. Then something suddenly clicked. 'Mother knew all about those funds from day one, didn't she?' she exclaimed.

'That's right.' Her father was right up there with her. 'Money has always been like a god to her. She worships the stuff, and was after Hadleigh's education fund too. And I nearly missed seeing it! But no more,' he said decisively. 'Over the years that woman has bled me dry. But *I* have taken as much as I'm prepared to take. From now on I shall take charge of finances. You, young lady, are not to give her any more. Yes, I know all about that. I'm afraid I caught Hadleigh at a weak moment over lunch. He was very down to start with, but after I'd explained about his fund, and how he was to have his chance, he opened up to me.'

'He's all right?' Taye asked, concerned.

'Never better. I told him I was coming here. He said to give you a big hug and a thank-you. I did ask him to come back with me to Warwickshire, to come and live with me, but he wants to be around to pick up his exam results, and he has his job and other loose ends he wants to deal with before October. Though I think he's ready to spend time with me during his student vacations.'

'Will Mother mind?'

'It's not her fault that she just doesn't have that maternal instinct, I suppose. But as to whether she'll mind...' He smiled suddenly. 'To quote Rhett, "Frankly, my dear, I don't give a damn." I've told her not to bother you or Hadleigh for money, and that if she's that hard up she can sell that big house. With the price it would fetch she'd have enough to purchase at least two very respectable properties and still be able to live comfortably on what's left over.'

'Will—?' Taye began, and then heard Magnus's key in the door. 'That will be my flat-share,' she broke off to tell her father. And was glad his glance went to the door, because as Magnus came in so she blushed scarlet. 'Hello, Magnus,' she said in a rush, aware of his eyes flitting from her visitor and then staying with her fading colour. 'Come and say hello to my father.' She then went on to introduce the two men.

'I seem to know your face,' her father commented. 'Have we met before?'

'I'm sure not. I think I must have "one of those faces,"' Magnus replied easily, as the two men shook hands.

In Taye's view he definitely did not have 'one of those faces'. He was much too good-looking, for one thing— though she did recall that Damien Fraser had seemed to think he knew Magnus from somewhere. But all that was forgotten as Magnus and her father exchanged one or two comments, and then her father was remarking that it was time he was off.

'But I haven't given you anything to eat!' Taye protested. 'You can't go without—'

'I had a huge banquet of a meal with Hadleigh at lunchtime,' Alden Trafford replied. And, smiling, 'I did phone Hilary earlier, but she'll be anxious to hear more.'

He and Magnus shook hands again, and Taye went out into the hall with her father. 'I'm still trying to take in your good news,' she said, and was on the receiving end of a warm hug.

'I wish there was some way I could make it up to you. When I think…' He shook his head regretfully.

'Oh, please don't! I think it's been harder for you than for me.'

'I doubt that,' he said solemnly, but was smiling as Taye hugged him back and asked him to give her best to Hilary.

Taye returned to the apartment half wishing that Magnus had gone to his room. He had not, but was still in the sitting room. And she was glad that he had not disappeared—loving him was turning her sane world on its head.

'Your father had lunch with Hadleigh?' Magnus commented, and she just had to smile.

'What you don't know, find out. Not that you're one to pry, of course.'

'So?'

'So my mother rang my father last night to tell him that Hadleigh did not want to go to university. Basically, Dad smelt a rat, and went to Pemberton today, took Hadleigh out to lunch, and informed him that he had made financial provision for his adult education when Hadleigh was a baby. I gather that by the pudding stage my brother was back on course to go to Oxford.'

Magnus took that on board in no seconds flat, and

was all too soon there with his summing up. 'Do I gather that the same provision he made for you went where Hadleigh's allocated finances were likely to go?'

This man Ashthorpe was too sharp for his own good! 'Brainy as well as good-looking!' she commented, with what was supposed to be acid.

'I cannot deny it,' he sighed. She turned away so he should not see her lips tugging upwards. But quickly turned back when, as sharp as she had thought, he added, 'I take it you now have no need to look for less expensive accommodation?'

Taye stared at him transfixed. She had not got that far in her thinking. But joy entered her heart. 'There's no need now, is there?' she answered, her voice strangely husky. She was having the greatest difficulty in holding in a beam of a smile that might have given him some indication of how she did not want to leave the apartment and now, more particularly, Magnus himself.

But all at once she noticed that his expression had gone to look deadly serious. 'You're not afraid, Taye?' he asked gravely.

'Afraid?' The only fear she had was that he would see just why she was so delighted they did not now have to part.

'I shouldn't have kissed you yesterday,' he said as pink seared her cheeks. And, while taking in her heightened colour, he was determined, it appeared, to give the subject the airing he seemed to think was required. 'You were in a vulnerable and emotional state before I kissed you. I should—'

'You didn't take advantage, if that's what you're thinking!' she exclaimed, not happy to be discussing what had happened, but too honest to let him take the blame when it had been she who had so loved that first kiss, and had pushed for a second. 'I was perfectly willing—' nay, eager '—about—about what went on. I wanted... Only... Only...' She ran out of steam.

Thankfully he seemed sufficiently convinced to let it go. He smiled suddenly. And as swiftly as he had got onto that subject he changed it. 'I'm having a coffee. Want one?'

In actual fact she didn't. The teacups were still on the table from her father's visit. 'Yes, please,' she accepted, and gave up wondering about the topsy-turvy world of being in love.

It took her a long while to get to sleep that night, and she thought it had very little to do with the caffeine in the coffee. There was just so much to think about. She did not wish to visualise the kind of conversation that had gone on between her parents. Her father was slow to anger, but when roused, Taye knew, would not back down again.

She thought of Hadleigh. Leaving it as late as he could, he had telephoned, his first words a fairly cautious, 'Have you seen Dad?'

'I hear you had a banquet at lunch,' she had replied, and listened while her ecstatic brother grew excited and repeated more or less the same that their father had told her. So much for Hadleigh not wanting to go to Oxford; he could barely wait to get there.

So much too, for her having to try to work out something with regard to getting Hadleigh to accept her financial help. She would no longer have to do that. And, for an added bonus, she did not have to find somewhere smaller to live, and so leave the apartment—and Magnus.

Ah, Magnus! She thought about him. How could she not? She thought of his smiles, his occasional laugh, the way he made her laugh—whether she wanted to laugh or not. She thought about his kisses, his tender caresses. She thought about him in all of his moods—and wondered how she had ever thought that she hated him. She eventually fell asleep, still thinking about him.

Taye still had Magnus in her head the next day. She was busy at her desk; then found she had drifted off to think of him again. At one time she might have banished him. This time she let him stay.

He went briefly from her head, though, when Damien Fraser, ever a trier, phoned. 'Are you still going out with that other bloke?' he asked.

'Yes,' she replied.

'Anyone I know?'

'No,' she said.

'Goodbye—no, *au revoir!*' he bade her.

'*Ciao*,' she responded, though goodbye just about covered it. And, with Magnus pushing Damien out of her head, she got on with some work.

Taye left her office early that night. She wanted to see Magnus. Not for any particular reason other than she had a need to see him. Much good did it do her! They passed in the hall—she coming in, he on his way out.

'Be late back!' he said in passing.

Good of you to come home at all! 'I won't wait up!'

He grinned. 'See you.'

Jealousy played havoc with her for the rest of the night. She was in bed—not sleeping—when her listening ears heard his key in the door. Half of her was glad Elspeth had kicked him out. The other half hated him that he had stayed out this long!

Wednesday and Thursday followed pretty much the same pattern. Magnus arrived home, had a quick shower and was off out again. She hoped his paintings never dried.

Magnus was not home when Taye went home on Friday. She got ready to go out with Julian, not looking forward to the evening in front of her one tiny bit.

Magnus was still not home when Julian came to call for her. She dragged her thoughts away from Magnus, knowing that the time had come for her to tell Julian what he had to be told. Now that the moment had arrived, though, she wanted it done now rather than at the end of the evening. But she knew she was just going to have to wait a little while. For all it would hopefully not take long to do, no way did she want Magnus to walk in in the middle of it. Julian deserved better.

'I thought we'd go somewhere a bit special tonight,' he announced enthusiastically as they drove in and out of traffic.

'I—um…' Oh, grief! How could she tell him in some place that was 'a bit special' that it was marking the last time they went out together?

She could not, Taye realised. She just could not. She could, she suppose, duck telling him, but… No. Do it now. They had just pulled up in a parking space when Taye took her courage in both hands.

Julian was just about to open the driver's door when—'Julian!' She stopped him, and plunged straight in while she could. 'I'm afraid this will be our last meeting outside of the office.'

'What?' He was shocked and, clearly having his own agenda, had not picked up that she had been backing away this last couple of weeks. 'You can't mean that!' he exclaimed and, in shock, blurted out, 'I was going to ask you to marry me!'

It was difficult to say then who was the more stunned. 'I…' she said helplessly. 'I'm sorry. But…'

'Is it something I've said? Something I've done?'

'Oh, Julian, you've been super to go out with,' she assured him—and spent the next half-hour trying to convince him that there was no fault with him, and that it was just that, while she cared for him, it was not enough to marry him.

She was all for cancelling the rest of the evening, but Julian would not hear of that. 'If I'm not to see you again, at least let me have this one last evening with you,' he insisted.

Weakly, she agreed. But the evening was not a success. They both tried. But she found Julian's sad eyes on her so many times, and she found that much too upsetting.

But she was more upset when, having driven her home, they stood outside her apartment building and he suddenly urged, 'Marry me, Taye?' And, when numbly she shook her head, 'Do please think about it?' he asked. 'I love you enough for two of us.'

'Oh, Julian, please don't!' she whispered, and wanted to give him a gentle kiss of healing but knew that she dared not. He had appeared to misunderstand that the dates she had been on with him were just that and nothing more. The state he was in now he would misunderstand totally any final kiss in the empathy of the moment. 'I'll still see you at work,' she said gently, while wondering even then if she was going to have to consider getting a job elsewhere.

Eventually he stood back, and she went indoors. Taye felt as close to tears as she had ever been. Julian was nice, kind and good, and despite not wanting to hurt him, hurt him she had. And that hurt her.

For once as she went in she would not have minded having the apartment to herself. But there was a line of light beneath the sitting room door. And, while her heart went squishy to know that Magnus was home, she did not want to see him.

From courtesy, however, she opened the door, but did not go in. She tossed an, 'I'm home!' in through the open doorway and went on to her room.

A few seconds later, after the briefest tap on her door, she found she had company. She had her back to the door when Magnus came in. She did not turn round. 'What's wrong?' he asked.

She supposed her voice had sounded a little choked. 'Nothing,' she answered—and discovered she was looking at Magnus when he did no more than come round and stand in front of her.

'Fraser? You've been out with Fraser again!' he accused.

She bridled at his tone. 'No, I haven't!' she retorted.

'Julian Coombs?'

'You're prying again!' she snapped.

'You've been out with Julian Coombs,' Magnus decided, and, his tone softening, 'You've told him you're not going to see him again?'

Leave me alone! Taye gave a shaky sigh. She somehow knew in advance that Magnus was unlikely to leave her alone until she had answered his every question. 'I don't want to talk about it,' she said stiffly.

'Oh, poor Taye. You told him, he took it badly—and now you're hurting that you've had to cause him pain.'

'What makes you so smart?'

'It comes naturally,' Magnus teased—the back of his hand stroking down the side of her face. 'I'd love to cuddle you better, but to be honest, sweetheart, you're much too heady a woman for me to try that again.'

That shook her. She raised her head to stare at him.

Magnus thought her a heady woman? She opened her mouth, her head empty of words. Then she found a few.

'In that case, you'd better clear off,' she replied.

He looked at her long and hard, observed that she did not look quite as disquieted as she had a minute or two ago, and then said softly, 'Perhaps I had better.' And did so.

When Taye lay down in her bed shortly afterwards she began to feel guilty. Because it was not sad thoughts of Julian that kept her awake, as she might have supposed, but thoughts of Magnus. He had wanted to give her a cuddle, a kind of hug, but thought her too heady to attempt it!

She remembered how their lovemaking had begun last Sunday with Magnus giving her a cuddle. And she knew he had been right not to give in to that sensitive impulse. Because a cuddle could so easily become a kiss—and what then? Should neither of them back away from what would naturally follow—where did they go from there?

Ultimately one of them would have to leave. She faced that square on. And Taye just did not want to think of her life without Magnus in it.

# CHAPTER EIGHT

IT WAS Saturday and there was no need for Taye to get up early. But already the sun was shining and she was awake and restless. She got out of bed and, remembering how the previous Saturday Magnus had remarked on her 'messed up hair', for all he had called it 'fetching', just in case he was up and about she dragged a comb through her hair before she donned her satin wrap and made for the kitchen.

There was no sign of him as she made a pot of tea and alternately thought of him and thought, sadly, of Julian. She recalled how last night Magnus had commented that he thought her a heady woman, and while just remembering that caused *her* a few heady moments, she then reflected how she had hurt Julian.

Taye poured herself a cup of tea and, feeling bad about Julian, put the cosy on the teapot and, taking her tea with her, padded to the sitting room.

While sipping her tea she mulled over what she should do that day. There were the usual chores, of course, but nothing that could not be shelved if she had a better offer.

She wondered what Magnus would be doing with his Saturday. He could be intending to work, she supposed. Being a self-employed artist wasn't the same as having a Monday-to-Friday nine-to-five occupation.

Or would he be taking his laundry to his mother? Taye was not so sure that she believed that was what he had done last Saturday—when he had come home and seen her in the bath. But she did not want to think about that!

It was true enough, though, that, while his linen was always clean, she had never seen him up to his elbows in soapsuds; she had an idea he would not know one dial on a washing machine from another.

Taye was on the point of returning her cup and saucer to the kitchen when she heard sounds that told her Magnus was on the move. He was up early too! Perhaps he was packing up his laundry to take to his mother. Jealousy struck! Perhaps he was eager to get to his lady love, Elspeth—Taye rather thought Pen-Penelope had long since had the old heave-ho.

Taye heard a nearer sound, and for no reason jumped up from her chair. Somehow she did not feel ready to see Magnus. She decided to wait until she heard the shower running and then she would slip back to her room.

It did not work out like that. For one thing Magnus did not go straight to take his shower but wandered into the sitting room, where she was. He was robe-clad—and terrific with it.

'I didn't know you were up,' he remarked casually when he saw her.

Her heart was pounding all at once, and she suddenly felt all emotional just from seeing him. She turned from him and ambled over to the window, as if finding the view from the sitting room of utmost interest. 'There's tea in the pot,' she thought to mention as she strove to get herself more of one piece.

But tea was of no concern to him just then, apparently, and she felt her heartbeats begin to pick up again when Magnus strolled over to her.

She had her gaze fixed firmly on the big old apple tree in the garden when Magnus quietly asked, 'Still feeling as upset this morning?'

He meant over Julian, of course. 'You know how it is,' she said over her shoulder.

'It upset you to have to hurt him,' Magnus sympathised. But, his tone sharpening, 'You *did* tell him you wouldn't see him again?'

'I'll have to see him at work sometimes.'

Magnus decided that was a yes. 'He took it badly?'

Taye was momentarily back with Julian. Yes, he had taken it badly. 'He asked me to marry him,' she said absently, but rapidly came to and quickly added, 'I didn't mean to tell you that!'

'Too late. I heard,' Magnus replied, and came a few steps nearer. But he was still having a mighty effect on her and she moved away—forward—which brought her that bit closer to the window. He was standing directly behind her when she felt his hands come and take a grip on her shoulders. How she did not leap a foot into the air she did not know, but she had herself outwardly under control when he demanded, 'And you said?'

'What?'

'When Coombs asked you to marry him. You said?'

Magnus's hands were burning on her shoulders through the thin satin material of her kimono. 'You know what I said,' she replied a little shakily.

There was silence for a moment before Magnus reminded her, 'You're aware that the Coombs empire is worth a mint? That he can give you everything?'

'I'm aware of that,' Taye responded. And found she was adding, 'But I don't love him.'

'You'd marry for love—not money?'

This was getting too serious. 'Don't be disgusting!' she said, with a trace of a laugh.

Magnus did not laugh, but questioned, 'You're still determined not to marry a poor man, Taye?'

She gave a small sigh. It seemed to her then that she had changed greatly since she had first known Magnus. It was no longer of importance to her whether the man she married was poor or rich, or even somewhere in between, so long as he loved her—as she loved him.

She looked out to the apple tree, saw what she had come to think of as her star, dazzling, twinkling away as the breeze turned it. And somehow found that either Magnus had taken a small step forward or she had taken a half-step back, because she was all at once leaning back against his chest.

She was so aware of him she could barely breathe. She did not want to jerk away; that would take away what for either him or her had been something sweet and natural. But something light was called for, so she pointed through the window to the apple tree.

'See that star?' She continued to point, then announced, 'I shall only marry the man who is brave enough to climb that tree and get it for me.'

With that, wanting to keep the mood light, but feeling self-conscious suddenly, she turned and discovered that Magnus still had his hands on her shoulders, and that his head was much too close to her.

Grey eyes smiled into worried blue ones and, as though to kiss away her fears, her worries, Magnus lightly touched his lips to hers. He pulled back, yet somehow seemed reluctant to let go his hold of her.

'Now see what you made me do!' he complained.

Her lips twitched. 'I get the blame for everything around here,' she complained in kind, but as he held her she found she was powerless to be the first one to make a move to break the moment.

'You know we're going to be in trouble if I do what I want to do and kiss you again?'

Taye swallowed hard. 'I somehow don't think there's been enough of that sort of trouble in my life,' she murmured huskily.

'Stop it,' he ordered. 'Behave yourself.'

She grinned up at him. 'Why should I?'

He looked down at her, down into her sparkling eyes, his glance straying to her inviting mouth, and back up to her eyes. 'Right now I can't think of one single solitary reason,' he breathed, and, gathering her into his arms, his head came down.

She felt the heat of him through her thin wrap, felt the warmth of his kiss, and was at once on fire for him as they exchanged, gave, received kiss for kiss. She was not thinking but was just one mass of loving emotion when Magnus led her to the large padded sofa. He held her close to him and they kissed and held and kissed—and held more closely.

And when Magnus moved with her she willingly lay down on the sofa with him, the ache in her heart for him for the moment quieted as he kissed her eyes, her face, his kisses straying to her throat.

'Taye,' he breathed, and she clutched on to him with no idea, as her bare feet touched the bare skin of his legs, of when she had parted with her slippers.

'Magnus.' She whispered his name, and as his hands undid her wrap, the closer to get to her, so she loosened his robe, her hands caressing his skin.

'Oh, sweetheart,' he breathed, and kissed her long and hungrily.

And she wanted more. She kissed him in return, her heart hammering as his hands caressed her breasts, a fire storming through her when he kissed her again, and once more breathed her name.

She was his, all his when, gently caressing her, those

tenderly caressing hands moved beneath her and she felt his touch on the pert globes of her buttocks, pulling her that bit closer to him.

Taye wanted to be closer to him; she felt his hard body against her and swallowed. She wanted him, oh, how she wanted him.

And yet there was a nagging something going on in her head. She felt his tongue on her lips and instinctively arched her body to him. She heard his groan of wanting and almost matched it with a moan of her own desire for him.

But that stubborn insisting annoyance in her head was thundering its way through—and Taye was struggling to sit up.

'No!' It was Magnus's voice in protest.

'Oh, Magnus!' she cried, as he too sat up.

She looked at him, and it seemed to her that he knew that the barrier she was trying to erect was only of the flimsiest. She thought he looked as though he might bring her to lie down with him again—when she knew she would be utterly and completely lost. Just one more kiss and her will to resist him would be gone.

But, manfully, when it still looked as though he would haul her back into his arms, haul her back against him, he made some space between them—and actually pushed her wrap back on to her shoulders. Though he still did not seem one hundred per cent in control when he commented, 'You're still determined to keep out of the tulip field?'

She had to smile. With her face still flushed from his lovemaking, she had to smile. 'Oh, Magnus,' she said softly, most of her defences still down. 'You must know that I want to make love with you. Only…' Her words dried. She knew she had to be careful, had to watch every word she said. But, as far as she could, she wanted to be honest with him, this man whom she loved.

'Only?' he prompted, before she was ready.

'Only—I seem to have grown a bit—er—attached to my flat-mate.'

Magnus's brow went back. Then his expression suddenly became never more serious as, sitting beside her, he looked into her eyes. 'You—have?' he asked quietly—and seemed as though he might move closer up to her.

'Don't come any nearer!' she exclaimed in panic. She was still striving to come down from that high plateau he had taken her to, and knew she would go rocketing up again if he came an inch closer. 'But if we did—you know—' She broke off, striving desperately to piece together and put into words that which was spinning around in her subconscious and wanting to take shape. 'If we did,' she picked up, 'th-then ultimately one of us would have to leave, and…' Words failed her.

But not Magnus, solemn now, intent somehow. 'And you don't want that?' he pressed.

Just then she had a feeling she would settle for anything. But deep down she knew that she wanted to be loved by Magnus, not have some brief and, to him, meaningless affair. Besides, he still had Elspeth.

Taye shook her head. 'No,' she agreed. 'I don't.' She stood up then, starting to get worried that if she said much more she would give away something of how much he truly meant to her. She rather thought she had given him some kind of a hint anyway, and she searched feverishly for some witty exit line. But all she could find to say was a rather staccato-sounding, 'As the song says—I've grown accustomed to your face.'

She looked at him, startled by her own words, and

hoped quite desperately that he would think she meant that because she loved living there she did not want to be the one to leave—and also that she would rather have him as her flat-share than have to start looking for someone new all over again.

But by then Magnus was on his feet also, and was looking at her as though he was under some kind of strain too. And abruptly it was as though he had just come to some kind of important decision. 'Taye,' he said, a note of some kind of deliberation there in his voice. 'Taye, there's something I need to tell you.'

No! She knew what that something was, and did not want to hear it. All too plainly he had seen her love for him, but needed to tell her that he was in love with Elspeth—quite possibly about to get engaged to her.

'No time!' Taye said quickly, and was already halfway to the door. 'Busy day,' she offered by way of explanation. 'Better go and get dressed.' She had been a bit of a sprinter in her school sports days; she discovered she could still move like lightning when the occasion demanded it.

Taye showered and dressed, trying with all she had to keep her thoughts and emotions at bay. But found to do so totally was impossible.

She had loved being in Magnus's arms, And, next door to being engaged to his lady-love Elspeth though he might be, Taye felt that he had liked her responding to him the way that she had.

She tried to hate him for that. He was a man, wasn't he? Why wouldn't he enjoy having some young woman clinging on to him, eager for his kisses?

But she could not hate him. Somehow, even with Elspeth somewhere in the background, Taye could not believe that Magnus was like that—a kiss-where-he-could type of man. She thought of the sensitive side she had witnessed in him many times, and somehow could not believe he had taken her in his arms just because she had been there, so to speak.

When Taye got around to thinking that in that case did it not follow that Magnus must have some kind of small caring for her, she knew she needed to get away from where he was and clear her head.

Not yet ready to see him again, she waited until she heard him taking a shower and then, taking up her shoulder bag and picking up her shopping basket *en route*, she went quickly from the apartment.

She might have put some space between them physically, but Magnus was in her head the whole of the time. Taye supposed she must have been away from the apartment for an hour when her resolve to spend the morning away began to weaken. She was no nearer to clearing her head than she had been. And her emotions were still in a scaled-down traumatic uproar. But somehow something seemed to be calling her back.

She did not question what that something was. It was bound to be connected in some way with Magnus anyway. But she had to return to the home she shared with him, simply because she could stay away no longer.

Though as she let herself in she determined to keep any conversation between them on a non-personal level. And also to keep her distance from him; at least three yards' distance. Although there was something so magnetic about him three yards did not seem nearly far enough away.

Disappointment awaited her in that when she went in there was no sign of him. She dropped her shopping basket down in the kitchen and stood and listened for any sound that would tell her that Magnus was about somewhere in the apartment. All was quiet.

She put her shopping away and wished she had come home sooner, while the proud part of her wished she had not come back at all. With the whole day in front of her and guessing, as her jealousy demon tormented her mercilessly, that he was spending *his* day with some female, Taye wandered from the kitchen into the sitting room.

She was proudly sure that she did not— Suddenly pride and all thoughts of anything else ceased, everything in her freezing in horror! For, on glancing through the sitting room window, while not being fully aware of doing so, a jumbled heap of clothes on the garden path suddenly took shape in her vision: a jumbled-up bundle of clothes that had not been there when she had looked out earlier. And as that clothes bundle at once started to take shape—one leg emerging, a head and an arm—so Taye was released from her momentary frozen spasm of horror and—with terror in her heart—she took off.

She reached Magnus's collapsed and crumpled-up figure in no time flat, and was not thinking, just feeling, as she sank to her knees beside him.

'Magnus!' she croaked hoarsely.

He opened his eyes, looked at her, saw her concern, her panic—and who knew what else?—and suddenly he smiled. 'And for my next trick…' he began, striving to sit up.

'Don't move!' she instructed urgently, striving hard to keep a lid on her panic as blood streamed down the side of his face. Had he passed out for some reason and banged his head? Or tripped and fallen over something? she wondered worriedly. 'I'll get—'

'I'm all right.' Magnus ignored her instruction and began to sit up.

'You're not supposed to move!' she admonished him. He was now bleeding profusely, she saw, her blue eyes agitatedly on his watching grey eyes.

'Love me?' Magnus asked, his eyes steady on hers.

Her heart somersaulted at his question. 'That was some bang on the head.' She sidestepped the question, her heart pounding in fear for him, for his head and a possible concussion. There was fear for herself too, and what in the stress of the moment she might unwarily let fall. 'Have you hurt yourself anywhere else?'

He shook his head—and shared some of his blood with her. 'You do love me?' he insisted.

'You're not safe let out on your own!' she complained, her emotions starting to get all tangled up again as she found her handkerchief and held it in the general direction of the source of the bloodflow.

'Then...' Magnus said, and took a deep breath before continuing, 'I think you had better marry me.' Taye froze again, and there was such a roaring in her ears just then that she could hardly believe she had heard what she thought she had just heard. Had Magnus just said what she thought he had just said? Apparently he had. Because while she was still staring at him, transfixed, although he paraphrased it, he repeated it. 'You are going to marry me, Taye, aren't you?'

He did not know what he was saying, what he was asking, she decided. That bang on his head, or whatever it was, had given him a slight concussion. But he was waiting. And, bang on the head, concussion or not, there was no way she could tell him no—particularly as, when he had got himself more of one piece, he was not going to recall any of this conversation. 'We'll—um—be poor.' She found her voice to answer him at last.

Magnus beamed the most wonderful smile at what he

saw as her acceptance of his proposal, and placed a hand over the one of hers that was holding the make-do handkerchief pad to his head. He looked quite delighted. 'We'll have babies,' he informed her.

'That'll be fun!' she retorted, thinking that maybe she should nip this kind of talk in the bud right now.

'Won't it, though?' Magnus answered wickedly—and suddenly they were both grinning idiotically.

But Taye, the one looking at the blood still streaming down his face, was the first to recover. 'We'd better see about getting you to hospital,' she said firmly.

'No chance,' he replied—and there was that in his tone that clearly told her she would be wasting her breath in arguing.

'Well, at least let me get you inside so I can inspect the damage!' she exclaimed shortly, and felt relief when he allowed her to help him to his feet.

She was not sure it was strictly necessary for him to place an arm about her shoulders as they went up the path, but she could not deny she liked his arm there. And, just in case he needed her as a prop, she put an arm around his waist.

'Kitchen,' she said as they went into the house. 'Sit here,' she suggested and, when he meekly complied, she went in search of a scrappy sort of first-aid box, hoping there was everything there that she would need. 'I'll try not to hurt you,' she said kindly when she returned.

'I'm sure you have the touch of an angel,' Magnus replied politely—and did not so much as murmur as Taye got busy with water and cotton wool and began to clean away the blood.

'Good heavens!' she exclaimed, when she eventually got to the source of the problem—the smallest cut, about an inch above his left eyebrow.

'Am I going to live?' he teased.

'All that blood, and it's only the tiniest nick!'

'You're not going to have to sew it up for me, then?'

She smiled, wanting to hug him, wanting to kiss him, and just to hold him he was so dear to her. 'I think, in my professional opinion, you'll get by without it needing a stitch. Though until it stops bleeding you're going to have to wear a plaster.'

'Anything you say, Nurse,' he replied—now that she had lifted the threat of a hospital visit ready to agree to anything she said, it seemed.

Taye loved the intimacy of the moment as, close up to him, she put a small adhesive dressing on his wound. She had to make quite an effort to stand back from him. 'I think you may want to change your shirt,' she commented of his blood-soaked shirt.

Magnus got to his feet, his eyes gentle on her. 'I've bloodied your shirt too,' he said apologetically.

'Not a problem!' she murmured, stepping further back to give him some space.

She thought he would go straight away, but he delayed to quietly ask, 'You won't try to avoid me again?'

She stared at him. From that she gathered that he knew she had been out, perhaps knew too that, all het-up from their lovemaking, she had not then been yet ready to face him. 'I'd better go and change too!' she said in a hurry, and was halfway to the door when his voice reached her.

'Got a kiss for your fiancé?' he asked.

Stunned, she halted. Then turned. His expression was serious, stern almost, as she tried to read his eyes. Her heart was pounding away so furiously she felt she could hardly breathe. 'I… You…' she gasped. And, whether he thought she was avoiding him or whether he didn't, it was just then all too much for her.

Her emotions had been on the jangle all morning. And that had been before he had kissed her and she had kissed him. She had bolted—ostensibly to shop—and had returned half fearing she had found him dead. And now this! It was all too much. Much too much! Taye turned about again—and fled.

# CHAPTER NINE

TAYE made it to her bedroom door and raced in, hurriedly closing the door behind her. Magnus could not be serious, could he? Agitatedly she collapsed on to a chair, could not sit still, and got up again. He had looked serious, though, she recalled, her mouth dry.

Yes, but he had just received a bang to his head, argued that piece of her she would much prefer not to listen to. She recalled all the blood on his clothes, albeit that the wound was such a small one.

No, he could not have been serious, argued her saner self. Somehow or other he'd had an accident, collapsed dazed and confused on the garden path, and had still been dazed and confused when she had found him.

There was every likelihood, Taye decided, that once he had recovered—most probably any time now—Magnus would remember nothing of what had taken place in the garden or, for that matter, the kitchen.

She had just begun to wonder if she should go back and check that he was all right, when she heard sounds of him moving around. Her fears for him momentarily abated, she then heard the shower running.

Taye listened, fear rising again in case, still not quite himself, Magnus might slip in the shower while rinsing the blood off. But he was safe. A few minutes later the plumbing noises stopped, and a few minutes after that she heard him leave the bathroom.

She looked down at her own blood-splattered self and

considered a quick shower would be the easiest way of cleaning herself up.

Fifteen minutes later, dressed in a fresh tee shirt and jeans, Taye was in her room wondering what to do for the best. She knew she would have to face Magnus some time, and she wanted to see him—of course she did. But the more she thought about it, the more she began to believe that he must have seen her love for him. But it would be just too utterly humiliating should he refer to it, yet feel nothing for her himself.

Yet would he do that? He was far more sensitive than she had at first given him credit for. And anyway, hadn't she already judged that he would most likely not remember any of what had taken place either in the garden or in the kitchen?

That last thought, spurred on by her need to see him and get this over with, saw Taye leaving her bedroom. Still the same she hesitated at the sitting room door, and had to take a moment to get herself a little together before she went in.

Magnus was there, as she'd hoped—not hoped. He was standing with his eyes on the door, clearly waiting for her. She felt her colour rising and hated that tell-tale blush that gave away that just seeing him again affected her emotionally.

She decided to get in first. 'How's the head?' she asked, her eyes on the strip of plaster above his left eye, her words sounding uneven and jittery even to her own ears. Feeling still too strung up to be able to sit down, she went to stand at the back of an armchair.

Magnus studied her, seeming calm where she was all over the place. 'No kiss yet?' he enquired politely.

He might have been trying to relieve her tension, might have been trying to make her smile, but what he had done was to remind her—and she had not forgotten—that his last words to her had been, 'Got a kiss for your fiancé?'

'I—um—wasn't sure you knew what you were saying,' she responded cautiously. 'I—thought perhaps you wouldn't remember any of what happened—er—in the garden.'

'I remember everything,' Magnus replied steadily. And, his eyes watching her face, he added deliberately, 'And that includes falling out of the apple tree and—'

'You fell out of the apple tree?' she gasped, her eyes huge in her astonishment. 'What on earth were you doing...?' Her voice faded. 'You—didn't?' she questioned huskily, trying to deny what her brain was endeavouring to tell her.

'I had to,' Magnus took up, when she had no more to say but just stared at him speechlessly. 'It was only this morning that you stated, quite categorically, that you would only marry the man brave enough to climb that tree for that star.' Taye was still staring at him open-mouthed when he added, 'I wasn't leaving it there for some other man to collect for you.'

'You—climbed the tree for it? For m-me?' she stammered, her head in a whirl.

'For you,' he confirmed, and, dipping his hand into his trouser pocket, he withdrew the star that for the last seven or so months had rested, snagged, in the old apple tree. 'So you see, Taye, my very dear Taye,' he said quietly, coming over and handing the star to her, 'that even without your earlier acceptance of my proposal, you are in receipt of that token which makes you honourbound to marry me.' Her heart was thundering. She wanted to speak—but was powerless to find her voice. 'You'd agree, I hope?' Magnus insisted.

He was serious. He *was* serious! 'It would seem I have

very little choice—but to agree,' she answered, with what breath she could find.

'Sweet darling,' Magnus murmured tenderly, and at his tone, never mind the spine-melting endearment, her legs went to water. He made to come nearer, but Taye was in such a state of wanting to believe she had just agreed to marry him, and in such a state of not believing he could have asked her to marry him, that she took a step back. And he halted, his expression questioning.

'You—um—care about me a little—then?' Taye found she just had to ask. She needed to know. Oh, how she needed to know.

'Oh, I care about you, Taye Trafford,' he assured her. 'You, and thoughts of you, have filled my head since that first day I met you.'

'Oh!' she sighed, and was ready to melt completely—until ice-cold reasoning plugged in, switched on, and gave her a jolt. 'From day one?' she questioned—would she ever forget the surly brute he had been when they had first met?

'From day one,' Magnus confirmed, his eyes fixed on hers, the cooling of her tone not lost on him. 'I wouldn't lie to you over a thing like that.'

Taye stared at him, her mind in something of a major turmoil. 'Are you intimating that you have lied about other things?' she asked.

And Magnus expelled a sharp breath. 'One of the things that attracted me to you, and there are many, is your quick intelligence,' he said after a moment, and while Taye's heart raced to hear that many things about her attracted him he went on, 'So I suppose I can hardly complain that you're not going to meet me at the altar without me first giving you the answers to some of the questions that are likely to crop up.'

Taye watched him, and wanted quite desperately then to be held and kissed by him. But it sounded to her very much as if he was admitting that he had lied to her—and that was no basis for a marriage, was it?

'You lied to me?' she queried, finding, even though she was still wilting at the thought of meeting him at the altar, that she could not let it go. There had been lies in her parents' marriage—there would be no room for them in hers.

'I've tried not to,' Magnus answered carefully.

'But you have?'

He nodded. 'I've avoided having to lie wherever possible, but, the situation being what it was, I'm afraid there have been times when to lie has been unavoidable.'

Situation? What situation? Taye stared at him totally uncomprehending. 'You're the one with the bang on the head, right? So why do I feel as if I'm the one who's disorientated? I'm sorry, Magnus, but I cannot see any logical reason why you should lie to me.' She strove hard to see, but still could not. 'I mean, I know you're an artist and probably see things a little differently, perhaps. But—'

'I'm not an artist,' he cut in quietly. 'I want to be completely honest with you now, T—'

'You're *not* an artist?' she butted in, feeling winded. 'But—but you asked me to pose for you—in the nude!' she exclaimed, vividly remembering how that had come about. She had been naked in the bath...

'Oh, I knew in advance you'd say no,' Magnus interrupted, to save her further blushes.

Her amazement seemed to increase with every word he uttered. 'So, you're not an artist,' she itemised when she came up for air.

'I had to tell you something,' he owned up. 'And you'd

spotted paint on one of my fingers. To be an artist was the first thing that came to mind.'

She was still having difficulty taking this in. 'But you're not—yet you had to tell me something?' She looked at him sharply. 'So what is it you do do—if you don't mind me asking? You're not a bank robber or anything shady like that?'

'Nothing at all like that,' he reassured her. 'The opposite, if anything.' But, before going on, 'Look, Taye, I realise I have a lot to tell you, a lot of explaining to do,' he said. 'It—humph—could take a little while. Shall we sit down over there?' he said, indicating the sofa where only that morning they had lain together.

Taye was unsure. She somehow felt a need to keep her head, but, remembering Magnus's kisses, the kiss he was still waiting for from his fiancée—oh, heavens, fiancée—how was she to keep her head if he kissed her again? Aside from anything else, she did not know when, if ever, she would come down to earth again had his proposal that she marry him been for real. Yet, crazily, she somehow found she had started to believe that it had been for real. 'I don't know…' she demurred, even as she wanted to hear everything he had to say. But, looking over to the sofa, 'You won't try any of that—kissing stuff…?' His sudden smile made her break off. She guessed he knew what the kisses they shared did to her.

Magnus held out his hand. 'I promise I'll hold off from kissing you for as long as I'm able,' he agreed.

Taye was not very sure what sort of security she should read into that kind of a promise, but she loved the man and, after a moment, moved from behind the armchair and let him take her hand in his and lead her over to the sofa.

She quickly retrieved her hand once they were seated,

however, and began to think it about time she started asking a few questions. She had no idea what Magnus had meant by 'the situation being what it was' but, first things first, she thought she would like to know why he had lied about being an artist.

'So,' she turned to him to enquire, 'what sort of job do you do that is the opposite of robbing banks?'

'I endeavour to make them burglarproof,' he promptly answered. 'I run a company that specialises in high tech security systems for the home and overseas commercial sector.'

'You run it!' Taye exclaimed.

'Somebody has to,' he answered modestly.

And suddenly then the fact that his clothes looked expensive all at once took on a new meaning. 'I thought you were broke!' she said, wide-eyed. 'But you're not, are you?'

'Not,' he agreed.

'You're—quite—um—well-to-do?' she pressed.

'Quite,' he replied, watching her as she took in the information that the man she'd believed struggled as she did to find the rent was in actual fact quite financially sound, and then some, thank you very much.

Taye looked at him, not feeling in the least amused. 'Then would you mind very much telling me exactly what you are doing living here in rented accommodation?'

'A question I have frequently asked myself,' Magnus replied, which to her mind was no sort of an answer.

'And would I be right in assuming that not only can you very easily afford to pay the quarterly rent, but that you could probably afford to buy this flat if it came up for sale?'

'And the rest of the building,' Magnus informed her pleasantly.

Taye closed her mouth, barely knowing when it had fallen open in shock. To be able to buy the whole of the building would make him some kind of millionaire!

She swallowed. 'You're joking, right?'

'Not joking,' he replied seriously, and stayed serious to ask quickly, 'You're still going to marry me?'

Her heart gave one of its giddy leaps, and she tried desperately to keep her feet planted firmly on the ground. 'I think it's high time, Mr Ashthorpe…' Her voice tailed off, something in his expression, that silent Oh his wonderful mouth formed, alerting her to perhaps another lie. 'What?' she asked.

'Hmm—Ashthorpe is my middle name,' Magnus replied.

'Ashthorpe is—' She broke off, stupefied. 'You're not Magnus Ash… Mr Ashthorpe?'

'I'm afraid not.'

Taye took a shaky breath. 'Then I suggest, Mr Who-ever-you-are…that you start talking,' she told him severely. She would much prefer that he took her in his arms. But it seemed to her—and confused wasn't the word for how she felt—that a lot had been going on here. And if they were to have any sort of a life together—her heart raced again at how wonderful that sounded—then that could only happen, for her anyway, from an open and truthful basis. And, by his own admission, Magnus had not shirked from lying to her.

Magnus looked at her, stretched out a hand and tenderly stroked a strand of white-blonde hair back from her face, and, while her heart did a giddy flip again at his tender gesture, 'I came here that first day…'

'Nick-Mick Knight didn't ask you to leave his flat, did he?' she butted in.

'He did not.'

'His girlfriend wasn't moving in with him?'

'I don't know that she exists.'

'You invented her?' Magnus nodded. 'And him?' Taye asked, and, sensing she was right, 'Is there any such person as Nick Knight?'

'Most likely. Though I've never come across him,' he admitted.

Taye looked at Magnus, her brain racing in competition with her heartbeats. 'So—if you weren't living at Nick Knight's address prior to moving in here, where were you living?'

'I have my own place,' Magnus replied, ready to at once answer her every question, it seemed.

'Then why…?'

'Why move in here?' Magnus took her next question. 'Well, for one—and for several—other matters had arrived to take precedence over the extended holiday I'd planned to take while my house was being redecorated throughout.'

Taye saw what he meant by for one—and for several. By the sound of it Magnus had a house and had booked decorators to do his place up while he went on holiday. Only something else had happened, arrived, to make him cancel his holiday. And, since he had probably waited some while to get a good firm of decorators to give him a start date, he had decided not to cancel the decorators.

'You decided, rather than put the decorators off, that you would rent for a short while?' Taye enquired, and, bridling suddenly, 'And you had the nerve to get umpty with me when I told you I would have to find somewhere smaller, cheaper to live, when you had no intention of staying yourse—'

'I had every intention then, as now, of continuing to live with you, and still do,' Magnus broke in, well and truly taking the wind from her sails.

'Oh,' she murmured, feeling just a tinge pink, though with the way her heart was misbehaving not at all surprised. 'You—um—didn't fancy going to a hotel while the decorators were in? Or to your mother's? Or—' as that demon green-eyed monster nipped '—your friend Elspeth?' Taye asked.

Magnus smiled, quite liking her shade of green, it seemed, though his expression was serious when, like balm over a deep wound, he informed her, 'Elspeth, is my sister.' His sister! 'She is going through an extremely difficult time right now.'

'Oh, I'm so sorry!' Taye was instantly apologetic. But, not wanting to pry into what was clearly a family matter, and particularly not wanting to say a word about Elspeth that would indicate how many times jealousy had swamped her, Taye went in another direction, 'So you saw the card advertising half a flat to let here, and—' Magnus shaking his head caused her to break off.

'I didn't see that card until after I'd left here that Saturday,' he said.

'You—didn't?' Bewildered wasn't the word for it! 'But how did you know there was a flat-share available?'

'I didn't know. In fact it wasn't until I had let myself in through the main door and, just in case the present occupant was in some state of *déshabillé,* had knocked on the door instead of coming straight in, that—'

'Just a minute!' she interrupted him quickly. 'Are you saying that you had a set of keys *before* I gave you a set?'

Magnus smiled at her. 'Are you sure you wouldn't like me to kiss you?' he asked.

Oh, stop it, stop it, stop it! Didn't he know how pathetically weak she was where he was concerned? 'I'm sure,' she lied—lying wasn't his sole prerogative. 'You already had a set of keys.' She managed to remember what they had been talking about. 'How?' she asked. 'Did Paula give them to you? I didn't think you knew her? You—'

'I don't know her,' he replied. And, solemnly then, he said, 'But I know her man-friend.'

Taye looked questioningly at him. 'You know Graeme?'

'He was married to Elspeth,' Magnus informed her quietly.

'He—he was married to your sister?' Startled to hear that, Taye thought for a moment. 'That would be before they divorced and he started going out with Paula?' It was the only thing that seemed to fit.

'My sister and Graeme Lockwood were never divorced,' Magnus revealed. 'Graeme was still married, and living with Elspeth, at the same time he was having an affair with Paula Neale.'

Taye was dumbstruck. 'They were still together while...?'

'Happily together, as far as Elspeth was concerned.'

'She had no idea that he...?' Words failed her.

'Not the smallest idea. She still doesn't know,' Magnus said. 'I intend to keep it that way.'

'You don't think Graeme will confess at—'

'Graeme's dead,' Magnus bluntly stated. And, at Taye's look of shock, for all she had never met his brother-in-law, 'He was killed in a motor accident,' Magnus said. 'He worked for me and—'

'He worked for you?' Taye exclaimed. Then something suddenly clicked in her brain and she was glad to find that the memory part of her brain was not as totally stupefied as she herself felt. 'Hadn't Graeme worked for a security equipment company? At Penhaligon's?' she questioned. Penhaligon's was a massive firm, so that part of it did not take too much memory retrieval to recall. But then something else struck her and she took a deep if shaky breath. 'If you're not Ashthorpe—well, you are, in the middle, but—pardon me if I sound muddled; I thought I was confused before but...' She swallowed. 'Tell me you're not Penhaligon at the end?'

Magnus looked a shade uncomfortable, she thought, but manfully owned, 'I am,' and while she stared at him dumbfounded he found a gentle smile for her and nicely offered, 'But I can change it if you don't fancy the name Mrs Penhaligon.'

'Stop!' Taye implored him. 'I feel in one totally bewildered maze from what you've told me so far without having to cope with the fact that you must be some kind of multimillionaire—who could eat at Claridges every day if you wished, and lodge at the finest of hotels, yet have chosen to live in this abode—' She broke off, not certain she wanted him to know how the fact he seemed to want to make her Mrs Penhaligon was affecting her. 'C-can we please concentrate on just one particular issue?' she asked shakily.

'Sweet love, anything you say,' Magnus answered, his eyes tender on her all-at-sea expression.

'You said Graeme worked for you.' She plucked that out from a head racing with But whys.

'He did,' Magnus took up. 'He was good at his job too. Elspeth at one time worked for the firm also. It was how they met. And though she still popped in to the firm from time to time, she thought it politic to resign when they married. But when Graeme died she was absolutely distraught—so distraught, in fact, that when she found what was obviously a desk drawer key amongst his belongings she just could not face going to his office to pick up his personal effects.'

'I can understand that,' Taye put in quietly, and received a warm smile from the man sitting next to her.

'I insisted that she didn't have to, that I would do it.'

'It was how you found out that he was having an affair?' she guessed. 'A letter or something…'

'A lease to this apartment, actually,' Magnus corrected her. 'And with it a set of keys.'

'A—lease? Paula's lease?' Taye stated that which her startled intelligence had brought her.

'The lease was in Graeme's name.'

'Oh!' Taye exclaimed, but after a moment or two recovered to ask, 'You began to suspect…?'

'For sure I didn't want to tell Elspeth what I had found until I'd made damned sure she knew nothing of it. She was and still is having difficulty in coming to terms with the fact her dear love will not be coming home any more. It would devastate her should she learn, as I began to realise, that he had some little love-nest tucked away somewhere.'

'The mud is starting to become a little clearer,' Taye murmured. 'You decided to come and investigate?'

'Too true! I was not,' he thought to mention, 'feeling at my sunniest that morning we met.'

'Funnily enough, I did notice.'

'I didn't know then that you weren't the one Graeme had been carrying on with. Are you sure I can't kiss you?'

Her heart fluttered. 'You were saying?'

'I shall make up for it later,' he threatened. 'Please. So there was I,' he resumed, 'without the first idea of Graeme's mistress's name, knocking on the door ready to tell whoever answered that I'd been to the agents, taken over the lease pro tem, and was throwing her out.'

'You've taken over the lease?' Taye gasped, open mouthed. 'But I—but all that—about me being a sub-let—about you… And all the time…'

'I know,' he acknowledged gently. 'I didn't want any comeback on Elspeth, so needed the matter dealt with properly. Which meant I gave the agents a quarter's notice to terminate the tenancy and paid the coming quarter's rent. But I couldn't tell you any of that. Not then. And later, well…' Magnus left it there and went speedily on. 'Anyhow, there was I, incensed on my sister's behalf, and more than ready to sort out the trollop who answered the door.' Trollop! 'Then, to thoroughly deflate me, this beautiful woman with the most gorgeous blue eyes opens the door…'

'Me?' Taye asked faintly, on the instant ready to forgive him the 'trollop' remark.

'You, my darling,' Magnus replied.

'Oh,' she sighed. But, remembering how it had been, 'You didn't look as if you thought me—um—beautiful,' she reminded him.

'I was having to cope with several matters all at once,' he explained. '"You've come about the flat," you said. Well, I rather supposed I had. But by then I'm trying to ignore how taken I am by your beauty, and endeavouring to get to grips with the fact that no sooner is your provider dead than his money-grubbing lover is trying to rent out half of the flat.'

'You thought…?'

'Forget what I thought then—I soon discovered that you were as beautiful inside as you were on the outside.'

Taye drew a sharp breath. 'Carry on like that Mr Ash...Penhaligon, and I shall start to melt,' she murmured, and, regardless, was tenderly kissed.

'Sorry,' he apologised, not looking at all sorry. 'I just had to do that. So...' he continued. 'Um...' he went on, as if trying to remember. 'There was I, more interested in saving Elspeth from hurting any more than she was already hurting, while knowing that I can throw this Taye Trafford out any time I choose.'

'Too kind,' Taye murmured, but said it with a smile— and risked being on the receiving end of another kiss.

Magnus managed to hold down the impulse, however, the sooner to get it all said. 'Before I did that, though, I first of all needed to discover if this woman had any power to make problems for my sister. Elspeth was particularly fragile just then. I, my love, was without anywhere to comfortably lay my head. I particularly wanted to keep out of my mother's way, and to go to a hotel had no appeal; although I did find myself using that option several times when I needed to put some space between you and me and—'

'That weekend? Those nights away? They were...?'

'On account of you, Miss Trafford. You,' he said softly, 'were getting to me big-time.'

'Good heavens,' she whispered huskily, and had to fight hard against the almost overwhelming urge to return his compliment and tenderly kiss him. 'So?' she found a moment of restraint to question instead.

'So it seemed to me that since, with the decorators in, I had no home to go to, I might as well stay and be your sub-tenant when, by living in the same dwelling, I'd be well placed to find out more about you and what more trouble and grief, if any, you were likely to cause for Elspeth. You wanted references—as soon as I hit the pavement I was on the phone to my mother, asking her, should you ring, to give me a splendid reference.'

'That lady—um—Mrs Sturgess—is your mother? The lady I spoke with, who said she had been at school with your mother, *was* your mother?' Was there no end to the shocks she was receiving? Taye wondered.

'She's incorrigible—a dear, and a woman who loves a bit of intrigue.'

'Is that why you wanted to keep out of her way?'

'Precisely. Graeme was killed the day before I was scheduled to fly to the Bahamas. I cancelled my holiday to be there for Elspeth and subsequently sort out the muddle of his affairs—no pun intended. My mother knew my place was awash with decorators, so I hoped she'd believe I was renting some place meanwhile, and under the name of Ashthorpe because I wanted to keep a low profile.'

'Your mother swallowed that?'

'Not the Ashthorpe bit; but I knew she would back me to the hilt. Though, knowing her mammoth curiosity to get to the root of everything, I had to limit our communications to the telephone—she would have been extremely upset on Elspeth's behalf had I told her the truth. But in any event she has been fairly preoccupied in supporting Elspeth as much as she can.'

'Of course,' Taye sympathised, but, after a moment or two, 'So you moved in here...?'

'Not before I'd walked around and found a newsagent with a card in his window advertising half this flat for rent.'

'You stole that card,' she documented.

'Quite easily done,' he owned, totally unblinking.

'And, yes, I moved in—and promptly had all my theories about Graeme Lockwood's mistress go sailing out the window.'

'You discovered I—'

'Before I moved in I discovered you were nowhere near as money-grubbing as I assumed. I knew by then that the rent to the start of the June quarter had been paid by Graeme. Yet when you could have asked me for two weeks' rent up to then, you didn't. Another surprise was the fact that the quarter's rent you asked for was a straight split down the middle. And, if that wasn't enough to have me rethinking my prior opinions of you, there was your sensitivity when you obviously felt awkward about prying into my relationships.'

'You were still being a—a grouch, though,' she reminded him.

'Why wouldn't I be? Elspeth was heartbroken, but you were so un-grief-stricken that you were soon dating someone else.'

'Julian?'

'The same,' he agreed. 'It soon became very clear that you must have been two-timing Graeme. So there am I, trying to learn as much as I can about you, trying to gauge what sort of a threat you represent to my sister's already fractured peace of mind—while at the same time I'm starting to be at war with myself in that I find I'm struggling not to like you.'

'You liked me—early on?' she fished, loving him so much, wanting to know his every thought, his every emotion.

'How could I help it?' he asked simply. 'In between going to check how the decorators are doing, looking in on the office, and keeping in contact with Elspeth, I find I'm not caring very much for you dating your pal Julian

Coombs. Is it any wonder I had to take myself off to a hotel to sort myself out?'

Her eyes were big and shining as she quietly asked, 'Did you really take your washing to your mother last Saturday?'

'She'd have told me what to do with it if I had,' he said with a smile. 'Though in actual fact it was my original intention to stay away for the weekend. Only…'

'Only?' Taye prompted when he seemed hesitant to continue.

'Only I found I couldn't settle and that nothing would do but that I check out of that hotel and come home.'

'Home?'

'Home—to you,' he answered. 'Crazy, I know. Even though I was sure you wouldn't be here—you had mentioned some party invitation—I just had to come back to you.' He paused then, and, looking levelly at her, stated, 'On Sunday morning I knew exactly why.'

Taye's heart began thundering in her chest at his look; she sensed that something pretty staggering was coming. 'Sunday morning?' she asked, her voice barely above a whisper.

'I said I'd take you out to lunch,' he reminded her. 'And you bounced my invitation back at me.'

'You'll make me blush. I thought then that you couldn't afford it.'

'Sweet darling,' he said softly. 'That was when it happened,' he murmured, his eyes adoring on her face.

'What—happened?' she asked chokily, her bones turning to liquid just from his look.

'You being you. You, when I knew full well that you were as broke as makes no difference, refusing my offer but saying you would take me for a pie and a pint. Sweet love, I knew then what it was that had been battering away at the brick wall I had tried to erect from our very first meeting.' He looked deeply, tenderly into her eyes, and softly he told her, 'My darling Taye, I knew then, accepted then, that I was in love with you with my whole heart.'

'Magnus!' There was a roaring in her ears as his name left her on a breath of sound.

'That's all right with you?' he asked.

Taye found her voice. 'More than all right,' she whispered.

He smiled, seeming relieved. 'And you? How do you feel about me?'

'I knew on Sunday too,' she answered shyly.

'What?' He seemed tense all at once.

'Last Sunday, when you borrowed a car—' She broke off. '*Did* you borrow that car?' she asked.

He shook his head. 'It belongs to me,' he admitted. 'Go on,' he urged, more interested in how she felt about him than the ownership of the vehicle. 'Last Sunday?' he prompted.

'Last Sunday,' she dutifully took up, 'you were so good, so kind, and I just knew, when I came to you in the garden of my mother's home, what all the jealousy and the mixture of other emotions that have bombarded me over you were all about. I,' she said softly, 'just loved and loved you.'

'Oh, Taye!' he breathed, and, whether all his lies had been explained or whether they had not, he just had to haul her joyously into his arms and hold her. 'Dear love, you're sure?' he asked.

'It's just there. For real. I can't help it. I just love you—am in love with you—and...'

'And you can't begin to know how relieved it makes

me to hear you say that. Sweetheart…' he murmured, and all was silent for long minutes as he just had to kiss her.

And Taye just had to kiss him back, and for uncounted minutes they kissed and held each other, Magnus pulling back from time to time to look into her face, to feast his eyes on the love he saw there.

'One way and another that was one very memorable Sunday,' he said after some while.

'As it happens,' she said on a sigh, 'everything has turned out wonderfully. For us, and for Hadleigh.'

'It would have been fine for Hadleigh without your father coming to the rescue,' Magnus commented, as if it was by the way. But, at her enquiring look, 'I couldn't tell you my plan before I had confessed all my lies to you, my darling, but my idea was to financially back Hadleigh through university and—'

'He wouldn't have taken your money,' Taye interrupted. 'He's proud and…'

'I know that,' Magnus said with a smile. 'Which is why I thought I'd make a binding agreement with him that in return for Penhaligon's sponsoring him he, at the end of his studies, would enter our graduate scheme and work for a two-year term at Penhaligon Security.'

Taye stared at him in love and amazement. 'You planned…? You had this up your sleeve the whole…?'

'I couldn't tell Hadleigh then. But I knew I would have to tell you everything before too long; then I could tell your brother…'

'You were going to tell me soon?'

'Dammit, woman, I'm in love with you,' Magnus growled. 'It *had* to be soon. I couldn't hold off much longer. I want to marry you. I *need* to marry you. It's got so bad just lately,' he confessed, 'that I haven't trusted myself in the same room with you. I've sometimes had to go out, make myself stay away from here, for fear I might give in and take you in my arms.'

'Oh, Magnus. Honestly?'

'The truth only from now on, my love.'

'Only the truth from now on,' she agreed, her heart still having a high old time within her. 'Er—why…?' she began, but just had to kiss him, and be kissed for her trouble.

'Why…?' Magnus was marginally the first to recover.

'Why—um—when I told you it was Paula who had been Graeme's girlfriend, when you knew it wasn't me that might hurt Elspeth, why did you stay on here? I mean, I can appreciate with you not knowing me all that well that you wouldn't want to confide about your sister and everything, but you continued to live here—to let me live here.'

Magnus cupped the side of her face with one hand and revealed, 'While I may have realised that I'd moved in for nothing, I still didn't have anywhere else I wanted to be.' He gave a self-deprecating shrug. 'Of course I told myself that I might as well live here as anywhere until the decorators had finished. But…'

'But?'

'But the plain truth is it began to feel right coming home to you. It began to feel right being here when you came home.' He gave that self-deprecating shrug again as he confessed, 'Then I kissed you—and while every scrap of common sense was telling me to pack up and leave, right then, I was somehow finding that love—what I now know is love—and common sense just don't mix.'

Taye smiled, her smile becoming a beam—and Magnus looked at her and, his heart full of love for her, he groaned and just had to gather her to him and hold her close.

'Love me?' he asked.

'You know I do.'

'So say it,' he growled.

And, while it amazed her that a man as confident as he should need reassurance that she loved him, 'I love you, love you, love you,' she lovingly obliged. Then asked, 'Who was Penny?'

'Penny?' He pulled back, a touch mystified.

'You answered the phone—that day I rang your mobile. It had been engaged the first time I tried. So I realised when you answered the phone with her name that you must have just been speaking to her and thought she had rung back. You said "Pen and—"' She broke off at his grin.

'Pen,' he said, 'is short for Penhaligon. I instinctively went to answer the phone "Penhaligon" but, having been waiting for your call, nearly blew my whole plot.' He did not have to say any more.

'Well, I shan't have to be jealous of her any more,' Taye commented.

'Fair's only fair,' he countered. 'I was not at all happy whenever I thought of you and Coombs together—only to get eaten alive by that green stuff when you take up with Fraser!'

'I only went out with him because you accused me of being jealous.'

'Little love,' he breathed, and held her close up against him for long, long, comforting, loving seconds.

Being in his arms was utter bliss; being held by him sublime. 'There was a letter for an M. A. Penhaligon,' she murmured dreamily.

'Blundering agents,' he muttered. 'I gave specific instructions not to send any communications to me here, but to use my office address. And what do they do when they decide to send a receipt for the cheque I gave them…?'

'My cheque?'

He shook his head. 'The quarter's rent was already paid by then. I'm keeping your cheque as a souvenir. Everybody was trying to blow my cover,' he informed her lightly.

She pulled back to look at him. 'They were—' She broke off. 'Damien Fraser thought he knew you from somewhere!' she exclaimed.

'As did your father. I can only assume they both must take the financial newspapers. There's a photo of me they trot out whenever anything newsworthy in the financial area crops up—as happened recently. As luck would have it neither your father nor Fraser associated Magnus Ashthorpe with Magnus Penhaligon.'

'Beware your sins will find you out,' she teased him. 'That's what you risk when you start telling lies.'

'I'll never lie to you again,' Magnus uttered, a sincerity there that melted her heart.

'Love me?' she asked, finding, as he had, that, trust him though she did, she still needed to hear him say it.

'So much,' he responded. 'I love you so much nothing else matters but that you are in my life.'

'Oh, Magnus,' she sighed, and kissed him, and was kissed in return. Her face was a tinge pink as they pulled back and looked into each other's eyes. 'This morning, and before, when to kiss and—make love with you seemed so right,' she began shyly, 'I needed to hear you say you loved me, that it wasn't just some meaningless affair that would end with one of us leaving.'

'Oh, my dearest darling,' he breathed. 'I loved you then and I love you now. And we'll leave together.'

'We—will?' she asked huskily.

'I want you with me always,' he told her tenderly. 'I've a home just waiting for you. Please say you'll come and be my house-mate—my wife?'

'You truly want to marry me?' she whispered.

'I'll settle for nothing less,' Magnus replied, his eyes never leaving her face. 'Please, my beautiful Taye, let me hear you say you will.'

Taye smiled at him, her heart full to bursting. 'Oh, Magnus. I will. I love you so, I can't think of anything or anyone I'd rather be than Mrs Magnus Ashthorpe—Penhaligon.'

'Darling!' he cried triumphantly, and gathered her close up to him once more.

# BETROTHED FOR
## THE BABY
### KATHIE DENOSKY

**Kathie DeNosky** lives in her native southern Illinois with her husband and one very spoiled Jack Russell terrier. She writes highly sensual stories with a generous amount of humour. Kathie's books have appeared on the Waldenbooks bestseller list and received the Write Touch Readers' Award from WisRWA and the National Readers' Choice Award. Kathie enjoys going to rodeos, travelling to research setting for her books and listening to country music. Readers may contact Kathie at: P.O. Box 2064, Herrin, Illinois 62948-5264, USA or e-mail her at Kathie@kathiedenosky.com.

This book is dedicated to my editor, Tina Colombo. Thank you for your unwavering support and encouragement. You're the very best. And a special thank you to my son, Bryan, for his help with the Spanish in this book.

*Te amo, mi hijo.*

# One

When Hunter O'Banyon glanced over at the pretty little blonde he'd met only moments ago, adrenaline began to pump through his veins. Her porcelain cheeks were flushed with a mixture of heat and excitement, and he could tell from the sparkle of urgency in her violet eyes that he was in for one hell of a ride.

"I hope you don't mind, but this is going to have to be faster than I'd planned," she said, sounding a little breathless.

Grinning, he nodded. "Bring it on. I can take it as fast as you want to go."

"I like the way you think." Her smile caused his

heart to race like a twelve-stroke engine hitting on all cylinders. "Hang on, big guy. This might get a little wild."

Hunter took a deep breath and braced himself. "Burn it, darlin'."

At the same time as she pushed the gas pedal all the way to the floor, she reached out to flip a switch on the dash. Lights and the keening wail of a siren competed with the sound of spinning tires kicking up a huge cloud of gravel and southwest Texas dust as the pickup truck careened away from the tarmac at Devil's Fork Community Airfield.

When Hunter had discovered there was no commercial air service to the little town, he'd wondered why the pilot of the Cessna Skyhawk he'd chartered to fly him to Devil's Fork from El Paso had laughed like a hyena when Hunter had called it an airport. Now he knew why. The entire thing consisted of an asphalt landing strip that he'd bet barely met FAA standards, a storage shed that leaned precariously to one side and a wooden pole with a tattered wind sock attached to the top just above the United States and Texas flags. As far as he could tell, there weren't even any lights for landing at night. He could only hope the Life Medevac operation looked better.

"By the way, I'm Callie Marshall, the flight nurse on the Evac II team," the blonde said conversationally.

Nice name for a nice-looking woman, he thought

as they approached the edge of town. "I'm Hunter O'Banyon."

"Thank God." She grinned. "When my pager went off, I didn't give you time to introduce yourself, and it suddenly occurred to me that you might not be the man I was supposed to meet."

His heart stalled and he had to clear his suddenly dry throat. When she smiled, Callie Marshall wasn't just pretty, she was drop-dead gorgeous.

"What were the chances of anyone else flying into Devil's Fork?" he asked when he finally got his vocal cords to work.

Her delightful laughter was one of the nicest sounds he'd heard in a long time. "Good point," she said, nodding. "I think you're the first person I've heard of flying into Devil's Fork since I arrived two months ago."

"Somehow that doesn't surprise me." He tightened his safety harness when she turned a corner, seemingly on two wheels. "Did you arrive by plane?"

"No way." She shook her head, causing her ponytail to sway back and forth. "I drove over from Houston. I wasn't about to take one of those puddle-jumper flights in here."

As they sped down Main Street, Hunter decided that if he'd blinked, he might have missed the entire town. Besides the fact that Callie was going so fast it wasn't much more than a blur, the business district was only a few blocks long and there wasn't much more than two or three blocks to the residential section.

"Mary Lou, our dispatcher, said you're from the Miami area. It might take a while for you to get used to Devil's Fork. It's about six hundred miles from the nearest beach and not exactly a hotbed of social activity."

"No kidding." He cringed when they sailed through a four-way stop on the opposite end of town without so much as slowing down. "I knew this place was small, but I expected something a little bigger than this."

"I did, too," she agreed. "After I drove through it the first time, I had a hard time believing there was enough of a call for a medevac operation to be based here. But I was wrong."

Hunter thought back to what he'd read in the file he'd been handed on the business his grandmother had given him to run. "The way I understand it, we're the only emergency service available for sections of five different counties."

She nodded. "The population is so sparse in this part of Texas, it isn't cost-effective for communities to have their own ambulance." Shrugging, she steered the truck onto a dirt-packed road leading up to a large aircraft hangar with Life Medevac Helicopter Service painted on the side. "Besides, if they had a ground unit, it would take too long to reach most of the people and even longer to get them to a hospital. We're their best hope for emergency medical care."

When she drove the truck around the side of the building, Hunter breathed a little easier. The Life Medevac base appeared to be in much better condition than the Devil's Fork airfield. Besides the well-kept hangar, there were two brand-new, top-of-the-line Bell EMS helicopters sitting on brightly painted helipads, and the entire area was ringed with what looked to be state-of-the-art lighting for night takeoffs and landings.

"I'll see you when we get back," she said, jamming the gearshift into Park at the same time she killed the engine and threw open the driver's door. "I have a flight to catch."

"Thanks for the ride," Hunter called, getting out of the truck.

Turning, she gave him another one of her killer smiles. "I almost forgot to tell you—beware of Mary Lou's coffee. She'll tell you it's the best you've ever had, but don't believe it." She grimaced. "It's awful."

As he stood there staring at Callie slowly jogging toward the waiting helicopter, he couldn't put his finger on what it was about her, but something bothered him. Aside from the fact that she'd driven the truck through town as though the hounds of hell were chasing them and she now moved as if she had all the time in the world, there was something about the snug way her navy-blue flight suit fit her around the middle that didn't seem quite right.

But when she disappeared inside the cabin space of the chopper and the door slid shut behind her, he quickly dismissed his concerns as Evac II lifted off the helipad. Although Emerald Larson had assured him that she'd seen to it that all the equipment was up-to-date and exceeded state requirements, he intended to order new flight suits in a color that could be more easily differentiated from other first responders that might be on scene when the Life Medevac crews arrived. And he'd make sure everyone wore the right size.

"You must be Hunter O'Banyon, the new boss of this outfit."

At the sound of the female voice behind him, Hunter turned to face a woman he'd judge to be somewhere in her late sixties or early seventies. With curly snow-white hair, a perfectly round face and a pair of narrow reading glasses perched on her nose, she looked as if she could easily play Mrs. Claus in a Christmas pageant.

He smiled as he extended his hand. "That would be me. And you must be Mary Lou Carson."

"The one and only." Grinning, she firmly shook his hand. "Come on in the dispatch room and rest a spell. I'll pour you a cup of the best coffee you've ever had, then I'll show you your quarters."

Reaching into the bed of the pickup truck, Hunter grabbed his luggage and followed Mary Lou out of the late-August heat and into the air-conditioned office of the hangar. When she led him into the dispatch room, he looked around at the framed military medals hanging on the wall beside the door.

"Did these belong to your husband?" he asked conversationally.

"Some of them." Mary Lou walked over to a small kitchen area on the opposite side of the room to stir the delicious-smelling contents of a huge pot on the electric range. "The rest are mine."

When she walked back over to where he stood, she handed him a cup of coffee, then motioned for him to sit in one of several chairs on the opposite side of a scarred wooden desk. "Take a load off, Hunter."

"What branch of the military were you in?" he asked, sitting down.

"Lester and I were both career Navy." She walked between the desk and a built-in counter filled with radio equipment, a computer and several telephones to settle herself into an old wooden desk chair that looked as if it might have been around since World War II. "He was an aircraft mechanic and I was a nurse. He died in an accident onboard an aircraft carrier not long before we were supposed to retire."

"I'm sorry." Hunter knew all too well what it was like to lose someone unexpectedly.

"Don't be sorry," she said, surprising him. "Lester died doing what he loved most—working on fighter jets. That's the best way any of us can hope to go out of this world." Before he could respond, she shrugged. "That's why I'm a dispatcher here. After my arthritis forced me to stop working the floor in a hospital, I took this job. When people call with an emergency, I sometimes stay on the line and talk them through whatever medical crisis they have until one of our crews arrives. It's almost as satisfying as nursing."

Hunter took a sip of coffee as he considered what Mary Lou said. But as the bitter taste spread over his tongue, he had to force himself to swallow. Quickly setting the cup on the desk, he barely controlled the urge to shudder. What Callie had told him about the coffee being awful had been an understatement. The stuff was as thick as syrup and tasted as though it had been made with quinine.

Coughing, he looked up to see Mary Lou watching him expectantly. He could tell she was waiting for him to tell her how good it was.

"You like your coffee strong, don't you?" he asked, trying not to grimace.

She shrugged. "I like my coffee to be just the way I like a man—strong and the best I've ever had."

If he'd thought her coffee was enough to send his system into shock, her outspokenness finished the job. He couldn't have been more dumbfounded if he'd tried. Unable to think of a thing to say, he waited to see what she'd say next. Unless he'd misjudged her, that shouldn't take very long.

Her knowing smile clued him in on the fact that she'd known her statement would render him speechless. "There's a few things about me you might as well know up front, Hunt. I don't mince words. I say exactly what I think because I'm old enough to get away with it and I've never been one to beat around the bush."

"I can respect that." Hunter had no idea where Mary Lou was going with this, but he could tell she had more on her mind.

"I'm glad to hear you say that, because what I'm going to tell you now might not set real well."

"I'm listening."

"I'm going to treat you like I treat everyone else around here because I'm not impressed by much of anything anymore. And that includes you being Emerald Larson's grandson."

Hunter frowned. He'd specifically asked Emerald not to divulge his relationship to her. For one thing, he didn't need the added pressure of living up to someone's expectations. And for another, he still hadn't fully come to terms with being her grandson.

"How did you learn about—"

"Emerald and I go way back. She hasn't always been on the top of the heap. When she was a teenager, she worked behind the soda counter in my father's drugstore." Mary Lou grinned. "She was like an older sister to me, and we've stayed in touch over the years."

Hunter wasn't particularly happy about having one of Emerald's lifelong friends working for him. He didn't like the idea of not being able to make a move without his manipulative grandmother knowing about it.

"If you're worried about me running to Emerald to report everything you do, don't waste your time," Mary Lou said as though she'd read his mind. "I don't carry tales. If she wants to know what's going on with you, she'll have to ask you herself."

"That's good to hear." Whether he should or not, Hunter believed the woman.

Draining the last of her coffee, Mary Lou placed her cup on the desk and stood up. "Now that we have that out of the way, I'll show you to your living quarters and let you get settled in while I finish up the beef stew I put on for our supper." She pointed to his cup. "Would you like that warmed up?"

He quickly shook his head. "I'm not much of a coffee drinker." He didn't want to hurt her feelings, but if he never drank another drop of the bitter brew, it would be all too soon.

She shook her head. "I don't know what's wrong with you young people. I'm the only one working here who likes coffee."

As Hunter grabbed his suitcase and followed her through a doorway and down a hall toward the back of the hangar, he suspected the others' reluctance to drink Mary Lou's coffee had everything in the world to do with self-defense and nothing to do with not liking coffee.

"This is your office," she said, passing a door on the way to the back of the building. Pointing to a door across the hall, she added, "And this is the on-duty crew's sleeping quarters. We have three crews working rotating twenty-four-hour shifts—two days on duty and four off. Of course, on the outside chance that we get a call while one crew is out, the first two days that a crew is off duty, they're on call."

"What about you? What are your hours?"

"I'm here round the clock. When I'm not dispatching a crew, I'm cooking and handing out advice that nobody seems to listen to." She laughed as she pointed to a door next to the crew quarters. "This is my room. I have a ringer in here that wakes me up when we have a night call or I decide to take a nap."

Hunter frowned. "Who's the dispatcher on your days off?"

She continued walking toward a door at the end of the hall. "On the rare occasions that I take a day off, one of the members of the off-duty crew fills in for me."

"You don't have regularly scheduled time off?" He didn't like the sound of that. Aside from Emerald taking advantage of Mary Lou, he wasn't sure that it was even legal for the woman to be working that much.

"Don't get your shorts in a bunch, Hunter," Mary Lou said as if she'd read his mind. "I don't have family, and working here at Life Medevac is what makes me happy and keeps me going. I love what I do, so don't go getting any ideas about making me take time off on a regular basis, because I won't do it." She opened the door to his room, then, stepping back, pointed to his luggage. "Are all your things in that one suitcase?"

He nodded. "I stored the rest of my things until I find a place in Devil's Fork."

"Good idea." The woman nodded her approval. "Now go ahead and get your gear stowed away while I radio Evac II and find out the status of their patient and what time they estimate they'll get back to base."

Hunter stared after Mary Lou as she breezed out the door and down the hall as if her working without regular days off was a nonissue. But he wasn't so sure. It wasn't just a question of the labor laws. Her age and well-being had to be taken into consideration, as well. She might seem like a dynamo with boundless energy, but working 24-7 would be hard on a much younger person, let alone a woman close to seventy.

As he lifted his suitcase and placed it on the edge of the bed to unpack, he decided there were several things he needed to do right away. Not only did he need to order the correct size flight suits for everyone, he'd have to check into Texas labor laws.

Putting away the last of his clothes, he looked around. It was a good thing he always traveled light. The room was barely big enough for the twin bed, small chest of drawers and bedside table. There was no way he'd have had room for anything but his clothes.

But then, he didn't need a lot of room. For the past five years he hadn't cared how spacious his accommodations had been or even where they'd been located. After working construction so hard each day that he'd been too tired to think or remember, all he'd needed was a place to sleep, shower and change clothes. With any luck, there would be enough work to keep him just as busy at Life Medevac.

At the sound of a helicopter landing outside, he walked down the hall to the dispatch room. "They weren't gone long."

Mary Lou nodded. "Juanita Rodriguez thought she was going to have her baby, but it turned out to be false labor." Smiling, she added, "She's only nineteen and it's her first pregnancy. She and her husband, Miguel, are worried they won't make it to the hospital in time."

"I hear that's a big concern for most first-time parents." A twinge of regret ran through Hunter. Anticipating the arrival of a child was something he would never experience.

But he didn't have time to dwell on the disturbing thought as the flight crew from Evac II entered the dispatch room. Besides Callie, the crew consisted of a sandy-haired man who looked to be in his forties and a fresh-faced kid of about twenty.

"The name's George Smith," the man said, smiling

as he walked over to shake Hunter's hand. Almost as tall as Hunter's own six-foot-three-inch frame, George was built like a heavyweight prizefighter, and if his grip was any indication, as strong as one. "I'm the pilot for the Evac II team." He nodded toward the younger man. "And that kid over there is Corey Timmons, the EMT on our crew."

"It's nice to meet you, Mr. O'Banyon," Corey said, stepping forward to pump Hunter's hand enthusiastically. "We've been looking forward to you taking over."

"Call me Hunter." He wasn't surprised to hear the employees had been looking forward to a change in administration. From the file he'd been given, when Emerald bought Life Medevac, the employees hadn't been paid their wages in several weeks.

Grinning, the young man's brown eyes danced mischievously. "We're glad to see you survived the drive across town with Callie behind the wheel."

Hunter chuckled. "Was there doubt?"

"After flying into Devil's Fork with Crash Jenson at the controls of that little four-seater prop job, we kinda wondered if her driving wouldn't finish you off," George added, laughing.

"If you two keep joking about my driving, I'll stop making those chocolate-chip-oatmeal cookies you love so much," Callie warned good-naturedly as she crossed the room to the kitchen area, where Mary Lou was putting the finishing touches on the crew's dinner.

"We take it all back," Corey said earnestly as he walked over to grab a plate for Mary Lou to fill with a generous helping of stew.

"You bet," George said, nodding vigorously. "We were just joking around, Callie. Whatever you do, don't stop making those cookies." Turning to Hunter, he confided, "You've never tasted anything as good in your entire life as her chocolate-chip-oatmeal cookies."

"I'll look forward to trying them," Hunter said, enjoying the easy banter.

As George moved to get a plate of stew, Hunter watched Callie open the refrigerator to remove a carton of orange juice and once again noticed the way her flight suit fit. The navy-blue fabric was fairly loose everywhere but in her midsection and she looked as if…

A sudden cold feeling of intense dread began to fill Hunter's chest and he had to swallow hard against the bile rising in his throat. Callie Marshall wasn't just carrying a few extra pounds around the middle. She was several months pregnant.

# Two

As she walked past Hunter to sit down in one of the chairs in front of Mary Lou's desk, Callie wondered what on earth she'd done to come under such close scrutiny. His intense stare had followed her from the moment she'd walked into the room and caused her skin to tingle as if he'd reached out and touched her.

Shaking her head to clear it, she decided her uncharacteristic reaction to him had to be because her hormones were all out of whack due to her pregnancy. It was the only reasonable explanation she could think of to explain it.

His concentrated stare had probably been nothing

more than the result of noticing her thickening midsection. He was no doubt trying to figure out whether she was just a bit plump or expecting a baby.

Careful to keep her voice low to avoid calling the others' attention to the fact that she'd caught him staring, she smiled as she turned to meet his intense green gaze. "In case you're wondering about my odd shape, I'm four and a half months pregnant."

Running an agitated hand through his dark brown hair, he looked a little uncomfortable. "I…didn't mean to—"

"Don't worry about it." She smiled, hoping to put him at ease. "It's not like it's a big secret. And, as you can see, I'm certainly not trying to hide my pregnancy."

"Your husband is okay with you flying while you're pregnant?" He shook his head. "I'm sorry. It's none of my business."

It was an odd question, but the concern on his handsome face and in his deep voice was genuine. "Don't worry about it. I don't have a husband, so it's a nonissue." She shrugged. "I'm unmarried, uncommitted and quite content to stay that way."

"I didn't mean to pry." He looked more uncomfortable than before.

"It's not a problem. I'm actually looking forward to single motherhood."

He looked as if he intended to say something, but Corey chose that moment to walk over and plop down in the chair beside her. "Have we sucked up enough to get more cookies or do we need to grovel a little more?"

Callie laughed at the likable young EMT. "No, I think you've redeemed yourself enough for another batch of chocolate-chip-oatmeal cookies."

"If you'll excuse me, I think I'll go check out my office," Hunter said suddenly, turning to walk down the hall.

Staring after her new boss, she wondered what had caused his abrupt change. When she'd met him at the airfield, he'd been congenial and outgoing. But within the span of a few minutes his mood had become pensive and troubled. Was he concerned that she would be unable to do her job?

She rose to her feet to follow him into the office and reassure him that she was perfectly capable of carrying out her duties, but the dispatch radio chose that moment to crackle to life.

"Looks like we have another run," Mary Lou said, crossing the room to answer the call.

As Callie listened to the highway patrol officer relay the location of the one-car accident on Interstate 10 and the patrolman's assessment of the driver's injuries, she, George and Corey started for the door. "Tell him we're on the way."

"ETA is fifteen minutes," George said.

"Keep the stew warm," Corey added.

Out of the corner of her eye Callie saw Hunter

reenter the room. His concerned expression reinforced her determination to set his mind at ease. But their talk would have to wait until later. Whether or not he believed she was capable of doing her job, she had an accident victim depending on her for emergency medical attention. And she wasn't about to let her patient down.

Drenched in a cold sweat, Hunter awoke with a jerk and, swinging his legs over the side of the bed, sat up. Propping his elbows on his knees, he cradled his head in his hands as he tried to chase away the remnants of his nightmare.

He hadn't dreamed about the accident in almost six months. But it was just as real now as it had been when he'd lived through it five years ago. He and his fiancée, Ellen Reichert, a second-year resident at the Mount Sinai Medical Center in Miami, had flown into Central America to deliver medical supplies and administer first aid to some of the remote villages hit the hardest by a category-four hurricane. Everything about the trip had been routine and uneventful until he'd circled the landing site for their last stop. That's when all hell had broken loose and the course of his life had changed forever.

The twin-turbine helicopter he'd been piloting had suddenly lost oil pressure, then, before he could get it safely set down, it stalled out. He didn't remember a lot of the details of what happened after that, only that he'd fought the controls with little success. The chopper had ended up tilting precariously in midair, then come down hard on its starboard side.

His first thought had been to make sure that Ellen was all right, then get them out of what was left of the helicopter. But the blood in his veins had turned to ice when he'd called her name and she'd failed to respond. He'd placed his fingers to the side of her neck and, detecting a faint pulse, scrambled to release their seat belts. Pushing the door on the port side of the chopper open, he'd carefully lifted her up through the opening, then carried her a safe distance from the wreckage.

When she'd regained consciousness, they'd both known she didn't have long, and that's when his devastating heartbreak had turned to total despair. She'd told him that she'd been waiting for the perfect time to tell him she'd recently learned she was pregnant. With her dying breath she'd told him how much she loved him and how sorry she was that she had to go, then, closing her eyes, she'd quietly slipped away.

The ensuing investigation into the crash had proven the accident had been caused by mechanical failure and there was nothing he could have done to prevent it. But he'd quit flying that day and struggled for the past five years, feeling guilty because he'd walked away with nothing more than cuts and bruises, blaming himself for living when the woman he'd loved and their future child had died. He'd spent countless hours going over every detail of the accident, wondering if there was something he could have done differently, something that could have lessened her injuries or saved her life. But try as he might, he couldn't think of anything that would have changed the outcome.

He took a deep shuddering breath and tried to relegate the disturbing memories to the back of his mind. There was no doubt why the horrific dream had returned, and he couldn't say he was overly surprised that it had. After discovering that Callie was pregnant, all he'd been able to think about was once again being responsible for the lives of a woman and her unborn child. Even though she wasn't on his flight crew, as her employer it was ultimately his job to see to her safety.

Fortunately her shift had ended right after the Evac II team had returned from transporting the car accident victim to a hospital in El Paso. That meant that he had four days to come up with a convincing argument to get her to ground herself. And unless her crew was called out as backup for Evac III, she and her baby would be safe.

Now all Hunter had to do was figure out a way to keep them that way.

"Give me a second," Callie called when it sounded as if whoever was at her front door would knock it off its hinges with their insistent pounding. Wiping the flour from her hands with her apron, she turned her CD player down and hurried from the kitchen to open the door. "What's so important that—"

She stopped short at the sight of Hunter O'Banyon standing on her tiny front porch. Lord have mercy, but he was one of the best looking men she'd ever seen. He was dressed in a black T-shirt and worn blue jeans. The soft fabrics fit him like a second skin and emphasized the width of his broad shoulders and his narrow hips. When she glanced at his arms, the sight of his bulging biceps stretching the knit sleeves of his shirt sent a shiver of awareness straight up her spine.

Callie gave herself a mental shake. What on earth was wrong with her? And why in the name of heaven was she ogling the man as if he were a fudge-nut brownie with rich chocolate frosting?

"Are you all right?" His expression was one of deep concern.

"Of—" she swallowed hard "—course. Why wouldn't I be?" Other than being embarrassed that her hair was piled on her head in total disarray, her shorts and T-shirt were the oldest things she had in her closet and she was coated with a fine dusting of flour, she was just peachy.

"I knocked for five minutes before you answered the door. I thought something might be wrong." He rubbed his hand over the back of his neck. "Never mind. Do you have a few minutes? We need to talk."

What could he possibly think they needed to discuss? And why did he have to show up after she'd received a phone call from her mother?

At least once a week since telling her mother she was pregnant they'd gone through the same old routine of her mother wanting to know who the father of Callie's baby was and why she was so insistent on keeping the man's identity a secret. Frustrated beyond words with her mother's persistence, by the time Callie had ended the phone call, she'd already measured the ingredients for several dozen sugar cookies and had pulled the box of oats from the cupboard for a double batch of chocolate-chip-oat-meal cookies.

Some women cleaned house when they were upset. Callie baked.

"Do you mind if I come in?" Hunter asked, returning her to the present.

"I'm sorry. Please come in." She stepped back for him to enter her small cottage. "I was just baking some—oh no! My cookies!" Remembering the peanut butter cookies she'd put into the oven just before hearing him pound on the door, she made a beeline for the kitchen with him hot on her heels.

"Damn! When you make cookies, you don't fool around, do you?" he said, looking around.

Taking the baking sheet from the oven, she placed it on the top of the stove, then glanced at the table and countertops. Plates of cookies covered every available surface.

Shaking her head at the sight, she nibbled on her lower lip. She must have been more upset over her mother's phone call than she'd realized.

"Would you like some milk and cookies?" She grinned. "I have plenty."

"No kidding." His deep chuckle caused a wave of goose bumps to sweep over her skin. "What are you going to do with all of them?"

"They won't last long around George and Corey."

She opened a cabinet to get something to store the cookies in, but the feel of Hunter's broad chest pressed to her side as he stepped forward to reach for several of the plastic containers on the top shelf sent a charge of excitement skipping over every nerve in her body. When he handed them to her, then stepped back, she had trouble drawing her next breath.

Unnerved, her hand trembled as she took the containers from him. "Th-thank you."

He gave her a short nod, then moved farther away. "I think I will take you up on that offer of some milk and cookies."

Pouring them each a glass of milk, she set one at the far end of the table and started to sit down at the opposite end. Hunter was immediately behind her, holding the chair, and his close proximity unsettled her so much that she almost turned over her glass.

What in blazes was wrong with her? She not only felt as jumpy as a frightened rabbit, she'd suddenly turned into a major klutz.

When he sat down across from her, he studied the plates of cookies between them. "What do you suggest I start with first?"

"I like the oatmeal cookies, but that's probably because I use chocolate chips instead of raisins," she said, reaching for one of the tasty treats.

He nodded as he took a cookie from one of the plates. "I'm kind of partial to peanut butter myself." Taking a bite, his eyes widened. "Corey and George weren't exaggerating—these are some of the best cookies I've ever tasted."

As they munched on the cookies, Callie wondered what it was he thought they needed to discuss. For the life of her she couldn't think of anything so important that he'd pay her a visit on her day off.

"What did you want to talk to me about?" she asked, hoping the sooner he stated the purpose for his visit, the sooner he'd leave. She desperately needed to regain her composure.

Taking a deep breath, he set his empty glass on the table, then caught her gaze with his. "I'm concerned that your job might be a little too much for a woman in your condition."

She laughed. "Contrary to what you might think, pregnancy is not a disability."

"I understand that," he said, nodding. "But at times I'm sure it's extremely tiring."

"I'm not going to pretend that it isn't." She rose to place their glasses in the dishwasher, then started stacking cookies in the containers for freezing. "But there are also times when we'll go for a day or two without an emergency call and I'm exhausted from sheer boredom. Besides, my obstetrician doesn't have a problem with me working as a flight nurse, so if you're worried that it's too strenuous for me, don't. Corey and George are both very conscientious and won't let me do any heavy lifting. And when we're not out on calls, I make sure to take regular naps."

"Yes, but there's other things to be considered, such as turbulence or pilot error," he said as he handed her plates full of cookies to be stored in the plasticware.

"I trust George. He's a good pilot."

"I'm not saying he isn't."

She snapped the lid shut on the box, then started filling another one. "What *are* you saying?"

He rubbed the back of his neck as if to relieve tension. "Aren't you worried about having to make a rough landing or a possible crash?"

"Not really." She couldn't for the life of her figure out why he was so overly concerned. Every pilot she'd ever known considered flying the safest mode of transportation. "In the event that something like that happens, I'm in no greater danger because I'm pregnant than I would be if I wasn't."

"But—"

"I see no reason why you're so worried about it, but if you think it's that important, why don't you review the employment records and put me on the crew with the best pilot?"

To her surprise, he placed his large hands on her shoulders and turned her to face him. But instead of arguing his point further, he stared at her for several long seconds before he muttered a curse and lowered his head to capture her lips with his.

As his mouth moved over hers in a gentle caress, Callie's pulse raced and her insides began to hum. The last thing she'd expected for him to do was kiss her. But instead of pushing him away as she should have, she reached out and placed her hands on his biceps to steady herself. The feel of his rock-hard muscles flexing beneath her palms sent a shiver of excitement up her spine and caused her knees to tremble.

If she had any sense, she'd put a stop to the kiss right now and demand that he leave. But his firm, warm lips were making her feel things that she'd only read about in women's magazines and romance novels, and she didn't want the delicious sensations to end.

When he wrapped his arms around her and pulled her against him to deepen the kiss, the feel of his superior strength surrounding her sent tiny little sparks skipping over every nerve in her body. Opening for him, she felt her heart skip several beats when he slipped his tongue inside to tease and explore her with a tenderness that made forming a coherent thought all but impossible.

Placing his hand at the small of her back, he urged her forward, but the feel of her round little tummy pressed to his stomach must have brought him back to reality. He suddenly went completely still, then, releasing her, he carefully set her away from him and took a couple of steps back.

"That shouldn't…have happened." He ran an agitated hand through his thick dark brown hair. "I think I should probably leave."

"Don't worry about it."

Embarrassed and more than a little confused by her uncharacteristic behavior, Callie began packing more cookies into the plastic containers. Why hadn't she stopped him instead of clinging to him as if she were desperate for a man's attention?

Hunter O'Banyon might be tall, dark and movie-star handsome, but she was no more interested in him than she was in any other man. But, dear heaven above, could he ever kiss.

Her cheeks feeling as if they were on fire from her sudden wayward thought, she shoved a container of cookies into his hands. "Take these back to the hangar for Mary Lou and the on-duty crew."

"Callie…I—"

If he didn't leave soon, she'd be up all night baking. "It's getting late and I'm sure you need to get back." She walked into the living room and opened the front door. "Thank you for stopping by. I appreciate your concerns and I will give them some thought."

"By the way, I know this is short notice, but I'm holding a staff meeting the day after tomorrow at 10:00 a.m.," he said, looking anything but happy. "Will you be able to be there?"

She shook her head. "I have a doctor's appointment. But I'll stop by after my checkup and someone can fill me in on what was covered in the meeting."

He stared at her for what seemed an eternity before he gave her a short nod. "Good night, Callie," he said, walking out onto the porch.

"Have a nice rest of the evening, Hunter," she said, closing the door behind him.

Walking straight to the kitchen, she stacked the containers of cookies on a shelf in her freezer, then pulled out the ingredients for a batch of brownies. Her phone conversation with her mother had been frustrating and caused her to make several batches of cookies. But Hunter's disturbing kiss was sending her into a baking frenzy, and for some odd reason everything she wanted to make was chocolate.

As she measured cocoa and flour, something she'd heard on a cooking show came to mind and caused her to knock over a cup of sugar. Eating chocolate released the same endorphins in the brain that were released while having sex.

"Not good, Callie. Not good at all."

Hurriedly opening a bag of milk-chocolate chips, she popped a handful into her mouth, and as the rich taste spread over her tongue, she decided that even if chocolate did make her gain too much weight, it was far less dangerous to her peace of mind than Hunter O'Banyon.

As he descended the steps and walked over to the white truck with Life Medevac painted on the side, Hunter shook his head. He didn't blame Callie one damned bit for giving him the bum's rush. Hell, he'd deserved more than that. He'd acted like an oversexed teenager on his first date. But what he was having the devil of a time trying to figure out was why.

Getting into the truck, he started the engine and, backing from the driveway, drove across town. But instead of turning onto the road leading to the Life Medevac hangar, he kept going until the lights of Devil's Fork faded in the distance behind him. He needed to think, and even though he could go into his room for solitude, he'd found that staring at the vastness of a starlit night always helped him put things in perspective.

When he parked the truck and stared out the windshield at the stars above the Apache Mountains in the distance, he couldn't help but wonder what the hell had gotten into him. He'd only stopped by Callie's place to try to talk some sense into her and get her to see the wisdom in grounding herself until after she had her baby. But when he'd placed his hands on her shoulders and looked into her pretty violet eyes, he could no more have stopped himself from tasting her sweetness than he could stop his next breath.

He took a deep breath. Although he wasn't overly proud of it, he hadn't exactly led the life of a monk since Ellen's death. But he'd always been careful to be with women who wanted nothing more from him than mutual satisfaction and had no expectations of their liaison leading to anything more. And Callie Marshall was most definitely *not* that type of woman. Instead of smoke-filled nightclubs, champagne cocktails and a meaningless one-night stand, she was a cozy little cottage, homemade cookies and a long-term commitment.

But come to think of it, he'd been so busy in the past several months that he'd completely abandoned any kind of a social life. And although he was far from being as randy as a seventeen-year-old boy, a man of thirty-two did have certain needs that couldn't be ignored.

He frowned. But he'd never in his entire life found a pregnant woman irresistible.

He stared at a shooting star streaking across the inky sky. He guessed it was only natural that he'd be attracted to Callie even though she was expecting a baby, considering his current state of celibacy. She was a very pretty woman with a killer smile, a delightful laugh and a pair of legs that could drive a saint to sin. Combine all those traits with his neglected libido and it was no wonder he'd felt compelled to kiss her.

Satisfied that he'd discovered the reason for his uncharacteristic caveman behavior, he started the truck and headed back toward the Life Medevac base. Now that he had things in perspective, there was no reason that he and Callie couldn't put what happened this evening behind them and move forward as employer and employee. Hell, maybe they could even be friends.

But much later, as he lay in bed trying to will himself to sleep, Hunter couldn't seem to forget the sweet taste of Callie's soft lips or that the blood in his veins had heated considerably when she'd kissed him back. And whether he liked it or not, the very last thing on his mind was friendship.

# Three

On the drive back from her appointment with the obstetrician, Callie thought about Hunter's visit and how foolish she'd been. The kiss they'd shared had been very nice, but it didn't mean anything. She knew he'd been frustrated with her refusal to ground herself and he'd been just as surprised by his actions as she had. There had really been no reason for her to get so flustered and read more into it than that.

But she'd spent the rest of the night baking everything from chocolate-fudge-nut brownies to chocolate cake. And by the time she'd gone to bed, the gray light of dawn had begun to chase away the shadows of night.

She shook her head. She hadn't baked that much since she'd discovered she was pregnant.

Thinking back on that day, she could still remember walking out of her gynecologist's office in a total state of shock. She'd always wanted children, but she'd envisioned herself happily married and anticipating the blessed event with the man she loved and who loved her in return. She wasn't supposed to have become pregnant by a man who put social status above a meaningful relationship.

When she'd first met Craig Culbertson, he'd swept her off her feet with his charm and thoughtfulness. But it hadn't taken long for her to discover that he wasn't the man she'd thought he was. He'd hidden his true nature behind a winning smile and charming ways, and by the time they'd parted company, *shallow, self-centered* and *selfish* were the nicest words she could think of to describe the conceited snake.

Then, when she'd discovered she was pregnant a month after their breakup, her disillusionment with Craig had turned to abject fear. One of the deciding factors in her ending their relationship had been the sickening disgust she'd felt when he'd confided in her that at the age of nineteen he'd gotten his girlfriend pregnant and that his twelve-year-old brother was actually his son. He'd told her that once his parents had learned of the pregnancy and discovered the girl wasn't the family's social equal, they'd used their money, as well as their position in Houston society, to gain custody of the baby, adopt him and raise the boy as their own.

A cold chill raced through Callie. She could only imagine the devastation and powerlessness the young mother must have felt at losing all contact with her child. And that was the very reason Callie had made the decision to leave her job as an emergency room nurse at one of the Houston hospitals and take the job as flight nurse with Life Medevac.

If Craig found out about her pregnancy, she wasn't sure he and his parents wouldn't try to do the same thing to her that they'd done to the mother of his first child. Callie hadn't been born into a life of wealth and privilege and therefore would no doubt be considered an undesirable candidate to raise a Culbertson heir. They'd take her to court and she'd come out the loser. She didn't have the kind of money it would take to fight a custody battle against their high-powered lawyers.

She'd come from a middle-class single-parent home where there hadn't been an endless supply of money, and social outings had consisted of making trips to the mall or attending a matinee at the movie theater. And even if her father hadn't been lost at sea during a storm while working on an oil platform in the Gulf of Mexico, her social status wouldn't have been a whole lot different.

As she steered her car onto the lane leading up to

the Life Medevac hangar, she placed her hand on her rounded tummy. She might not have been born with a silver spoon in her mouth, but she loved her little boy with all her heart, and no one was going to take him away from her.

Parking the car, she took a deep breath and forced herself to forget about Houston and the ruthless Culbertsons. She was about to face Hunter O'Banyon and tell him that she'd given a lot of thought to his request that she ground herself. She'd even gone so far as to discuss her physical limitations with her obstetrician, and together they'd concluded there was no reason for her to go on maternity leave for a few more months. Now all she had to do was explain that to Hunter.

"Hi, Mary Lou," Callie said as she entered the dispatch room. "Is Hunter in his office?"

The older woman nodded. "I suspect he's back there compiling a list of everyone's size and the number of new flight suits he's going to order." She laughed. "How do you look in red?"

"We're going to wear red flight suits?"

"That's what he says." Mary Lou looked thoughtful. "Come to think of it, though, our crews will be more easily identified among other emergency personnel at an accident scene."

"It does get confusing sometimes when some of the other services wear the same shade of dark blue that we do," Callie agreed.

"Did everything go okay at the doctor's office?" Mary Lou asked. Since learning of Callie's pregnancy, the woman had taken it upon herself to monitor Callie's progress and well-being.

Smiling, Callie nodded. "The obstetrician did a sonogram and said the baby's size is right on target for a four-and-a-half-month fetus." She laughed. "But I doubt that I can get away with blaming my five-pound weight gain on my son."

"No, that would be due to all those cookies you bake," Mary Lou said, grinning.

As Callie walked down the hall to Hunter's office, she decided that Mary Lou was right. If she didn't stop baking, there wouldn't be a flight suit big enough to accommodate her expanding form, whether she was pregnant or not.

Knocking on Hunter's office door, she waited a moment before entering the office. "Do you have the time to fill me in on what took place at the staff meeting or should I come back later?"

He shook his head and pointed to the brown leather chair in front of his desk. "Have a seat. I've been waiting for you."

"That sounds ominous."

"Not really." His intense green eyes held hers as she lowered herself into the oversize armchair and tried not to notice how good-looking he was or that the sound of his deep voice had caused her insides to start humming. "Before I can order the new flight suits for everyone, I need to know if you've given any more thought to my suggestion that you ground yourself until after your baby is born."

"Yes, I have." She met his questioning gaze head-on. "I even discussed your concerns with my obstetrician this morning."

"And?"

Hunter held out little hope that she'd changed her mind, but since it had been the uppermost thing on his mind for the past two days, he had to know.

"The doctor and I both agreed that as long as I avoid heavy lifting, eat a healthy diet and get plenty of rest, there's no reason that I can't continue as a flight nurse on the Evac II team."

"But—"

"But nothing." Her determined expression warned him that she wasn't going to budge on the issue. "I'm not only capable of doing my job, I need the money I'll make between now and when I give birth to pay for the doctor and hospital."

He had to concentrate hard to keep his mind off the fact that she had the prettiest violet eyes he'd ever seen. "And there's nothing I can say to change your mind?"

"No. But as I told you the other night, if my continuing to fly bothers you that much, pair me with your best pilot. That should eliminate some of your concerns about pilot error."

Hunter took a deep breath, then slowly released it as resignation set in. "I anticipated your decision and I've already made arrangements for you and Corey to be switched to Evac I."

"That's your team." If the dismay on her pretty face was any indication, he'd shocked her.

Not at all happy about the situation, he nodded. "George and Mike—the Evac III pilot—are good, but I'm better."

"Don't you think your assumption that you're a better pilot is a bit arrogant?" She didn't look any happier with his decision than he was.

He shook his head. "Not in the least. It's a matter of experience. I have more flight hours in a Bell helicopter than George and Mike combined. Until he retired from the Air Force a couple of years ago, George flew Sikorskys. And Mike flew Apaches for the Army. I've flown a Bell almost exclusively for the past twelve years." He stopped short at adding that if he'd been behind the controls of a Bell the day of the accident, instead of a reconditioned military chopper given to the hurricane relief organization for aid missions, his fiancée would probably still be alive.

"When does this reassignment take place?"

"Effective immediately." Glancing down at the list of everyone's flight suit sizes, he asked, "What size flight suit do you think you'll need until after you have the baby?"

As he watched her thoughtfully nibble on her lower lip, sweat popped out on his forehead. The memory of Callie's softness and sweet taste when he'd kissed her was doing a real number on his neglected libido.

Giving him the size she thought she'd need to accommodate her advancing pregnancy, she asked, "Was there anything else discussed during the staff meeting that I should know about?"

He sat back in his desk chair. "Mary Lou served your cookies, and everyone agreed that if you ever decide to give up nursing, you should open a bakery shop."

She gave him a half smile as she stood up. "I don't think that would be a good idea. I only bake when I'm…" She stopped suddenly and shook her head. "It doesn't matter. What's my new schedule?"

Hunter rose to his feet. "Instead of coming in this evening, you'll need to be here day after tomorrow."

"At the usual time? Or did you change that, too?"

"Six in the evening," he said, nodding. When she turned toward the door, he said, "By the way, the other night I noticed you have a loose board on one of the porch steps. You'd better have your landlord fix it. You don't want to run the risk of falling."

"If I had a landlord, I'd have him take care of the repair." She shrugged one slender shoulder. "But since I bought the place when I moved to Devil's Fork, I guess I'll have to buy a hammer and a few nails and see what I can do about it myself."

For reasons he didn't care to contemplate, he didn't like the idea of her trying to make the repair herself. "I'll be over this evening to fix the step."

"Don't worry about it." She edged toward the door. "Upkeep is part of a homeowner's job. I don't think hammering a couple of nails into a board will be all that difficult."

Hunter figured he knew what the problem was and, rounding the desk, walked over and put his hands on her slender shoulders. He realized he'd made a huge error in judgment the moment he touched her. An electric charge zinged straight up his arms, and he had to fight an overwhelming urge to draw her closer.

"Callie, about the other night—"

"Please, don't." She shook her head. "It was just a simple kiss and I'm sure it didn't mean anything more to you than it did to me."

Whether it was a matter of stung pride, a bruised ego or the fact that he hadn't been able to forget how soft and yielding she'd been in his arms, her statement hit like a physical blow and he was determined to prove her wrong. "Darlin', that kiss was anything but simple." Slowly lowering his head, he felt as though he just might drown in her violet eyes. "And I think you know it as well as I do."

The moment his lips touched hers, it felt as if a spark ignited somewhere deep inside of him and heat spread throughout his entire body. If he had any sense at all, he'd call Emerald Larson, tell her that he'd changed his mind about taking over the air-ambulance service and put as much distance as he could between himself and Callie Marshall.

But instead of setting her away from him and apologizing for acting like an oversexed teenager, Hunter slid his arms around her and pulled her to him. Callie's soft, petite body nestled against his much larger frame sent blood racing through his veins and caused his heart to pound hard against his rib cage.

When her perfect lips parted on a soft sigh, he took advantage of her acquiescence and deepened the kiss. Slipping his tongue inside, he tasted the sweetness that was uniquely Callie and reacquainted himself with her tender inner recesses.

To his satisfaction, she circled his waist with her arms and melted against him as he gently coaxed her into doing a little exploring of her own. But with each stroke of her tongue to his, the fire that had begun to burn in his belly spread lower and his body tightened with desire faster than he could have ever imagined.

Shocked by the intensity of his need, he eased away from the kiss. Staring at the confusion on her pretty face, he had a feeling he looked just as bewildered.

"I, um, think…it might be a good idea…if we didn't do that again," she said, sounding suspiciously breathless.

"I think you're right." Releasing her, he rubbed at

the tension gathering at the base of his neck. Why did he turn into a Neanderthal every time he was around her? "I'll…see you later this evening…when I come by to repair the step."

She hurried over to the door. "It's really not necessary. I can handle fixing the—"

"I said I'd take care of it." He shook his head. "I can still fly a helicopter with a swollen finger. But if you smash your thumb, you'll have trouble starting an IV or splinting a broken limb."

She stared at him for several more seconds before she nodded, then quickly walked out of his office.

As Hunter watched Callie leave, he closed his eyes and counted to ten, then twenty. Why the hell couldn't he have left well enough alone? What on God's green earth had he thought he was going to prove, besides the fact that he had all the finesse of a bulldozer? Hadn't he sorted through what happened the other night and come to a reasonable conclusion for his attraction to her?

He hadn't been with a woman in almost a year, and that was long enough to make any normal adult male ready to crawl the walls. But even as he thought about finding a willing little lady to help him scratch his itch, he rejected the idea. A one-night stand might help him with his basic needs, but a meaningless encounter couldn't fill the void of companionship in his life.

Shaking his head, he walked back to his desk and sank into his chair. He wasn't looking for any kind of romantic relationship and neither was Callie, but he saw no reason why they couldn't be friends. They were both new in town, alone, and she needed someone to help out with the upkeep on her house from time to time.

Now if he could just keep that in mind and stop grabbing her like a caveman and kissing her until they both needed CPR, everything would be just fine.

As he sat there trying to convince himself that he could do just that, the phone rang. Checking the caller ID, he groaned when he recognized one of Emerald Larson's private numbers.

Switching the speakerphone on, he greeted his grandmother. "Hello, Emerald."

"Good afternoon, Hunter. How is my oldest grandson?"

He almost laughed. He wasn't fool enough to think that the old gal had called him just to say hello and shoot the breeze. Emerald Larson had a purpose behind everything she did. And that included placing a phone call to one of her grandsons.

"I'm doing okay. How are you?"

"Planning a little dinner party for my grandsons and their wives for the end of next month." She paused. "You will attend, won't you?"

"Sure," Hunter said, suddenly feeling more alone than he had in his entire life.

He'd only learned about his brothers a few months

ago, and although they'd formed a bond of friendship that he knew would stand the test of time, Caleb and Nick had both recently married. And that made Hunter the odd man out. Unfortunately he'd always be the odd man out. Marriage and family weren't in the cards for him. Not now. Not in the future.

Loving someone only opened a person up to more pain and heartache than it was worth. His mother had loved Owen Larson and ended up suffering a lifetime of loneliness for her efforts. Owen had run out on her, to leave her facing motherhood alone, and never looked back when he returned to Harvard after sweeping her off her feet during his spring-break in Miami. Then, Hunter had damned near lost his mind from the guilt of surviving the helicopter crash that had taken the lives of Ellen and their unborn child.

No, the emotional investment and risks that went along with loving someone weren't worth the high price a man had to pay.

"Hunter, are you still there?"

"Sorry." He took a deep breath. "What was that you were saying?"

"I said I'm on my way back to Wichita from Houston and I thought I would stop by to see you and my old friend Mary Lou."

He should have known that she wouldn't be able to resist checking up on him from time to time. She'd done the same with his brothers and the companies she'd given them. Why should he be any different?

Even though she'd given him Life Medevac to run as he saw fit, it still came under the umbrella of Emerald Inc., and she hadn't become one of the richest, most successful businesswomen in the world by sitting back and letting others oversee her holdings.

"When will you be here?" he asked, barely resisting the urge to cuss a blue streak.

"My pilot said we should be landing at the Devil's Fork airfield in five minutes."

Rubbing the tension at the base of his neck, Hunter sighed heavily. "I'll be there in a few minutes to pick you up."

"There's no need." He could envision her waving her bejeweled hand dismissively. "I had a limousine service send a car down from Odessa to drive me to the Life Medevac hangar."

"Then I guess I'll see you shortly," he said, resigned to his fate of spending the afternoon with his indomitable grandmother.

Fifteen minutes later, when he met the limousine in the Life Medevac parking lot, Hunter wasn't surprised to see Luther Freemont, Emerald's trusted personal assistant, standing ramrod-straight beside the open back door of a sleek black limousine. "Hey there, Luther. How's it going?"

"Very well, sir," the man answered, as formal as

ever. Once he helped Emerald from the backseat of the limo, he gave Hunter a short nod. "It was nice seeing you again, sir."

When his grandmother slipped her hand in the crook of Hunter's arm and started walking toward the office entrance, he noticed that her assistant got back into the limo. "Do you think old Luther will be all right out here on his own? After all, this place is to hell and gone from a corporate office."

"Poor Luther, he's a proper gentleman and very set in his ways." Emerald laughed. "He doesn't quite know what to make of you and your brothers."

"The feeling's mutual."

"And he's not at all sure what to think of southwest Texas."

Hunter opened the door and waited for her to precede him into the building. "Is Luther always such a tight…uptight?"

As she laughed, her silver-gray eyes twinkled merrily. "Yes, he's always very formal."

"I'll bet he was just a barrel of laughs when he was a kid," Hunter said as he escorted Emerald into the dispatch room.

He introduced her to the on-duty Evac III team as they passed through on the way to his private office, but purposely avoided calling her his grandmother. He still wasn't entirely comfortable thinking of her as a family member, nor did he need the added pressure that went along with others knowing he was her grandson.

"Where's Mary Lou?" she asked, seating herself in the chair in front of his desk.

"When she found out you were dropping by, she decided to run into town to pick up something for refreshments. She'll be back soon."

"Good. I haven't seen her in quite some time and I'm looking forward to catching up."

As they stared at each other across the desk, Hunter couldn't help but think how out of place Emerald Larson looked. She was professional elegance from the top of her perfectly styled silver hair to the soles of her Italian pumps. His office furnishings were light-years away from the opulence she surrounded herself with at Emerald Inc. headquarters.

"A few months ago, when you learned I'm your grandmother and I told you about your father, you weren't as vocal about your feelings as your brothers, Caleb and Nick."

She gave him a look that he had no doubt intimidated the hell out of anyone facing her in a corporate boardroom. But he wasn't one of her loyal lackeys and she was on his turf now.

"I'm here to clear the air once and for all," she said bluntly.

"Do we have to?" he asked before he could stop

himself. He knew for certain she wouldn't want to hear what he thought of her interference in his life.

"Yes." There was a steely determination in her voice, and whether he liked it or not, he knew come hell or high water she was going to have her say. "I'm sure you'd like to know why I insisted that your mother keep her silence about your father's identity until I was ready to tell you myself."

He glared at the woman who until three months ago he'd known only by reading about her in newspapers and national magazines. He hated dancing to her tune. But as his mother had pointed out before he'd left Miami, if he hadn't taken Emerald up on her offer of giving him one of her companies to run, the sacrifices she'd made to ensure his birthright would have been in vain. Keeping his father's identity a secret from her close-knit Irish family had caused a breach that had never been reconciled.

Hunter clenched his back teeth together so tightly his jaw ached. "I'm still having a problem with that. What gave you the right to coerce my mother into signing a paper stating that she wouldn't tell anyone—not even me—who my father was?"

"I know you're bitter about the way I handled everything," Emerald said patiently. "I'd probably feel the same way. But believe me, it was the best for all concerned parties."

Anger, swift and hot, burned at his gut. "For who? You or your son?"

"I never once considered the effect it would have on me or Owen." She shrugged. "My only concern was you and your mother."

"What you did to my mother, as well as to Caleb's and Nick's mothers, amounts to blackmail." He hadn't meant to sound so harsh, but the truth wasn't always pretty.

To his surprise, Emerald didn't seem the least bit offended by his accusation. "You see it as blackmail. I saw it as protecting my grandsons and their mothers from the hazards of dealing with the paparazzi and a corruptive lifestyle." She sighed. "I was determined to see that you and your brothers didn't turn out to be anything like your father. Owen might be alive today if I had given him more of my time and attention instead of everything he thought he wanted."

Hunter took a deep breath in an attempt to bring his temper under control. "Did he even know that he'd gotten three women pregnant?"

For the first time since meeting the mighty Emerald Larson and learning that she was his grandmother, Hunter watched her lower her head as if she might be ashamed of her philandering offspring. He could almost feel sorry for her. Almost.

"Yes, Owen knew he had three sons. But, as usual, he relied on me to bail him out of taking responsibility for his actions." When she raised her eyes to look at him there was unapologetic defiance in their gray depths. "I'll admit that I've made a lot of mistakes and have more than my share of regrets, but whether or not you approve of my methods to insure you boys were nothing like him, you can't deny that it worked. And I didn't exactly coerce your mother into signing the agreement to remain silent about your father. I just made it clear that should word get out that I'm your grandmother, I would have to deny it in order to protect you from the media frenzy it would create."

Hunter could see her reasoning, but that didn't change the fact that she'd waited thirty-two years before she'd clued him in on who had fathered him or that all that time she'd had private investigators reporting his and his brothers' every move. "Why did you wait so long to tell us?"

"I wanted all three of you to gain some life experiences of your own instead of having to live down your father's reputation of being an international playboy," she said pragmatically. "That would have been a huge burden for all of you. Not to mention how it would have affected you to learn that you had a multimillion-dollar trust fund and would eventually inherit a sizable part of my business holdings."

As Hunter mulled over what she'd said, he couldn't help but agree with her. Handling the knowledge that he'd become an overnight millionaire and owner of his own business was hard enough to grasp at the age of thirty-two. He couldn't imagine the effect it would have had on him at a much earlier age.

But before he could comment, Emerald added, "And before you ask, it was extremely hard for me to read about your accomplishments in a private investigator's report while you were growing up and not be there to see them for myself." She leaned forward as if to emphasize her point. "What I did and the way I went about it I did out of love. Believe me, nothing would have pleased me more than to have had a traditional grandmother's relationship with you and your brothers. But I had to give that up in order to protect you."

Thinking it over, Hunter realized that as difficult as it had been for him growing up not knowing who his father was, it had to have been much harder for Emerald. She'd known all about him and his brothers but hadn't been able to let any of them know how she felt.

"I guess all we can do now is move forward," he said, thinking aloud.

"I believe that would be wise," Emerald agreed. "Taking over the Life Medevac Helicopter Service is a good start for you, and I expect you to do quite well." She surprised him when she rose from the chair and rounded the desk to kiss his cheek. "It's time to get back to what you do best—flying helicopters and helping those in need—and leave the past behind,

Hunter. It's history and can't be changed. But the future is an unwritten page and sometimes found where you least expect it."

# Four

"If you don't stop letting Hunter O'Banyon kiss you, you're going to be as big as a barn," Callie muttered, poking another snickerdoodle into her mouth as she measured the ingredients for a double batch of chocolate-chocolate-chip cookies.

The minute she'd arrived back home from her meeting with Hunter, she'd walked straight into the kitchen, put on her apron and started baking. Five dozen snickerdoodles, a double batch of sugar cookies and a pan of brownies later, she still hadn't been able to forget how his lips had felt on hers. Warm, firm and deliciously male, his mouth could very easily be classified as a lethal weapon. At least for her.

Spooning chocolate dough onto cookie sheets, she wondered what there was about Hunter that caused her to abandon every ounce of common sense she possessed. All he had to do was touch her and she clung to him like a piece of plastic shrink-wrap on a hot plate.

She slid the pan of cookie dough into the oven and set the timer. Then, sitting down at the table while she waited on the cookies to bake, Callie stared off into space.

It wasn't uncommon for a woman in her second trimester to find herself feeling more sensual than ever before, but she didn't think her pregnancy hormones could account for the compelling attraction she experienced with Hunter. With just a look he could make her heart flutter. And when he touched her, she practically melted into a puddle at his feet. She hadn't had that kind of reaction to Craig, and he was her baby's father.

Lost in thought, it took her a moment to realize someone was knocking on her door. Hurrying to remove the pan of cookies from the oven, when she walked into the living room and opened the door, she found Hunter squatted down beside the steps. He had replaced the loose board with a new one and was pounding nails into the wood with no more than a couple of whacks with a hammer. She swallowed hard when she noticed how his bicep and the muscles in his forearm flexed with each blow.

"That should last a while," he said, straightening to his full height. "And it'll be a lot safer for you."

When she finally found her voice, she nodded. "Thank you."

He wiped the sweat from his forehead on the sleeve of his T-shirt. "Is there anything else that needs fixing or that you'd like me to take a look at while I'm here?"

"I can't think of anything." She motioned toward the door. "Would you like to come in to cool off and have a glass of iced tea?"

Smiling, he nodded. "That sounds like a winner." He put the hammer and a small sack of nails in the back of his truck, then climbed the steps to Callie's cottage. "It's not as humid here in southwest Texas as it is in Florida, but it's still hotter than hell."

Callie laughed as they walked inside the house. "It's late August. What do you expect?"

"Good point," he said, grinning.

When they walked into the kitchen, she poured them each a glass of iced tea. "Having lived close to the Gulf all my life, I'm not used to all this dry heat."

"Thank God for air-conditioning."

"Amen to that." She smiled as she placed her hand on her rounded stomach. "I've been hotter this summer than I've ever been in my life."

"It's no wonder you're hot, with the oven on all the time." Chuckling, he looked at the plates of cookies and brownies sitting on the counter. "I see you've been at it again."

She smiled wanly. There was no way she was going to tell him that just the thought of him kissing her could send her into a baking frenzy.

He reached for a brownie. "What are you going to do with all this stuff?"

Thinking quickly, she shrugged. "Schools are always having bake sales. I thought I'd donate some of the things I've baked for their fund-raisers. And after the baby is born, I doubt that I'll have a lot of time, so I've frozen a lot of what I've made."

"Good idea." He grinned. "I'm sure Corey will appreciate that."

"I'm sure he will. He eats constantly but never seems to fill up." She frowned. "Do all boys eat like they have a bottomless pit for a stomach?"

"Pretty much." Hunter reached for one of the chocolate-chocolate-chip cookies on the baking sheet she'd removed from the oven earlier. "My mom said that once I hit puberty, I ate everything in sight."

"I guess that's something I have to look forward to." Callie smiled at the fluttering in her stomach. It was as if the baby knew she was talking about him.

"You're having a boy?"

She nodded. "That's what the sonogram indicates."

"When are you due?"

"Around the first of the year." She turned to spoon cookie dough onto a baking sheet. "Of course, that doesn't mean he won't decide to come a couple of weeks early or late."

"That would be anywhere from a week or so before Christmas to mid-January."

She wondered why Hunter was taking such an interest in when she'd give birth, until it occurred to her that he would need to find someone to cover her shifts at Life Medevac. "I'm planning on taking maternity leave at Thanksgiving and being back to work no later than mid-February. Mary Lou suggested that I bring the baby to work with me and she could watch him when I go out on a call. Is that all right with you?"

He nodded. "But are you sure it's a good idea to wait that long to take your leave?" He frowned. "I don't mean to offend you, but won't it be difficult climbing in and out of the helicopter when you're that…far along?"

"No offense taken. I know I'll be quite large." She slipped the pan of cookies into the oven, then turned to face him. "If I see that it's a problem, I'll…take my leave earlier than…I'd planned."

He took a step toward her. "Are you all right?"

Laughing, she nodded. "It's just the baby moving. He seems to be particularly active today."

"Does it hurt?" He looked and sounded genuinely concerned.

"No. If anything, it tickles." She lovingly placed her hand on her stomach. "At this stage of pregnancy it's like having a butterfly flapping its wings inside of me. Later on, I'm told it will feel like I have a prizefighter in there."

"I'll bet that does feel weird." When the timer on the oven went off, he reached for a hot pad. "Why don't you sit down and put your feet up?"

"I'm fine."

Hunter pointed to one of the kitchen chairs. "Sit."

He could tell she wasn't happy about it, but while she sat down and propped her feet up in one of the other chairs, he removed the cookies from the oven. "Damn! That's hot!" he cursed when the back of his hand touched the top of the oven.

She was at his side in a flash. "Let me see."

Reluctantly letting her examine his hand, he tried to ignore how nice her soft palms felt holding his calloused one. "It's nothing."

"It's already starting to form a blister," she said, reaching for a bottle of some kind of clear lotion.

"What's that?"

"Aloe vera. It will stop it from hurting and help it heal faster." She flipped the top of the bottle open, then glanced up at him and grinned. "And don't worry, it won't make you smell like a flower."

As he watched her gently spread the clear gel on the small burn, a warmth began to fill his chest. It had been a long time since he'd had a woman fussing over him. And whether it was wise or not, he liked the feeling more than he cared to admit.

"That should take care of it," she said, closing the bottle.

Amazed at how much better it felt, he flexed his hand. "That stuff really works. Thanks."

"Not…a problem."

She sounded slightly winded, and he figured their close proximity had the same effect on her that it had on him. He was having the devil of a time trying to keep from taking her in his arms and kissing her senseless.

"I think I'd better be going."

"How much do I owe you for fixing the step?" she asked, reaching for her purse on the table.

"I ate enough cookies and brownies to more than pay for the job."

He edged toward the door. If he didn't get out of there soon, he was going to take her in his arms—and that could spell disaster to his good intentions. And he'd have succeeded, too, if she hadn't touched him.

"Hunter, stop being so darned stubborn."

Her small hand resting on his forearm sent a wave of heat streaking throughout his entire body. Without a single thought to the consequences or that he'd promised himself he'd be able to keep his hands to himself, he pulled her into his arms.

"Darlin', friends help each other all the time." He

kissed her forehead. "And they don't ask for anything in return."

She stared at him for several long seconds before she shook her head. "I'm not sure that you and I could ever be just friends. And right now I'm not looking for anything more."

"That makes two of us, Callie." He brushed her perfect lips with his. "But I think as long as we keep that in mind, we'll be just fine." He kissed her soundly, then forced himself to set her away from him and walk to the door. Turning back, he smiled. "I'll see you at work tomorrow evening, *friend*."

"Where's Corey?" Callie asked when she arrived at work the next evening. "I didn't see his truck in the parking lot."

"He called to say he'd be a few minutes late," Mary Lou answered as she opened the container of brownies Callie had placed on the table by the coffeepot. Removing a double-fudge-and-nut chocolate square, she took a bite and shrugged. "I told him that if we get a call before he reports for his shift, I'd give him a talkin' to he won't soon forget."

Callie frowned. "It's not like Corey to be late. Did he say what's up?"

"He said he and his girlfriend were on their way back from talking to her parents up in Odessa. He should be here in about a half hour or so." Mary Lou lowered her voice and leaned forward. "Can you keep a secret?"

"Of course."

The older woman grinned. "Corey is going to be a daddy in about seven months."

"You're kidding." Callie laughed. "He's not much more than a boy himself."

Mary Lou grinned. "I've always said he's twenty-two going on ten."

"What's up?" Hunter asked, walking into the dispatch room.

Callie's heart came to a skittering halt, then took off double time. If she'd thought he looked good in jeans and a T-shirt, it was nothing compared to the way he looked in his flight suit. The one-piece coverall emphasized the impossible width of his muscular shoulders and narrowness of his trim waist.

"Just some girl talk," Mary Lou said, winking at Callie.

"Which one of us guys are you dissecting?" Hunter asked, grinning.

His comment had been for both she and Mary Lou, but when his gaze caught Callie's, she felt warm all the way to her toes. If he wanted to, she had a feeling Hunter O'Banyon could charm a little old lady right out of her garters with that smile of his.

And he thought they could be *just* friends? She

almost laughed. The way he was looking at her, there was a better chance of elephants roosting in trees.

"Don't worry, big guy." Mary Lou cackled. "We weren't taking you to task for anything. This time."

He arched one dark eyebrow. "This time?"

"We were discussing when Corey would show up," Callie added.

Hunter's skeptical expression turned to one of understanding. "Corey had some important personal business to take care of up in Odessa. He'll be here as soon as he can."

"You know what's going on, don't you?" Callie guessed.

"He came by yesterday evening to ask me and Mike what we thought he should do about the situation," Hunter said, nodding.

"That little skunk told me I was the only one he'd talked to about it," Mary Lou said, obviously put out that the confidence wasn't as big a secret as she'd thought. "Just wait until I—" Mary Lou stopped abruptly when the emergency phone rang.

Callie listened as Mary Lou asked several questions in Spanish. Great. Corey wasn't back yet and on the Evac II team he'd been the only one fluent in Spanish.

"Come on, Callie. We don't have time to wait for Corey," Hunter said, heading for the door. "As it is, we're going to have to race the stork to the hospital."

"Is it Juanita Rodriguez again?" Callie asked,

thankful that Hunter had obviously understood Mary Lou's end of the conversation and would be able to interpret for her.

He nodded as they climbed into the helicopter and put on the headsets that would enable them to communicate over the engine noise. "She's definitely in labor this time. From Mary Lou's questions, I could tell that Juanita's water broke and she's home alone."

"Where's her husband Miguel?"

"He's in El Paso at a National Guard meeting this weekend. We can radio his armory and have him meet us at the hospital."

While Hunter started the engine, Callie strapped herself into one of the jump seats in the back and listened to Mary Lou's voice give the coordinates for the Rodriguez ranch to Hunter. They had about a fifteen-minute flight to reach their destination, then another thirty minutes on to El Paso. Mary Lou was going to stay on the phone with Juanita until they got there, and hopefully Baby Rodriguez would wait to make his or her grand entrance into the world until after they made it to the hospital.

When they lifted off, Callie began to mentally run through emergency birthing procedure on the outside chance that she would have to deliver Juanita's baby, and it took a moment for her to realize Hunter had spoken to her. "I'm sorry. What did you say?"

"I asked if you've delivered a baby before." His

deep baritone coming through the headset was oddly intimate and sent a shiver straight up her spine.

She gave herself a mental shake. Hearing Hunter's voice through the headset was no different than when she'd communicated with George or Corey on a flight.

"I've delivered a few babies—one of them in the back of a taxicab when the E.R. doctors were busy treating victims from a bus accident."

"But you don't speak or understand Spanish?"

She sighed. "No."

They fell silent, and in what seemed record time, Hunter was setting the helicopter down in a field next to the Rodriguez ranch house.

Removing her headset and unfastening her seat belt, Callie grabbed one of the medical cases containing sterile dressings, latex gloves and other medical supplies and hurriedly slid the side door back. She bent slightly to avoid the rotor blades, then, once she was clear of the helicopter, she jogged the short distance to the house. Fortunately the front door was unlocked, and she walked inside without so much as a second thought.

"*¡Por favor ayúdeme!*"

Callie followed the frantic cries and found Juanita in one of the bedrooms. Drenched in sweat, the young woman was practically hysterical and instead of working with the contractions she seemed to be fighting them.

"*¡El bebé está listo!*" Juanita repeated, clutching at Callie's hands.

"What's she saying about the baby?" Callie asked Hunter when he appeared in the narrow doorway.

"She said the baby is ready."

"Tell her that I need to check to see how close she is to having the baby," Callie said, slipping on a pair of sterile latex gloves.

While Hunter assured Juanita that everything was going to be all right, Callie checked to see how many centimeters the woman had dilated. "The stork is going to win this one," she said, reaching into the medical case for clamps, a sterile drape and antiseptic. "The baby's head is crowning."

As she arranged the medical supplies she would need for the birth of Juanita's baby, Callie listened to Hunter reassure the woman. She had no idea what he was telling her, but it seemed to calm Juanita as well as send warmth throughout Callie's body. She'd always thought Spanish was a beautiful language and she didn't think she'd ever heard a more sexy sound than Hunter's deep voice flawlessly pronouncing the words.

"Do you have any kind of experience being a breathing coach?" Callie asked as she prepped Juanita for the delivery.

He shook his head. "No. We covered it briefly in EMT training, but that's it."

"You'll do fine." Using the two-way radio clipped to the epaulet on the shoulder of her jumpsuit, she advised the hospital in El Paso of the situation, then turned her full attention on the task at hand. "Tell Juanita to breathe, then show her how. She's tensing up instead of relaxing her pelvic floor and allowing the baby to pass through the birth canal."

"*Respira,* Juanita. *Respira.*"

When Hunter showed the young woman what he meant, she trustingly stared into his eyes and began to concentrate on doing as he requested. Once she stopped fighting the pain, she rapidly progressed to the pushing phase of the delivery. Moving into position to lift her shoulders when it came time to push, he continued to reassure her that everything was going to be all right.

"*Todo será bien,* Juanita."

"Tell her to stop the shallow breathing and start pushing," Callie said, showing the woman how to position her hands on her knees for leverage.

Encouraging Juanita to push with all her might, he supported her shoulders, and after only a couple of tries, the baby's dark head emerged from the young woman's lower body. Hunter watched Callie quickly and efficiently suction the infant's nose and mouth before it was time for Juanita to push the rest of her baby out into the world.

With one more mighty push from Juanita, the baby slid out into Callie's waiting hands. Without being prompted, the baby girl opened her mouth and wailed at the top of her tiny lungs.

"*Mí bebé,*" Juanita murmured tearfully.

"You have a beautiful daughter, Juanita," Callie said, placing the baby on her mother's stomach.

Awed by the miracle he'd just witnessed, the moment was so bittersweet Hunter couldn't have pushed words past the lump clogging his throat if his life depended on it. Although he was happy for the Rodriguez family and their new addition, he'd never know what it was like to watch his own son or daughter come into the world. After losing Ellen and their unborn child, he never intended to put himself in the position of loving someone and taking the risk of losing them. He'd been down that road before and had barely survived. There was no way in hell he could go through that again.

"Hunter, could you please hold the baby while I get Juanita ready for transport?" Callie asked, breaking into his disturbing thoughts.

The last thing he wanted to do was hold a baby. He knew for certain it would only compound his sense of loss and regret that he'd never hold his own child. But before he could protest, Callie placed the baby in his arms. As he stared down at the red-faced little girl wrapped in a soft white blanket, instead of the sorrow he expected, Hunter couldn't help but marvel at how small she was, how perfect.

Gently touching her little hand, he was thoroughly amazed when the baby curled her perfectly formed tiny fingers around one of his. "She's holding on to me."

"Babies do that," Callie said, smiling.

He watched Callie and Juanita exchange an indulgent glance. Apparently there was no language barrier when it came to women's opinions of men. It must be universally accepted that men didn't have a clue about these things. But that was okay with him. Men didn't understand women, so he supposed that made the genders pretty equal.

While Callie radioed the hospital to report a successful, complication-free birth, Hunter contemplated how they were going to get Juanita into the helicopter without Corey. He wasn't about to let Callie lift anything heavier than her nurse's bag or the baby, and the door and hallway were too narrow to get the stretcher into the bedroom. That left only one alternative.

"Are we ready for transport?" When Callie nodded, he handed her the baby. "You take your nurse's bag and the baby while I carry Juanita to the chopper."

"That would probably be best," Callie said, lifting the nylon bag's webbed strap to her shoulder. "You'd probably have to carry her to the front door before you could put her on the stretcher anyway."

Telling Juanita what was taking place, Hunter scooped her slight body into his arms and carried her out to the helicopter. Once he placed her on the stretcher and Callie handed her the baby, Juanita and her new daughter both drifted off into a peaceful sleep.

The flight to El Paso was uneventful, and once they

had Juanita and her new daughter safely checked in to the hospital, Callie and Hunter boarded the helicopter and headed back to the Life Medevac base.

"You did a wonderful job of calming Juanita down," Callie said as she stared through the windshield at the vast blue sky ahead of them. Riding in the front seat next to Hunter on the trip back to Devil's Fork, she enjoyed the view of the rugged Texas mountains that she missed when riding in the back with a patient.

"It didn't show that I had no idea what I was doing?" he asked, grinning sheepishly.

Smiling, she shook her head. "Not at all. Juanita is young and had no idea what to expect when her contractions started. Factor in that she was home alone and miles away from help and it was no wonder she was frightened half out of her mind. You were able to put her at ease and that made it a lot easier for her."

He shrugged. "I just did what I thought would help." They were both silent for some time before he asked, "Who's going to be with you when you have your baby?"

It was the last thing she'd expected him to ask. "Are you volunteering for the job?"

"Hell no."

She laughed at his horrified expression. "But you're a great labor coach."

He grunted. "Only because Corey wasn't there to take over for me. I'm the pilot, remember?"

"You're also a certified EMT."

"Only because my grandmother strongly suggested that it would be a good idea since I was taking over an air-ambulance service." He shrugged. "Besides, whether or not you and the father of your baby are together, I'm sure he'll want to be there when his son is born. He can be your breathing coach."

A cold chill ran the length of her spine at the thought of Craig Culbertson being anywhere near her or her child. "I can assure you, he won't be anywhere around when I give birth."

"Maybe he'll change his mind."

"It's not an issue."

Hunter was quiet for a moment, then turned his head to give her a questioning look. "He doesn't even know he's fathered a child, does he?" His mouth flattening into a disapproving line, he shook his head. "Forget that I asked. It's none of my business."

She hadn't discussed with anyone—not even her mother—why she'd made the decision not to tell Craig about the baby. But she needed to make Hunter understand, without divulging too many details, why she felt she had no choice but to keep her silence.

"Believe me, it's for the best." Placing her hand protectively over her son, she shook her head. "Even if I told him about the baby, he wouldn't care."

"Don't you think you owe him the chance to prove you wrong?"

"No. He's too selfish and self-centered to care about anyone or anything but himself."

Hunter stared straight ahead and she could tell he was thinking over what she'd said. "There must have been some substance to the man or you wouldn't have become involved with him," he finally said.

Callie sighed heavily. "In the past several months I've spent countless hours wondering why I allowed myself to be fooled by his insincerity."

She could feel Hunter's intense gaze as surely as if he'd reached out and touched her. "And?"

"I came to the conclusion that he was the consummate charmer who was more interested in the chase than in a meaningful relationship."

"I know the type," Hunter said disgustedly. "Let me guess—he asked you out several times and you turned him down. That's when he pulled out all the stops and did everything in his power to convince you that he was wild about you."

"That's exactly what happened. I became a challenge that he was determined to conquer." She took a deep breath. "And like a fool, I allowed him to wear down my resistance and charm me into believing that we could have a future together."

When Hunter took her hand in his to give it a gentle squeeze, a warmth like nothing she'd ever known filled her all the way to her soul. "Don't be so hard on yourself, darlin'. It's not the first time a woman has been taken in by a player. And it's sad to say, but it won't be the last."

She knew he was right, but that didn't make her feel any less foolish for allowing it to happen, especially since she was now facing motherhood alone. "Then you understand my reasoning for keeping my pregnancy a secret?"

"Not entirely." He released her hand, then, remaining silent for several long seconds, he finally added, "Don't you think you should at least give him the opportunity to redeem himself? I know if I was in his shoes, I'd definitely be angry if I discovered a woman had denied me the right to know my own son."

Callie knew for certain she couldn't take the chance of telling Craig. But she wasn't ready to outline her reasons to Hunter. "He'd only view the baby as an inconvenience, and my child deserves better than that."

"Do you ever intend to tell your son who his father is?"

"He'll be better off not knowing."

"Every kid has a right to know who they are and where they came from," he said forcefully. His tone left no doubt that he felt very passionately about the subject. "He'll grow up wondering if every man he passes on the street is the one responsible for his existence."

"Why do you feel so strongly about this?"

She watched him take a deep breath, then slowly release it. Just when she thought he was going to tell her it was none of her concern, he spoke. "I grew up not knowing anything about my father, and it wasn't until just recently that I even learned who he was—after he'd been dead for six months."

"Oh, Hunter, I'm so sorry." She began to understand why he felt it was so important that she inform Craig about the baby. "Your mother didn't tell him about you?"

"He knew." There was an edge to his voice. "He just chose to ignore the fact that he'd fathered three sons with three different women." Hunter gave her a meaningful glance. "But the point is, they gave him the opportunity to know about us. He was the one who made the decision to stay out of our lives."

"But she didn't tell *you,*" Callie guessed.

He shook his head. "She had her reasons and she knew that one day I would learn who he was. But that didn't make it any easier on me when I was growing up or stop me from resenting the fact that I wasn't given the choice to know anything about the man."

She could understand why Hunter felt the way he did, but her circumstances were different. If she told Craig about the baby, there was a good chance that he and his parents would try to separate her and her son the way they'd done that poor girl and her baby twelve years ago. And that was a chance Callie wasn't willing to take.

"I will tell my son about his father when I feel he's ready," she said carefully. "But until that time we'll be just fine on our own."

# Five

For the next few days Hunter couldn't stop thinking about the conversation he'd had with Callie on the way back from El Paso. There'd been something in her voice that had alerted him to the fact there was more to her refusal to tell her baby's father about the pregnancy than she was letting on. He couldn't quite put his finger on what that something was, but it was serious enough that she felt silence was her only option.

Hunter's heart stalled. Could the man have been abusive?

Fury stronger than he could have ever imagined coursed through his veins. He wasn't a violent man by nature, but just the thought that the jerk might have mistreated Callie in any way was enough to make Hunter ready to tear him limb from limb.

Suddenly needing to move before he put his fist through the wall, Hunter grabbed his sunglasses and, taking his ball cap from a hook beside his office door, jammed it onto his head. He felt as if he had enough adrenaline coursing through him to bench-press a 747 fully loaded with passengers and cargo. What he needed was some good, hard physical labor to help him work off his anger. And he knew exactly what he was going to do.

As he drove to the lumber yard, he mentally reviewed all the things in need of repair or replacement at Callie's place. Besides the steps he'd fixed a few days ago, he'd noticed the place could use a coat of paint and a new deck at the back door to replace a badly deteriorating concrete stoop.

Purchasing everything he needed to make the improvements, Hunter scheduled a delivery for the lumber to build a new deck, then loaded his truck with a new extension ladder, several buckets of paint, brushes and scrapers. Satisfied that he had everything he needed, he headed toward Callie's house at the edge of town.

He'd thought about talking to her before he started buying supplies and making plans, but if her protest over the simple repair he'd made to the step was any indication, she would have refused his offer. And whether she liked it or not, he wasn't taking no for an answer. In the case of the back stoop, it was a matter of safety.

When he parked the truck and positioned the ladder against the side of the house, he wasn't surprised when she came out to glare at him. "Why on earth are you making so much noise and what are you doing to my house?"

With her shoulder-length blond hair in delightful disarray, her eyes soft with sleep and her feet bare, she looked as if she'd just crawled out of bed. She also looked sexy as hell.

"Good morning to you, too." He grinned as he grabbed one of the scrapers. "Did you stay up late last night making cookies?"

"As a matter of fact, I did."

"What kind?"

She shook her head. "Don't change the subject. What are you doing here at the god-awful hour of seven-thirty in the morning? And why is that ladder propped against the side of my house?"

"One thing at a time, darlin'," he said, climbing the ladder. "Contrary to popular belief, seven-thirty isn't all that early. Did you know the lumber yard and hardware store here in Devil's Fork open every morning at six?"

Glaring at him, she propped her fists on her shapely hips. "Since I've never had occasion to go into either establishment, no, I didn't know that."

He scraped off a long strip of peeling paint close to

the peak of the roof. "The other day I noticed that the paint on this place had started to crack and peel."

"So you just decided to take it upon yourself to paint my house?" Clearly fit to be tied, she looked mighty damned cute standing there in an oversize pink T-shirt and a pair of mint-green camp shorts, tapping her bare foot against the hard-packed dirt.

"You can't do it," he said as he continued to remove strips of weathered paint from the board siding. "And it needs to be done before winter sets in."

"It could wait until after I have the baby."

He shook his head. "You'll be too busy once the baby gets here. Besides, I might as well do something constructive on my days off."

"But I can't afford this right now."

"You don't have to pay for it."

"Yes, I do."

"I've already taken care of it."

She made a noise that sounded suspiciously like a growl. "Tell me how much you've spent and I'll pay you back."

He grinned. "Nope."

"Are you always this—" she stopped as if searching for the right word "—this meddlesome?"

He stopped scraping to stare down at her. "Are you always this stubborn when someone is trying to help you?"

Rubbing her temples with her fingertips, she shook

her head. "I do appreciate you trying to help. But I can't afford all the improvements right now and I can't let you pay for them."

"Consider it a housewarming gift," he said, sending more flakes of paint falling to the ground.

"That's absurd." She frowned. "You're newer in town than I am."

He chuckled. "Minor technicality."

"I can't let you do this."

"You can't stop me." He climbed down the ladder, then, placing the scraper on the tailgate of the truck, walked over to stand in front of her. "Look, there are things around here that need attention and you're not able to do them in your condition."

She rolled her eyes. "I've told you before, I'm pregnant, not disabled."

"Whatever. You can't do them and I need something to keep me busy on my days off."

He could tell he was wearing down her resistance when she sighed heavily. "Yes, but it isn't fair for you to pay for the materials to make improvements to my house."

Unable to resist taking her into his arms, he smiled as he pulled her to him, then pushed the brim of his ball cap up out of the way. "If it bothers you that much, why don't we strike a deal?"

She looked suspicious. "What kind of agreement are you talking about?"

"I'll do some work around your house and you can make me a few home-cooked meals." He used his index finger to raise her chin until their gazes met. "Does that sound fair?"

"Not really. I still think that I'm getting the better end of this deal."

Her soft body pressed to his was playing hell with his good intentions, and before he could stop himself, he lowered his mouth to hers. "Throw in a couple dozen brownies—" he brushed her perfect lips with his "—some chocolate-chip-oatmeal cookies—" she parted for him on a soft sigh "—and we'll call it even," he finished as he deepened the kiss.

The combination of Callie's sweet taste and the fact that she was kissing him back sent blood surging through his veins and had his lower body tightening with a need that threatened to buckle his knees. Never in all his thirty-two years had he been aroused as fast or as completely as he was at that very moment.

But when she raised her arms to his neck and tangled her fingers in the hair at his nape, her feather-light touch caused a jolt of hunger to fill every fiber of his being and the need to touch her became overwhelming. Sliding his hand beneath the tail of her T-shirt, when his calloused palm met the satiny skin along her side, his heart thumped hard against his ribs. They'd been so embroiled in their argument over him doing repairs to her house that he hadn't paid attention to the fact that she wasn't wearing a bra.

When he cupped her full breast, then gently slid the pad of his thumb over her tight nipple, her moan of pleasure mingled with his groan of frustration. What the hell did he think he was doing?

Not only was he making out with his flight nurse for God and everybody to see, she was pregnant with another man's child. He wasn't looking for a lasting relationship with any woman. And Callie wasn't a woman who engaged in meaningless flings.

Reluctantly removing his hand from beneath her shirt, he broke the kiss to stare into her wide violet eyes. "Darlin', I think you'd better go back in the house and I'm going to get back to work."

Her porcelain cheeks colored a deep rose and she backed away from him. "I'll be…gone for…a little while," she said, sounding out of breath. "I need to go…to the grocery store."

He frowned. "What for? Your cabinets and freezer are full of food."

She took several steps backward. "I have to see if the store carries fifty-pound bags of flour."

Repositioning his ball cap, Hunter watched her turn and hurry around the side of the house toward the front porch. He'd never seen a woman bake as much as Callie. Maybe it was some kind of hormonal nesting thing.

He shook his head as he grabbed the scraper from the back of the truck and climbed the ladder. Whatever it was, as long as she was inside the house baking and he was outside painting, there wouldn't be any more encounters like the one they'd just shared. And if he repeated it enough times, he just might start to believe it.

When she heard someone knocking on the front door, Callie glanced at the clock on the stove. Hunter couldn't possibly have driven out to the Life Medevac hangar, showered and changed clothes, then driven all the way back to her place in such a short time.

After he'd finished the arduous task of scraping away the peeling paint, he'd told her he was going to go back to the hangar and clean up while she finished dinner. Although she couldn't imagine what it would be, he must have forgotten something.

Wiping her hands on a towel, she checked the pot roast she'd put in the oven earlier, then hurried to open the door. "I'm afraid dinner isn't quite…" Her voice trailed off as icy fear froze her vocal cords and filled every cell in her being.

"Hello, Callie." Craig Culbertson flashed his practiced smile as he brushed past her. "Since you didn't know I was coming for a visit, I didn't expect you to make dinner for me. But I'm sure whatever you're cooking up will be delicious."

"Wh-what are you doing here?" she asked, gripping

the doorknob so hard she wouldn't be surprised if she left her fingerprints embedded in the metal.

"I've missed you." He looked around her small, tidy living room. "What were you thinking when you left Houston for this? It's not even as nice as that minuscule apartment you had."

She ignored his insult and repeated her question. "Why are you here, Craig?"

Turning to face her, his charming smile disappeared; it was replaced with an expression of utter disgust. "Good God! You're pregnant."

Drawing on every ounce of courage she'd ever possessed, she squared her shoulders and placed a protective hand on her stomach. "Yes, I am."

"It's mine, isn't it?" he asked, his tone accusing.

Knowing full well that he wouldn't believe her, she shook her head. "No. The baby belongs to—"

"Me."

Callie had never been so relieved to see anyone in her entire life as she was when Hunter walked through the open door and put his arm around her shoulders. Nor had she ever been as shocked when she heard his claim to be her baby's father.

"This is Craig Culbertson from Houston," she said, silently thanking Hunter for intervening. "Hunter O'Banyon is my—"

"Husband," Hunter interrupted, giving her a look that asked for her to trust him.

"You're married?" Craig shook his head. "You can't be. Your mother said you only moved here a couple of months ago. That's not nearly long enough to find yourself a husband and get knocked up."

"I take exception to the phrase 'knocked up' in reference to my wife's pregnancy," Hunter said, his voice hard as granite.

"Sorry." His tone was anything but apologetic, but Craig apparently decided that Hunter meant business and wasn't one to be trifled with, because he immediately began to backpedal. "It was just an expression, no offense intended."

A fresh wave of fear coursed through Callie as she thought about her last conversation with her mother and how she'd tried to get Callie to tell her who the baby's father was. Had her mother inadvertently hinted to Craig that Callie might be carrying his child?

"Why did you call my mother?" she asked, surprised that her voice was fairly steady considering the state of her nerves.

Craig gave her the smile that she used to think made him look endearingly handsome. Now it only made her feel ill.

"When I discovered your old phone number was no longer in service, I remembered your mother's name, looked up her number and called her to ask how to get in touch with you." He shrugged. "She was reluctant to tell me about your move to Texas until I told her that we'd been seeing each other before you left and how much I missed you. That's when she suggested that if I was ever in the Devil's Fork area that I should look you up. I decided to clear my calendar for the rest of the week and make the drive out here to no-man's-land to see how you're doing."

Callie did a slow burn. She wasn't as angry with her mother as she was with Craig. He'd obviously fed her mother a line about how much he cared, and her mother had fallen for it. Unfortunately Nancy Marshall had never met Craig and had no idea what a snake he was. He wasn't interested in how Callie was doing. His ego was still smarting from the fact that Callie had been the one who'd rejected him instead of the other way around.

"Actually your mother and I talked for some time and I found her to be a very nice lady," Craig added solicitously.

"Oh, really?" Callie shook her head. "It's amazing to me that you carried on a lengthy conversation with my mother when you never would take the time to meet her when you and I were seeing each other."

"You've always been close with your mother, haven't you, Callie?" Craig asked.

She gritted her teeth. "You know I have."

"That's the main reason I find it odd that she didn't know anything about your marriage." He rocked back on his heels as he pointed to Hunter. "It seems to me that she would be the first one you told about your marriage to O'Banyon."

When the timer on the stove went off, indicating that the pot roast was done, Callie reluctantly left the two men standing in her living room glaring at each other. She had no idea what was going to take place or how to deal with it. Hunter's expression from the moment he'd walked through the door had been dark and foreboding. And Craig, as was his usual fashion when he felt threatened, had become arrogant and condescending.

Removing the roast from the oven, she hurried back into the living room before punches started flying. "Craig, I'm sure you have better things to do with your time than stand here debating my marital status."

He shook his head. "Not really. But I will take you up on that offer of dinner."

"I didn't—"

Hunter pulled her to his side and pressed a quick kiss to her lips. "I'm sure we have enough for three, don't we, darlin'?"

Had Hunter lost his mind? The last thing she wanted to do was spend more time in the presence of a snake like Craig Culbertson.

"Well, yes, but—"

"Good." Hunter turned to Craig. "Why don't you have a seat while I help my wife finish getting things on the table?"

Craig gave her a triumphant smile as he plopped down on the end of the love seat. "I think I'll do that."

As soon as she and Hunter entered the kitchen, she turned on him. "What on earth were you thinking?" she demanded, careful to keep her voice low. "I want him out of this house, out of this state and out of my life. For good."

Hunter nodded. "That's the plan."

She looked at him as though he might not be the sharpest knife in the drawer. "And having him stay for dinner is the way to do that?"

"I believe so."

Taking in a deep breath, Hunter still couldn't believe that he'd claimed to be Callie's husband and the father of her baby. But when he'd walked up the porch steps and heard the disgust in Culbertson's voice and the fear in Callie's, Hunter had done the only thing he could think of that didn't involve putting his fist in the man's nose.

"Would you care to explain your reasoning?" she asked as she reached for a pair of oven mitts. "Because I'm having a really hard time understanding."

When he noticed how badly her hands trembled, he took the mitts from her and removed a roasting pan from the oven. Placing it on a hot pad, he tossed the mitts on the counter, then cupped her cheeks with his palms. "The first thing I want you to do is calm down, Callie. I give you my word that as long as I have breath left in my body, I won't let him do anything to harm you or the baby. Is that clear?"

She gazed at him for several long seconds, and the fear he saw in her eyes just about tore him apart. "Yes," she finally said, nodding.

"Good." He reached into the cabinet for a platter. Handing it to her, he explained. "It's clear that Culbertson needs some convincing that you and I are married."

"That came as a surprise to me, too," she said, slicing the roast.

He rubbed the tension building at the back of his neck. "Then it's unanimous, because I was pretty damned shocked about it myself. But it's the only thing I can think of that might make him leave you alone. And that's what you want, isn't it?"

"Absolutely." There wasn't even a heartbeat's hesitation in her voice, and Hunter had no doubt that she didn't want Craig Culbertson anywhere near her.

"The way I see it, if we can convince him how happy we are and how much we're looking forward to our first child, he'll get the message, go back to Houston and you'll never hear from him again." He carried the platter of pot roast over to the small kitchen table while Callie set another place. "Now all we have to do is get a few things straight."

"Like what?"

He removed three glasses from one of the shelves, filled them with ice, then reached for a pitcher of iced tea sitting on the kitchen island. "He'll want to know how we met, when we got married and what we're going to name the baby."

She stared at him openmouthed. "We don't have time to coordinate all that."

Thinking quickly, Hunter said, "Just tell me what you intend to name your son and when you discovered you were pregnant. I'll take care of the rest. Just follow my lead and agree with the line I feed Culbertson."

"This is never going to work," she said, plunking a bowl of mashed potatoes onto the table. "There are too many ways he can trip us up."

Hunter caught her by the shoulders and turned her to face him. "Trust me, Callie. Unless you can think of something else, this is the only way."

He watched her close her eyes, take a deep breath, then opening them, she gave him the information he requested. "You'd better be right about this, Hunter. I won't let him take my baby away from me."

"There's no way in hell, darlin'," he said, giving her a quick hug.

Hunter's heart twisted at the fear he'd heard in her soft voice. He wanted to know what had caused her to be so terrified that Culbertson would try to get custody when the man clearly had no use for children. But that would have to wait until later. Right now they had to con the man into leaving Callie alone for good.

* * *

By the time dinner was over, Callie's nerves were stretched to the breaking point. Sitting between the two men, she'd listened to them discuss everything from baseball player stats to the size of engine they preferred in their vehicles. She wasn't sure whether to be relieved or disappointed that the subject of her and Hunter's marriage had yet to come up.

But that hadn't stopped Hunter from playing his part as the devoted husband to the hilt. Throughout dinner he'd given her smiles that threatened to melt her bones and he'd found every excuse imaginable to touch her. She'd caught Craig taking it all in with great interest, but not once had he asked any of the questions she knew for certain had to be running through his mind.

"Why don't we have dessert in the living room?" Craig asked when Callie rose from her chair to slice pieces of German chocolate cake for them.

"Go ahead and have a seat in there while I help Callie clear the table," Hunter said, rising to gather their plates. "We'll join you in a few minutes."

"It's not going the way we planned," she whispered when Craig left the room.

"Be patient, darlin'." Hunter rinsed the dishes to put in the dishwasher, then measured grounds from one of the canisters for a pot of coffee. "If he doesn't get around to asking, I'll bring up the subject myself."

"I should have never let you talk me into this." She shook her head at her own foolishness. "I'm sure he can see right through this little farce."

"Don't worry. Everything is going to be just fine."

As she allowed Hunter to carry the tray she'd arranged with dessert plates, cups and saucers and a carafe of coffee into the living room, she prayed he was right. Her nerves couldn't stand much more. She already had an almost uncontrollable urge to preheat the oven and start measuring sugar and flour.

"I have a question for you two," Craig said when he placed his empty dessert plate back on the tray. "If you're married, why doesn't Callie wear a wedding band?"

Sitting beside Hunter on the love seat, she had just taken a sip of milk from the glass she'd brought with her from the kitchen and it was all she could do to keep from choking at his blunt question. Panic seized her. She'd been right. Craig knew they were only pretending. Now what were they going to do?

"She had to take her wedding ring off when her fingers started getting a little puffy," Hunter said without missing a beat. He took her left hand in his and brought it to his lips to kiss her ring finger. "Once she has the baby, it will be right back where it belongs."

A wave of tingling heat traveled up her arm, then spread throughout the rest of her body at the loving gesture. She was glad that Hunter had been able to think fast because at the moment she wasn't sure she could think at all.

"When and where did you meet?" Craig asked.

Hunter held up his hand. "See that little scar on my palm? I had to go to the emergency room in Houston when I had a run-in with a fish hook. As soon as I saw Callie, I knew she was the woman for me." Giving her a smile that made her insides feel as if they'd turned to warm pudding, he lightly kissed her cheek. "We were married a few days later and pregnant a few weeks after that."

"Why the rush?" Craig asked, sounding more than a little suspicious.

"Once I see what I want, I don't let it get away from me." Hunter put his arm around her shoulders and held her close to his side. "I'm afraid you're going to have to face facts, Culbertson. She's with me now and I'm not about to let her or our baby go."

Callie watched Craig. She knew him well enough to know that he wasn't entirely convinced. There was a huge hole in their story, and although he hadn't asked again why she'd failed to tell her mother about her marriage to Hunter, Callie knew it was on his mind. But gaining strength from the man holding her so possessively against him, she decided that if the matter came up again, she'd simply tell Craig that she didn't have to explain herself to him or anyone else.

"Well, I suppose I should be going," Craig said as

he rose to his feet. "As always, your cooking was delicious, Callie."

When Hunter stood, then helped her up from her saggy love seat, she began to believe they might have pulled off the ruse. Craig would be leaving town and, with any luck, she'd never have to see or hear from him again.

"Have an enjoyable trip back to Houston," Hunter said as they all walked to the door.

Craig shook his head. "Oh, I'm not leaving the area for several more days. While you two were finishing dinner, I checked the phone book and found a little bed-and-breakfast just up the street." His smirk made Callie want to scream with frustration. "I thought I'd stick around for a while and take in the sights." He laughed as he opened the door. "It's been my experience that you can learn a lot from talking to the locals in a town the size of Devil's Fork."

As Craig walked down the steps and out to his sleek red sports car, Callie felt like crying. How could her life have gotten so out of control in such a short time?

Turning to Hunter, she sighed heavily. "Any more bright ideas?"

He didn't look any happier about the turn of events than she was. "The way I see it, we don't have a whole lot of choice. I'm going to have to move in with you until that sorry excuse for a human being leaves town."

# Six

Two hours later, after helping Callie clean up the kitchen, Hunter found himself trying to fold his six-foot-three-inch frame into a comfortable sleeping position on her lumpy love seat. Muttering a word he reserved for extreme situations, he sat up, propped his elbows on his knees and cradled his head in his hands. What the hell had he gotten himself into? And why?

If he'd kept his mouth shut, he'd be sleeping on a fairly comfortable, albeit narrow, bed at the Life Medevac hangar instead of torturing himself on the most uncomfortable piece of furniture known to man. And he for damn sure wouldn't be locked into playing house for the next week with a woman that he was already finding it all but impossible to keep his hands off.

But even as he castigated himself for getting involved, he knew he'd done the right thing. After meeting Culbertson and listening to Callie explain how he and his parents had used their money and influence to take the baby away from the first girl Craig had gotten pregnant, Hunter knew as sure as he knew his own name the Culbertsons wouldn't think twice about trying to do the same thing to Callie.

Shaking his head, Hunter couldn't believe how arrogant they were. What gave them the right to take a baby from his mother simply because Culbertson blood ran through the child's veins? What kind of people thought that it automatically made the mother unfit just because their bank account dwarfed hers?

As he sat there thinking about how ruthless and selfish they were, he realized that if Emerald Larson had wanted to, she could have taken him and his brothers away from their mothers at any time. She certainly had more money and power than the Culbertsons ever dreamed of having and she would have had very little trouble gaining custody of her grandsons.

But instead of viewing the three of them as possessions, Emerald had cared enough to content herself with watching Hunter and his brothers grow up in pictures and P.I. reports in order to ensure they turned out to be as normal and well-adjusted as possible. And for the first time since learning the details of his parentage he began to appreciate the sacrifices that had been made by Emerald on his behalf.

Any lingering traces of anger he still carried from being denied the right to know who his father was dissipated. Although Hunter would always have a problem with any man walking away from a woman when she needed him most, he came to the conclusion that Emerald and her philandering son weren't entirely responsible for the anger and confusion he'd grown up with.

It had been Marlene O'Banyon's choice to agree to Emerald's terms. And although Emerald hadn't required that his mother remain single, Hunter sometimes wondered if she'd signed the confidentiality agreement secretly hoping that one day Owen Larson would come to his senses and return to Miami for her and Hunter. But Owen had never laid eyes on any of his children, nor had he seen their mothers again. And with his death in a boating accident somewhere in the Mediterranean eight months ago, it was never going to happen.

Of course, his mother had no idea that old Owen had sown more than just one wild oat. Although she was the first woman he'd gotten pregnant, she certainly hadn't been the last. Hell, Hunter doubted that Emerald was completely certain that he, Nick and Caleb were Owen's only offspring.

But that was immaterial now. The fact of the matter was, in light of the way the Culbertsons had dealt with a similar situation, he understood and could even commend his grandmother for handling everything the way she had.

Lost in thought, it took a moment for Hunter to realize that Callie had gotten out of bed and was tip-toeing her way through the living room into the kitchen. "Can't sleep?" he asked, careful to keep his voice nonthreatening so as not to frighten her.

Her startled cry was loud enough to wake the dead. So much for trying not to frighten her.

"It's just me, Callie."

"Dear heavens, you scared me out of a year's growth," she said, clutching something to the front of her robe.

"I'm sorry." He switched on the lamp at the end of the love seat. "I didn't mean to…" He stopped to stare at her when he realized what she was carrying. "What the hell are you doing with your apron at—" he checked his watch "—midnight?"

"I'm too keyed up to sleep," she said defensively. "I thought I'd find something to do."

He frowned. "So you're going to start cooking?"

She breezed past him to enter the kitchen. "Every-one deals with stress in their own way. Some people drink. Some eat. I bake."

That explained why she'd made enough baked goods to stock a chain of grocery stores, he thought as he followed her. She'd been scared witless since learning she was pregnant that Culbertson would find out about the baby. Now that he had, it appeared that Callie would be making enough cookies to feed every man, woman and child in the whole damned state.

"Our shift starts in a little less than eighteen hours." He yawned. "Don't you think it would be a good idea to be well rested when we go to work?"

She shook her head as she reached for a set of measuring cups and the canister of flour. "Don't worry about me, I'll be fine. You're the one who needs rest to pilot the helicopter. Go back into the living room and get some sleep."

"That's easier said than done," he muttered.

"I promise I won't make much noise," she said, knocking over the cup of flour she'd just measured.

"That's not the problem." He pulled out a chair and sat down at the table. "I'm too tall."

"Excuse me?"

She looked thoroughly confused and so darned cute standing there in her nightclothes and apron, he had to force himself to remember what they were talking about. "The love seat is roughly fifty inches long and I'm six foot three. You do the math."

Her eyes widened. "Oh, dear. I'm sorry. I hadn't thought of it being too short for you." She shook her head. "But it's not a problem. You can take my bed and I'll sleep on the love seat."

"Like hell." He wasn't about to sleep on a comfortable bed while she endured that instrument of torture in her condition.

"Why not?" she asked as she cleaned up the flour she'd spilled. "I'm at least ten inches shorter and shouldn't have nearly as much trouble getting comfortable."

"You're pregnant."

"And you're bossy." She grinned. "But I'm trying not to hold that against you."

Her pretty smile sent a wave of heat straight through him, and he could think of several things he'd like for her to hold against him—every one of them soft, warm and deliciously feminine. He swallowed hard. Thinking along those lines could only accomplish one of two things. It would either get him in a whole lot deeper than he was comfortable with or drive him completely insane. And he wasn't altogether sure that he hadn't already crossed the line in both areas.

"I can sleep in one of the chairs and—"

"Wake up with a terribly stiff neck," she interrupted, dropping an egg on the counter. "Darn." Grabbing a paper towel, she cleaned up the mess. "If I'm going to be flying with you, I not only want you well rested, I'd like for you to have your full range of motion."

"I can manage in the chair." He stood up and started toward the living room, but her soft hand on his back stopped him dead in his tracks and sent a jolt of electric current throughout his system.

"I think we're overlooking the obvious here," she said, turning to measure more flour into a bowl. "I'll probably be up for hours before I'm relaxed enough to go to sleep. There's no reason for you to be uncomfortable when there's an empty bed that you could be sleeping in. And if I want to go to sleep before you get up, I'll be careful not to wake you when I lie down."

She had a point. It was pretty silly for him to try to sleep in the chair when he could be stretched out. But just knowing that she'd eventually be getting in bed with him was enough to send him into orbit.

"I guess that could work," he said, thinking aloud. "And we're both adults. There's no reason we can't handle this." And maybe if he repeated it enough, he'd start to believe it.

"Exactly." She waved her hand toward the other room as she reached for a spoon and promptly knocked over a container of baking powder. "You're distracting me. Now go to bed and let me get started on these cookies."

Yawning, he scratched his bare chest and headed for her bedroom. Hopefully he'd be out like a light as soon as his head hit the pillow. And if he believed that, he was sure somebody had a piece of beachfront property in the middle of Arizona that he'd be fool enough to buy.

* * *

A couple of hours after Hunter went to lie down in her bed, Callie turned off the light in the kitchen and quietly walked into the bedroom. Making several dozen cookies had helped, but her nerves were still on edge and she expected they would remain that way until she was certain Craig was out of her life for good.

As she removed her slippers, then turned to pull back the cover, she forgot all about her current problem with Craig and focused on the sight of Hunter's broad back. From the muted moonlight filtering into the room through the sheer drapes she could see that he was lying on his stomach with the sheet covering him from the waist down.

Her heart stalled and she swallowed hard as the sight of all that delicious masculine skin reminded her of earlier in the kitchen when she'd first seen his bare chest. The play of his perfectly defined chest muscles beneath a light sprinkling of dark hair had fascinated her beyond words and distracted her to the point she'd been about as coordinated as a bull in a china shop.

How on earth was she going to be able to sleep with all that raw masculinity mere inches away? And why did her double bed suddenly seem as though it had shrunk to the size of a cot?

Wishing she had bought a two-bedroom house instead of a charming one-bedroom cottage, she shook her head as she jammed her feet back in her slippers.

She'd go into the kitchen, grab a handful of chocolate chips and lie down on the love seat.

"Are you going to stand there the rest of the night or are you going to get into bed?"

She jumped at the sound of Hunter's voice and her cheeks heated with embarrassment at being caught staring at him. Thank heavens there wasn't enough light in the room for him to see her guilty expression. "I…didn't want to…disturb you."

He rolled to his back and gazed up at her. "I wasn't asleep."

"What's wrong?" The way he'd been yawning before he'd gone to bed, she'd have thought he'd be asleep before he had a chance to close his eyes. "Is the mattress too soft for you?"

"No, it's quite comfortable."

She frowned as she gingerly sat down on the side of the bed. "Then what's the problem?"

"I've been thinking—"

"I'm not altogether sure I want to hear this," she interrupted warily. "The last time you shared your thoughts is what got us into this mess."

"Are you going to take off your robe and lie down?"

She swallowed hard. It would have been hard enough to stretch out beside him if he'd been asleep. But awake? Just the thought caused a tingling sensation to skip over every cell in her body.

"That's what you've been thinking about?"

"No." His deep chuckle sent a shiver straight up her spine. "But you've been going on adrenaline all evening, and I think it would probably be a good idea for the baby's sake if you tried to relax."

Callie knew he was right. But she wasn't sure that was going to be an option, especially with him so close.

"Are you going to keep me guessing or are you going to tell me what you've come up with this time?" she hedged.

He shook his head. "Not until you lie down."

Exasperated beyond words, she shook her head. "I think it would be best if I slept on the love seat."

"Why? You aren't afraid of sleeping in the same bed with me, are you?" She couldn't see much of his expression in the darkened room, but she'd heard the laughter and good-natured challenge in his voice.

"Don't be silly," she lied. "I just think since we're clearly attracted to each other, it might not be a good idea."

"Remember, we're both adults," he said softly. "I give you my word that nothing is going to happen that you don't want to happen."

It shouldn't be a problem, she told herself as she stood up to remove her robe. She wasn't sure why, but she trusted him. And she knew for certain she didn't have to worry about herself. The last thing she wanted or needed was to become involved with another man.

When she slipped into bed, he turned to his side,

propped his elbow on the pillow and rested his head against his palm. His proximity sent a delicious little thrill from the top of her head all the way to the tips of her toes. She did her best to ignore it.

"I think we should get married."

His voice was low and intimate, and it took a moment for her to realize what he'd said. When she did, her heart slammed against her ribs.

"You can't be serious."

When she started to get out of bed, his hand on her arm stopped her. "Think about it, darlin'. It won't take much effort on Culbertson's part to discover that we aren't married or that I've never been to Houston."

"And this just occurred to you?" She rubbed at her suddenly throbbing temples. "Why did I let you talk me into this? I told you it wouldn't work."

"That's why I'm suggesting we get married," he said patiently. "It doesn't matter when we got married, we'll still be husband and wife."

"I can't see where that would do anything but add one more complication to an already impossible situation." A sudden thought caused a chill to race through her, and she had to take a deep breath in order to get words passed the tightness in her throat. "He could ask for a DNA test to prove paternity."

"He might, but something tells me he won't."

Her breath caught on a soft sob. If he and his parents learned that her son had been fathered by Craig, the

Culbertsons were the kind of people who would intervene and take her baby away from her—not because they loved the child, but because they viewed him as one of their possessions. They'd find an excuse to find her unworthy or unfit to raise their heir, the same as they'd done that poor girl twelve years ago.

"There's no way out of…this." A chill ran the length of her spine. "They're going to take my child away from me and there's nothing I can do to stop them."

Hunter reached out to wrap his strong arms around her and cradle her to him. "Not as long as I'm around to stop them, they won't."

"I can't see how—"

"Taking a child away from a single parent isn't as difficult as it is from a married couple."

"Yes, but the Culbertsons are quite wealthy and can hire the best lawyers. And I'm sure they'll see that the case is heard by a judge who travels in the same social circle they do." She placed her hand over her stomach. "We'd be fighting a losing battle."

"Let them hire whoever they want or get whatever judge they think will go along with their request." He kissed her forehead. "It's not like I don't have a few connections of my own."

Pulling back to look at him, she shook her head. "I'm not sure who you think you know, but it's going to take more than a connection or two to keep them from taking my son."

"You might be surprised." He gently brushed a strand of hair from her cheek with his index finger. "Let me worry about dealing with the Culbertsons and their lawyers. I'm going to do some checking, but I suspect there's more to his visit than what he's saying."

Anger and frustration filled her. "This is the very reason I detest rich people. They think that because they have money it gives them the right to do anything they please."

"Not all people of means are like the Culbertsons, Callie," he said quietly. "My father's family had money, but there was never a threat of them taking me or my brothers away from our mothers."

Remembering their conversation on the trip back from El Paso, Callie bit her lower lip to keep it from trembling as a fresh wave of fear coursed through her. "I'd say your father's family is the exception, not the rule."

"Maybe, but I'm betting it's closer to being the other way around." He lightly ran his palm up and down her arm, sending a wave of tingling warmth to every part of her. "At any rate, I promise you have nothing to fear from the Culbertsons as long as I'm around."

"I hope you're right," she said, hiding a yawn behind her hand.

He kissed the top of her head. "We'll talk more in the morning. Right now we both need to get some rest."

Within moments his deep, even breathing signaled that Hunter had fallen asleep. But, as tired as she was, Callie couldn't stop thinking about the threat that Craig posed or Hunter's offer of marriage.

Everything he said made perfect sense and could very well solve her problem. But friendship only went so far. She couldn't believe he was willing to enter into something as serious as marriage simply to help her. What did he expect to get out of it for himself? And what would happen if they were successful in keeping the Culbertsons from taking her baby away from her? How long before Hunter asked for an annulment or a divorce?

Thoroughly exhausted from the tension of Craig's unexpected visit and the speculation of what would happen if she did go along with Hunter's insane suggestion, Callie felt herself begin to drift off to sleep. But instead of having nightmares of her baby being taken away from her by Craig and his family, she dreamed of marriage to a tall, dark-haired, handsome man with a sexy-as-sin voice and devastating kisses.

The feel of thin, downy-soft hair against her cheek, the steady beat of a heart beneath her ear and the scent of clean masculine skin assailed Callie's senses as she floated in the surreal world between sleep and wakefulness. When a pair of strong arms tightened around her, she smiled and snuggled against the hard male body beside her.

"Good morning, sleepyhead."

The sound of Hunter's voice caused her eyes to fly open and had her tilting her head to meet his incredible green gaze. She was lying with her head pillowed on his broad chest and her arm thrown over his flat belly. But it was the realization that her leg was draped over his muscular thigh—his bare muscular thigh—that sent a shiver of excitement up her spine and had her wondering if she'd be able to draw her next breath.

"H-how long have you been awake?"

"About an hour."

Goose bumps shimmered over her skin at the vibration of his rich baritone rumbling up from deep in his chest. But it was the feel of his hard arousal straining at his briefs that had her gingerly moving her leg away from his. They were treading in dangerous territory and it would definitely be best to put some distance between them.

"Where are you going?" His warm breath stirred the fine hair at her temple and caused her heart to skip several beats.

"I, um, should probably get up and cook something for breakfast."

He held her firmly against him when she tried to pull from his arms. "I've got a hunger, but it's not for food."

A delightful heat like nothing she'd ever known began to flow through her veins at his candid comment.

"I—it wouldn't be a good idea to complicate things more than they already are."

His deep chuckle caused the warmth inside of her to pool in the pit of her belly. "Darlin', kissing isn't complicated." He brushed her lips with his, sending a delightful tingling sensation all the way to her toes. "It's one of the purest forms of pleasure a man and woman can share."

The sound of his voice, his provocative words and the feel of his calloused palm caressing her side through her thin cotton gown were like a drug and she suddenly had a hard time remembering her own name, let alone why it would make their current situation more difficult. But she ceased thinking at all when his mouth settled over hers and he tenderly traced the outline of her lips with his tongue.

"This is…insane," she murmured, trying to draw some much-needed air into her lungs.

He nibbled kisses along her jawline to the sensitive hollow below her ear. "Do you want me to stop?"

"I should demand that you stop and get out of my house immediately."

His lips blazed a trail down her neck to her collar-bone. "But you aren't going to do that?"

With a myriad of delightful sensations coursing through her, she had to concentrate on his question. "N-no."

"Why not?" he asked as he ran his palm back down

her side, then slipped his hand beneath the hem of her gown.

His fingers sliding along her bare skin made breathing all but impossible and caused the heat in her lower belly to intensify. "Wh-what you're doing…feels too good."

"Do you want me to stop?"

Unable to think clearly, she shook her head. "Don't you dare."

He caressed her hip, then her ribs as he slowly moved his hand up her body. "Are you aware of what's going to happen if I continue?"

When he covered her breast with his hand, then chafed her puckered nipple with the pad of his thumb, need coursed through her to settle deep in the most feminine part of her. "W-we'll make love."

His hand continued to caress her overly sensitized skin. "Is that what you want, Callie?"

Staring into his dark green eyes, her heart pounded hard in her chest. From the moment they'd first met there had been a magnetic pull drawing them together, a chemistry they'd both tried but found impossible to deny. And with each kiss the tension between them had heightened until it had become a force that was impossible for either of them to fight.

Whether it was her pregnancy hormones that caused a desire stronger than anything she'd ever known or something more, she didn't want him to stop. She wanted to feel the warmth of Hunter's kisses and the passion of his loving touch.

"It's pure insanity. But yes, I want to make love with you, Hunter."

# Seven

At Callie's admittance that she wanted to make love with him, Hunter's heart slammed against his rib cage so hard he was surprised it hadn't jumped right out of his chest. Throughout the night he'd lain with her in his arms, and with each tick of the clock her soft body and sweet womanly scent had increased the tension he'd been fighting from the moment he'd laid eyes on her. But when she'd awakened and stared up at him with her sexy violet eyes, he'd become harder than he'd ever been in his life and could no more have stopped himself from tasting and touching her than he could stop the sun from rising in the east each morning.

But as much as he wanted to sink himself deep inside of her, to hear her call his name as he pleasured her, he couldn't bear the thought that she might regret one minute of what they would share. "Are you sure that making love is what you really want, Callie?"

His heart stalled and he found himself holding his breath when she closed her eyes and remained silent for several long seconds. Then, to his relief, she opened her eyes and nodded her head.

"I think I'll go into total meltdown if we don't."

Taking a deep breath, he tried to slow the liquid fire racing through his veins. "I know I should have asked this before things went this far, but would your doctor be okay with our making love?"

Her porcelain cheeks colored a pretty pink as she nodded. "The obstetrician has given me the go-ahead for normal activity with no restrictions. And that includes lovemaking."

Hunter couldn't believe the level of relief that washed over him. If she'd told him there was even the slightest possibility of a problem or the tiniest bit of discomfort for her, he'd have found some way—no matter how difficult—to walk away. But knowing there was nothing to prevent them from having a pleasurable and satisfying experience sent a fresh wave of heat straight to his groin.

Unfortunately it was short-lived. He hadn't planned on spending the night with Callie, let alone making love with her, and protection hadn't even crossed his mind when he'd left the hangar yesterday evening. But he was thinking about it now. Or, more accurately, the lack of it.

But as he gazed at the woman in his arms, he realized there was no possibility of him making her pregnant. And truth to tell, it wouldn't matter to him if she wasn't already expecting a child.

The thought of Callie carrying his baby appealed to him more than he could have ever imagined and should have scared the living hell out of him. It was something he didn't understand, wasn't entirely comfortable with and, at the moment, didn't intend to analyze. All that mattered was bringing her pleasure, cherishing her as she was meant to be cherished.

Without a moment's hesitation he gathered her close and covered her mouth with his. Her soft lips molded to his with a hungry desperation that matched his own and sent fire racing through his veins with the swift-ness of a raging river.

When she parted for him to deepen the kiss, Hunter thought his head might come right off his shoulders as she boldly stroked his tongue with hers and engaged him in an erotic game of advance and retreat. She was letting him know that she felt the passion as deeply as he did, that she wanted him as much as he wanted her.

Breaking the kiss, he nibbled his way to the base of her throat as he reached for the hem of her gown.

"Lift your hips, darlin'," he whispered against her satiny skin.

When he'd whisked away her panties and thin cotton gown, he quickly removed his boxer briefs, then tossing the garments to the floor beside the bed, gathered her back into his arms. At the feel of her satiny skin against him, desire raced through his veins, and he had to fight an almost uncontrollable urge to cover her with his body and sink himself deep inside of her.

His entire being pulsed with the urgent need to claim her, but he was determined not to rush things no matter what his body demanded. "You feel so soft...." He trailed kisses down the base of her throat, then past her collarbone to the slope of her breast. "So sweet."

As he teased her with a light swirling motion, the fire of need in his belly grew when she threaded her fingers in his hair and pulled him closer. Arching her back, she gave him better access to the hardened tip, and taking her into his mouth, he chafed her with his tongue and caressed her with his lips.

"P-please, Hunter."

"Not yet, darlin'." Moving his hand down her side to her hip and beyond, he cupped her at the apex of her thighs. "I want to make sure you're ready for me."

"If I was any more ready...I'd burn to a crisp." Her voice sounded wispy and breathless and he had no doubt she was as turned-on as he was.

Parting her, he stroked her, then touched her intimately. Her moist warmth and moan of pleasure assured him that she needed him as much as he needed her.

"I want you to promise me something," he said as he continued to stroke her.

"Anything." He watched her close her eyes and catch her lower lip between her teeth a moment before she whimpered, "You're driving me…crazy."

Her response to his touch heightened his own passion, and he had to take several deep breaths in order to force himself to slow down. "I want you to promise me that if there's even the slightest bit of discomfort, you'll tell me."

"I promise." When she opened her eyes to gaze up at him, the desire in the violet depths robbed him of breath. "Please…make love to me, Hunter."

Unable to deny either one of them any longer, he nudged her knees apart and levered himself over her. As he moved his lower body into position, he settled his mouth over hers at the same time he pressed himself forward.

Slowly, carefully, he pushed into her, and the feel of her tight body melting around him as he sank deeper and deeper had him clenching his teeth as he struggled for control. But when she raised her hips for more of him, the slender thread of his restraint snapped and he buried himself completely within her feminine depths.

With every muscle in his body taut with the need to complete the act of loving her, Hunter forced himself to remain completely still. She needed time to adjust to him and he needed time to savor the feeling of being completely one with the most desirable woman he'd ever known.

Gathering her close, he kissed her sweet lips. "I'm going to try to go slow, but I want you so damned much I'm not sure that's an option."

Her smile caused the fire threatening to consume him to flare out of control. "I want you just as much."

He held her gaze with his as he eased his hips back then forward, thrusting into her again and again. As he felt her respond by meeting him halfway, he increased the rhythm with each stroke, and in no time he felt her body tighten around his, signaling that she was poised to find her release.

When she wrapped her legs around his waist to hold him close, the pressure in his body increased tenfold and it was all he could do to hold himself in check. But he wasn't going to find his satisfaction without her, and sliding his hand between them, he touched her as he thrust into her one last time.

Her moan of pleasure and the quivering of her tiny inner muscles rippling around him as she found her satisfaction triggered his own completion. Heat and light flashed behind his tightly closed eyes as he surrendered to the storm, and feeling as if his world had been reduced to just the two of them, he emptied himself deep inside of her.

As Hunter slowly drifted back to reality, an emotion filled his chest that he didn't dare put a name to. He'd never experienced anything as amazing as what he'd just shared with Callie. Her passionate response to his touch had excited him in ways he'd only dreamed of and he felt more alive than he had in years.

"Are you all right?" he asked when he finally found the strength to move to her side.

"I-I'm fine."

A slight crack in her voice had him rising up to look down at her beautiful face. The tears he saw welling up in her eyes scared him as little else could. If he'd hurt her in any way, he'd never forgive himself.

"Callie, darlin', what's wrong?"

"Nothing. Making love with you was one of the most beautiful experiences I've ever had." She cupped his cheek with her palm, and her smile lit the darkest corners of his soul. "Thank you."

Weak with relief, he shook his head. "I should be thanking you. You were incredible."

When she hid a yawn behind her delicate hand, he kissed the top of her head. "You were up pretty late and it's still early. Why don't we take a nap, then we can talk over breakfast." He hadn't much more than gotten the words out before her shallow breathing signaled that she'd drifted off to sleep.

As he watched the predawn shadows in the room melt away with the light of day, Hunter held Callie close and thought about what they would be talking about later. After the accident and Ellen's death, he'd never intended to ask another woman to marry him. But these were a different set of circumstances. He and Callie wouldn't be marrying for love. They would be doing the only thing he could think of that might discourage Craig Culbertson from trying to take her baby away from her.

He closed his eyes and tried to think of some other way to help Callie. From the time he'd gone to bed until she'd entered the bedroom a couple of hours later, all he'd been able to think about was how they could stop Culbertson and his family.

Hunter had no idea what the man's motive was, but he must have learned about Callie's pregnancy from her mother and shown up to confirm his suspicions that he was the father. Considering the disgust in his voice when he'd accusingly asked her if the child was his, Hunter was surprised that Culbertson hadn't jumped at the chance for someone else to take responsibility. But he hadn't, and Hunter had every intention of pulling out all the stops to find out why. And he knew exactly who to contact to help him start making inquiries into the matter. He'd get the name of a discreet private investigator from Emerald's trusted assistant, Luther Freemont, and see what they could dig up on Culbertson.

If he'd wanted to, Hunter could have asked outright for Emerald to intervene on Callie's behalf and he had no doubt that she would have. But that wasn't his style. Whether it was pride or bullheaded stubbornness, he fought his own battles. He'd offered to help Callie and he'd be the one to see the matter through to the end.

Another reason he didn't want to get Emerald involved was that he wasn't ready for anyone—and especially Callie—at Life Medevac to learn of his relationship to the indomitable Mrs. Larson. For one thing, he had yet to prove himself with the business she'd given him to run. And for another, Callie had trust issues with anyone who had money. If she were to discover that he was Emerald Larson's grandson and had been given a trust fund large enough to make a dent in the national debt, as well as being in line to inherit part of Emerald Inc., she'd automatically assume he was like the Culbertsons and refuse his help. And that was something they both knew she couldn't afford to do.

Gazing down at her sleeping so peacefully in his arms, he fleetingly wondered if getting married would pose a threat to either of their hearts. But he immediately dismissed the concern. They wouldn't be marrying for love, and as long as they kept things in perspective and their emotions in check, there shouldn't be a problem for either of them.

Satisfied that he had everything under control,

Hunter relaxed and closed his eyes. They'd stay together as long as it took to settle this business with Culbertson once and for all, then evaluate the best way to handle the dissolution of their marriage.

An unexpected twinge of regret tightened his chest at the thought, but he ignored it. He and Callie were friends now and they would remain friends once they parted ways. And that's just the way it had to stay.


"Where's your husband, Callie?"

Callie went perfectly still at the sound of the familiar voice. Needing a refill on her prenatal vitamins, she'd stopped at the drugstore on her way to start her shift at Life Medevac. She didn't have the time nor the desire to deal with the likes of Craig Culbertson.

"Not that it's any of your business, but Hunter owns the air-ambulance service and had some paperwork to deal with," she said, heading back to her car.

She could pick up the vitamins another time. Right now she wanted nothing more than to put as much distance between her and Craig as humanly possible.

But before she could get the driver's door open, he caught her by the arm. "What's your hurry? Surely you have enough time to talk to an old friend."

Extricating herself from his grasp, she turned to face him. "We aren't friends and never will be. Now if you'll excuse me, I need to get to work."

His knowing smirk was enough to make her want

to scream. "If your husband owns the business, going in late shouldn't be a problem for you."

She reached for the handle on her car door. "I need to be there on time to relieve the on-duty crew."

He shook his head as he placed his hand on the driver's door to hold it shut. "What you need to do is answer a few questions."

"No, I don't."

"Oh, I think you do." He reached out to trace his index finger down her cheek. "It seems that none of the people here in town knew anything about you and O'Banyon being married. In fact, Mr. Jones over at the grocery store was quite surprised to hear the news."

A cold chill slithered up her spine at Craig's touch. She must have had blinders on not see that his charm was a weapon, not an endearing quality. How could she have ever found herself attracted to such a reptile?

Batting his hand away, she shook her head. "Don't ever touch me again."

"You used to like for me to touch you, Callie," he said, trying to affect an injured look.

"That's ancient history." She tried to remove his hand where he held the car door. "All I want from you now is to be left alone."

His eyes narrowed and a sneer replaced his wounded expression. "Now is that any way to talk to your baby's daddy?"

"Just because you can fertilize an egg doesn't make

you father material. That takes someone special." She jerked the car door from his grasp and started to get in. "Someone who is actually capable of loving a child."

"Like O'Banyon?"

"Yes. Exactly like Hunter."

His sarcastic laugh caused her to clench her fists until her knuckles ached. "Why don't you give up the charade, Callie? We both know you're no more married than I am. If you come back to Houston now, maybe I'll forget that you and O'Banyon tried to dupe me into believing the baby belongs to him." He shrugged. "Who knows? I might even be persuaded to let you have visitation rights."

Fear so strong it threatened to the buckle her knees ran through her. "As long as I have breath left in my body, you won't take my child away from me," she said, doing her best to keep her voice steady.

His knowing smile made her skin crawl. "That remains to be seen, my dear."

As Callie got into the car, her hands shook so badly that it took a couple of tries before she was able to fit her key into the ignition. Everything she'd feared for the past several months was coming true.

As she backed the car from the parking space and drove the short distance to the Life Medevac hangar outside of town, her body trembled and tears ran unchecked down her cheeks. For reasons she didn't have time nor the inclination to analyze, all she could think of was getting to Hunter. She knew it made no sense at all considering the short time they'd known each other, but with him she felt more secure than she had in her entire life. And although she hated being vulnerable and dependent in any way, his reassuring presence gave her strength.

Parking her car at the side of the hangar, she hurried into the dispatch room. Thankfully the on-duty crew and Mary Lou were occupied with a game of Texas Hold 'Em poker. She knew she looked more than a little upset and she didn't particularly want to endure a barrage of questions from Mary Lou.

"Is Hunter in his office?" she asked as she breezed past them.

"He's been in there all afternoon making phone calls," Mary Lou answered without looking up from her cards.

When Callie came to Hunter's office, she didn't even hesitate as she opened the door and walked into the room. Craig might think he had the upper hand, but she wasn't going to stand by and let him take her son away without a fight. And if that meant entering into a marriage with a man she barely knew, then that's exactly what she was going to do.

"If you're still willing to marry me, my answer is yes."

# Eight

Hunter was on his feet and rounding the desk in a flash. Callie looked as if she'd seen a ghost, and the tears streaming down her cheeks just about tore him apart.

"What's happened?"

When he took her into his arms, she burrowed into his embrace. As she told him about meeting up with Culbertson and the man's arrogant attitude, pure fury burned at Hunter's gut.

"Do you honestly think we would have a chance of stopping him if we were married?" she asked, trembling against him.

"There's not a doubt in my mind, darlin'."

If he could have gotten his hands on Culbertson at

that very moment, Hunter would have choked the life out of him for putting her through that. The man was without question the sorriest excuse for a human being he'd ever had the misfortune to meet, and it was going to give him great pleasure to deal the arrogant jerk a good dose of reality.

Hunter had spent the entire afternoon on the phone with Emerald's personal assistant, Luther Freemont, and the private investigator Emerald Inc. hired for running background checks on potential employees for Emerald's various companies. After speaking with the man at length, Hunter was confident that if there was anything they could use to combat Culbertson's attempt to gain custody of Callie's baby, the P.I. would find it.

And on the outside chance that Culbertson was squeaky-clean—which Hunter knew damned good and well he wasn't—he and Callie would establish them-selves as a married couple with a stable home life that no lawyer, judge or social worker could argue wasn't perfect for raising a child.

"I don't want you spending any more time worrying about Culbertson or what he's going to do," Hunter said as he soothingly rubbed at the tension along her spine.

She leaned back to look at him, and the anxiety he saw in the depths of her expressive eyes caused his gut to twist into a tight knot. "Th-that's easier said than done."

"Do you trust me, Callie?"

"Yes." There wasn't so much as a hint of uncertainty in her answer.

"I give you my word that everything is going to work out." He gave her a reassuring smile. "By the time this is settled, Craig Culbertson will be running back to Houston like a tail-tucked dog."

"I hope you're right."

"I am."

He sealed his promise with a kiss, and by the time he raised his head, his body was as hard as a chunk of granite. Taking a deep breath, he rested his forehead against hers. He had no idea how she'd managed to get under his skin so quickly, but there was no denying that he found her to be the most exciting woman he'd had the good fortune to meet in the past five years. And the thought of making love to her every night, then holding her as she slept, was enough to send a laser of heat straight through him.

"Why…are you willing…to do this for me, Hunter?" she asked, every bit as breathless as he was. "What's in this for you?"

He'd asked himself the same question at least a dozen times and the answer had been surprisingly simple. "Even though my father's family is well off, my grandmother felt that my brothers and I would be much better off being raised by loving mothers who taught us a solid set of values, instead of giving us everything we wanted, like she'd given our father." He grinned. "Her logic must have worked, because we all turned out to be well-adjusted and productive, instead of selfish and hopelessly irresponsible like her son."

"Your grandmother must be a very special, very wise lady."

"She's definitely one of a kind," he said evasively, thinking that was an understatement. "But the point is, I believe every kid deserves the same chance she gave me and my brothers."

"In other words, you're doing this for the sake of my son?"

Hunter nodded. "I know you'll be a great mom and raise him with the love and guidance he needs. He wouldn't get that from Culbertson and his family."

She shook her head disapprovingly. "He'd turn out to be just like Craig—hedonistic, selfish and shallow."

"Exactly." Hunter kissed her forehead. "And to answer your second question, the only thing I expect to get out of our marriage is the satisfaction of knowing that I stopped that from happening."

"How long—"

Placing his finger to her lips, he shook his head. "Let's take it one day at a time. After we take care of this business with Culbertson, then we'll discuss how we want to handle…things." He had no idea why, but he couldn't bring himself to say the word *annulment* or *divorce*.

He watched her nibble on her lower lip as she gazed

at him for several seconds. "Does that mean you'll be moving in with me for a while?"

"Husbands and wives usually live together, darlin'." He grinned. "Of course, you could always move into my room here at the hangar."

For the first time since walking into the room she smiled. "I don't think that would work very well considering you have a twin-size bed."

"Oh, I think it might work out real well." Sharing any bed with Callie sounded good to him. He brushed her lips with his. "When we aren't making love, I can hold you close while we sleep."

He watched a spark of awareness replace the worry in her violet eyes. "That might work for a time. But what happens when my tummy is as big as an overinflated balloon?"

"Good point," he said, wondering what it would feel like to have her baby moving under his hands. A sharp pang of regret that he'd never feel his own child move inside her knifed through him, but he did his best to ignore it. Suddenly feeling as if he might be drowning, he added, "Maybe your bed would be best."

"When do you want to do this?"

He laughed, relieving some of his tension. "If it had been left up to me, we wouldn't have gotten out of bed this morning."

Her cheeks coloring a pretty pink fascinated the

hell out of him. "I meant, when do you think we should get married?"

"I know." He gave her a quick kiss, then stepped back before he gave in to temptation and took her down the hall to test out his narrow bed. "How does tomorrow afternoon sound?"

"Impossible." The sound of laughter in her sweet voice was like a balm to his soul. "Besides the fact that we'll be on duty, there's a three-day waiting period in the state of Texas from the time we obtain a license until we get married."

"I happen to know there isn't a waiting period in New Mexico." He took her by the hand and led her over to the door. "And remember, I'm the boss. I can have the Evac II crew come in on standby for the day while you and I make a trip up to Carlsbad."

She looked a little dazed as they walked out into the hall. "This is all happening so fast."

"Things will slow down after tomorrow." He put his arm around her slender shoulders and held her to his side. "Now put on your best smile, darlin'. We have an announcement to make to our coworkers."


"Do you, Calantha Marshall, take this man to be your lawful wedded husband? To have and to hold…"

The rotund judge droned on, but Callie had no idea if he recited the words of the traditional wedding ceremony or if he was trying to auction off a pile of dirt.

She was way too nervous to think of anything but the fact that she'd not only let Hunter talk her into marrying him, they were actually going through with it.

When the Honorable Juan Ricardo cleared his throat and looked at her expectantly, she swallowed hard and forced herself to concentrate on what he'd asked. "I do," she said, surprised that her voice sounded fairly steady considering the state of her nerves.

Judge Ricardo nodded his approval, then turned to Hunter and asked the same question.

Giving her a smile that curled her toes inside her cross trainers, Hunter's voice was strong and sure when he answered. "I do."

"Do you have a ring?" the judge asked, giving Hunter an expectant look.

Callie's cheeks heated as Hunter shook his head. They were probably the most ill-prepared couple to be getting married that the judge had ever seen.

"As soon as she said she'd marry me, I didn't want to take the time to pick out a ring," Hunter said, giving the man a conspiratorial grin. "I was afraid she might change her mind."

Judge Ricardo chuckled. "Then, by the power vested in me by the state of New Mexico, I pronounce you husband and wife. You can kiss your bride, son."

When Hunter took her into his arms to seal their union, his kiss caused her head to spin and her knees to feel as if they were made of rubber. Raising his head, he gazed at her for several long seconds before he turned and thanked the judge, then took her hand in his and led her out of the courthouse.

As they got into the Life Medevac truck for the drive back to Devil's Fork, she still couldn't believe how quickly everything had taken place. "What in heaven's name have we done?"

When he reached out and covered her hand with his, a sense of well-being coursed through her. It was completely unexpected and caused her to catch her breath. Dear heavens, was her attraction to Hunter more than a case of overactive prenatal hormones?

Being a registered nurse, she knew that due to an imbalance in hormone levels, during the second trimester some expectant mothers felt more sensual and sexy than they'd ever felt in their lives. She'd naturally assumed that was the reason she'd given in to desire and passion when she'd made love with Hunter. But now? Could she actually be falling for him?

No, that wasn't possible. She'd only known him a short time, and although her attraction to him was stronger than anything she'd ever felt, that didn't mean she loved him.

"You're awfully quiet," he said, bringing her hand to his lips to kiss the back of it.

Thinking quickly, she smiled. "I was contemplating whether to keep my last name, hyphenate it or change it to yours."

He nodded. "I did an Internet search this morning and found a Web site with a list of things that a bride needs to do after the wedding. Changing her personal documents and identification was on the list." He gave her a seductive smile. "It's up to you, darlin'. But I think Callie Marshall-O'Banyon or just Callie O'Banyon sounds pretty good."

"Since our marriage is only temporary, I suppose it would make more sense to hyphenate."

"Then Callie Marshall-O'Banyon it is."

"For now."

"Right. For now."

As they rode in relative silence on the way back to Devil's Fork, Callie couldn't help but wonder why the thought that her name change wasn't going to be permanent caused her to feel a deep sadness. She'd known up front that they were only getting married in order to thwart Craig's efforts to take her baby away from her. So why was she feeling so darned melancholy?

But as she analyzed her reaction, she supposed it was only natural to feel a bit depressed. She'd always thought that once she got married and took her husband's name it would be for the rest of her life. Of course, that had been when she'd been idealistic and thought the only reason she would ever marry was for love.

Glancing over at Hunter, she couldn't help but think that he had all the qualities she'd ever dreamed of in a husband. He was kind, considerate and, above all, caring. Very few men would have cared enough about an unwed mother keeping her baby to give up their freedom indefinitely.

Sighing, she stared out the windshield of the truck. She wasn't sure what lay ahead of them once they returned to Devil's Fork or how long they'd be husband and wife. But there wasn't a doubt in her mind that no matter what happened, she could count on Hunter being right there beside her to face whatever Craig Culbertson tried to do.

When Callie and Hunter walked into the Life Medevac dispatch room, Mary Lou and the on-duty crew gave them a standing ovation. "Congratulations!"

Grinning like a Cheshire cat, Mary Lou stepped forward. "We've all talked it over and we're giving you two the night off."

"Yeah, we decided you couldn't have a decent wedding night here at the hangar with all of us hanging around," Corey chimed in. His knowing smile made Callie's cheeks heat with embarrassment.

"I'm taking over for you, Hunter," George said. "And Mark, the Evac III paramedic, is coming in to take over for Callie."

"What about standby?" Hunter asked. "We have to have a crew on call in case we have overlapping runs."

"We've got that covered," Mary Lou said, stepping between them. She slipped her arms through theirs and started walking them toward the door. "The rest of the guys are going to take care of that. Now I think you should go back to Callie's place and spend the rest of the night having a little honeymoon fun."

Callie felt as if the heat in her cheeks would burst into flames at any moment. She might have known that Mary Lou would cut to the chase and tell them exactly how she thought they should be spending the evening.

"Hunter?" She felt bad about everyone giving up their day off to cover for them. The least he could do was put up a token protest.

But his sexy grin sent a streak of heat thrumming through her veins and spoke volumes of what an excellent idea he thought the Life Medevac staff had come up with. "Sounds good to me," he said, nodding. He took her hand in his and led her through the door, then, turning back, added, "We'll be back at eight tomorrow morning to finish out our shift."

When they walked into her house several minutes later, Callie took a deep breath and turned to face Hunter. "I don't feel right about this."

He frowned as he reached to take her into his arms. "We're married, darlin'. Making love is something husbands and wives do."

She shook her head and tried to remember what she'd been about to say. With him holding her close, it seemed to short-circuit her thought process. "I was talking about our coworkers giving up their day off."

"Why?" He bent his head to nibble at the sensitive skin along the column of her neck. "I thought it was a nice gesture."

"It…is." A shiver of excitement slid up her spine when he kissed his way to the wildly fluttering pulse at the base of her throat. "But they have no idea…that we aren't making…a lifetime commitment."

Raising his head, he held her gaze with his as he cupped her cheek with his large palm. "Don't worry about it, Callie. We're committed to each other now and for as long as it takes to make sure Culbertson never bothers you again."

"But—"

"Giving us the night off was something they wanted to do, and they know we'll do the same thing for them when they need time off."

His deep, smooth voice and the look in his dark green eyes quickly had her forgetting her guilt or the reason for it. The feel of his hands sliding the length of her back sent shivers of delight coursing through her, and it suddenly didn't matter why they'd gotten married or that it wasn't forever. God help her, but she wanted to spend the night in Hunter's arms again, wanted to feel his hands on her and the sense of being cherished as he made their bodies one.

She would have told him, but when his mouth settled over hers, the contact was so tender it caused tears to flood her eyes and robbed her of the ability to speak. He deepened the kiss, and as his tongue stroked hers, the mating was filled with promises of things to come. He wanted her and he was letting her know in no uncertain terms how much.

When he swung her up into his arms and walked into the bedroom, their lips never broke contact, and as he gently lowered them both to the bed, Callie's heart skipped several beats. With his legs tangling with hers, the strength of his arousal pressed against her thigh and had her own body responding with wanton pulses of need.

His lips clung to hers a moment before he raised his head to smile down at her. "I want you so damned much I can taste it."

"And I want you just as much." Her body tingled with such need she trembled from it. "Please, make love to me, Hunter."

His slumberous look thrilled her to the depths of her soul as he rose from the bed to remove their shoes and socks, then, taking her by the hand, he pulled her to her feet. Bringing her hands to rest on his chest, he gave her a smile that caused her knees to wobble.

"Let's do this together, darlin'."

Excited by the prospect of removing his clothes, Callie rose up on tiptoes to kiss the skin just above the neck band of his red T-shirt at the same time she tugged the tail of it from the waistband of his jeans. Sliding her hands under the soft cotton garment, she felt his muscles contract as she slowly pushed the shirt up along his lean sides. When he raised his arms to help her, she allowed him to pull the garment over his head and toss it aside.

"Your body is perfect," she said, lightly running her fingertips over his well-defined pectoral muscles.

When she traced circles around his flat male nipples, he sucked in a sharp breath. "As good as having your hands on my chest feels, it's my turn."

Reaching for her, he gently pulled the blue scrunchie holding her ponytail free and threaded his fingers through the shoulder-length strands. "Your hair is like fine threads of golden silk."

He tilted her head for a quick kiss, then with painstaking care worked the three buttons at the top of her oversize polo shirt through the buttonholes. Slowly, carefully lifting it up and over her head, his gaze held hers captive as he reached behind her to unfasten her bra. By the time he slid the silk and lace from her shoulders to toss it on top of their shirts, their breathing sounded as if they'd both run a marathon.

The look in his eyes warmed her all over as he filled both of his hands with her breasts and chafed the sensitive tips to harden peaks with his thumbs. "You're so beautiful, Callie."

He dipped his head to capture one of her nipples with his mouth, and she had to brace her hands on his shoulders to keep from melting into a puddle at his feet.

He teased first one, then the other tight nub with his tongue, and it felt as if her blood turned to warm honey as tendrils of desire threaded their way through her limbs to pool with an aching emptiness between her thighs. When he finally raised his head, the hungry look in his dark green eyes stole her breath.

Without a word, she reached for his belt and quickly worked the leather through the metal buckle. But when she popped the snap at the top of his jeans, she forced herself to slow down. Glancing up at him, she smiled as she traced her fingernail along each metal tooth of his bulging zipper. "This looks a bit uncomfortable. I think you'd probably feel better if we got you out of these."

"I don't *think*, darlin', I *know* I'd feel better," he said, his voice sounding raspy.

Easing his fly open, she pushed the jeans down his lean hips, then past his muscular thighs and calves. When he stepped out of them, she trailed her hands along his hair-roughened skin on her way back up to his navy-blue boxer briefs. She loved the way the sinew flexed and bunched at her touch.

"Is that better now?"

His sexy grin sent heat spiraling straight to her core. "Oh, yeah," he said, reaching for the waistband of her maternity jeans.

His heated gaze held hers captive as he slid his fingers under the elastic. His warm palms felt wonderful brushing against her skin as he knelt to push the jeans down her legs, then slowly skimmed his hands along her legs on his way back to her silk panties. Touching her between her legs, he applied a light pressure against the most sensitive spot on her body, sending waves of pleasure radiating through her.

"Does that feel good, Callie?" he asked when a tiny moan of pleasure escaped her.

Unable to form a coherent thought, all she could do was nod.

When he stood up, his gaze captured hers, and as if by unspoken agreement they both reached for the last barriers separating them. Never losing eye contact, together they disposed of his boxer briefs and her panties.

Callie's eyes widened at the sight of his magnificent body. When they'd made love the other morning there hadn't been enough light for her to see his physique. But as she gazed at him now, she marveled at how perfectly made he was.

His wide shoulders, chest and thighs were well defined by muscles that she somehow knew hadn't been honed by working out at a gym. As her gaze drifted lower, past his lean flanks, her breath caught at the sight of his proud, full erection. He was impressively built, thoroughly aroused and, as she lifted her eyes to meet his, looking at her as if he thought she was the most beautiful creature on earth.

"You're amazing," he said, his voice thick with passion.

"I was thinking the same thing about you." She might have felt a bit unsure about her expanding shape had it not been for the gleam of appreciation in his eyes and the reverence she detected in his voice.

Reaching out, she tentatively touched him. Shivers of hot, hungry desire streaked through her when she circled him with her hand and his warm, thick strength surged at her touch. Measuring his length and the softness below, she glanced up at him when a groan rumbled up from deep in his chest. His eyes were closed and a muscle ticked along his jaw as if he'd clenched his teeth against the intense sensations her touch created.

"Does that feel good, Hunter?"

When he opened his eyes, the feral light in the green depths caused her to shiver with a need stronger than anything she'd ever experienced before. But when he cupped her breasts, then lowered his head to circle each nipple in turn with his tongue, swirls of heat coursed through her and she abandoned her exploration to place her hands on his shoulders for support.

"P-please…"

"What do you want, Callie?" His warm breath on her sensitized skin made her feel as if she'd go up in flames at any moment.

"You."

"When?"

"Now!" He was driving her crazy and he wanted to play twenty questions?

Chuckling, he raised his head and, wrapping his arms around her, pulled her to him. The instant soft female skin met hard masculine flesh, Callie moaned with pleasure.

"Let's get in bed while we still have the strength," he said hoarsely.

When he helped her into bed, then stretched out beside her, waves of sheer delight danced over every cell in her being at the feel of his calloused palms caressing her ribs and the underside of her breasts. Feeling as if she were burning up from the inside out, she pressed her legs together in an effort to ease the empty ache he'd created there. He must have realized what she needed because he reached down to gently cup her, a moment before his fingers parted her to stroke the tiny nub of hidden pleasure. Waves of heat streaked through her and she felt as if she'd go mad from wanting.

Raining kisses along her collarbone, then up the side of her neck, he moved his finger deeper to stroke her inside. "Is this where you want me, Callie?"

"Y-yes."

"Do you want me there now?"

"Hunter…please—"

"Just a little bit more, darlin'," he said as his relentless fingers continued to stroke her inner core.

"I can't…stand anymore."

When he moved his hand away, he immediately nudged her thighs farther apart with his knee and eased himself into position. He covered her lips with his, and Callie closed her eyes at the exquisite feel of his blunt tip against her a moment before she felt him slowly, surely slip inside.

"Look at me, Callie."

When she opened her eyes, his heated gaze held hers as he set an easy pace, and all too soon she felt her body straining for sweet liberation from the tension he'd created within her. He must have noticed her tightening around him because he steadily increased his thrusts until the coil of need within her snapped and she was cast into the realm of intense pleasure. She heard him call her name at the same time his big body stiffened, then quivered inside of her as he found his own release.

Wrapping her arms around Hunter's broad back, she held him close as her body pulsed with sweet satisfaction. When their bodies began to cool, she bit her lower lip to keep from crying. She'd done the unthinkable. She'd fought against it from the moment they'd met, but there was no sense denying it any longer.

She'd fallen in love with Hunter O'Banyon.

# Nine

The next morning, when Hunter and Callie walked into the dispatch room, Mary Lou pointed to a slip of paper on her desk. "Hunter, you have a message from someone by the last name of Barringer." She shook her head disapprovingly. "He wouldn't tell me what the nature of his business was. But he said it was important that you call him as soon as possible." She pointed to a huge box over in the corner. "And the new flight suits you ordered were delivered yesterday afternoon."

"Good," Callie said, walking over to gaze into the box. "I can barely zip the one I have now."

Recognizing the name of the private investigator

he'd hired, Hunter nodded. "While I return his phone call, why don't you and Callie sort through the new flight suits and match them against the list of everyone's sizes." He walked over to kiss Callie's cheek. "I'll be back in a few minutes to help."

Her cheeks colored a deep rose and he didn't think he'd ever seen her look prettier. "Mary Lou and I can handle this. Go make your phone call."

"I can sure tell the two of you are newlyweds," Mary Lou said, laughing. "If you can't be away from her long enough to make a phone call, you've got it bad."

Hunter had no idea why, but he couldn't seem to stop smiling as he picked up the slip of paper with Barringer's number on it and walked down the hall toward his office. Maybe it was because the investigator was reporting back so quickly. But he had a feeling that it had more to do with the fact that he'd just spent the most incredible night of his life with his amazing wife.

Callie was the most responsive, sensual woman he'd ever met, and he couldn't wait for the end of the day when their shift ended and they could get back to her place. Unless they were called out for a standby run, they had four days to resume their honeymoon and he had every intention of making the most of their time off. His body tightened at the thought and he cursed the fact that they had eight hours before they were off duty.

When he closed the office door behind him, he took several deep breaths to calm his runaway libido, then walked over to the desk and dialed Barringer's number. He'd no sooner given his name to the man's secretary than Joe Barringer came on the line.

"I've discovered several things about Culbertson that I think you'll find very interesting," he said without preamble.

"You've got my attention," Hunter said, sinking into the desk chair.

"Craig Culbertson is broke. He's gambled away the trust fund his grandfather left him and it appears that he's started siphoning money out of the one set aside for his son."

"But aren't his parents in control of that money?" Hunter asked. He could've sworn that Callie told him the Culbertsons had adopted Craig's son and raised the boy as their own.

"They were," Barringer said. "But there was a stipulation in his grandfather's will that when Craig reached the age of thirty, he gained control of that fund, as well."

"Anything else?" Hunter asked, wondering how he could use the information to help Callie. So far, he hadn't heard anything worthwhile.

"Yes. It appears that provisions have been made for future children."

Hunter sat up straight in his chair. He had a feeling

he was about to learn the motive behind Culbertson's visit to Devil's Fork. "What kind of provisions?"

"Just a second." It sounded as if Barringer was shuffling papers a moment before he added, "Any future offspring of Craig Culbertson will have a million-dollar trust fund set up and—"

"Let me guess," Hunter said. "Culbertson is the administrator."

"You got it." The disgust in Joe Barringer's voice was evident. "His grandfather must have expected Culbertson to sow more wild oats. Instead of leaving him the lion's share of his estate, the old man stipulated that the majority of his money would be held in trust for future heirs." He paused as if consulting his notes. "And Culbertson has to have custody of each child before a trust will be set up in his or her name."

"That explains a lot," Hunter said, thinking aloud.

"Something else you might find interesting—Culbertson has some pretty shady characters breathing down his neck for past gambling debts. I'm not sure he can wait for Ms. Marshall to give birth. He needs the money now," Barringer finished.

"What about his parents? Can't he go to them for the money?" To Hunter, that would be the obvious choice if the man was in that kind of trouble.

"Harry and Alice Culbertson have pretty much washed their hands of their son," Barringer said. "They've bailed him out several times, and from what I can gather, they put their foot down the last time and told him that was it. They wouldn't pay off any more gambling debts."

"In other words, he's desperate for cash and if he can stall his bookies until Callie has her baby, he'll have one more trust fund to steal from," Hunter said, shaking his head at the man's foolishness.

"That's about it. If I find out anything else, I'll give you a call," Barringer added. "But I think you have the most relevant information now."

When Hunter ended the connection, he immediately called the bank, Luther Freemont, Emerald's assistant, then the bed-and-breakfast where Craig Culbertson was staying. Satisfied that he had everything under control, as soon as the fax came in from Emerald Inc. headquarters, he left the office and walked back into the dispatch room.

"I have some business I need to take care of," he said, putting his arms around Callie. "When I get back from town, there's something I need to tell you."

Concern lined her forehead. "It sounds serious."

"Nothing for you to be worried about, darlin'." Not caring that Corey and Mary Lou were avid spectators, he gave her a quick kiss. "I'll be back as soon as I can."

"If we need you, we'll page you," Mary Lou said, pouring herself a cup of her god-awful coffee.

As Hunter drove into Devil's Fork, he couldn't wait to confront Culbertson. He was about to make the man an offer Culbertson couldn't afford to turn down. And within the next couple of hours Hunter fully expected for Craig Culbertson to be headed back to Houston and out of Callie's life for good.

"I have to admit, your demand that we have this meeting came as a bit of a surprise, O'Banyon."

Seated in a booth at the back of the Longhorn Café, Hunter stared across the table at the most despicable human being he'd ever had the displeasure to meet. With his slick good looks, sophisticated air and boyish smile, Hunter could understand why women would find Craig Culbertson attractive.

But Hunter knew the type. Guys like Culbertson used their assets to hide their true nature, and Hunter never thought he'd ever admit it, but the man seated across from him was even lower than Owen Larson. As irresponsible as Owen had been about impregnating women, then leaving them to face single motherhood alone, he'd never used his offspring as pawns to bail himself out of a jam.

"I'm going to make you a one-time offer, Culbertson. And if you're as smart as you try to lead people to believe, you'll take it."

"Oh, really?" The man's sneering expression made Hunter want to reach across the table and grab him by the throat.

"I'm going to write you a check for five hundred

thousand dollars, then you're going to sign a document relinquishing all rights to Callie's baby." Hunter knew the moment he mentioned the money that he had the man's attention. "You'll leave town and never bother Callie or her child again."

"What makes you think I can be bought off that easily?" Culbertson asked, not even bothering to sound offended by Hunter's demands. "And who's to say that once I sign that paper, I won't discover that your check is no good?"

"Believe me, the check is good." Leaning forward, Hunter lowered his voice to a menacing growl. "And I happen to know that if you don't get your hands on some money, and damned quick, your life won't be worth spit."

Culbertson paled visibly. "What makes you say that?"

"It's amazing what a good P.I. can uncover, like the bookies coming after you for your gambling debts." Hunter removed the fax he'd received from Emerald Inc.'s legal department from one of his pockets and shoved it across the table. "This is a confidentiality and custody agreement. Sign it, accept my check and clear out of town or run the risk of not only losing the trust fund that would be set up for Callie's baby but your life, as well."

"Is that a threat, O'Banyon?"

Hunter shook his head. "Not at all. Although I'd like

to take you apart limb by limb, I won't have to do a damned thing. Your bookies will take care of that for me." He held up his hand to get the waitress's attention. "I'm going to order a cup of coffee. By the time I'm finished with it, you'd better have signed that document or the offer is rescinded and you can take your chances with the bookies and the court system."

After the waitress brought Hunter's coffee, Culbertson gave him a cocky grin. "Why should I settle for half a million? If I wanted to, I could get custody of Callie's brat in a heartbeat and end up with a full million at my disposal."

"I wouldn't count on that." Hunter gave the man a confident smile. "For one thing, Callie and I really are husband and wife. That will go a long way in her favor."

"Oh, that's rich," Culbertson laughed. "You own a run-down air-ambulance service in Nowheresville that I'm sure barely makes ends meet and you expect me to believe that my lawyers and good friend Judge Howell would rather see a child raised by you and Callie than in the lifestyle I could provide."

Hunter took a sip of the coffee, then slowly set his cup back on the saucer. "You don't get it, do you, Culbertson?"

"What's to get? I can tie this up in court for years and I know for certain Callie doesn't have that kind of money." His expression condescending, he shook his head. "And I seriously doubt that you do either."

"You might be surprised who could tie who up in court." Hunter laughed harshly. "Besides, I doubt that your bookies would want to wait that long before they start taking their money out of your worthless hide."

Hunter could tell that he'd given Culbertson something to think about. But the man was more arrogant and self-absorbed than Hunter had given him credit for.

"What if I say half a mil isn't enough? What if I want more?"

"It's up to you." Hunter took a healthy swallow of his coffee. "But I'm getting close to finishing this coffee. If you haven't signed that paper by the time I get done, Callie and I will see you in court." He grinned. "That is, if there's anything left of you by the time the case comes up on the docket."

When Hunter started to pick up his cup, he watched Culbertson glance at the contents, then eye the document in front of him. "And you're sure the check is good?"

Hunter nodded. "I can guarantee it."

"How do I know I can trust you?"

"That's something you'll just have to take on faith," Hunter said, lifting his cup. He almost laughed out loud when Culbertson quickly took an ink pen from the inside pocket of his sports jacket and hastily scrawled his name on the designated line of the document before Hunter could take the last sip of the coffee.

Shoving the paper back at him, Culbertson glared at

Hunter as he folded it and put it in his pocket. "You're welcome to Callie and her brat. Now where's my money?"

Hunter removed a check from a zippered pocket on his flight suit, then, before he could stop himself, he reached across the table and grabbed Culbertson by the front of the shirt. Pulling him forward until they were nose to nose, he made sure there was no mistaking the menace in his voice. "Don't ever let me hear you use that tone of voice again when you refer to my wife or our baby. You got that?"

"You really love her, don't you?"

"Yes, I do." When Hunter realized what he'd said, he released Culbertson's shirt and shoved him away. Then, sliding out of the booth, he tossed the check on the table. "Now get the hell out of Devil's Fork and don't let me see you again."

As he walked out of the café and got into his truck, Hunter's heart pounded hard in his chest and he had to force himself to breathe. He loved Callie.

When he'd lost Ellen, he'd vowed never to love another woman and run the risk of losing her. But as much as he'd cared for his fiancée, his feelings for her couldn't compare to the depths of what he felt for Callie. In the past couple of weeks he'd felt more alive than he had in his entire life and he knew for certain that if he lost her he'd never survive.

How the hell had he let himself get in so deep?

When had it happened? And why hadn't he seen it coming?

Somewhere between that wild ride from the airfield when she'd picked him up the day he'd arrived in Devil's Fork and yesterday when they'd exchanged wedding vows he'd let go of the past and reached for the future. A future with Callie and her son.

Steering the truck out onto Main Street, he shook his head. He wasn't fool enough to think that just because he realized he loved her they could work things out and make a go of their marriage. At the time he'd suggested they get married, she'd had just as many reservations, if not more, than he'd had. And the sole reason they'd married in the first place was to keep Culbertson from taking her baby away from her. Now that he was no longer a threat, their reason for staying together was gone.

He took a deep breath as he turned onto the drive leading up to the Life Medevac hangar. He knew that Callie cared for him. Her response to his kisses and the passion they shared when they made love was proof of that. But did she love him?

She'd told him that she trusted him, but that didn't mean she wanted to stay with him for the rest of her life. And he distinctly remembered her telling him the first day they met that she was quite content to remain single.

He also recalled Callie had a problem with anyone

who had money. How would she take it when she discovered that she was married to a man with a multimillion-dollar bank account and who stood to inherit a sizable portion of Emerald Inc., the multibillion-dollar enterprise his paternal grandmother had built from the ground up?

As he parked the truck, got out and walked toward the hangar, he wasn't sure how things would turn out for them. But he had every intention of finding out. He'd tell her how he felt, explain everything about himself and pray that she understood and loved him anyway.

"I was just about to page you," Mary Lou said, hanging up the phone.

"There's been an accident on the Thompson ranch and they need us there as soon as possible," Callie added as she breezed past him on the way out the door.

"Where's Corey?" he asked, following her.

"Right here, boss," Corey called, running after them.

When they were all strapped into their seats, Hunter revved the helicopter's engine and took hold of the stick. He wasn't happy about having to postpone his talk with Callie, but it couldn't be helped. They had an accident victim waiting on them and that took precedence over matters of the heart.

After stabilizing the compound fracture on Carl Thompson's leg and transporting him to the hospital in El Paso, Callie was more than ready to get back to base. It had taken everything she and Corey could do to convince the man that he wasn't on a joyride and couldn't sit up to look out the window during the thirty-minute flight.

"I hope old Carl isn't overly accident-prone," Corey said as they climbed back into the helicopter.

Callie nodded. "If it had taken much longer to get here, I would have radioed for a doctor's order to give him a sedative."

"Well, that's something you won't have to give me," Corey said, taking off his headset and settling back in his seat. "I intend to catch a few winks on the flight home."

When Corey closed his eyes and fell silent, Callie turned her attention to Hunter. As she watched, he put on his headset and flipped switches on the control panel. Her heart skipped a beat and she had to remind herself to breathe. If she lived to be a hundred, she didn't think she'd ever see a man look as sexy as he looked in his flight suit and aviator sunglasses. But then, she thought he was sexy no matter what he did or didn't wear.

She took a deep breath. As hard as she'd fought to keep from loving him, he'd managed to get past her defenses and fill a void in her life that she hadn't even known existed.

Unfortunately that didn't mean they could have a future together. He'd made it quite clear that he was only marrying her to help her retain custody of her son and that once the threat from Craig was over, so was their marriage. Besides, pretending to be happily married and anticipating the birth of a child was one thing. Permanently accepting the role of loving husband and expectant father was something else entirely.

Her chest tightened as she thought of her life without Hunter. She didn't want to think about not being able to see his handsome face every day, hear his hearty laughter or feel the warmth of his touch. But did she have the nerve to tell him how she felt and that she wanted to stay married after her current problems were resolved?

"Damn!" Hunter's vehement curse coming through her headset broke through her disturbing introspection.

"What's wrong?"

"We've got some weather moving in that I don't like," he said, pointing to a bank of clouds.

As she listened to him radio for a weather report from the control tower at the El Paso airport, she was relieved to hear the storm front was moving away from them. She'd never been overly frightened by heavy turbulence in an airplane, but she wasn't sure she wanted to experience it in a helicopter.

"Looks like we're in the clear," he said, lifting off the helipad and steering the helicopter back toward Devil's Fork.

"Did you get your business taken care of this morning?" she asked conversationally.

He nodded. "When we get back to base, we have some things we need to discuss."

"That sounds rather ominous." She wasn't sure from the serious tone of his voice that she wanted to hear what he had to say.

"Don't worry, darlin'. It's not as bad as it sounds."

His endearment reassured her, and they flew in companionable silence for some time before Hunter rattled off a string of blistering curses, ending with a word that most men saved for extreme circumstances.

"I'm almost afraid to ask, but what was that for?" she asked.

"The winds have shifted and we're about to fly right into the middle of that weather front," he said as a gust of wind buffeted the helicopter.

As Hunter fought the stick, Callie tightened her shoulder harness and did her best not to scream when they swayed precariously. Praying they were close to the Life Medevac base, her heart sank when she glanced out the side window and saw the jagged peaks of the mountains.

"I hope like hell I can find a place to set down," Hunter said as he continued to struggle with the controls. "We need to ride this out on the ground."

"That sounds like a good idea to me," she readily agreed.

Glancing over at Corey, she couldn't believe he was still asleep. No wonder Mary Lou complained about trying to wake him up when their crew had a night run to make.

"This is going to be risky," Hunter said, sounding as if his teeth were clenched. "I want you and Corey to hang on tight."

She gripped the sides of the jump seat. "I don't know how, but Corey is still asleep."

"Does he have the shoulder harness buckled?"

"Yes. But he disconnected his headset."

"That's okay," Hunter said tersely. "All that matters is that he's strapped in."

Callie felt as if her heart was in her throat. She knew enough about helicopters to know that landing in a mountainous area was tricky under the best conditions. But during a storm with strong wind gusts it was going to be extremely hazardous.

She felt the helicopter suddenly lurch to one side, and closing her eyes, she prayed as hard as she could while she waited for whatever happened next.

When Hunter spotted a relatively level area at the base of one of the mountains, he clenched his teeth and used every ounce of strength he had to hold the chopper as steady as possible. Fleeting images of another emergency landing and the devastating outcome flashed through his mind. But this time would be different. He was determined that this time the woman he loved and her unborn child would be safe and unharmed.

When the skids bumped the ground hard, then bounced up to come down again with a bone-jarring thud, Hunter killed the rotor engine and released the latch on his shoulder harness. Saying a silent prayer of thanks to the powers that be for a safe, albeit rough, landing, he climbed into the cabin area to check on his passengers.

Taking Callie into his arms, he held her close. "Are you all right?"

She clung to him as she nodded. "Y-yes."

Turning to Corey, Hunter asked, "What about you? Are you okay?"

Pale as a ghost, his eyes wide with shock, the young man nodded. "Wow! That was one hairy landing. Where are we?"

Hunter looked out the starboard windows at the surrounding mountains. "About halfway between El Paso and Devil's Fork."

The adrenaline high he'd been on since realizing they were on a collision course with the storm began to wane, and Hunter felt as if his muscles had turned to jelly. Reaching for the microphone clipped to the epaulet on Callie's flight suit, he radioed Mary Lou to advise her of the situation. Then, after assuring her they were all okay, he told her they would start back as soon as the storm let up.

Unable to stop thinking about how close he'd come to reliving the nightmare he'd been caught up in five years ago and not wanting Callie to see that his hands were beginning to shake, he made up a lame excuse about doing a systems check and climbed back into the pilot's seat.

He was vaguely aware that Callie and Corey were discussing Corey's sleeping habits, but Hunter paid little attention to the conversation. He was too busy thinking about what could have happened if he'd been unable to land the chopper safely.

What would he have done if he'd lost Callie the way he'd lost Ellen? How could he have lived with himself?

He took a deep breath, then slowly released it. The answer was simple. He couldn't. And with sudden insight he knew exactly what he had to do.

As soon as they returned to the hangar, he'd hand Callie the document Culbertson had signed, tell her she was free to pursue an annulment, then terminate her employment at Life Medevac.

# Ten

$B$y the time she, Hunter and Corey returned to the hangar, it was time for their shift to end, and Callie was more than ready to turn over the watch to the Evac II crew and go home. Her nerves were still jangled from narrowly escaping a crash landing and she needed to talk to Hunter. He hadn't said more than a handful of words since the incident, and she could tell something was bothering him.

Well, that made two of them. While they'd waited out the storm, Corey had chattered about everything from being hard to wake up to his pregnant girlfriend and their impending wedding, but Callie hadn't paid much attention. She'd been too preoccupied with thoughts of her baby and how close she'd come to losing him.

"I've got a couple of things to take care of here at the office," Hunter said, walking up behind her. "If you don't mind, I'll be over a little later."

Turning to face him, her smile faded at his serious expression. "Is there a problem?"

He hesitated before shaking his head. "No. I'm just not looking forward to the paperwork I have to do."

"We left my car here last night and I need to get it home anyway. I'll see you in an hour or so." When he gave her a short nod and started to turn to walk back down the hall to his office, she asked, "What would you like for dinner?"

"Don't worry about anything for me. I'm not hungry." Then without another word he disappeared down the hall.

She'd only known him for a couple of weeks, but that didn't matter. There was no doubt in her mind that something was terribly wrong, and she had every intention of finding out what it was.

But a hangar full of people wasn't the best place to have a heart-to-heart talk with her husband, and Callie decided that biding her time would be her best option. When Hunter came over, she'd find out what was bothering him, then tell him her news. She was going to grant his wish and ground herself, at least until after her son was born. And, unless she changed her mind, there was the strong possibility that she might give up being a flight nurse permanently.

As she drove the short distance to her house, she placed her hand on her rounded stomach. She knew it would take Hunter some time to find a replacement for her, but that couldn't be helped. Effective immediately, she was resigning her position at Life Medevac to concentrate on becoming a mother and being there for her son as he grew up.

Parking his truck in Callie's driveway, Hunter sat for several minutes staring at her little house. In the past couple of weeks he'd been happier visiting the cozy little cottage than he'd been in five long years, and it was tearing him apart to think that after tonight he would no longer be welcome there.

But what he was about to do was best for all concerned and he knew that Callie would eventually understand that. And even if she didn't, he could at least sleep at night knowing that he'd done everything in his power to protect her and the baby.

When he got out of the truck, he gripped the folder with the papers he was about to give her and slowly climbed the steps to knock on the door. As soon as he got this over with, he had every intention of driving out to that spot he'd found a few days after he'd arrived in Devil's Fork where he could stare at the stars. Maybe if he stayed there long enough, he'd come to terms with the fact that to protect the woman and child he loved with all his heart, he had to give them up.

"Why did you knock?" Callie asked when she opened the door and stood back for him to enter. "Why didn't you just come on in?"

Standing there with her silky blond hair down around her shoulders, flour streaked across her blue maternity top and the prettiest smile he'd ever seen, she was causing his heart to twist painfully in his chest and she didn't even know it.

Walking past her into the living room, Hunter waited until she closed the door, then turned to face her. "We have to talk."

Her smile faded. "Does this have something to do with what happened this afternoon? Because if it does—"

"We were damned lucky this afternoon," he said, cutting her off. He hadn't meant to sound so harsh, but it was taking every ounce of strength he had not to take her in his arms and abandon the course of action he knew he had to take.

"Hunter?"

She extended her hand and took a step toward him, but, shaking his head, he moved away. He knew beyond a shadow of doubt that if she touched him, he'd lose his internal battle. And it was one he knew that he had to win.

"I think you'd better sit down for this," he said, tempering the tone of his voice.

Sinking onto the love seat, she stared up at him with troubled eyes. "You're beginning to frighten me."

"I don't mean to." He took a deep breath and opened the folder in his hand to remove the document that Culbertson had signed earlier in the day. Handing it to her, he explained what he'd learned from the private investigator and about his meeting with Culbertson. "You won't be hearing any more from Craig Culbertson. He's gone back to Houston and won't bother you or your son again."

She gave him a disbelieving look. "You paid him off?"

Hunter shrugged. "I guess you could call it that."

"My God, I can't allow you to do that. That's an exorbitant amount of money."

"Too late, darlin'. It's already done."

Staring at the paper for several seconds, when she looked up at him, she shook her head. "You can't afford this and I can't possibly pay you back."

"I'm not asking you to," he said firmly. "Consider it a baby gift."

"A baby gift is a set of bibs or a high chair. It's certainly not as extravagant as half a million dollars to get someone to leave me alone."

"Don't worry about it. I'm not."

"Hunter, please—"

When she started to rise from the love seat, he shook his head. "I'm not finished yet. Now that the threat from Culbertson is over with, you're free to petition the courts for an annulment."

She sucked in a sharp breath. "Is that what you want?"

It was the last thing he wanted, but he couldn't tell her that. "I believe that was our agreement."

Standing up, she walked over to him. "You didn't answer my question."

"It doesn't matter what I want." He handed her the folder. "After you take a look at this, I'm sure you'll agree that an annulment is for the best."

When she scanned the termination of employment papers he'd drafted and the severance check for a year's wages, she glared at him. "Why am I being fired? And why are you giving me so much money?"

"Because it's the only way I can think of to keep you from flying. There's enough money that you should be able to pay for the birth, as well as stay home with your son for several months." He'd known she wouldn't be happy about it, but that couldn't be helped. It was for her own good and his peace of mind.

"This won't keep me from flying," she said, tossing it onto the coffee table. "I'm an experienced flight nurse. If I wanted to, I could get a job with another air-ambulance service. But I've decided—"

"You'd better not." Before he could stop himself, he reached out to take her by the upper arms. "What happened today was just a glimpse of what could happen every time you climb into a helicopter to make an emergency run. Promise me you'll find a job in a hospital somewhere."

"Hunter, why…are you…doing this to me?" she asked haltingly.

He closed his eyes for a moment, and when he opened them, the tears on her porcelain cheeks caused a pain to knife through him that threatened to knock him to his knees. He didn't like talking about the accident, but he had to make her understand why he couldn't bear the thought of her flying.

"Five years ago I was behind the controls of a helicopter that went down in Central America. It was a mechanical problem and there wasn't a damn thing I could do to stop the crash from happening. I lost my fiancée and our unborn child that day." Wrapping his arms around Callie, he pulled her to him. "I can't and won't let that happen to you."

"That's why you've wanted me to ground myself from the day you got here."

Unable to get words past the cotton lining his throat, he nodded.

Leaning back, she looked up at him. "Why, Hunter? Why can't you let that happen again?"

"Because I love you, dammit." Realizing what he'd said, he immediately released her, stepped back and, reaching up, rubbed the tension gathering at the back of his neck. "Whenever you get ready, stop by the hangar and clean out your locker."

"Are you finished saying what you came here to tell me?"

Fully expecting her to demand that he leave, he started for the door. "Yes."

"Good." She walked up to him and stabbed her finger at his chest. "Now you're going to listen to me."

"I won't change my mind."

Her violet eyes sparkled with anger. "I don't care. You've had your say and I'm going to have mine."

He guessed it was only fair, but it didn't make standing there wanting to hold her and knowing he couldn't any easier. "All right. Make it quick."

"Number one, I'll take as long as I want to tell you what I think. And number two, you need to stop being so bossy and learn to listen." She waved one delicate hand toward the door. "From the minute you walked in here I've been trying to tell you something and you wouldn't let me get a word in edgewise."

"I can't see that it will make a difference."

She folded her arms beneath her breasts and tapped her bare foot against the floor. "Why don't you sit down and hear me out before you start making judgments."

He shook his head. "I don't think—"

"Sit!"

Lowering himself into the armchair, he gazed up at

her. She was working up a full head of steam and he
didn't think he'd ever seen her look more beautiful. But
then, when a man loved a woman the way he loved
Callie, there was never a time when she didn't look
beautiful to him.

"If you had let me talk earlier, I could have spared
us both a lot of anguish." Standing in front of him, she
propped her hands on her hips. "I was going to tell you
that after what happened today, I realized that I no
longer want to be a flight nurse. So you can take that
termination notice and your severance check and stick
them where the sun doesn't shine."

Suddenly feeling as if a heavy weight had been
lifted from his shoulders, he sat up a little straighter in
the chair. "You don't want to fly anymore?"

"No, I don't." She placed her hand on her stomach.
"What happened today reminded me of what's important."

Hunter couldn't believe the degree of relief coursing
through him. "You have no idea how glad I am to hear
you say that."

"And something else." She began to pace. "What
gives you the right to tell me what I should do about
our marriage? Did it ever occur to you that I might not
want an annulment?"

He couldn't believe that she might want the same
thing he did—to try to make their marriage work.
Almost afraid to hope, he asked cautiously, "You don't?"

"No. An annulment is the last thing I want." She shook her head. "Although, at the moment I'm questioning my sanity and the reason why I love you, you big lug."

Hunter couldn't have stayed in that chair if his life depended on it. Jumping to his feet, he took her into his arms and held her close.

"Thank God!" Giving her a kiss that left them both gasping for breath, when he raised his head, he felt as if his soul had been set free at the love he saw shining in her pretty eyes. "I want to live the rest of my life with you, darlin'." He placed his palm over her rounded stomach. "And if you're agreeable, I'd like to be a father to your baby."

"I'd like that very much." Tears filled Callie's eyes as she reached up to touch his lean cheek. When she'd come to Devil's Fork, she'd had no idea that in running from her past, she'd find her and her son's future. "You're a special man, Hunter O'Banyon."

"I don't know about that, but I promise I'll be the best husband and father I can be," he said, kissing her. "And the first thing I'm going to do for my new family is add a couple of rooms onto the house." He nibbled tiny kisses to the hollow below her ear. "Or, if you'd like, I can build us a new home with lots of bedrooms for babies, as well as guest rooms for grandmothers to visit."

"Could we afford something like that?" Shivering

with desire, she closed her eyes when Hunter cupped her breast to tease her taut nipple through the fabric of her shirt. "You had to spend a lot of money to get rid of Craig."

When his hand stilled, she opened her eyes to look at him. "What?"

"There's something else you don't know about me," he said, looking a bit uncomfortable.

"You mortgaged Life Medevac to pay off Craig," she guessed, hating that he'd put his business in jeopardy for her sake. "Don't worry, I'm a registered professional nurse. After the baby's born, I'll see what jobs are available."

"That won't be ne—"

"I promise I'll make sure the job is on the ground," she hurriedly reassured him.

"But, darlin'—"

"There might be a traveling nurse's position with the tricounty health department. At any rate, I'll be able to help with the loan payments and I can cut a few corners here and—"

His deep chuckle sent a streak of heat straight to her core as he placed his hand over her mouth. "Now which one of us isn't letting the other get a word in edgewise?"

She playfully touched the tip of her tongue to his palm and watched his eyes darken to forest-green. "I love you," she murmured, letting her lips brush his calloused skin.

He shuddered against her a moment before he took his hand away. "I love you, too, Callie." His expression turned serious. "But there's something more I need to tell you about myself."

Her heart stalled at the apprehension she detected in his voice. "What is it?"

"Remember me telling you about not knowing who my father was until just a few months ago and that his family had money?"

She nodded. "That's when you found out you have two brothers and your grandmother's reason for keeping your father's identity a secret."

"Right." His wide chest rose and fell against her breasts as he drew in a deep breath, and she could tell he was reluctant to say more.

"Surely it can't be all that bad."

He shook his head. "Most people wouldn't think so, but you might feel differently."

"Why do you say that?"

"Because you're not overly fond of wealthy people." He gave her a sheepish grin. "Darlin', I'm rich." He shook his head. "Actually I'm not just rich, I'm filthy rich."

"You're what?" Of all the things that had run through her mind, his being wealthy wasn't one of them. He certainly didn't act like any of the wealthy people she knew.

"When my grandmother finally told me and my

brothers who our father was, she also informed us that we each have a multimillion-dollar trust fund and will one day inherit part of a multibillion-dollar enterprise."

Callie's mouth dropped open and she couldn't have strung two words together if her life depended on it. When she finally found her voice, she asked, "Who is your grandmother?"

He smiled. "Emerald Larson."

"*The* Emerald Larson?"

"The one and only," he said nodding. "I hope you won't hold that against me."

She shook her head. "I can't believe…I mean, you never acted any differently than anyone else and I had no idea—"

He silenced her babbling with a kiss, and by the time he raised his head, she couldn't have cared less how much money he had or who his grandmother was. All that mattered was the man she loved more than life itself was holding her securely against him.

"Hunter, I don't care how much money you have or if you have any at all. I love you and that's all that matters."

"And I love you. Never doubt that." His smile heated her from the top of her head all the way to her bare toes. "By the way, what do you have planned for the end of next month?"

"The same thing I have planned for the rest of my life—loving you." He nuzzled the side of her neck, sending shivers of delight skipping over every cell in her body. "Why?"

When she kissed the strong column of his neck, he groaned and swung her up into his arms. "It doesn't matter. Right now I can't think past taking you into the bedroom and getting started on the rest of our lives."

"I like the way you think, flyboy." Circling his wide shoulders with her arms, as he carried her into the bedroom, she whispered close to his ear, "I love you, Hunter."

"And I love you, Callie." Gently lowering her to the bed, he stretched out beside her, then gathered her into his arms. "And I intend to spend the rest of my life showing you just how much."

# Epilogue

As Emerald Larson watched her three grandsons and their wives circulate among the guests at the dinner party she'd put together in their honor, she gave herself a mental pat on the back for a job well done. She'd specifically chosen the companies she'd given each of them to run, as well as arranged for them to meet the women she'd known would be perfect for them, and she couldn't have been more pleased with the results of her efforts.

Glancing at her youngest grandson, Caleb, she smiled fondly. He'd proven to be a genius with his innovative and creative approach to management and had not only improved morale at Skerritt and Crowe

Financial Consultants, he'd increased productivity by fifty percent in just a few months. Along with his wife, Alyssa, he was building a solid reputation as a force to contend with in the financial world.

Turning her attention to her middle grandson, she couldn't have been more proud. Upon his return to the Sugar Creek Ranch, Nick had not only reclaimed his birthright, he'd courageously faced his nemesis and found vindication after thirteen long years. With the help of his wife, Cheyenne, Emerald had no doubt that his plans to turn the cattle company into a free-range operation would meet with complete success. And in the spring, when their first child was born, they'd finally realize their dream of raising a family in that big, charming ranch house under the wide Wyoming sky.

When her gaze landed on Hunter, her oldest grandson, Emerald sighed contentedly. He'd been the one she'd worried about the most. After losing his fiancée and their unborn child, he'd given up flying the helicopters he loved and built a wall around his heart that she'd feared might never come down. But when he'd arrived to take over running the Life Medevac Helicopter Service, he'd not only recaptured his love of flying, he'd met Callie, a young expectant mother whose love had helped him let go of the past and healed his wounded heart.

"You wanted to see me, Mrs. Larson?" Luther Freemont asked, walking up beside her.

As a personal assistant, Luther was highly efficient, his loyalty unsurpassed. But as a man, he was the biggest stuffed shirt she'd ever met.

"I want to thank you for helping me accomplish my goal," she said, continuing to watch her grandsons and their wives. "Our efforts have worked quite well, don't you think?"

"I'd say they've been a resounding success," Luther agreed with her.

"I rather enjoyed watching my grandsons prove themselves with the businesses I gave them to run, as well as helping them find the loves of their lives." She sighed. "It's a shame that I don't have more grandchildren."

Her breath caught and her mood lightened considerably when Luther gave her one of his rare smiles. "Well, as a matter of fact…"

* * * * *